THEATRES ON FILM

MANCHESTER
1824

Manchester University Press

Theatres on film

How the cinema imagines the stage

Russell Jackson

Manchester University Press

Manchester and New York

*distributed in the United States exclusively
by Palgrave Macmillan*

The right of Russell Jackson to be identified as the author of this work has been asserted by him in accordance with the Copyright, Designs and Patents Act 1988.

Published by Manchester University Press
Oxford Road, Manchester M13 9NR, UK
and Room 400, 175 Fifth Avenue, New York, NY 10010, USA
www.manchesteruniversitypress.co.uk

Distributed in the United States exclusively by
Palgrave Macmillan, 175 Fifth Avenue, New York,
NY 10010, USA

Distributed in Canada exclusively by
UBC Press, University of British Columbia, 2029 West Mall,
Vancouver, BC, Canada V6T 1Z2

British Library Cataloguing-in-Publication Data
A catalogue record for this book is available from the British Library

Library of Congress Cataloging-in-Publication Data applied for

ISBN   978 0 7190 8879 7   hardback

First published 2013

The publisher has no responsibility for the persistence or accuracy of URLs for any external or third-party internet websites referred to in this book, and does not guarantee that any content on such websites is, or will remain, accurate or appropriate.

Typeset
by Carnegie Book Production, Lancaster
Printed in Great Britain
by CPI Antony Rowe Ltd, Chippenham, Wiltshire

To Patricia Lennox,
co-voyeur

Contents

List of illustrations

Acknowledgements

WORK on this book has been supported by a period of study leave granted by the School of English, Drama and American and Canadian Studies at the University of Birmingham. An invitation from the Folger Shakespeare Library, Washington DC to offer a seminar in the Folger Institute's programme enabled me to conduct research there and in other libraries. I have benefited from the expertise of the staff of the Billy Rose Theater Collection of New York Public Library at Lincoln Center, the University of Birmingham Library Services (including the Shakespeare Institute's library in Stratford-upon-Avon) and the City of Birmingham's central reference library, and the Fales Collection, Bobst Library, New York University.

I am grateful to friends and colleagues who have viewed and discussed films with me, and in particular to the students who have participated in a study option on the book's topic in the University of Birmingham's Department of Drama and Theatre Arts. I am especially obliged, for their lively and perceptive comments, to my dear friends Gemma and Lewis Hall and Lita Semerad, who have watched some of these films with me; to James Walters, Peter Holland, Pierre Kapitaniak and John Horn for valuable advice; and to Sara Peacock for her sympathetic and meticulous copy-editing.

My greatest debt is to Patricia Lennox, who has been in on the work from the beginning, a constant source of advice and support and – to adopt John Ellis' term to indicate the cinema audience's engagement with each other as viewers of the spectacle before them – my most valued co-voyeur.

Note: Unless otherwise indicated, translations are my own.

Russell Jackson
Birmingham
May 2012

Introduction:
the lure of the theatre

All films are about the theatre: there is no other subject.
(Jacques Rivette)[1]

T HE present study does not attempt to be a comprehensive survey of films in which theatre figures: rather, it proposes a framework within which this dimension of the cinema can be addressed. The chapters that follow focus on films that draw on the theatre as a source of thematic material, atmosphere and narrative structure, or as a metaphor for experience and its perception. They range from earnest exploration to exuberant celebration, and from psychological profundity to cheerful virtuosity in the cause of entertainment. Two examples – not discussed in detail in subsequent chapters – will serve to suggest some of the opportunities afforded to film-makers when they evoke the theatre: Ernst Lubitsch's *To Be or Not to Be* (1942) and Alfred Hitchcock's *Stage Fright* (1950).

Lubitsch's film opens with the announcement 'We're in Warsaw...' and a view of a handsome though clearly studio-built set of a street with a grand building at its focal point. The date is September 1939 and the fact that this is a Hollywood film released three years after the German invasion reinforces the sense of artifice. The apparently omniscient narrator plays the film's first joker: what is this figure, clearly identifiable as Hitler, doing on the street in a city under threat but not as yet attacked or occupied? 'It all started in the general headquarters of the Gestapo in Berlin.' We cut to a scene in which uniformed Nazi officers interrogate an eager Hitler Youth about his parents. As the scene becomes increasingly ludicrous, Hitler himself is announced. When he enters he returns the officers' greeting with '*Heil* myself'. The scene is interrupted by the voice of the director, and it is now clear that this is a theatrical rehearsal: 'This is a serious play', he insists, adding that the actor's makeup is not convincing enough. The actor, Bronski, stalks off, intending to test its effect out on the street.

We return to the initial scene, but now as the amazed crowd keeps its distance from the 'dictator' the spell is broken by a little girl, who tugs at his sleeve and asks 'Mr Bronski' for his autograph.

The performance of the trappings of tyranny, with its rituals and uniforms, recalls Chaplin's *The Great Dictator* (1941), but here it is part of an intricate but always lucid pattern of disguises and deceit in a film that develops into a combination of cinema genres: spy adventure, screwball comedy, bedroom farce, and wartime evocation of the plight of a country. These intersect and complement each other.[2] The satirical comedy with its stage full of *ersatz* Nazis is banned by a censor afraid to offend the Germans, but its costumes and props are subsequently turned to good effect with the advent of Hitler's forces ('There was no censor to stop him') and the need to intercept intelligence that will be lethal to the underground. Scene after scene turns on the acting abilities – on and off stage – of Josef Tura (Jack Benny) and his wife Maria (Carole Lombard). Her clandestine romance with a young Polish airman is subsumed in another kind of subterfuge when he returns on an undercover mission and is parked in Tura's bed. The latter's image of himself as a 'great Polish actor' is constantly under threat, not only from the sudden exit from the audience of his wife's lover as soon as he begins 'To be or not to be', but from almost everyone else, including the real chief of the local Gestapo, who saw him in Berlin: 'What he did to Shakespeare we are doing now to Poland.' On a more serious level, made uncomfortable in hindsight by knowledge of what was in fact happening to Jews in Europe, a Jewish actor gets his chance to 'perform' Shylock. He causes a disturbance in the foyer during the film's climactic masquerade in which 'Hitler' (Bronski again) is offended by the breach of security during his visit to the theatre and insists on being taken straight to his plane. Now 'Hath not a Jew eyes?' serves as both a dignified act of defiance and part of a comic strategy that will enable the Turas and their company to escape to Britain. Theatricality and deceit, often in the service of comic amorous intrigue, and the doubleness of double entendres that evaded censorship are integral to Lubitsch's sophisticated story-telling in many of his films, a major element of 'the Lubitsch touch'. Here the doubling is enhanced by the specifically theatrical context.

The opening credits of *Stage Fright* are shown over a theatre's safety curtain as it slowly rises, but what it reveals is not a stage set. The screen is filled with a long shot of a London street, with St Paul's Cathedral in the background, largely surrounded by bomb sites (Figure 1). As the curtain reaches the top of the screen, a car appears in the distance and speeds towards the camera, now at the level of the

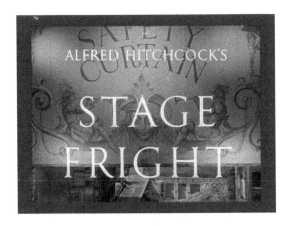

1. *Stage Fright* (1950):
the safety curtain rises

roadway. Just as the car seems about to hit the camera a swift cut takes us inside the vehicle, to a couple who we discover are fleeing from the police. In one quick exchange their immediate situation is set up, and presently a flashback takes over the passenger's story. Hitchcock has begun his story as he means to end it, with a device summoning ideas of suspense, the revelation of secrets and the excitement of theatrical performance. Even the words 'Safety Curtain' are ironic: safety is about to be threatened, as indeed we might hope from this director. The story we then are told is in fact untrue, and Hitchcock has been reproached for deceiving his cinema audience.[3] As the film progresses, performances of various kinds will take place, in private and public venues from a class at RADA to the stage of a West End theatre, and the heroine, an aspiring actress, will assume the role of a dresser in order to come closer to uncovering the mystery of the crime that has been committed. The villain, cornered in a theatre after a performance, will take refuge in a property room under the stage and then meet his fate on stage before an empty auditorium, beheaded by the relentless fall of just such an iron curtain as we saw at the beginning.

In other films Hitchcock uses the theatre as one of the public places in which he likes us to savour the discomfiture of his characters, but in *Stage Fright*, as he told François Truffaut, what appealed to him in the story was 'the idea that the girl who dreams of becoming an actress will be led by circumstances to play a real-life role by posing as someone else in order to smoke out a criminal'.[4] Although it has not been reckoned among the director's outstanding films – Robin Wood remarks that 'one feels the creative impulse at a comparatively low ebb' – *Stage Fright* is exemplary in co-opting the theatre for the cinema's ends.[5] Here, as often in the cinema, the theatre is a place of personal transformation, whose physical qualities – the stage and what lies behind it – offer extraordinary possibilities for atmospheric as well as narrative effects.

Playgoing and picturegoing

The relationship between film and theatre has been analysed in terms of the viewer's relationship with the images and sounds of the film, attempting to differentiate the effect of 'liveness' in the theatre from the cinema audience's alleged experience of distance or – in less sympathetic accounts – passivity. André Bazin pondered the effect produced by identification with such figures as Tarzan:

> The cinema calms the spectator, the theatre excites him. Even when it appeals to the lowest instincts, the theatre up to a point stands in the way of the creation of a mass mentality. It stands in the way of any collective representation in the psychological sense, since theatre calls for an active individual consciousness while the film requires only a passive adhesion.[6]

John Ellis, in *Visible Fictions* (1982) suggests a less diminished role for the cinema audience, in which 'the spectator is separate from the film's fiction, able to judge and assess; separate from the filmic image, which is absent even whilst it presents itself as present.'[7] This is a state of play that one might expect the most determined Brechtian to welcome, detachment in the face of a medium whose primary aim seems paradoxically to command assent. Bazin's essay, published in two parts in the summer of 1951, argues around the film/theatre relationship in terms of the adaptation of stage plays for the cinema as well as the distinctions between the two media and the vexed question of theatricality in film. Distinguishing the film's screen from the stage/auditorium division, Bazin seems to treat the fourth-wall theatre as normative, but nevertheless his formulation of the comparison has been influential:

> The screen is not a frame like that of a picture but a mask which allows only a part of the action to be seen. When a character moves off screen, we accept the fact that he is out of sight, but he continues to exist in his own capacity at some other place in the décor which is hidden from us. There are no wings to the screen. There could not be without destroying its specific illusion, which is to make of a revolver or of a face the very center of the universe. In contrast to the stage the space of the screen is centrifugal.[8]

This contention that there are no 'coulisses' to the screen, where the term denotes the backstage in general rather than the established translation's 'wings', is particularly significant for the ways in which the theatre is figured by film-makers: the critical writing and film work of Jacques Rivette, discussed in Chapter 6, amount to a dialogue with the terms and arguments of Bazin's essay, situated in the post-war cinematic avant-garde and informing the more radical subsequent departures of the *Cahiers du cinéma* group.[9] Christian Metz proposes 'the impression of reality experienced by the spectator' as one of film theory's 'most important problems': 'Films give us the feeling that we are witnessing an almost real spectacle – to a much greater extent … than does a novel, a play, or a figurative painting.' In comparison with the products of other arts, films engage directly with a wide and numerous public, and have 'the *appeal* of a presence and a proximity that strikes the masses and fills the movie theatres'.[10]

From the other direction, asserting the need to revivify its own art-form, the theatrical avant-garde has sometimes disparaged the new medium in corresponding terms. In 1933 Antonin Artaud announced his campaign for a 'theatre of cruelty' as a response to the damage done by both the 'psychological theatre, derived from Racine' that had 'rendered us unaccustomed to the direct, violent action theatre must have', and the baleful influence of cinema: 'Cinema, in its turn, murders us with reflected, filtered and projected images that no longer connect with our sensibility, and for ten years has maintained us and all our faculties in an intellectual stupor.'[11] Less dismissive, but equally concerned to identify the specific qualities of live performance, in 1968 Jerzy Grotowski described his quest for a 'poor theatre' and 'performance as an act of transgression' in terms of locating theatre in contradistinction to the other performance media:

> The theatre must recognize its own limitations. If it cannot be richer than the cinema, then let it be poor. If it cannot be as lavish as television, let it be ascetic. If it cannot be a technical attraction, let it renounce all outward technique. Thus we are left with a 'holy' actor in a poor theatre.[12]

The premium placed on the audience's direct and often physical involvement has in some cases led to the discounting of any possibility of participatory spectatorship in the film experience. Paul Woodruff, in *The Necessity of Theater* (2009) supports the primacy of what his subtitle calls 'the art of watching and being watched' in live performance: 'The art of filmmaking seeks to make the film worth watching, not the action it is supposed to represent. In film there is only the art of making film. There is no art of film watching.'[13] This fails to acknowledge that a film – like a theatre performance – is not complete until interpreted by the audience. Meaning is deferred until the gaps between distinct elements, even those between adjacent shots, have been closed by the viewer.[14] A more radical suggestion, addressing the common proposition that 'to be a spectator is to be separated both from the capacity to know and the power to act', is Jacques Rancière's contention that 'every spectator is an actor in her story; every actor, every man of action, is the spectator of the same story'.[15] Cinema figured variously as a stimulus and threat to the theatre for the advocates and chroniclers of the 'New Theatre' of the 1920s and 1930s. Huntley Carter's accounts of Russian theatre hailed Soviet Russia as the exemplar for the 'new spirit' in the theatre, including the contribution of 'the kinema' and radio. Although he emphasized content and social engagement rather than technique, for Carter the cinema's potential was as an extension of drama's ability to encompass great social themes on a scale commensurate with the developing soviet theatre.[16] In *New Theatres for Old* (1939) Mordecai Gorelik identifies elaborate scenic naturalism of the kind associated in the early decades of the century with the American manager David Belasco as a dominant element of popular film well into the century's third decade. There is hope, though, both in the moves towards an engagement with 'real life' and in the development of a distinct filmic medium.[17] Allardyce Nicoll, in his pioneering study *Film and Theater* (1936) argues that naturalism, which the cinema simply does better and with greater subtlety, is no longer part of the theatre's future:

> Is, then, the theater, as some have opined, truly dying? The answer to that question depends on what the theater does within the next ten or twenty years. If it pursues naturalism further, unquestionably little hope will remain; but if it recognizes to the full the condition of its own being and utilizes those qualities which it alone possesses, the very thought of rivalry may disappear.

At the same time, Nicoll proposes a version of spectatorship in the cinema that does not characterize it as passive or inferior: 'Our illusion in the picture-house is certainly less "imaginative" than the illusion which attends us in the theatre, but it has the advantage of giving increased appreciation of things which are outside nature.'[18]

The theatrical avant-garde, of whatever period or persuasion, rarely appears in films, although various unconventional kinds of theatrical performance have been a vehicle for the exploration of wider issues of personal identity and expression in the work of some directors, notably Jacques Rivette and Ingmar Bergman. Although since the early twentieth century many if not most innovations in theatre and drama have encompassed radical alterations in the configuration of the performance space and the relationship between spectators and performers, it is the picture-frame, 'fourth wall' theatre, with its proscenium arch and curtain that has dominated the cinema's represen-tations of the theatre. As represented on film this conventional division of the theatre's realm – like the figure of the emotionally engaged actor – remains powerfully suggestive. The moment when the house lights dim and the curtain is raised, heralded in France by the 'three blows' (*les trois coups*), generates a mysterious excitement especially among those who, like Jean Renoir, have experienced it in early childhood. Baz Luhrmann's identification of a group of his films, including *Moulin Rouge* (2001), as the 'Red Curtain Trilogy' testifies to the attractive power of this element of the traditional theatre.

Because the films discussed here often play on their audience's perception of the nature of theatrical space it is important to consider some fundamental distinctions between the physical and social experiences of playgoing and picturegoing. Conventionally, theatre buildings consist of an acting space, with a more or less concealed area from which players will emerge, both separated from the space in which the audience assembles.[19] This persistent basic configuration, although subject to constant reshaping in response to changing conceptions of theatrical performance, has been a source for metaphors relating to experience in the 'real' world – that of the audience when they are not in the theatre's environs – and the world of imagination. It has also been the basis, especially in its medieval and early modern incarnations, of the perceived symbolic relationship between stage action and the grander framework of the cosmos. It is a surprisingly short step, via Jacques' speech in *As You Like It*, from the concept of *theatrum mundi* to the cliché voiced in the lyrics of the song 'That's Entertainment': 'The world is a stage/ The stage is a world/ Of Entertainment.'

When the theatre is represented in films, the building itself and the work done in it represent elements absent from the cinema-going experience. The topography of the theatre's premises lends itself to a variety of thematic and symbolic purposes. All the related and subtly differentiated domains of the building are explored: backstage areas (including scene docks, prop rooms and the flies), dressing rooms, front-of-house offices and foyers and the different social zones within the auditorium itself. There are thresholds that can only be crossed by permission and sometimes with peril. Stage doors are defended against intruders, as are dressing rooms. Passage from the front-of-house to behind the scenes is available for a privileged few. Stage doors are approached by way of unpromising alleys, but once passed they admit the visitor to a world that is both commonplace and glamorous. The demarcations of the backstage social world correspond in many ways to the upstairs/downstairs division in upper-class households. The cinema building has less potential for this kind of thematic exploration or the drawing of social or psychological analogies. There is no backstage, except what may serve for storage, equipment or administration. What lies 'behind' the screen image exists only in the now distant time and place of the film's production. Most of the films discussed in this book were made and distributed when cinema-going had more in common with the experience of theatre. Uniformed attendants presided in the foyers; ushers led the way to the seats; live music might be performed, often on a formidably resourceful cinema organ; there might be more than one feature film on the bill, with newsreels, cartoons and advertisements, and a stage show sometimes supplemented the screen entertainment. When older films celebrate the theatre or draw on it for thematic material, there is a sense of both kinship and rivalry between the live and the recorded media, and a respect for the glamour and mystique of the theatre and its actors.

The aspects of the theatrical experience and theatre life that have lent themselves to exploration in films constitute an identifiable repertoire of narrative elements, character types and situations. These are shared with other forms of fiction and their constructions of theatre history match those of popular historiography, if not academic theatre studies. Beyond this, the theatre's liveness, rendering every performance an event whose essence cannot be defined or recaptured by mechanical reproduction, makes it both a challenge and inspiration to the film-maker. Marvin Carlson, in *The Haunted Stage: The Theatre as Memory Machine*, notes that 'all theatre ... is a cultural activity deeply involved with memory and haunted by repetition'. His study points to a characteristic that many theatre films explore and exploit: 'a simultaneous awareness of something previously experienced and of something being offered in the present that is both the same and different, which can only be fully appreciated by a kind of doubleness of perception in the audience.'[20] The cinema, in speaking of the theatre, not only deals with this sense of the past in the present, but also brings its own paradoxes to bear.

In most feature films the sequences of events have been constructed in editing, even when (as in Hitchcock's *Rope*, 1948) long continuous takes have been used. Invariably, theatrical performance may be said to have *happened* on each occasion in real time. However, although the projected movie (the recorded vision and sound) may be the same at every repeated viewing, the experience of it is susceptible of modification by circumstances. Contrary to Bazin's view of the passivity of audiences, the film-viewing event itself has its own 'liveness', a blending of individual experience and membership of a group. The audience members in a cinema may not influence what runs through the projector but a full house in a cinema generates a sense of occasion very different from the privacy of a living room or study. Philip Auslander's contention that 'communality is not a function of liveness' supports this argument: 'The sense of community arises from being part of an audience, and the quality of the experience of community derives from the specific audience situation, not from the spectacle for which that audience has gathered.'[21]

Show folks:
the personnel of the theatre

There are, to quote the lyric from *Annie Get Your Gun*, no people like show people. They perform heroically in adverse circumstances, even when they find themselves stuck out of town in 'a turkey they know will fold'. As well as fostering resilience, the conditions of show business have been held to elicit and magnify quirks of character rarely evident in other walks of life, often in a comedic or melodramatic mode. Joseph L. Mankiewicz, director and script writer of *All About Eve* (1950), discussed in Chapter 3, went so far as to wonder 'why serious students of the human psyche look to anything *but* theatre folk for most of the answers they seek'.[22] The typology of theatre characters is discussed more fully below in the chapter on 'backstagers', but some general observations may be made at this point. Most commercial theatre films centre their attention on performers rather than other theatre staff. Managers are rare as the leading interest of popular films: Florenz Ziegfeld, in the 1936 MGM biopic, and Danglard in Renoir's *French Cancan* (1954) are notable examples, as is the begetter of the Windmill Theatre, the formidable heroine of *Mrs Henderson Presents* (2005). Directors seldom appear in anything more than supporting roles, with the director of *Andromaque* in Jacques Rivette's *L'Amour fou* (1969), Julian Marsh in *42nd Street* (1933) and Oscar Jaffe in *Twentieth Century* (1934) among the distinguished exceptions. (Jaffe is more extravagantly histrionic than any of the actors he directs: his 'creation' Lily Garland points out that if his throat were cut greasepaint would come out.) Although directors and other staff may be frustrated by personal problems and relationships, and challenged by the pressures they are under, for the most part in film depictions of the creative processes their psyche, however troubled, remains intact. (Rivette's films, discussed in Chapter 6, are an important exception.) Few films have centred on the tribulations of authors, for all their vulnerability in the context of the production process: notable exceptions include biographical treatments of Shakespeare and Molière, the hapless playwright in Woody Allen's comedy *Bullets over Broadway* (1994) and the author of the play almost destroyed by the leading actress in John Cassavetes' *Opening Night* (1977). As for critics, apart from Addison de Witt in *All About Eve* and the noxious collaborator Daxiat in Truffaut's *Le Dernier Métro* (1980), they have attracted little attention, except as peripheral and often annoying elements of the theatre scene.

The privileging of performance and self-conscious theatricality over the exploration of character psychology, an impulse common to Brecht, Meyerhold and many subsequent innovators, has had its counterpart in radical film-making, but the older theatrical modes have dominated representations of the theatre in the cinema. Ariane Mnouchkine, director of the Théâtre du Soleil, described how in her work on Shakespeare in the mid-1980s she had to deal with actors who were 'deformed' by their training and experience: 'The poison of psychology is injected very deeply into us, by cinema and television' – again, the new media appear as enemies of true theatre.[23] For the most part, though, the European and North American cinema has shown little interest in actors of the kind Mnouchkine hoped to find or train, focussing rather on those whose work is informed by the investment of their personality in their roles. Moreover the stage actor's direct engagement with a live audience and the need to command them – in vaudeville parlance to 'kill the people' – make for a sense of drama and danger that is observed with fascination in its representation through the medium of the screen actor's differently modulated skills of pretence and (to varying degrees) self-exposure. It is this quality that makes the bravura of Laurence Olivier's Archie Rice in *The Entertainer* (1960) even more powerful than his *Richard III* (1955), where a stylized setting supports a thrilling characterization of a self-dramatizing political performer. An outstandingly successful actor of the 'classical' English repertoire appears here as a stage performer no longer able to communicate with his audience and with nothing left to convey except aggression disguising his own desperation. What Archie should be as a 'pro' is expressed by Archie's father, the retired music-hall veteran Billy Rice, when he declares that 'a real pro' is 'like the general run of people, only he's a lot more like them than they are themselves'.[24] The actress heroine of W. Somerset Maugham's 1938 novel *Theatre* – filmed by István Szabó as *Being Julia* (2004) – embodies in comic form a truism about the profession:

'Beginners, please.' Those words, though heaven only knew how often she had heard them, still gave her a thrill. They braced her like a tonic. Life acquired significance. She was about to step from the world of make-believe into the world of reality.[25]

Maugham's sly reversal of the two worlds reflects centuries of fascination with the actor's psychology. A similar treatment of the actor's inability to live a 'real' life without performance is the mainspring of George S. Kaufman and Edna Ferber's *The Royal Family* (1927) where the members of a stage dynasty – modelled on the Barrymores – are unlikely to fulfil such promises as 'From this time on I'm going to live life, and leave imitation behind me!'[26] Jean-Paul Sartre's 1953 adaptation of Alexandre Dumas' play *Kean* (1836) has moments and scenes of brilliant comedy, but (as might be expected) inflects the actor's situation in existential terms. 'You don't act to make your living', his Kean exclaims, 'You act in order to lie, to lie to yourself, to be what you can't be and because you've had enough of being what you are … Acting! Do *I* know when I'm acting? Is there a moment when I stop acting?'[27]

The resilience of actors is legendary, but its obverse is a sense that acting like all performance can be regarded as a form of compulsive behaviour ('Gotta dance!') reflecting the expression of desires not normally admitted or exposed by non-actors. In this connection, C.G. Jung's concept of the *persona* – a term adopted from the Greek word for the actor's mask – can be invoked: 'a complicated system of relations between individual consciousness and society, designed on the one hand to make a definite impression upon others and, on the other, to conceal the true nature of the individual'. Jung observes that 'people really do exist who believe they are what they pretend to be'.[28] Even without reference to specifically Jungian psychological theory, in its resonance with commonplace notions of performance the persona has clear relevance to the image of the performer. In this context, the dressing-room mirror becomes a powerful symbol, present in many films and exploited tellingly in *A Double Life* (1948), *Opening Night* and (in an act of homage and imitation of Cassavetes' film) Almodóvar's *All About My Mother* (1999). Al Jolson's character in *The Jazz Singer* (1927) experiences a crisis not merely of personal but of cultural identity, compounded by parental love and guilt, giving a special quality to his moments in front of the mirror.

The actor's potential as a representative figure is enhanced by a related consideration: his or her simultaneous involvement and self-possession in the process of performance in general and impersonation in particular. Fascination with the topic informs Hamlet's reflections on the Player King's false but convincing passion, and is the subject of the discussion in Denis Diderot's *Paradoxe du comédien*, written in the 1770s but first published in 1838. The spokesman for Diderot in the dialogue argues for detachment as a prime virtue in performance:

> The man of sensibility [*l'homme sensible*] obeys the impulse of Nature, and gives nothing more or less than the cry of his very art; the moment he moderates or strengthens this cry he is no longer himself, he is an actor.[29]

Joseph Roach, in *The Player's Passion: Studies in the Science of Acting*, observes that the 'concepts originating in or at least taking their modern form' in Diderot are 'emotion memory, imagination, creative unconsciousness, ensemble playing, double consciousness, concentration, public solitude, character body, the score of the role, and spontaneity' – in other words, a good many of the ideas explored by and contested among theorists and teachers of acting since the end of the nineteenth century.[30] Among the various mid-twentieth-century developments of the notion of a divided consciousness one of the most concise and at the same time far-reaching is that of the actor's being simultaneously 'not me' and 'not not me'. The consequence of this, as Marvin Carlson points out, is that 'performer and audience alike operate in a world of double consciousness'.[31]

As well as furnishing the terms for theoretical and analytical discourse, the actor's divided self has often been a source of mystery and comedy in other media. It can disrupt the general quality ascribed to show people, their sense of solidarity and cheerful resilience, but it can also be soothed by it. For this reason, the theatrical troupe is itself a powerful image of theatre at its most benign, a family to which those oppressed by their natural family may be able to escape. In Théophile Gautier's novel *Le Capitaine Fracasse* (1862–1863), informed by his study of Scarron's *Le Roman comique* (1651–1657), a *commedia* troupe of the time of Louis XIII provides shelter for a romantic hero, an impoverished and unworldly young aristocrat who finds an unsuspected outlet for his histrionic talents and emotional impulses. 'A players' cart contains a whole world', the author reflects, and its crude, worn-out costumes and pasteboard finery are the 'wretched treasures' (*misérables trésors*) in which the poet is content to dress his fantasy and which are sufficient, with candlelight and fine language, to entrance the most difficult audiences.[32] Here and in many similar fictional examples, the acting troupe thus offers a space in which division between the 'real' and the 'unreal' may be beneficial and supportive.

Theatrical life has not always been treated as sympathetically as in these more-or-less romantic accounts of the vagabondage of the strolling players, or the elegant amusement evinced by Maugham and

Kaufman at the expense of sophisticated stage stars. Several films draw on the theatre and theatrical ambition as powerful metaphors for the lure of the big city and its dangers and attractions. Arguably the backstagers produced by Warner Bros in the 1930s, with their acknowledgement of the Depression and the street-smart manners of their characters, suggest that the theatre offers a refuge from the hazards of city life, even though it is part and parcel of it. Many backstage films deal with the tensions of life as a 'hopeful', but there is little sense of the situation that prompted actors to campaign for and organize alternatives to the system in the West End or on Broadway. Elia Kazan described the establishment of the Actors Studio in terms of its providing a focus of artistic activity and, effectively, a shelter as well as a source of training: 'The great body of the profession, like the longshoremen on the waterfront, shaped-up every morning, hoped to be lucky, made the rounds, waited for a phone call, lived on the curb, had nowhere to come in out of the rain.'[33] Celebrated one moment and 'on the curb' the next – to put it in melodramatic terms – the actor's lot has lent itself to the shaping of narratives in popular fiction in every medium.

Fascination with the actors' social vulnerability and equivocal status as artists has coincided with the residue of the moral anxiety found in Victorian commentary and fiction. The element of gender anxiety and prejudice haunts fictional treatments of women in show business. Charlotte Brontë's novel *Villette* (1853) includes a vivid description of Vashti, a French actress based on Rachel Félix, whose performance in the title role of *Phèdre* takes the spectators into new and hazardous regions. The heroine Lucy Snowe is thrilled and appalled, recalling that 'It was a marvellous sight: a mighty revelation' and at the same time 'a spectacle low, horrible, immoral'. The duality in her reactions expresses concisely the tension between admiration and revulsion underlying antitheatrical prejudice, here as often with the element of an ideal of female integrity and virtue being undermined: 'I had seen acting before, but never anything like this: never anything which astonished Hope and hushed Desire; which outstripped Impulse and paled Conception'.[34]

Henry James' fraught relationship with the theatre offers a less emphatic, more sophisticated example of a complex of attitudes that persisted into the twentieth century. In *The Tragic Muse* (1890), anxieties about the social and moral character of the actress combine with an acute analysis of more general attitudes to art as a 'respectable' and 'serious' pursuit, as against the more obviously worthy goals of political and diplomatic life. The central female character, Miriam Rooth, is continually discussed in terms of the deception and self-presentation that mark the actress as 'unwomanly' by most conventional measures. James does not implicitly endorse such attitudes in their more simplistic form, but remains equivocal in his account of Miriam. 'As soon as she stepped on the boards a great and special alteration usually took place in her – she was in focus and in her frame: yet there were hours in which she wore her world's face before the audience, just as there were hours when she wore her stage face in the world.' The narrator, like the novel's principal male characters, is clearly in awe of this disturbing dualism, Miriam's ability to be 'read' on stage and off according to different and (it seems) mutually exclusive codes: 'She took up either mask as it suited her humour.'[35]

This Jamesian balancing act contrasts with the hostile account of the actress and theatrical life in Émile Zola's *Nana* (1879–1880), filmed in a remarkable adaptation (1926) by Jean Renoir. Zola's title character is effectively a prostitute, for whom the theatre is the means of launching a career of sexual, financial and moral degradation that threatens to destroy a nation on the brink of the disastrous war with Prussia. The melodrama of the novel's plot is complemented by the lurid details of the backstage world, and is also supported by the theatricality of Nana's entire way of life. Her apartment has a distinctive backstage/onstage dimension, as do her dressing room and the luxurious town house Count Muffat buys for her when she becomes his mistress. All these, with their closets, curtained doors and entrance halls, serve her for the enticement and management of her rival lovers. Bordenave, the manager of the theatre where Nana makes her début, frankly admits that he is running what amounts to a brothel, and Zola describes its squalor with characteristic relish. Nana's dressing room has a low ceiling and looks out onto a 'leprous wall'. The atmosphere is stifling, with the heat from the flaring gas jets on either side of the mirror, its 'odeur de femme' and the smells of the makeup that litters the dressing table.[36] As Jane R. Goodall points out, the characterization of Nana and her world is part of Zola's wider ethnological scheme in the Rougon–Macquart novels, co-opting familiar images of the theatre and the actress in his encyclopedic depiction of degeneration, destructive passion and duplicity in society.[37] Renoir follows Zola's tactics in conducting the viewer from the performance and its effect on the audience to the corridors and dressing rooms backstage. The film deftly characterizes the tenebrous backstage areas and the provocatively ambivalent relationship between privacy and availability that gives the dressing-room world its erotic charge. Nana is the incarnation of male anxieties about women who perform, and Renoir's script – but not the film as released – even anticipates in the deathbed scene a vision of Christ pardoning the penitent Magdalene, an effect worthy of D.W. Griffith or Cecil B. de Mille.[38] The image of the erring actress is bound up, as it had been in the nineteenth century, with the representation of her working environment as a tawdry trap, even (or especially) at its most glamorous. The social status of the theatre, the disparity between front-of-house and backstage, and the moral dilemmas of the profession are inextricably bound together. The stage door leads to a world that is glamorous in the older sense of being magical and potentially dangerous.

Theatre audiences on film:
a view from the new medium

Given that the definition of the spectator's experience of the two media has been so vigorously contested by theorists of theatre and film, it is hardly surprising that the characterization of audiences has a special significance in films about theatre. In the case of historical subjects this raises questions of priority: artistic effect must prevail over documentary accuracy. In any case, the foundations for accurate depictions of the audience are themselves by no means secure. For historians of the theatre, recovering an accurate picture of audience behaviour in earlier periods is a complex undertaking, and contemporary reports of the reception of performances need to be rigorously examined and in many cases revised. In films, however, depictions of audience behaviour in specific historical periods often perpetuate long-established and attractive clichés, sometimes giving them a degree of adjustment in terms of current attitudes.

The characterization of audiences is commonly a significant dimension of films with a historical setting, especially when the principals' careers are charted by representing a succession of eras and the social constituencies of the theatres they play in. When there is a more specific focus on social and political history, film-makers have attempted careful reconstructions of the audience, with differentiation of their place and influence in the performance space. Laurence Olivier's script for *Henry V* (1944) indicates that in the opening playhouse sequence 'it should be made clear that there is far more intimate interplay between actors and audience than can be imagined in today's theatres'.[39] (His Elizabethan groundlings are neater and less unruly than their equivalents in *Shakespeare in Love*, released in 1999.) In *Nana* Renoir shows a fashionable stalls audience transported by the heroine's erotic performance, with the gallery audience expressing their enthusiasm with even less restraint and, although he does not have the time to develop for the screen every one of Zola's characteristically meticulous details of theatre life, he establishes the broad outlines with skilfully selected details. In other cases where active involvement is to be depicted, such as *Les Enfants du paradis* (1945), Richard Eyre's *Stage Beauty* (2004) or the Molière films by Ariane Mnouchkine and Laurent Tirard (respectively 1978 and 2006) the audience's social identity is a significant element in the narrative, and calls for elaborate treatment. An opera-house scene in *Farinelli il castrato* (1994) shows the packed and glamorous audience responding with rapt attention to the singer's astonishing voice: one woman even falls back in an ecstatic faint. When an insultingly detached book-reading lady in one of the boxes clinks her coffee cup against its saucer, Farinelli stops, waits for silence, then launches a sustained high note that has a positively erotic effect. (After the performance, she is ready to be bedded by him, a situation that calls for some legerdemain by him and his more fully equipped brother.)

Luchino Visconti's *Senso* (1953) characterizes the opera audience at La Fenice during the Risorgimento in political terms, with the white-unformed officers of the occupying Austrian army in the front rows and the Venetian populace, to whom Verdi's 'Di quella pira' is addressed as a rallying call, behind and above them. Here the politics of spectatorship are to the fore. In Martin Scorsese's *The Age of Innocence* (1993) important social and emotional transactions take place in the opera house (twice) and the theatre: in the latter we see the principal characters as they are illuminated by the lights from the stage as the curtain goes up on a scene from a melodrama they are watching. The social composition and behaviour of the spectators are established with the detail appropriate to Edith Wharton's novel. In this society it is normal to arrive late and talk during the performance in the privacy of one's box, exercising the privilege of observing closely the rest of the audience while Gounod's *Faust* takes its course on stage as a background and counterpoint to one's own preoccupations. Similar care is taken in Mike Leigh's *Topsy-Turvy* (1999), attentive to the social dimension of theatre history to an unusual degree.

Carefully researched scenes of lower-class spectatorship include the 'children of the gods' in Carné's film, the audience shown in striking detail at the beginning of Mamoulian's *Applause* (1929) and the rowdy elements tamed by the young Gertrude Lawrence in a music-hall sequence in Robert Wise's *Star!* (1968). *Applause* is unusual in its specific and unflattering characterization of male spectatorship. The film begins with a burlesque troupe on tour, parading their shop-worn chorus girls through a small town and playing to an audience of avid oglers. In a remarkable backstage sequence the heroine (Helen Morgan) gives birth, and a top shot shows the company circling her with protective awe and affection. Subsequently the illegitimate child is placed in the safety of a convent, and knows nothing of her mother's career. In due course the mother has made it to New York but is still stalled in the exploitative world of burlesque. Her daughter, having left the convent, comes in search of her mother and is told at the hotel that she is on stage. Naively assuming that performing in the city means the achievement of respectability, she goes to see the show and is cruelly undeceived. We see her averting her eyes as the happy males around her focus enthusiastically on the spectacle. Giant close-ups of women's legs and the faces of performer and audience members are edited in a dizzying sequence (22 shots in 30 seconds) that culminates in the horrified girl pushing her way out along a row of protesting spectators.[40]

Even where theatre audiences are not involved, the sense of theatrical spectatorship has frequently been invoked as an enriched variation on the point-of-view shot. Sometimes a door or window frame in a shot is just that, rather than a proxy (or metaphorical) proscenium arch, but the theatrical implications of the 'framing' effect are easily made specific. In this respect, there is kinship between Eve Harrington, the *hypocrite voyeur* in Mankiewicz's *All About Eve*, and Alexander, the magic lanternist and seer of visions in Bergman's *Fanny and Alexander* (1989). Both characters cross the line between imagining things and pretending to others that they exist in ways that correspond to the cinema's own art but are made more forceful by their theatrical milieu. They cross into the spectator's realm, sharing temporarily the audience members' position as (in John Ellis' suggestive definition) 'co-voyeurs'.[41]

Patrice Pavis points out that the 'vast cosmogonies of theatre and cinema [have been] opposed according to criteria that were "specific" and metaphysical rather than historical and material'. Rather than trying to define them once and for all 'we are interested in the exchange of procedures that characterizes their incestuous relationship and in the relativity of notions of "theatricality" or "filmicity" (as the neologism might go)'.[42] The tensions or 'exchange' Pavis identifies inform the ways in which we imagine theatrical activity in all its aspects. The films discussed in the following chapters capitalize on the sense of differentiation in pleasurable tensions between the film and theatre as well as those between backstage and on stage, audience and performers or (more globally) theatre world and 'real' life. At the same time, they contribute to the historiography of the older medium – the stories audiences enjoy hearing about it and the values they ascribe to them.

As has been noted already, the present work does not attempt to offer a comprehensive account of films that represent and – crucially – imagine the theatre. Necessarily selective, it addresses dominant patterns of these representations through detailed accounts of particular films. In the first two chapters, elements of the mythology of the theatre are identified in their simplest and most influential cinematic expression, in 'backstagers' and biographical films ('biopics') from the heyday of the Hollywood studios. The essential optimism of these derives from their commercial origins, and their fictions are formulated in terms of the prevalent ideology of their time and place. These are stories in which the good end happily, the bad unhappily. (As Wilde's Miss Prism observes, 'that is what fiction means'.) The final section of Chapter 2 considers three more recent films that have some claim to vary the Hollywood model, though it is argued that only one of them, Mike Leigh's *Topsy-Turvy*, is truly radical in its approach. Chapters 3, 4 and 5 discuss ways in which the underlying patterns of the backstager and the biopic have been appropriated in films addressing darker aspects of theatre: the complexities of the actor's personality in the specific situation of the actress; the theatre as a place of mystery and psychological disturbance; and the political dimension of theatre in relation to the theatricality of politics. The concluding chapter discusses films by three French directors – Marcel Carné, Jean Renoir and Jacques Rivette – whose innovative and influential work has been marked consistently by engagement with the theatre.

Notes

1 'Tous les films sont sur le théâtre: il n'y a d'autre sujet': 'Entretien avec Jacques Rivette. Le temps déborde' (*Cahiers du cinéma*, no. 204, September 1968), in Antoine de Baecque and Charles Tesson, eds, *La Nouvelle Vague. Textes et entretiens dans les Cahiers du cinéma* (Paris: Cahiers du cinéma, 1999), p. 295.

2 Peter Barnes, in his study of *To Be or Not to Be* (London: BFI Film Classics, 2002) observes that the film 'reminds us that the theatre precedes reality: it doesn't copy it' (p. 77). On the reception of the film in 1942, see the summary of reviews – some hostile – in the American Film Institute Catalogue.

3 François Truffaut, *Hitchcock*, with the collaboration of Helen G. Scott, revised editon (New York: Simon and Schuster, 1984), p. 189.

4 Ibid.

5 Robin Wood, *Hitchcock's Films Revisited*, revised edition (New York: Columbia University Press, 2002), p. 80.

6 André Bazin, *What is Cinema?*, essays selected and translated by Hugh

Gray, 2 vols (Berkeley, Los Angeles and London: University of Los Angeles Press, 1967), vol. I, p. 99.

7 John Ellis, *Visible Fictions. Cinema, Television, Video* (London: Routledge and Kegan Paul, 1982), p. 89.

8 Bazin, *What is Cinema?*, vol. I, p. 105.

9 On Rivette and Bazin, see Alain Ménil, 'Mesure pour mesure. Théâtre et cinéma chez Jacques Rivette', in Suzanne Liandrat-Guigues, ed., *Jacques Rivette, critique et cinéaste* (Paris and Caen: Lettres Modernes Minard, 1998), pp. 67–96.

10 Christian Metz, *Film Language. A Semiotics of the Cinema*, translated by Michael Taylor (New York: Oxford University Press, 1974), pp. 4, 5. (Emphasis in the original.) In the first quotation, Metz is citing an observation by Albert Laffay in an essay first published in 1946.

11 Antonin Artaud, *The Theatre and its Double*, translated by Mary Caroline Richards (New York: Grove Press, 1958), p. 84. Richards' translation captures the manner in which Artaud's language slides from one metaphor to another. Artaud's attitudes to the cinema shifted from enthusiasm to antagonism with the advent of synchronized sound.

12 Jerzy Grotowski, *Towards a Poor Theatre*, edited by Eugenio Barba with a Preface by Peter Brook (London: Methuen, 1969), pp. 19, 41. The quotations are from essays published in 1965 ('Towards a Poor Theatre') and 1964 ('The Theatre's New Testament').

13 Paul Woodruff, *The Necessity of Theatre. The Art of Watching and Being Watched* (Oxford: Oxford University Press, 2009) p. 43. Susan Bennett's landmark study *Theatre Audiences. A Theory of Production and Reception*, 2nd edition (London and New York: Routledge, 1997) includes a more circumspect consideration of the relationship between film and theatre in the context of theories of spectatorship.

14 Graeme Turner, *Film as Social Practice*, 3rd edition (London and New York: Routledge, 1999), p. 130.

15 Jacques Rancière, *The Emancipated Spectator*, translated by Gregory Elliott (London and New York: Verso, 2009), pp. 2, 17. The work was first published in 2008 as *Le Spéctateur émancipé*.

16 Huntley Carter, *The New Spirit in the Russian Theatre, 1917–1928* (New York, London and Paris: Brentano's, 1929), part five, 'The New Auxiliaries'. Carter was revisiting the subject of his 1923 work, *The New Theatre and Cinema of Soviet Russia, 1917–23*.

17 Mordecai Gorelik, *New Theatres for Old* (New York, 1940; London: Dennis Dobson, 1947) p. 427.

18 Allardyce Nicoll, *Film and Theater* (New Haven, CT: Yale University Press, 1936), pp. 184, 188.

19 Marvin Carlson examines the variations on the 'essential spatial dialectic' between the actors' and audiences' spaces in *Places of Performance. The Semiotics of Theatre Architecture* (Ithaca, NY and London: Cornell University Press, 1989), chapter 5, 'Interior Spaces'.

20 Marvin Carlson, *The Haunted Stage. The Theatre as Memory Machine* (Ann Arbor: University of Michigan Press, 2001), pp. 11, 51.

21 Philip Auslander, *Liveness. Performance in a Mediatized Culture* (London and New York: Routledge, 1999), p. 56.

22 Joseph L. Makiewicz, *More About All About Eve, a colloquy by Gary Carey with Joseph L. Mankiewicz, together with his Screenplay 'All About Eve'* (New York: Random House, 1972), p. 8.

23 Quoted by Adrian Kiernander, *Ariane Mnouchkine and the Théâtre du Soleil* (Cambridge: Cambridge University Press, 1993), p. 113.

24 John Osborne, *Plays 2* (London: Methuen, 1998), p. 76.

25 W. Somerset Maugham, *Theatre* (Garden City, NY: Doubleday, Doran and Co., 1938), pp. 82–83.

26 Laurence Maslon, ed., *Kaufman and Co. Broadway Comedies* (New York: The Library of America, 2004), p. 78.

27 Jean-Paul Sartre, *Kean*, edited by David Bradby (Oxford: Oxford University Press, 1973), Act 2, scene 3, p. 91 (my translation). Bradby points out that Sartre's Kean was first played by Pierre Brasseur, who had appeared as the actor Frédérick Lemaître – the creator of Dumas' character – in *Les Enfants du paradis*.

28 'The Relation between the Ego and the Unconscious' (1928) cited from Anthony Storr, ed., *The Essential Jung* (1983; London: Fontana, 1998), pp. 94–95.

29 Denis Diderot, *'The Paradox of Acting' by Denis Diderot and 'Masks or Faces?' by William Archer. Introduction by Lee Strasberg* (New York: Hill and Wang, 1957), p. 37. The French text's 'l'homme sensible' encompasses the notion of response to emotional stimulus, which Diderot sets against the great actor who observes the 'l'homme sensible' as a model for the performance, while at the same time observing himself as he performs.

30 Joseph Roach, *The Player's Passion: Studies in the Science of Acting* (Newark, NJ: University of Delaware Press / Associated University Presses, 1985), p. 117.

31 Marvin Carlson, *Performance. A Critical Introduction* (London and New York: Routledge, 1996) p. 54.

32 Théophile Gautier, *Le Capitaine Fracasse*, ed. Antoine Adam (Paris: Gallimard / Folio Classique, 2002) p. 122.

33 Elia Kazan, quoted in David Garfield, *A Player's Place. The Story of the Actors Studio* (New York: Macmillan, 1980), p. 46.

34 Charlotte Brontë, *Villette*, edited by Herbert Rosengarten and Margaret Smith (Oxford: Clarendon Press, 1984), pp. 370, 371.

35 Henry James, *The Tragic Muse*, edited by Philip Hoare (London: Penguin, 1995), p. 381. On James' treatment of Rachel/Miriam see Rachel M. Brownstein, *Tragic Muse. Rachel of the Comédie Française* (Durham, NC and London: Duke University Press, 1995), pp. 246–258.

36 Émile Zola, *Nana*, ed. Henri Mitterand (Paris: Gallimard / Folio Classique, 2002) p. 152. Noël Burch discusses the film in terms of the

establishment of off-screen space in *Praxis du cinéma* (Paris: Gallimard, 1969), translated by Helen R. Lane as *Theory of Film Practice* (New Brunswick, NJ: Princeton University Press, 1981), Chapter 2, '*Nana*, or two kinds of space'.

37 Jane R. Goodall, *Performance and Evolution in the Age of Darwin* (London: Taylor and Francis, 2007), pp. 159–166.

38 *Nana, un film de Jean Renoir*, the screenplay published with the Arte DVD (Paris: Arte Éditions, 2004), pp. 102–104.

39 *Henry V*: 'Revised Treatment for Technicolor Film [...] Copy no. 7,' Birmingham Shakespeare Library S322.8F, p. 2.

40 The sequence is analysed, with frame enlargements, by Rick Altman in *The American Film Musical* (Bloomington and Indianapolis: Indiana University Press, 1989), pp. 218–222.

41 Ellis, *Visible Fictions*, p. 88.

42 Patrice Pavis, *Theatre at the Crossroads of Culture*, translated by Loren Kruger (London and New York: Routledge, 1992), p. 128.

1

The backstage movie
and the patterns of theatre life

Films about the theatre made in the sound era during the Hollywood studios' ascendancy – between the late 1920s and the 1950s – draw on many enduring elements of plot and character types. The persistence of these in backstage movies from other regimes of production and in subsequent eras suggests not only that Hollywood's products were widely influential but also that they tapped into an underlying set of ideas about the theatre. In particular we can identify the sense of the theatre's glamour, the magic relationship between what is seen 'in front' and what goes on behind the curtain, and the attractions of the actors' way of life. Some of these aspects of the mythology of theatre have been outlined in the introduction: this chapter examines further the formulaic building blocks in the 'backstager' narrative. The invocation of a location – Broadway – and its rewards and perils corresponds to a more general sense of the theatre and its sites as special, apart from the ordinary activities or even the moral strictures that govern most people's lives but at the same time representing aspirations that only depictions of the life of the stage can fully articulate.[1]

The recurrent narrative structures can be summarized. The careers of those performing in the theatre are fraught with various obstacles, both in their personal advancement and in the accomplishment of their tasks, the latter usually consisting of putting on a show of one kind or another. The personal career may encompass: a rise from low status in social and artistic terms; progress from the provinces to the metropolis; achieving acceptance among peers and employers (the audition); coping with envy and rivalry, and with complications in private (usually, love) life; finding inspiration and energy; securing and maintaining critical and audience approval. The specifics corresponding to these general features of theatrical life may involve locations or personalities (particular rivals and employers) with their own associations. Along the way the protagonists of backstage drama encounter blockers and helpers: inherited from older dramatic genres, the *senex* and the

scheming servant have their equivalents in the obstructive parent/
manager/rival and the supportive comic friend/dresser/partner. The
folk-tale hero or heroine entrusted with a quest or task, embarking on
a journey and needing to obtain support or – in a more mundane form
– some kind of clue or talisman has much in common with the hopeful
hoofer heading for the Great White Way. Unlike the heroes of some of
the tales analysed by Vladimir Propp in *The Morphology of the Folk
Tale* (1927),[2] the hoofer is unlikely to need to possess a talisman, still
less be told (like one of the Russian folk heroes) where to find a magic
duck, but he or she is going to need an entrée to the magic backstage
kingdom via the forbidding portals of the stage door or to placate the
gatekeeper who guards the impresario or agent.

The theatre is figured as a liminal space between a real and an
idealized world, and the cinema dwells on the relationship between
the realisations of dreams and the often quasi-industrial means of
achieving them. The thresholds the aspiring performer must cross are
in themselves exciting and seductive. Rick Altman observes that

> [W]hereas backstage space serves as an intermediary for the actor
> striving toward the stage, for the [cinema] audience it is the stage that
> mediates between our limited workaday world and that imaginary
> ever-so-glamorous life lived by the stars. Stage and backstage space thus
> serve as a reversible intermediary between two real worlds, that of the
> audience and that of the actors.[3]

Some 'backstage' activities are favoured more than others by film-makers.
The work of scenic and costume designers is dealt with only when it
is material to the behaviour of the principal subject of the film or
represents one among many incidental aspects that fill in the sense of
purposeful toil. For really tough rehearsal work, one has to wait for
the new wave, with John Cassavetes' *Opening Night* (1977). Although
rehearsal scenes are common, sequences depicting or even alluding
to training for the stage are rare, except for such situations as that in
Easter Parade (1948), where Fred Astaire's seasoned vaudevillian has
to instruct the tyro played by Judy Garland in routines more sophisticated than those she has been performing in a rowdy (but decorous)
bar-room.

Not infrequently in Hollywood's accounts of the stage the would-be
actor enunciates some version of the theatre's mythology, either in
general terms – wanting to make the Big Time – or in parodic detail.
In *Stage Door* (1937), Katherine Hepburn plays an idealistic young
woman whose consciousness of the dignity of the theatre and more
elevated social background make her at first an awkward member of

the community in a New York guest house for actresses. Hepburn had won an Oscar in *Morning Glory* (1935) as a much more naïve, gauche and pushy aspirant whose statement of intent embraces a theatrical myth rare among Broadway's hopefuls. Eva Lovelace ('I've acted ever since I was a child') 'reverences' Shaw above all modern dramatists:

> There will always be a Shaw play in my repertoire as long as I remain in the theatre. I expect to die at my zenith. My star shall never set. I've sworn that, too. And when that moment comes when I feel that I've done my best, my very best, I shall really die by my own hand some night at the end of the play – on stage.

Taken to a first night party by her tutelary spirit, an old English actor (C. Aubrey Smith), Eva gets drunk and insists on performing Shakespeare ('To be or not to be' and the balcony scene from *Romeo and Juliet*) to the astonishment of a roomful of Broadway luminaries. The film is franker than most of its period in intimating that she gets a part by sleeping with a powerful agent (Adolphe Menjou). She fails miserably in the minor role her indiscretion won for her, and comes near to being ruined by her illusions, but she sticks with show business, descending from the Shakespearian and Shavian heights to a job as a glamorous assistant to a team of acrobats. She finally wins through by the copybook method of going on as an understudy and making a huge hit. Warned by her dresser, herself once a Broadway star, that success is fleeting, the 'morning glory' of the film's title, she nevertheless embraces her future with determination: 'I'm not afraid of just being a morning glory.' Eva has made a false entry into the magic kingdom, been cast out to the darkness of vaudeville, but made her return. In its schematic form the film is a theatrical *Pilgrim's Progress*, a Broadway folk tale.

Broadway itself, invoked relentlessly in these and many other popular films, symbolizes not only personal success *per se*, but the bringing together of diverse talents and impulses in the great new city. Although the rules of New York's Tony awards now distinguish between theatres on the basis of audience capacity rather than location, they still invoke the division between 'Broadway' and 'off-Broadway'. The gossip columnist Walter Winchell, writing when abundant newspaper columns were there to be filled extravagantly, rhapsodized in 1928 on the glories of Broadway:

> The great thoroughfare is all things to all men. ... It is the street of opportunity, of gilt paint, of color, of high lights and deep shadows. It countenances the vulgar, when the vulgar is rich, it tolerates art, but does not endorse it. It laughs with the spendthrift while his money lasts, and forgets him when he ceases to be interesting.

'To omit Broadway', Winchell opines, 'is a calamity, to survive Broadway is an achievement.'[4] Alongside the hymns of praise to Broadway there has been no lack of reproach and admonition. In 1936 the theatre critic George Jean Nathan, after a paragraph evoking 'a great boulevard whose million dazzling lights outshine the stars of night and evening, whose gay restaurants and brilliant theatres are crowded with celebrities in the world of fashion, belles letters and public affairs' (etc.), settled down to a block-by-block description of the tawdriness of the real Broadway, 'one of the ugliest, cheapest and most thoroughly unromantic streets in the whole world'. After several pages relentlessly listing cheap eating places, downmarket cinemas and gimcrack stores, Nathan perorates with a reminder of the Broadway that once was that of George M. Cohan, Lillian Russell and others, before concluding that 'Broadway is dead'.[5]

Nevertheless, so far as the MGM's 'Broadway Melody' films – and countless others – were concerned, the name signified not only Big Time, but also the peak of the performer's career. Typically, the progression was envisaged as being from the provinces (or the sticks) to New York, and from the lower levels of burlesque *via* vaudeville to revue. (In 'legit' theatre terms, the equivalent was from summer stock to Broadway.) Vaudeville has been construed as a force in urban life that assimilated immigrants and their cultures. Albert F. McLean in *American Vaudeville as Ritual* (1965) sees it as 'a symbol of the modern American's search for commonalty of vision, as an expression of the mechanical containment of vast energy and frantic rhythms, and as an invitation to the dazzling wonderland of comfort and convenience brought about by technology and capitalism, vaudeville took a permanent place in the popular imagination.'[6] Robert W. Snyder in *The Voice of the City* (1989) identifies in vaudeville an expression of New York's spirit at the turn of the century, 'an arena for communications between otherwise separate people. ... Influences flowed back and forth in the kind of reciprocal cultural exchange that scholars have called "circularity."'[7] In the historiography of American popular entertainment vaudeville has commonly been construed as a more respectable successor to the 'variety' entertainments of the mid-nineteenth century. (In Britain the terms are different, variety being the staider successor to the music hall.) M. Alison Kibler, addressing the development in terms of gender, observes that it 'uplifted low culture and unravelled high culture; it aspired to bourgeois standardization but did not neglect working-class, immigrant pride'.[8] Lewis A. Erenburg, concurring with this view of vaudeville as a signifier of upward mobility, notes that, like the new restaurants and other elements of the booming consumer culture centred on Broadway, it was part of an 'urban state of mind: a sense of sharing a community and a set of behaviors without the need for intimacy and actual experience'.[9]

The Great White Way has its own peculiarities and rites of passage, but the diverse theatrical cultures represented in films – in Paris, Berlin or London – have many features in common with it. There is a hierarchy of genres with corresponding clienteles and signs of status in audiences and backstage; a conservative element in the art-form must be overcome by innovation; the company has its own solidarity and sense of unity in the face of the customers; the backers of the theatre must be convinced that individuals or projects are worth investment; the different constituencies within the theatre's audiences (stalls patrons and 'the gods' for example) must be wooed; prevailing social and political circumstances (war, economic hardship, etc.) must be dealt with. The overarching imperative is, unsurprisingly, that the show must go on.

As the introduction has suggested, the theatre building, with its demarcations between front-of-house, stage and backstage areas, is a rich source not only of social detail but also of symbolic meanings. This is a world of contrasts in which reflections on appearance and reality are among the simplest and most obvious level of discourse, on the basis of which statements of political and social – not to say existential – import can be made. Unsurprisingly, explicit allusions to such matters are rare in Hollywood backstagers, but they are present implicitly in the films' structures of plot and representation. Within the theatre, where backstage areas may be either luxurious or tawdry, the stage space will be empty but numinous during the day and glamorous at night, sometimes (as in the Warner Bros musicals) with an implausible but significant expansion of scenic space and orchestral resources that take the theatre-on-film beyond what the theatre-on-Broadway can do. At the very least, the camera has more privileged access than the on-screen audience. The cinema audience is admitted not only to the mechanics of stage production but also to an emotional life that is usually hidden, satisfying the desire to be in the know and at the same time to share vicariously in the performers' ability to overcome adversity. Another commonplace consequence of admission backstage is the indulgence of voyeurism and fetishism, particularly in relation to the intimacies of the dressing room. The theatre world is often figured as a haven for irregular sensation and passions, tolerated because they produce pleasures that are more or less guilty but are felt to be safe. Although such matters are not explicitly addressed in most of the earlier films from the Hollywood studios dealing with Broadway, there is often an underlying sense of the moral complexities and erotic charge of the theatre world.

Performing against the odds:
42nd Street and Gold Diggers of 1933

Released in 1933, *42nd Street* staked the claim of Warner Bros as a leading producer of musicals: in short order what was considered a moribund genre was revitalized by subsequent productions from this studio and its rivals, many of them offering variations on its situations and character types. As Richard Barrios observes, Warners delivered 'a glossy package of mythmaking that has lasted for decades'.[10] *42nd Street*, which initiated the series of 'Gold Digger' films from the studio, was derived from a lurid novel by Bradford Ropes, whose leading characters have been described as 'bastards and bitches'.[11] *Gold Diggers of 1933* (1933) adopted the leading idea and some of its incidents from Avery Hopwood's Broadway success of 1919, *The Gold Diggers*. Hopwood's play is a sentimental comedy with sufficient acknowledgements of the facts of theatrical life to raise it above the run-of-the mill musical comedy theme of the chorus girl who marries an upper-class heir or, in European contexts, a royal or aristocratic wooer. His chorus girls may be on the make, but they work hard and are not without principle. In the central action of the play the heroine skilfully pretends to be the kind of girl she is assumed to be by the strait-laced family of the young man who is wooing her. The type has been defined early on by these enemies of pleasure: 'A gold digger is a woman, generally young, who extorts money and other valuables from the gentlemen of her acquaintance, usually without making them any adequate return.'[12] The play had already been adapted with additional musical numbers (in sound and colour) by Warners as *Gold Diggers of Broadway* (1929), of which only a few minutes survive. In the 1933 musical the material has been reshaped to make on-stage performances integral to the plot and the emphasis has shifted to the family's objections to their scion's inappropriate liaison with a chorus girl to the more complicated attempt to prevent him from going on the stage himself. Robert Treat Bradford (Dick Powell), under the assumed name of Brad Roberts, has been composing songs and then participating as juvenile lead in a show he has supported financially. Consequently, whatever gets in the way of him as a performer, composer and producer – and, as it happens, as the lover of the ingénue Polly Parker (Ruby Keeler) – will work against the imperative to get the show, *Forgotten Melody*, on stage. Overcoming the prejudices of his stuffy family will be the task of the film's second act. Variations of this situation, with an inevitable link between the thwarting of young love and the denial of resources to a show, and the more or less significant but always recurrent theme of show girls seeking rich husbands, provide the basic structure for the subsequent musicals in this series, produced in rapid succession: *Footlight Parade* (1933), *Gold Diggers of 1935*, *Dames* (both 1934), *Gold Diggers of 1937* (1936) and *Gold Diggers in Paris* (1938).

In *42nd Street* the backing for *Pretty Lady* has already been obtained by its star Dorothy Brock (Bebe Daniels), who is seen persuading her sugar daddy Abner Dillon (Guy Kibee) to gratify her and further her career by signing a contract. As he hesitates, a shot shows his view of Dorothy's shapely legs and his fate is obviously sealed: to this extent, the 'gold digger' motif is already in place, even though it will not be the mainspring of the plot. It resurfaces when Abner threatens to withdraw his investment after Dorothy has dismissed him. Angrily, the director Julian Marsh (Warner Baxter) faces him down over this betrayal. Unfortunately, Dorothy breaks her ankle, and it looks as though the show cannot go on, but Abner turns up at the theatre with 'Anytime Annie' (Ginger Rogers), whom he offers triumphantly as a replacement for Dorothy. Nobly and surprisingly, she turns down the chance and hands it over to the young beginner Peggy Sawyer (Ruby Keeler). In *Footlight Parade*, Chester Kent (James Cagney) is the tireless producer of lavish live-action 'prologues' for movie houses, his answer to the slump in the market for musical comedies.[13] He is being swindled by his backers, but the main obstacle to be overcome is the skullduggery of a rival producer who is stealing his ideas. The opening night towards which the film is propelled consists of his staging three of these prologues at three different cinemas on the same night, a feat of logistics which climaxes in his having to go on himself in the final prologue ('Shanghai Lil') because the leading man has been made drunk by a treacherous chorine working for the opposition. *Gold Diggers of 1935* also moves away from the gold-digging trope as the central armature of its plot, but compensates with a relentless emphasis on money-making and chiseling in the grander environment of a resort hotel where a moneyed but avaricious widow has the strange habit of staging an annual entertainment. Within this scheme the extraction of money from men by the exercise of 'feminine wiles' plays no more than a minor part, but everyone except the innocent principals seems to be digging for gold, including the pretentious European director Nicoleff. (He boasts of 'a priceless silver fruit dish given me by the Grand Duke Alexis after seeing my production of *A Midsummer Night's Dream* with an all-Eskimo cast'.)

These examples illustrate the changes rung on the 'getting the show on' plot, with the admixture in varying proportions of some other recurrent elements. The money man – in the parlance of the time, a 'butter-and-egg man' besotted with the glamour of the big city – is clueless about show business and its realities. His business tends to be given a comic title (Abner in *42nd Street* is 'the Kiddie Kar King') and he may be under pressure from his domineering relatives or subject to other influences that have nothing to do with either the theatre business or his own concerns. In some cases Puritanism rather than social prejudice is a problem, in which case leverage may be provided by the obstructive person's succumbing to the blackmailing allure of a show girl or the undermining of his defences by other means. Consequently, the success of the show will entail the defeat of those whose claim to be wiser is mistaken, of rivals within the company, and of social prejudices. And it will result, inevitably, in the success in love and on stage of the young leads.

Measured simply in terms of productions opened, Broadway had suffered in the wake of the 1929 stock market crash and continued to experience hard times through the next decade. From 239 openings in 1929–1930 the output of the New York stage fell to 187 in 1930–1931 and was down to 100 in 1938–1939.[14] *42nd Street* and *Gold Diggers of 1933* are more forthright than the subsequent films in situating the show business world in the context of the Depression. The former is sprinkled with references to the economic situation, but soon leaves them behind. The latter opens with a full rehearsal of the number 'We're in the Money' that is broken up by the Sheriff and his men serving the producer Barney Hopkins (Ned Sparks) with 'a legal attachment to pay creditors' and impounding the sets, props and costumes – to the extent of trying to detach the costume from a chorus girl who is wearing it. (In a neat symbolic touch, the garment in question consists mainly of a large dummy coin attached to her briefs.) Subsequent scenes emphasize the effect of the Depression on Broadway – a notice board lists the theatres that are closed – and the girls who share lodgings and struggle to pay their rent also have to share beds and clothes. Once the show is on, however, money is no longer a problem and the girls can move into a more luxurious apartment. Although after the first twenty minutes or so *Gold Diggers of 1933* seems to leave the Depression behind, it concludes with 'My Forgotten Man', a spectacular and impassioned plea for the recognition of men who returned as heroes from the First World War but found themselves thrown out of work by the Depression.[15]

In *Footlight Parade* the main causes of anxiety are the effect of talking pictures on live musical comedy and the rivalry within the profession, but the New Deal is vividly represented in the finale of 'Shanghai Lil', with a platoon of marines who march and counter-march elaborately before joining with the female chorus to form what is seen in a series of top shots as, successively, the Stars and Stripes, a portrait of Franklin D. Roosevelt, and the eagle emblem of the National Recovery Administration. This is not so much an integral element of the film as a grand gesture of support on the part of Warner Bros, because the financial worries of the professionals have little to do directly with the country's situation. Nevertheless, money remains a problem. Show business, although treated with greater simplicity than the real workings of Broadway finance would require, is still definitely a business. Somehow getting has to precede spending. This account of the financial dimension of the musicals' plot lines has necessarily included some indication of recurrent character types. Here, as in other respects, *42nd Street* establishes – or confirms – important elements of the theatre as viewed from Hollywood. The characterization of backers reflects the precarious nature of financial support and its susceptibility to influences in the wider commercial world or in the personal lives of the providers. Given that unless the show does go on the cinema audience is going to be denied the pleasure it expects from it – as well as from the happiness of the leading characters – the obstacles rarely seem very formidable.

More interesting are the figures that can be described in folk-tale terms as 'helpers' or as fulfilling the ancient comedy role of an *eiron* – the scheming slave or servant – partly because this function can be located not merely in individuals but also in the prevailing supportive ethos of show business. Once the newcomer has passed the initial test – in *42nd Street* as in many other films, the audition – she (rarely, he) becomes one of the family. Significantly, one of the divergences of this film's script from Ropes' novel is that the heroine does not become swollen-headed once she has achieved her great success: Ruby Keeler/ Peggy Sawyer 'goes out there a youngster' and does come back a star but remains a youngster at heart. For no very good reason except a conversion to the good-heartedness she has hitherto concealed under a cynical exterior – and certainly not on account of any outstanding talent we have seen on Peggy's (or Keeler's) part – Annie gives up her chance of replacing the injured star in favour of the young hopeful. Later, after Peggy has been put through the mill by the director and is resting before curtain time, Dorothy appears in her dressing room on crutches and demands to see her alone. Rather than excoriate the lucky girl, Dorothy now acts with surprising generosity: 'I'm going to

2. *42nd Street* (1933):
Marsh motivates Peggy

wish you only one thing, my dear. Go out there – and be so swell you'll make me hate you!' Peggy's principal helper is of course the juvenile lead, Billy Lawler (Dick Powell), whom she 'meets cute' on her first morning in the theatre when she barges into his dressing room while he is in his underwear. He protects her as he leads her to the stage by fielding the wisecracks made at her and his expense by a group of 'hard-boiled' chorus girls (so described in the script) and then she is handed over to the other girls, led by Lorraine Fleming (Una Merkel), who take pity on her naïveté and quickly accept her. Billy soon has a rival in supporting Peggy, a pushy chorus boy called Terry who later makes a crude and futile pass at her during a cast party, and she also receives moral support from Pat Denning, an unsuccessful vaudevillian who is Dorothy's secret lover.

Peggy thus attracts sympathy and support on a scale that helps the cinema audience to overlook the limitations of her dancing and (more drastically) her feeble singing. Eventually, when Julian Marsh has been persuaded against his better judgement to give her a try as Dorothy's substitute, she is put through a tough training session that leaves her exhausted before first Billy and then Dorothy come to see her. Only by kissing her suddenly and passionately has Marsh been able to overcome Peggy's failure to put any energy and expression into the banal first line of her part – '*Jim*! They didn't tell me *you* were here! It was grand of you to come!' Before she goes on, though, he delivers the admonition that has become the film's best-known speech, insisting that 'two hundred people – two hundred jobs – two hundred thousand dollars – five weeks of grind – and blood and sweat – depend on you', and ending with the order 'you're going out there a youngster – you've GOT to come back a star!' (Figure 2).

The pattern of the plot and the identity of the actress all make her fulfilling this demand a forgone conclusion: we *know* she will succeed. All the same, as helpers go Marsh is remarkably uncompromising: it is tempting to suppose that Peggy triumphs despite this harangue rather than because of it. His character combines two stereotypes important in the genre, the superior who has to be convinced (just as he had to be at auditions) and the artist with problems. He is a driven and complex personality, a sick man whose health and financial security ride on *Pretty Lady* and a tyrant who seems more exasperated and exhausted in successive rehearsal scenes as he twists in agony on his bentwood chair and repeatedly denounces the ineptitude of his cast. Peggy collapses and has to be carried off as he drives the dancers through a prolonged late-night rehearsal. She is lucky: in the shooting script an old actor playing a cabman reminiscing about the glorious past of Broadway keels over and dies during a rehearsal, an incident that is passed over by Marsh until he is sitting alone on the empty stage with the dance director Andy and admits: 'My back's against the wall ... I've cursed them – driven them – worn their feet off and torn their hearts out – who knows (thinking of the old trouper) I may even have killed one of them.'[16] Marsh is the stage director of *Pretty Lady*, and the choreography – such as it is – is taken over by Andy and an assistant. One of their chief duties seems to be shouting at the chorus, repeating Marsh's orders. So far as the book of the show is concerned, we see very little of it except for a brief rehearsal scene in which Marsh is taking the principals through a dialogue scene and allowing the leading lady to overrule the irate author of the script. His imperious approach to the material is reinforced when he stops a staggeringly banal number ('It must be June') and berates the composer and lyricist, played in a charming gag by Al Dubin and Harry Warren, the film's song writers. Doesn't he like the song? – 'Sure I like it. I've liked it since 1905. Like it...? What do you think we're putting on ... a revival?' The key elements of Marsh's technique are a zest for angry expostulation and being prepared to push everyone around him to their physical and mental limit. In the closing moments this sick man, who has already had one breakdown and is directing *Pretty Lady* against doctor's orders, sinks onto the steps of the fire escape as playgoers jostle past him expressing the opinion that the show's success is all down to Peggy Sawyer and Marsh will be taking more than his share of the credit.

That Marsh's working methods should remain one of the mysteries of the theatre (along with whatever plot *Pretty Lady* has) is typical of the way his kind of work is shown in most of the films featuring musicals. Clark Gable, as the director Patch Gallaher in *Dancing Lady* (1933), MGM's response to *42nd Street*, has comparable material to work with, the same bentwood chair perched on the edge of the stage or on a plank over the orchestra pit, and a faithful assistant to convey his orders to the company. Unlike Marsh, Gable's character is not chronically ill but simply exhausted, and the love plot plays to the actor's strengths and screen image: he has to admit to himself that he has fallen for the determined 'dancing lady' (Joan Crawford) who is made the show's star. (Marsh has no relationship with Peggy beyond his professional one, and the kiss he uses to startle her has no ulterior purpose.) In its depiction of how directors operate, though, *Dancing Lady* follows the same pattern as its rival. In the Warner Bros films there is a similar lack of concern with the director as an artist. The nearest approach to this is in *Footlight Parade* when Chester Kent, whose background (like Cagney's) is as a dancer in vaudeville, takes over a rehearsal from his loyal but perpetually overstretched dance director (Frank McHugh). Here there is in any case no need for a book for the show-within-a-film, as the 'prologues' stand alone as numbers to be staged in a cinema, and we see vestiges of stage sets that correspond to the end product. In these circumstances, it may matter less – if it really matters at all – that the numbers devised by Busby Berkeley would be impossible to put on any stage and are seen from angles and vantage points inconceivable for a theatre audience. Martin Rubin notes that the establishment of a distinct stage space rather than any realistic representation of it is all that is required for what he identifies as the 'Berkeleyesque' spectacle that the films contain:

> The film must work to establish a space (or a series of homologous spaces) that are, to a certain extent, self-enclosed and independent of the surrounding narrative. This renders the space accessible to spectacular extensions and distortions that can be clearly in excess of the narrative without necessarily distorting it. The main requirement is that this space can be a special or bracketed space, adjoining the primary space of the narrative but not completely subordinated to it.[17]

Not only does this effect a demarcation of performance space from the realm of the 'off-stage' narrative, as Rubin observes, but it also sets it apart from the backstage established before we see the numbers. The fantasies of the grand numbers – and after 42nd Street they get even grander – could not be produced by the more or less realistically rendered facilities and rehearsal procedures shown to us. Effectively, the 'backstage' musicals have three rather than two distinct worlds: off-stage, backstage and imaginary. It is perhaps significant that the one film in the series directed by Berkeley himself, *Gold Diggers of 1935*, has virtually no 'backstage' element: he had nothing to say about the work of the stage director and the mechanics of 'putting on a show' that form the pretext for his own work. The only rehearsal scenes are those led by Nicoleff, a comic mixture of modern dance and 'Russian' ballet with no connection to anything seen on stage.

The backstage architecture of the theatres in *42nd Street* and *Gold Diggers of 1933* is shown with convincing realism. We see brick walls, a sense of height and the empty space that is to be filled – shots look down onto the stage from the flies and across the footlights – and there are sparsely furnished dressing rooms, trunks piled in passages and corners of the stage and along passages, and flats leaning against walls. The lighting board is a simplified version of the real thing, 'industrial' enough for strong, determined men to move big levers at the word of command, and the curtain is raised and lowered with a hemp rope in the prompt corner. The stage crew (as it would have been at the time) is exclusively male, and we see very few women backstage, even as dressers or wardrobe mistresses, and no people of colour apart from Dorothy's 'colored' maid, with her appropriately stereotypical dialogue. In this theatrical economy, women are a raw material that may be shaped into a chorus or selected for stardom. There are iron galleries and stairs leading to the dressing rooms, allowing shots from below as chorus girls run up and down them. The chorines have attractive rehearsal outfits of shorts and blouses, some more ornate than others – this is not the world of leg warmers and lycra leotards that we find in the corresponding situations in *All That Jazz* (1979) and *A Chorus Line* (1985) – and the routines consist for the most part of combinations of steps and hammering tapping. The male gaze is gratified not only in the numbers by Berkeley but, as matter of routine, in the auditioning process when the women in their street clothes are asked to raise their skirts so that their legs can be appraised. (The process is hardly necessary in the 'cattle call' auditions of the two later films, but returns in a cruder form in *Showgirls* [1995] when the conventionally tyrannical director requires a display of breasts rather than calves.) The director and his assistants wear street clothes, formal by twenty-first-century standards, the men invariably with hats which for the most part they keep on during work: this makes Marsh's growing dishevelment all the more striking.

All this goes with a sense of purposeful workaday bustle on the part of stage staff and anxious waiting (more bentwood chairs) or determined hoofing from the dancers. One convention of the stage-on-film, however, demands that just before the curtain goes up a milling crowd has to be shouted at to take 'places' and orders have to be delivered with stentorian urgency. The world of illusion is grounded in a sense of workaday reality, even if in the big musical numbers it is about to depart from it, while the auditorium on a first night is filled with the top-hatted and evening-gowned clientele. The Big Time deserves no less, and although this maybe the street where 'the underworld can meet the elite', there is no sign of the former on this occasion.[18]

The plot structures and character types of *42nd Street* recur with variations in subsequent movies in the Warner Bros series and those of other studios. It is useful to consider again the counter-measure taken by MGM in the form of *Dancing Lady*. Not only does the film adapt the 'exasperated director' figure, Patch Gallagher, to suit Clark Gable's potential as a strong but reluctant lover, but it also benefits from Joan Crawford's presence. She is superior to Keeler as a dancer and actor, and her role is that of an experienced – not to say, hardened – and dedicated dancer who has to work her way up from burlesque to the Big Time, an archetype of backstage narrative which will be discussed presently but which Peggy Sawyer has nothing to do with. Crawford's character, Janie Barlow, refuses to allow love to deprive her of a career, but only when she discovers that she has been cruelly deceived by an upper-class backer who attempts to wreck it after she has agreed to marry him if it is not a success. Finding true love and artistic as well as personal integrity with Clark Gable is a far more bracing and grown-up proposition than spending the rest of one's life cosseted on Park Avenue.

MGM's art department, led by Cedric Gibbons, creates a theatrical environment that is palatial compared to that available in the Warner Bros studio, with a spacious backstage area, a chorus dressing-room that looks like the ladies' lounge in a fancy night club, a star dressing room to match, and an auditorium that is the latest in art deco good taste. By contrast the burlesque house in which Janie is first seen dancing has a rough male audience, runways for the girls to parade down (and be lunged at by overwrought clients) and a blaring orchestra. The first scene shows uptown ladies and their silk-hatted escorts braving this preserve of downtown raunchiness, slumming so that Tod (Franchot Tone), the moneyed young man-about-town, can show them his discovery. But Crawford is born to dance and her ambition is expressed in geographical as well as artistic terms. Later, as she undresses before going to bed in the shabby apartment she shares with a fellow burlesque artiste, she announces 'I'm through dreamin' – I'm goin' to start doin' – I'm goin' up where it's art. Uptown.' Tod has used his influence with the show's backer to get her in to see Gallagher despite the 'No girls wanted' sign on the stage door. Once in the theatre she braves an audition, which Gallagher sabotages by saddling her with a parody of accompaniment. (Two of the Three Stooges are employed as stage hands, the third as a rehearsal pianist.) Despite the cacophony, she shows she is a marvelous dancer, and reinforces the effect when Gallagher insist on her being given a proper chance. Her obvious talent overcomes his justified resentment of the pressure brought to bear on him through the show's backers: 'These very important friends who want to put their dames in the front row so they can show their friends how well they can pick 'em.' Like Peggy Sawyer, who neither smokes nor drinks and hates being 'pawed' by men, Janie needs to keep free and sober to defend herself in a hostile world: she will not sell herself cheap and she is put off by Tod's habitual tippling. When Gallagher decides his leading lady is not up to the job, her place is offered to Janie. The pressure on her is as great as that applied to Peggy, but expressed in terms of personal danger rather than duty to a company: 'The top spot, where if you drop you've got twice as far to fall.' The show is heading for success when Tod selfishly pulls out his money and calls on her promise, taking her off to Cuba on a (chaperoned) holiday that should result in marriage. Gallagher responds bitterly to the news of the backer's withdrawal and Janie's decision to honour her promise to Tod, wishing her 'better luck with his show than you had with mine', and dismisses her ruefully in a line to his assistant Steve as 'a girl who traded Broadway for Park Avenue'. Watching Cuban dancers makes her homesick for the stage where her soul belongs, and when she learns of Tod's perfidy she hastens back to New York in time to save the show and her relationship with Gallagher. It is especially satisfying that in the final scenes she is able to confront her would-be lover with the truth. 'Dancing's my racket, Tod', she insists, reminding him of the Pygmalion-style lessons in grammar he tried to teach her when he first wooed her: 'I'm afraid them things won't mix with those things.' Life with Patch Gallagher will be demanding. Even in the moment of triumph she has sensed his unremitting professional commitment: 'I saw your face once in the wings – made me feel as if everything I was doing was wrong.'

The spectacular musical numbers in *Dancing Lady* lack the imaginative quality of Berkeley's fantasies.[19] Their 'bolted-on' quality is reflected in the use of what are evidently substantial outtakes in the opening credits – among them a roller-skating routine that must have been moved from its logical position at the end of the film. Here an important distinction suggests itself. In the Warner Bros films the 'realist' storylines and dialogue make more or less explicit reference to the erotic commerce that is part of the gold-digger type and also, more generally, of the mythology of the theatre. Jerome Delamater, in *Dance in the Hollywood Musical* (1981), hails Berkeley as 'the consummate surrealist of the American screen', pointing to the manner in which 'the worlds of fantasy, irrationality and eroticism so important to the surrealists are the controlling forces in Berkeley's work'.[20] The musical numbers develop this erotic dimension, much as they extend the imaginary space of performance: it is as though what might be hinted at in the business relations and/or love lives of the show folks is transposed into the magic realm of gushing waterfalls, 'crotch shots', displays of female underwear and implicit variations on the sexual consequences of 'spooning'.[21] Then there are the sleeping cars that help newlyweds 'shuffle off to Buffalo' in *42nd Street* and the coyly erotic haven of 'Honeymoon Hotel' with its clientele of couples registered as Mr and Mrs Smith in *Footlight Parade*. (Keeler and Powell, of course, are shown being married before they go upstairs.) In this respect, then, the surreal qualities of the numbers intersect with the routine love story of the plot, filling out its unspoken dimensions. The chorus lines, Patricia Mellencamp argues, 'are a combination of Freud's sexual fetish and Marx's commodity fetish, linking up with mechanical studies of human labour [i.e., Taylorism] but taken into leisure and pleasure – like the cinema itself.'[22] To summarize: a great deal of psychological and ideological work is being done here.

Above all, these are success stories for hard times. Andrew Bergman argues persuasively for continuity between the gangster films and the musicals produced by Warner Bros: 'The gangster world and the backstage world of Warner's big three musicals of 1933 were, in effect, success preserves. From triggerman to Boss of the North Side, from back row of the chorus to the opening night lead, from office boy to chairman of the board: it was the same dynamic at work.'[23] Broadway is a magic realm within which, for all the hardships and impoverishment its inhabitants have endured, personal achievement is possible by legal means. This ultra-optimistic individualism is in tune with one of the popularly entertained solutions to the social and economic situation of the early 1930s, a conservative 'Horatio Alger' agenda. At the same time it may be the case that, as Morris Dickstein points out, the elaborate numbers are 'hymns to collective planning and precision movement, not to individual initiative'.[24] Whatever else they are, Berkeley's extravagant musical numbers are also a dream of theatre. One of the most extraordinary, 'Lullaby of Broadway' in *Gold Diggers of 1935*, is seen as if in a dream with canted camera angles and initiated by a shot that slowly brings the face of the singer (Wini Shaw), at first isolated as a speck of light in cavernous darkness, into a screen-filling close-up. She turns her head, inserting a cigarette between her lips, and her image mutates into a vignette of the city with the 'Great White Way' identifiable by its diagonal path across the grid. A series of episodes illustrate the early-morning bed-time and night-time revelling of a 'Broadway Baby', the culminating sequence being a performance in a night-club whose immense floor space, steps and rostra resemble a set design by Adolphe Appia. The 'baby' (also played by Shaw) and her escort (Dick Powell) are the only guests, watching from a high rostrum. The dancers on the floor below insist that she join them, and he follows her. Finally, she runs up to a balcony overlooking the city and playfully shuts the French windows against him and the crowd. When they surge against the windows, she is pushed over the edge of the balcony and falls to the street, many stories below. The concluding images take us back to the room she no longer inhabits, the kitten she is no longer there to feed, and the face of the singer. The 'baby' of the number is not a performer but an audience member, her lifestyle one of cocktail bars and night-clubs, implicitly aimless and hedonistic and divorced from the manifest hard work done by workers we see commuting, eating a hurried breakfast and clocking in during the prelude to the story itself. Do the dancers by whom she is effectively killed execute a vengeance on their behalf?

This moral tale not only violates the real spatial and technical resources of the stage on which it is supposedly presented, but also goes further than many other Berkeley numbers in exploring the possibilities of cinematic story-telling.[25] Some reviewers admitted to being bemused. 'It's not entertainment at all, it's something that happens to you, like an earthquake', wrote John C. Mosher in the *New Yorker*, disturbed by the number and the apparition of Wini Shaw's face that begins it: 'That the song which the face gravely chants on its journey through space is that harmless jingle, "The Lullaby of Broadway," makes the whole thing somehow a little more terrifying. I don't know why.'[26] In the *New York Times* André Sennwald hailed Berkeley as 'the master of scenic prestidigitation' and expressed amazement at the 'kaleido-scopic pageant' of the sequence: 'Some of us had begun to fear that Mr. Berkeley's effects were intended to club the fancy instead of beguile it, but here his work is notable for its imaginative qualities, as well as its technical brilliance.'[27]

'Lullaby of Broadway', like many Berkeley numbers, is not so much a depiction of the theatre as a reflection on it, a gesture away from the more limited resources of the 'live' stage that simultaneously acknowledges its importance. In the films Berkeley contributed to, characters succeed in the theatre they inhabit in the realistic backstage scenes, while – without their knowing it – Berkeley's fantasies project that success in terms that acknowledge but exceed the theatre's capabilities. Within *Gold Diggers of 1935*, set in a fashionable country hotel, 'Lullaby of Broadway', seems to constitute yet another hybrid film-within-a-stage-show, enacted in a psychological or at least allegorical theatrical space.

Other styles and aspirations:
Astaire and Rogers at RKO, the *Broadway Melody* series, and Rooney and Garland putting on the show at MGM

The Warner Bros films refer to vaudeville and its less glamorous antecedents in passing, but other variations on the backstage musical situate the culminating show more firmly in the range of popular entertainment, from burlesque to cabaret, or (with Rooney and Garland) incorporate it in a distinctive narrative of maturing talent and youthful resourcefulness. Nine RKO films, made between 1933 and 1938, pair Fred Astaire and Ginger Rogers: *Flying Down to Rio* (1933), *The Gay Divorcée* (1934), *Roberta* and *Top Hat* (1935), *Follow the Fleet* and *Swing Time* (1936), *Shall We Dance?* (1937), *Carefree* (1938) and a biographical film, *The Story of Vernon and Irene Castle* (1939). The first eight of these offer a far ritzier milieu than the Warner Bros series, but retain an element of the social tensions present in the other 'show business success' narratives and share some of their characteristic plot devices and character types. (The last, essentially a 'biopic', has the variation on these patterns specific to that genre.) Although the basic pattern allows of significant variations, *The Gay Divorcée* and *Top Hat* share plot characteristics outlined by Edward Gallafent: 'The mingling of romance and farce works similarly in the two films to create an apparent antagonism between the man and the woman as soon as they meet, to let them seduce each other with the dance, to let there be a misunderstanding over who or what he is and to let the misunderstanding be resolved.'[28] John Mueller, in *Astaire Dancing* (1985), offers an even more concise description of the formula: 'ABC', or 'Attraction, Breakup, Conciliation', and notes that it is repeated with more or less (usually less) sophistication in the subsequent films.[29] There are varying degrees of professional experience in Rogers' characters but she always reveals a 'natural' or trained accomplishment to complement that of Astaire, who usually plays an established professional. Superlative performing ability is acknowledged and rewarded, and it only needs the right occasions to be revealed.

However, there is little to suggest the backstage world itself in the RKO cycle. Astaire's character may find his way temporarily blocked by a romantic entanglement, but his performing aspirations are already more than satisfied. The impediments are the misunderstandings in his love life noted above, and the connection between these and his dancing – and attractive and persuasive singing – lies in his ability to woo by exercising his art. *Top Hat*, with a score by Irving Berlin, is exemplary in this respect. Jerry Travers (Astaire) is an American dancer making his London début in a show produced by Horace Hardwick (Edward Everett Horton). There is no doubt about the success of the production, although for a few moments it looks as though its run may be jeopardized by Jerry's pursuit to Venice of the woman with whom he has fallen in love, Dale Tremont (Rogers).

Most of the action unfolds in series of spaces that are effectively theatrical. Van Nest Polglase's sets provide spacious and ornate hotel rooms and lobbies, and above all his fantasy Venice, the last of these more rococo than deco. A park bandstand that becomes a stage shared by a dancing couple may be private (the rain has driven away potential onlookers) but its suitability as a performance space is unmistakable. The transition from dialogue first to song and then to dance seems 'natural' with only a token regard for realistic pretexts: this is, after all, what these performers (and/or characters) do for themselves and for us. In 'Cheek to Cheek' Astaire and Rogers begin dancing among other guests then segue into a transitional passage when he begins the song, before moving – on their own – to a stage that is suspended above the studio floor and the 'Venetian' canals (Figure 3). The 'stage' here, whatever justification it may have in the architecture of the hotel, is there to support their developing relationship and to offer it up to the camera and its audiences. At the end of the number the couple lean against a balustrade and then walk through a gate that opens onto a balcony with a palpably fake view of the moonlit city – as though they are on a stage in front of a backdrop only slightly less stylized than the outline of the Eiffel Tower and row of streetlamps that backed Jerry's 'Top Hat' number in the London theatre. A reverse angle shows the Venice set and its canals. No one can ever have wished this setting were more realistic, nor its dramatic pretext more probable: both contribute to the other-worldly sublimity achieved in the combination of music and dance. It exemplifies the comprehensive theatricalization of the world in *Top Hat*. Like the Berkeley numbers, it is not so much a depiction of the theatre as the annexation of some of its features. Dancing in private and public is an irresistible impulse and is unquestionably good for you. In the theatre, truth resides, and it can be invoked even when its day-to-day activities and labours are not shown. The cabaret situation facilitates a smooth transition from private to theatrical behaviour. As Lewis A. Erenberg observes, cabarets 'modified the

3. *Top Hat* (1935):
Astaire and Rogers move
across the canal onto the
'stage'

formal boundaries that existed between audience and performers in the theatre'.[30] The rooftop nightclub set designed by John Harkrider – a Ziegfeld associate – for *Swing Time* delivers an even clearer and literal suggestion of the cabaret's elevation of the guests and performers it brings together: James Sanders in *Celluloid Skyline* points out that New York night-clubs – with the notable exception of the Rainbow Room in the Rockefeller Center – were not perched at or near the top of high buildings. In the dynamic of social and artistic success represented by the movies, though, imagination won out over actuality in this as in many other respects.[31]

The world in which Astaire and Rogers achieve success in the RKO films is 'high hat' even when their breadwinning involves (at least at first) a period spent in less elevated social circles. By the end of each movie, the pair will have performed in at least one grand night-club or theatre: in *Follow the Fleet* this is achieved by having them appear in a parable of Monte Carlo, 'Let's Face the Music (and Dance)', at a benefit performance on board the ship whose refitting is being financed. Beyond such sequences marking their achievement of an ultra-sophisticated Big Time, the two principals can be seen as members of another level of aristocracy, a paradox within America's democratic society that is never invoked in the Warner Bros films. Joseph Epstein comments that 'Alexis de Tocqueville would doubtless have had fascinating things to say about the mixed democratic-aristocratic element in the Astaire-Rogers team'.[32] The lyrics of 'Top Hat, White Tie and Tails' in *Top Hat* amount to an unequivocal announcement of high status: 'an atmosphere / That simply reeks of class'. But the high class is, of course, that of an American entertainer, a distinction emphasized by Astaire's disruption of the decorum of the stuffy Thackeray Club in the film's first sequence and his 'conquest' of its members as they watch this number from a box. Part of the appeal of such stories during the Depression surely lay in the improbable ease with which talent finds its rewards. The situation is also traditional in musical comedies and films such as *Sally* (1929), where rapid achievement of recognition leads to more and fancier singing and dancing, which is after all what the audience has paid for.

In MGM's 'Broadway Melody' movies the sense of a real place and entertainment industry predominates, one distinct from the fairy-tale-like world conjured up by RKO and at the same time charged with a romantic energy largely absent from the Warners' films. The series was inaugurated with an early talkie, *The Broadway Melody* (1929), and revived with *Broadway Melodies of 1936* (1935), *1938* (1937) and *1940* (1939). *Broadway Rhythm* (1943) was originally intended to be *Broadway Melody of 1944*. The title song of the 1929 film, introduced by Charles King in an opening scene in Tin Pan Alley, recurs – along with some other numbers – with shameless regularity, and because studios drew liberally on their musical properties for background music, it permeates the cycle and persists into later productions such as *Singin' in the Rain* (1952). The lyrics of Arthur Freed and Nacio Herb Brown's song are relentlessly optimistic: 'Broadway always wears a smile' and there are 'No skies of grey on the Great White Way'.[33] Nevertheless, *The Broadway Melody* delivers its share of grey skies, if only for its female lead, played by Bessie Love.

Publicity promised that 'the pulsating drama of Broadway's bared heart speaks and sings with a voice to stir your soul', and for all the jauntiness of the title song, there is a degree of bitterness in the story of the initial *Broadway Melody*, with its not altogether likeable leading man and a spunky heroine, 'Hank' (Love), whom the Big Time scarcely treats well. After working their way west to New York she and her 'sister act' partner Queenie (Anita Page) are holed up in what a title card identifies as a 'theatrical hotel', washing their underwear in the bathroom sink and contriving to use room service without tipping the bellhop. They team up with Eddie (Charles King), a songwriter and singer who is not quite the big shot he claims to be, but despite setbacks, including a spiteful chorine who 'crabs' their audition, they manage to get as far as a revue staged by 'Zanfeld'. When a showgirl posing as its figurehead faints and falls from a galley in the rehearsal of an 'Antony and Cleopatra' number, Queenie takes her place and gets promoted on the basis of her figure. (The professional Hank is miffed by this evidence of the phenomenon she dubs 'Broads Way': 'We ain't ever got by on our legs before.') Queenie almost falls prey to a stage-door playboy but is rescued. Eddie professes his love to

Hank by singing 'You were meant for me' to her in her hotel room, and they go to the company's birthday party for Queenie – a festivity she off-handedly cuts in favour of a high-class affair hosted by her would-be beau in an art deco apartment. Knowing that Queenie really belongs with Eddie, Hank sends him to rescue her. After a sequence including 'The Wedding of the Painted Doll' and a number for the sister act, the film veers back to the plot, with Hank laughing and crying in the dressing room as she takes off her makeup. In the final scenes Hank sacrifices herself for the other half of her 'sister act' and admits in the final sequence to being 'happier on the road' and 'opening in Peoria, four shows a day'. Broadway wants Queenie and she needs it, but Hank is a 'born trouper' and, when all is said and done, she does not belong there.

The 1929 film goes further than the Production Code would subsequently allow in depicting the perils and peculiarities of the stage. The 'theatrical hotel' is distinctly down market. In the theatre the chorines are casually referred to as gold diggers, and one of the backers is a permanently drunk 'swell' who sits ogling the chorus girls and is addressed as 'Unconscious' as if it were his name. There is even a costume designer characterized as a conventional comic 'fairy'. In the dressing room the women are bossed around by a brusque wardrobe mistress and the backstage conditions are unglamorous. Still, this is Broadway, and Hank is conscious of the difference between New York and the road: 'Can you imagine putting on all this makeup for only one show a day?'

The later *Broadway Melody* films, picking up some of the same musical material seven years later, are in the much grander and far less realistic style associated with MGM in the 1930s. They offer by contrast a relatively uncomplicated version of the performers' hard-won achievement of stardom, and in them no one is dispatched back to the sticks they came from. A range of miscellaneous talents strive for recognition, from odd speciality acts (the expert snorer or sneezer) to eccentric dancing (Buddy Ebsen), child prodigies (Judy Garland) and – as a kind of vaudevillian aristocracy – dancers like Eleanor Powell and Fred Astaire.[34] *Broadway Melody of 1938* has the veteran Sophie Tucker as a presiding genius, affirming the illustrious history and career open to talents that the street represents. For Astaire himself *Broadway Melody of 1940* begins in circumstances less glamorous than those of the RKO cycle of musicals, paired with George Murphy in a double act at the 'Dawnland Ballroom', which also offers a fast-track wedding facility. They are spotted by an agent who picks Astaire to partner Eleanor Powell in his big new show.

Unfortunately a misunderstanding delivers the job to Murphy. Astaire, in the first of a series of self-effacing gestures, goes along with this. After a number of twists and turns, this confusion is cleared up, Powell realizes that it is Astaire who is the better dancer and should have had the contract – he substitutes for Murphy at a rehearsal – and in a somewhat unpleasant episode Murphy gets drunk on opening night and Astaire goes on again, this time for a number in which, being masked, he would not be recognized. The resolution delivers success and happiness as appropriate: the reformed Murphy feigns drunkenness so that Astaire will get his chance on stage in the film's climactic performance, 'When they Begin the Beguine'.

The 1940 film differs from the two that precede it in having a plot resembling the RKO 'ABC' pattern, albeit at a lower wattage: Powell and Astaire dance superbly together but lack the erotic chemistry of the Astaire/Rogers partnership. As Alastair Macaulay observes, Rogers was Astaire's ideal partner 'not simply because of her beauty as a dancer, but because of her complete responsiveness, the way she paid attention, sometimes without moving a muscle'.[35] There is never any doubt that the show will be a success and the only point to be resolved is which of the men will star alongside Powell. The previous films had Powell, along with other hopefuls, making her way in New York. In 1936 she is a girl from Albany, a gifted dancer who hopes that her high school sweetheart, now a major Broadway producer and director, will give her a break in his new show. Unfortunately, out of a misguided sense that Broadway is no place for a nice girl from Albany (unlike a passable boy from the same city), he refuses to help her: 'New York and Broadway, they're not what we thought they were – they're hard and cold.' He puts her on the train to Albany at Grand Central, but she gets off at 125th Street and heads back. She impersonates a mythical French star, Mademoiselle Arlette, who has been invented and touted by a news-hungry gossip columnist (Jack Benny) as the next big thing. The producer is convinced that Arlette will attend a grand party he is giving in a rooftop night-club, but Powell, attending as Benny's guest, slips behind the scenes and reappears in top hat and tails to perform a dance routine. 'Broadway Rhythm', sung by Frances Langford, which opens this spectacle, is prefaced now with the invocation to 'Broadway, street of a million lights' and goes on to include 'nights of pain and tears and sorrow' as part of the experience, but the film has not ventured beyond disappointment and mild anxiety. At the lodging house Powell teams up with Buddy Ebsen and his sister Vilma, whose perky song and dance 'Sing Before Breakfast' becomes one of the film's keynote tunes:

performed on the rooftop where they have prepared their frugal meal, it symbolizes the pluck and high spirits of – yes – show folks. The Ebsens can transform poverty-stricken surroundings into a vital and celebratory space for performance. Later, in a turn at the upscale night club, his lanky figure, homely looks and eccentric dancing make him a parody of the swells whose milieu this is.

In 1938 Powell's character is a superlative dancer and a gifted trainer of race horses. Teaming up with two other vaudevillians (one played by Ebsen) who are down on their luck, she hitches a ride in the horse box attached to the train from Philadelphia to New York, where she finds digs in a theatrical guest house run by Sophie Tucker and populated by a miscellany of vaudeville hopefuls. The view from the window is encouraging: 'Look, Broadway. We're going to put a ring round Broadway's nose and lead it around.' Here the obstacles to be overcome include an agent's office far more stylish – and art deco – than that in the 1936 offering, but its barriers can be breached by talent: Sophie Tucker encourages her niece (Judy Garland) to lead the entire clientele and even the snooty gate-keeper in a rendition of 'Everybody Sing' and then strides into the august presence as if by right. The film's finale is performed on a stage set that represents a vivid art deco version of Manhattan skyscrapers and features a grand flight of steps running the width of the proscenium. Sophie Tucker offers the benefits of Broadway to the new generations: 'It's My Broadway and It's Your Broadway', she sings, gesturing towards the neon signs celebrating great names from the theatre's past and embarking on a rhymed inventory of the celebrities of her pre-war heyday. In the final moments, with Powell centre stage and framed by the chorus, giant letters spelling 'Broadway Melody' rise from stage behind her, and the skyscrapers, which have grown miraculously during the last sequence, are suddenly augmented by the outlines of still taller buildings to provide a stunning image of metropolitan glamour. In the course of the film the city has become on occasion a performance space – notably in a charming set representing Bryant Park, where Powell dances with her would-be beau – and now at the end the stage presents a vision of the city in its most modernist form. The same parallelism – city-as-stage / stage-as-city – had been represented in the 1936 film by the number on the lodging-house roof and the finale in the night-club, whose high windows look out onto the glittering cityscape and which also features a décor with stylized representations of Times Square signs. Effectively this and similar backstagers enfold in a backstage narrative the kind of miscellany represented by such films as *The Hollywood Revue of 1929* (1929) or *The Goldwyn Follies* (1938) with its lame vestigial story line of the studio head wanting an outsider's view of the acts he is lining up. At the same time the message remains that Broadway, for all its alleged hardness and coldness, is at heart generous: talent and pluck will see you through. The reward takes one to sophistication and (literally) high society.

In *Broadway Melody of 1938* Garland sings 'You Made Me Love You' to her album of photographs of Clark Gable, conveying the intimate relationship between fandom and the performer's aspiration. The scene also registers as Hollywood's tribute to itself from within a film paying homage to the live theatre: in the 1936 film the exasperated producer exclaims 'I'm going to find a star for this picture if I have to steal Garbo', and complains that 'everybody's in pictures. It's getting impossible to cast a show any more'. Where the Ebsens (in this film, only Buddy) represent the yearning of troupers for Broadway, and Powell's characters are mature and amazingly talented absolute beginners from out of town, Garland typifies youthful pluck and ability, as yet undaunted and unscathed. By virtue of the less inimical world that their protagonists must cope with, these are films about aspiration, distinct from the fighting-against-the-odds stories of the Warner Bros series.

Youthful promise is acknowledged and rewarded even more fully in the series of films in which Garland appears with Mickey Rooney. There were eight in all, of which the most memorable are *Babes in Arms* (1939), *Strike Up the Band* (1940), *Babes on Broadway* (1942) and *Girl Crazy* (1943). The basic pattern of managing to put on a show is harnessed to narratives in which young people exercise their talents on various pretexts: playing in aid of themselves and retired vaudevillians (*Babes in Arms*); entering a swing-band contest judged by Paul Whiteman and staging a floor show (*Strike Up the Band*); coping with hard times and incidentally putting on a benefit to fund a summer trip for disadvantaged children (*Babes on Broadway*); and getting together a performance at a rodeo to raise money for the ranch school a rich kid (Rooney) has been sent to. (*Girl Crazy* follows the plot and includes numbers from Gershwin's 1930 Broadway musical of the same name.) The formidable talents of the two stars and the forceful and inventive staging of the big musical numbers in these films almost make the hackneyed and often mawkish plots palatable. The 'book' scenes do, however, include some important elements of theatre mythology, notably the propositions that success in performance can be a significant expression of maturity (as distinct from sentimental and erotic satisfaction, as in most musicals), that prevailing over the obstacles to success can be a generational triumph, and that vitality will always win out over entrenched social or artistic attitudes.

The wholesomeness of the Garland and Rooney characters, the latter in a show-business version of his Andy Hardy persona, guarantees respectability. Being 'fresh' and showing off mutate into more socially acceptable forms in the frame of performance, deviousness becomes resourcefulness, and the ego is indulged in the context of laudable teamwork. The kids win over authority figures in show business (Broadway agents, Paul Whiteman, etc.) and in day-to-day life (parents, school principals, etc.) The forward-looking zest of the juveniles is enhanced by appropriate reverence for their predecessors. In *Babes on Broadway* Garland and Rooney reflect on the past glories of the semi-derelict Duchess Theatre, where they intend to put on their show: evocations of some worthies of Old Broadway follow, including Sarah Bernhardt and Sir Harry Lauder. (Garland's Bernhardt is a collector's item of embarrassment, topped only by Ginger Rogers' impersonation of the actress reciting the Marseillaise in *The Barkleys of Broadway*.) Both *Babes in Arms* and *Babes on Broadway* (the latter more elaborately) include blackface minstrel show sequences, with Garland and Rooney as 'Mr Bones' and 'Mr Tambo'. Like similar sequences in other films of the period, despite their inherent racism they are intended as a lavish act of homage to a major element of American popular theatre, a part of the theatrical past that Hollywood has to acknowledge and reproduce. Garland's remarkable gifts, which included the ability to make her characters be seen to suffer and survive, are joined with homage to the past again in *For Me and My Gal* (1942), where she plays a vaudevillian, no longer paired with a fresh kid but sorely tried by a partner (and prospective husband) who spends most of the picture being a selfish, deceitful heel – Gene Kelly, in his first screen part and bringing to it elements of his successful Broadway role as the antihero of *Pal Joey*. The opening titles promised to do justice to 'a chapter in American history which has never been amply recorded', and to embrace 'one of America's greatest loves – that part of show business called "Vaudeville."' The subject had in fact been amply, or at least repeatedly, recorded on screen many times, though the 1942 film does include numbers given at length and in the appropriate theatrical space with a fair representation of the conditions of touring performers in the 1900s. In the context of a patriotic film – the action encompasses the 1914–1918 war with direct implications for the situation after Pearl Harbor – it was particularly appropriate to propose vaudeville as typically American in its harnessing of energy, loyalty and the building of character.

Backstage themes revisited:
The Band Wagon, Singin' in the Rain and *A Star is Born*

Three notable post-war films include further developments of the basic patterns of the influential Hollywood version of the roads to success, and one of them is a joyous proclamation that, after all, sincere artistry conquers all, including the damage done by High Art. *The Band Wagon* (1953), directed by Vincente Minnelli for MGM, looks back at Broadway's illustrious past from the perspective of a film star returning to New York in an attempt to revitalize his career.[36] In the opening scene the props associated with the song-and-dance man Tony Hunter (Fred Astaire) are failing to find a buyer at auction: they are in fact Astaire's own top hat, gloves and cane. Tony is then seen on his way to New York. In the parlour car, hidden behind his newspaper, he overhears passengers commenting on him as a has-been. When he arrives at Grand Central he at first delays getting off, but is pleasantly surprised by the bustling reporters who greet him as he alights. Then it turns out that they are there to meet another, more glamorous film star (Ava Gardner, as herself). Keeping up his spirits with a song, he saunters along the platform to be met by his friends Lily and Lester Marton (Nanette Fabray and Oscar Levant) who have come equipped as his fan club with noise-makers and placards. They have plans for a show and hope to confirm a deal with the multi-tasking, theatrically omnivorous actor-director-producer Jeffrey Cordova (Jack Buchanan). A rendezvous is arranged for later that evening, after the curtain of Cordova's grandiose production of *Oedipus Rex* – in which of course, he stars. Before Tony reaches this acclaimed masterpiece of highbrow art, he spends some time on 42nd Street. It is hardly recognisable:

> I just can't get over it. I can't understand it. This used to be the great theater street of the town. The New Amsterdam – I had one of my biggest successes there. Noel and Gertie were over there in *Private Lives* at the Selwyn. Strictly carriage trade, you know what I mean? Why, the first show I ever did was at the Eltinge, and I don't even believe that's here any more.[37]

After Lily and Lester have left him, Tony walks into one of amusement arcades that have taken over from 'legit' theatres – the sleazier aspect of the street is not visible – and is soon engaged in a song and dance with a shoeshine man, 'A Shine on Your Shoes'. He seems to have rediscovered his roots as a dancer in exuberant and uninhibited public performance, and although his encounter with the absurdly pretentious and egotistical Cordova is at first disheartening, another number with the actor, Lily and Lester, 'That's Entertainment', reassures him by celebrating the all-inclusive nature of the theatre, embracing shtick, slapstick and Shakespeare.

The plot of *The Band Wagon* plays variations on these themes. Betty Comden and Adolph Green, the film's scriptwriters, combine several familiar tropes in a screenplay that accommodates song and dance numbers of different kinds, tap, lyrical 'ballroom' and even bebop. The history of films as well as of the theatre is evoked, and the plot's driving force is the need to get a show right. Clashes of temperament, artistic taste and romantic entanglement are resolved. Early in the film Cordova is shown persuading potential 'angels' to fund his vision, in a finely conceived sequence where every time a door to his drawing room is opened we see him in full histrionic flight before a group of prospective backers.

Tony is at first alienated by the ballet dancer Gabrielle Gerard (Cyd Charisse) with whom he is to be paired, and the feeling is mutual: eventually they find harmony as dancers and in romance. The key moment comes when they take a horse-drawn carriage to Central Park, walk past a bandstand where couples are contentedly dancing on an open-air dance floor, and then find themselves moving – at first tentatively, then lyrically – to the non-diegetic orchestral version of 'Dancing in the Dark'. The simplicity of the number, representative of the couple's sincerity of feeling, contrasts with the extravagance of Cordova's conceptions. The megalomaniac director takes over the lively scenario written by Lily and Lester – about an author of children's books who writes thrillers on the side – and turns it into an overblown 'modern musical morality play' based on the *Faust* legend. It becomes a classic out-of-town disaster. The younger cast members, authors and show-business veterans, and Gabrielle (by now, more familiarly, Gaby), with Cordova's blessing transform the show into a straightforward revue, take it on a whirlwind national tour and open triumphantly on Broadway. A series of brilliant numbers are shown, interspersed with shots of trains speeding from city to city. When New York is regained – fulfilling the territorial imperatives of the backstage genre – we see the 'Girl Hunt Ballet', which presumably has some relation to the Martens' original concept as it parodies the thrillers of Mickey Spillane. Within the number the detective (Astaire) is led from a desolate city street to an uptown fashion house, a luxurious apartment and a Greenwich Village dive, before returning to the mean street where his adventure began. There is even a comic gunfight ballet on a subway platform beneath Times Square.[38]

In the brief scenes that follow, Tony at first assumes he has been left alone by his colleagues and deserted by Gaby, then comes out of his dressing room to see the entire company assembled on the stage below. 'That's Entertainment' is reprised, confirming his romantic and artistic success and – in the film's final gesture – the performers extend their arms towards the camera to embrace the cinema audience as well as each other. Everything, everyone and every medium and genre is being celebrated at once. In his *New York Times* review Bosley Crowther applauded the film's script as 'a grown-up and witty exposition of the modern musical stage, with its egocentric pretensions and commercial uncertainties', implying the rescue of an excessively conceptualized spectacle by recourse to the creation of what is in the end an old-style revue.[39] The Hollywood backstager has come back, like Tony, to its roots. Paradoxically, almost all the routines and numbers shown in *The Band Wagon* could be performed in a theatre. Only two episodes break this rule. One is Cordova's misconceived morality play which – when the elevators and pyrotechnics fail to function at rehearsal – practically breaks the stage itself. The other is the 'Girl Hunt Ballet', which begins and ends on a credible theatre set but moves for the first time in this film into settings and camera set-ups that could not be imitated in live performance. Minnelli's film is a summation of the energies, techniques and thematic obsessions of the backstager as Hollywood had defined it. What may sometimes seem a banal assertion – fulfilment in love accompanies fulfilment as a performer – takes on that additional dimension of liberation identified by Leo Braudy: 'the potential of the individual to free himself from inhibition at the same time that he retains that sense of limit and propriety in the very form of the liberating dance'.[40] One might add that in the backstager the disciplines of the theatre play their part in this, so that all get their reward by joining the team, accepting the rigours of rehearsal and preparation, and undergoing the heartache and the dozens of shocks that trouping flesh is heir to.

Sequences in two films not primarily concerned with the theatre reflect Hollywood's deeply felt need to keep on invoking it. They also encapsulate the narrative of the performer's career that will be discussed more fully in Chapter 2, with reference to biographical films. *Singin' in the Rain*, directed by Gene Kelly and Stanley Donen for the Arthur Freed Unit at MGM, combines nostalgia for the early days of synchronized sound with the bringing together of two talented performers in a traditional 'backstage romance'.[41] The year is 1927 and Hollywood is shaken by the advent of sound. When it is decided to rescue the silent film *The Duelling Cavalier* by adding dialogue, the result is laughed off the screen by a preview audience. The bright idea occurs that it can be salvaged by turning it into a musical while at the same time dubbing the shrill, squeaky voice of the leading lady without her knowing it. But more is needed. Don Lockwood (Gene Kelly) outlines his concept for a 'ballet' number to 'R.F.', the head of the studio. Given that the swashbuckling romance is set in the eighteenth century, the number Lockwood proposes would seem utterly out of place, but a pretext for the anachronism is supplied: the main action of the film will be 'imagined' by an actor who has been concussed by a backstage accident.[42]

Any reservations are forgotten in the exuberance of what follows. As he speaks, we see the number as it might be realized, the saga of a young dancer's arrival in New York, his rise through burlesque via vaudeville to Ziegfeld-style revue. Lockwood sings the opening of the 'Broadway' song, apparently elevated in an undefined space, which is presently identified as Broadway itself (or Times Square) by the neon signs that flash on. At street level, he stands in front of the bustling crowds, and sees a newcomer – his *alter* (younger) *ego*, with Harold Lloyd spectacles and a straw boater. The young hopeful pauses to insist that he's 'Gotta dance' and makes straight for a row of doors leading to the offices of theatrical agents. The third agent he auditions for introduces him to a speakeasy, where his charismatic performance rouses the crowd to frenzied emulation. However, he meets what might well prove to be his nemesis, when his dance brings him nose to toe with the very long leg of the vampish, ultra-sophisticated moll (Cyd Charisse) of a scar-faced gangster. After a comic dance of erotic encouragement, he is completely under her spell, but the gangster's henchmen close in on him and he makes his exit. Now he begins his journey towards stardom, represented by choruses repeated in the increasingly sophisticated styles of the shows he is in. Having achieved success, he is welcomed to a high-class nightclub. The woman of his dreams now reappears dressed in white as if for a wedding and in his imagination (and possibly hers) they dance a 'dream ballet' of romantic love in a seemingly limitless space. But the dance has to end: in the 'real' world of the night-club, she turns away from him to the gangster. Sadder and wiser, he makes his way to the door, but dancing is the cure: magically, he is back on Broadway, where he sees another bespectacled young man, dressed as he was when he arrived, striding across the screen towards the agent's door, proclaiming his destiny by singing 'Gotta dance!'

The sequence ends with Kelly leading a singing and dancing chorus in a reprise of 'Broadway Rhythm' with its insistence 'Everybody dance!'

until he is raised into air above the dancing crowd as the camera keeps him in a medium shot that slides into a climactic close-up. Then we are back in the studio chief's office, waiting for his reaction. 'Sounds great', he says, 'but I can't quite visualize it. I'll have to see it on film first.' Don's buddy Cosmo (Donald O'Connor) replies with 'On film, it'll be better yet.' As Gerald Mast observes, 'the ballet is unimaginable as descriptive sound and unvisualizable without movies. The movie has already visualized it for us.'[43] This long sequence revisits a scene early in the film when Don had given a radio interviewer a glamorized account of his rise to stardom – 'Dignity, always dignity'. A montage undercut this with scenes of him and Cosmo doing their double act as kids in a bar-room and then in burlesque and not very Big Time vaudeville. Steve Cohan persuasively connects this validation of Cosmo and Don as troupers with the film's assertion of popular values and definitively heterosexual masculinity.[44] It also returns Don to the show-business roots he forsook when he 'went Hollywood' – a phrase not heard in this film, but common elsewhere to describe the seductive appeal of life on the coast. His feet are back on the ground.

A complementary version of this vaudeville-to-Broadway (and beyond) career is presented in the far less genial context of George Cukor's 1954 remake of the 1937 film *A Star is Born*. Halfway through Cukor's film the two leading characters, the downwardly mobile movie actor Norman Maine (James Mason) and his protégée Vicki (Judy Garland) go to the preview of his latest picture. Vicki appears in a film-within-a-film – all we see of the movie – as the leading singer and dancer in the finale of a stage musical that is reaching its climax. On the final note the audience bursts into rapturous applause. The chorus urge her to take a solo call and she emerges, diffidently, from between the curtains. She sits down on the edge of the stage and modestly but firmly, in lines of rhyming verse, reminds the audience that her blazing success was the result of years of toil in a hard business. She segues into the song 'I Was Born in a Trunk'. As she sings we see episodes from her career as a child performer appearing with her parents; the constant practising after hours; the weary round of agents; the seemingly endless series of variations on the same, tired chorus line singing the same 'Black Bottom'. By the end of this 'curtain-speech' solo, she has brought us back to 'Swanee' and the number concludes as it began, with the singer sitting at the front of the stage, and we realize that only the preview audience (and we, in the cinema-outside-the-cinema) have seen and heard the 'illustrations' to her story.

In the film-within-a-film, 'Born in a Trunk' begins as a stage performance that then relies on film to invoke the traditions of theatre. It does so yet again in terms of a progression from turn-of-the century vaudeville to what is obviously a very high-class form of revue.[45] It adds nothing to Vicki Maine's character but is memorable as the kind of combined *cri de coeur* and triumph that accords with Garland's personality and with the view of show business that the singer embodied: laughter through tears, performance as destiny and the show that must go on. (The studio cut a brief episode which would have pushed the show-must-go-on cliché to its limit: immediately after the mother of the star of the 'film-within-the-film' died, her daughter would have gone on in her place.) In the middle of a film about stardom in Hollywood, the cherished mythology of the show world is rehearsed in the most hackneyed but at the same time most powerful way. The sequence may well be, as Jane Feuer suggests, 'a questioning of the boundary between dream and reality, onstage and offstage, in order to emphasize the "reality" of cinematic illusion and the "fantasy" of actual experience (and vice versa).'[46] It moves the audience into and out of another medium, framed by the film industry fable of *A Star is Born* itself.

The episodes in both films, like the comparable montage showing the success of a vaudeville act (with Garland and Astaire) in *Easter Parade*, evoke careers that parallel the biographical films discussed in the following chapter. There is also an element of autobiography, in that the performers, like Hollywood itself, are looking back at a vaudeville world they themselves have come from. From one perspective, it might be objected that after all there's no cliché like a show-business cliché, and that the Hollywood film industry merely marshalled all its resources to promulgate a sentimentalized version of the theatre. Although the vulnerability of women to the casting couch is represented – usually in comic terms that do not reflect the brutality of the situation – other less savoury aspects of Broadway were ignored. In particular, the movies barely acknowledge the hard working conditions and exploitation that led after a struggle (and a strike) to the founding of Actors' Equity; or the cut-throat rivalry and ruthless methods of impresarios like Klaw and Erlanger, the Syndicate and the Shubert brothers.[47] The celebrations of the allegedly palmy days of the stage have dated badly. Nevertheless, in films about the theatre the patterns set so powerfully by Hollywood have remained influential.

Notes

1 Three accounts of the film musical during the period are of particular relevance to the subject of this chapter: Rick Altman, *The American*

Film Musical (Bloomington and Indianapolis: Indiana University Press, 1989); Jane Feuer, *The Hollywood Musical*, 2nd edition (Bloomington and Indianapolis: Indiana University Press, 1993); and Richard Barrios, *A Song In the Dark. The Birth of the Musical Film* (New York: Oxford University Press, 1995).

2 Vladimir Propp, *The Morphology of the Folktale*, translated by Laurence Scott, 2nd revised edition, edited by Louis A. Wager (Austin: University of Texas Press, 1968).

3 Altman, *The American Film Musical*, p. 208.

4 *Daily Mirror* (New York), 31 March 1928, reprinted Michael Kantor, *Broadway. The American Musical, based on the documentary film by Michael Kantor* (New York and Boston: Bulfinch Press, 2004), p. [127].

5 George Jean Nathan, *The Theatre of the Moment. A Journalistic Commentary* (New York: Alfred A. Knopf, 1936), pp. 141–142; 157. Similar reflections on the decline of the Times Square section of Broadway are cited by Anthony Bianco, *Ghosts of 42nd Street. A History of America's Most Infamous Block* (New York: Harper Collins, 2004), p. 94.

6 Albert F. MacLean Jr, *American Vaudeville as Ritual* (Lexington: University Press of Kentucky, 1965), p. 211.

7 Robert W. Snyder, *The Voice of the City. Vaudeville and Popular Culture in New York* (New York and Oxford: Oxford University Press, 1989), p. xvi.

8 M. Alison Kibler, *Rank Ladies. Gender and Cultural Hierarchy in American Vaudeville* (Chapel Hill and London: University of North Carolina Press, 1999), p. 5.

9 Lewis A. Erenberg, *Steppin' Out. New York Nightlife and the Transformation of American Culture, 1890–1930* (Chicago: University of Chicago Press, 1984), p. 55.

10 Barrios, *A Song In the Dark*, p. 371. Barrios quotes press comments lamenting the working to death of the backstage theme in the immediate aftermath of synchronised sound (pp. 212–213). On the business and production practices of the studio, see Nick Roddick, *A New Deal in Entertainment. Warner Brothers in the 1930s* (London: British Film Institute, 1983).

11 On Ropes' novel, see Rian James and James Seymour, *42nd Street*, edited by Rocco Fumento (Madison: University of Wisconsin Press, 1979), pp. 9–14. Subsequent quotations from the film's shooting script are from this edition.

12 Avery Hopwood, *The Gold Diggers. A Comedy in Three Acts*, Lyceum Theatre, New York, 30 September 1919: NYPL typescript. Act I, p. 56.

13 Berkeley had worked briefly for the firm of Fanchon and Marco, who produced these shows: see Tony Thomas and Jim Terry, with Busby Berkeley, *The Busby Berkeley Book* (London: Thames and Hudson, 1973) p. 25.

14 Brooks Atkinson, *Broadway*, revised edition (New York: Macmillan, 1974), p. 289.

15 The number concludes the on-stage show and the film itself: it was originally to be placed much earlier, preceding the girls' discovery of Brad's identity and the family's attempt to prevent him carrying on with his stage career, but would have made what followed seem trivial: see Erwin Gelsey and James Seymour, *Gold Diggers of 1933*, edited by Arthur Hove (Madison: University of Wisconsin Press, 1980), pp. 13–18. The significance of the number is discussed on pp. 27–30. See also Patricia Mellencamp, 'Sexual Economics: *Gold Diggers of 1933*', in *A Fine Romance. Five Ages of Film Feminism* (Philadelphia, PA: Temple University Press, 1995), pp. 50–73.

16 Gelsey and Seymour, *42nd Street*, p. 147.

17 Martin Rubin, *Showstoppers. Busby Berkeley and the Tradition of Spectacle* (New York: Columbia University Press, 1993), p. 36.

18 Marsh calls on a gangster friend to warn off Dorothy's lover but the incident does not take place near the theatre, although in *Gold Diggers of 1933* a bootlegger, Gigolo Eddie, makes a brief appearance backstage.

19 On the film's troubled production, see Barrios, *A Song In the Dark*, pp. 396–398.

20 Jerome Delamater, *Dance in the Hollywood Musical* (Ann Arbor, MI: UMI Press, 1981), pp. 36–37.

21 On the 'crotch shot' see Altman, *The American Film Musical*, pp. 217, 223; and Nadine Wills '"110 per cent woman:" the crotch shot in the Hollywood musical', *Screen*, 42/2 (Summer 2001), pp. 121–141.

22 Mellencamp, 'Sexual Economics', p. 64.

23 Andrew Bergman, *We're in the Money. Depression America and its Films* (New York: Harper, 1972), p. 168.

24 Morris Dickstein, *Dancing in the Dark. A Cultural History of the Great Depression* (New York: Norton, 2009), p. 240.

25 On the origins of the sequence, see Thomas and Terry, *The Busby Berkeley Book*, pp. 89–90.

26 *The New Yorker*, 23 March 1935.

27 *New York Times*, 15 March 1935.

28 Edward Gallafent, *Astaire and Rogers* (New York: Columbia University Press, 2002), p. 33.

29 John Mueller, *Astaire Dancing* (New York: Knopf, 1985), p. 101. Mueller gives detailed choreographic analyses as well as information from studio records. A concise and influential discussion of the films is Arlene Croce, *The Fred Astaire and Ginger Rogers Book* (New York: Vintage Books, 1972.) Hannah Hyam, in *Fred and Ginger. The Astaire-Rogers Partnership 1934–1938* (Brighton: Pen Press Publishers, 2007) pays particular attention to dramatic effect in the numbers.

30 Erenberg, *Steppin' Out*, pp. 124–125.

31 James Sanders, *Celluloid Skyline. New York and the Movies* (New York: Knopf, 2003), pp. 257–264.

32 Joseph Epstein, *Fred Astaire* (Princeton, NJ: Princeton University Press, 2008), p. 145.

33 'Broadway Melody', lyric by Arthur Freed, music by Nacio Herb Brown in Robert Gottlieb and Robert Kimball, eds, *Reading Lyrics* (New York: Pantheon Books, 2000), p. 169.

34 In 1975 Powell described the circumstances of her casting in an interview with John Kobal, published in his *People Will Talk*, 2nd edition (London: Aurum Press, 1991), pp. 98–100.

35 Alastair Macaulay, 'Nice Work, Darling, Nice Work', *Times Literary Supplement*, 27 February 2004, pp. 18–19; p. 18. Macaulay insists that after Rogers 'there is never again a moment when the dance is completely suffused by the love which the film at that point is usually about'.

36 For details of the production process, see Hugh Fordin, *MGM's Greatest Musicals. The Arthur Freed Unit* (New York: Da Capo, 1995), pp. 397–419.

37 The Selwyn on the north side of the street had become a 'grind house' movie theatre by the early 1950s, but has been restored and is now the American Airlines Theater. The frontage and elements of the Eltinge were moved 168 yards west in 1997 to form the entrance to the AMC cinema multiplex. (See Lynne B. Sagalyn, *Times Square Roulette. Remaking the City Icon* (Cambridge, MA: The MIT Press, 2001), pp. 364–365.

38 Mueller (*Astaire Dancing*, p. 361) dissents from the generally favourable reception accorded this number, finding it 'dazzlingly colourful in design, but … misguided in conception and confused in execution'.

39 'Top Notch Musical. Metro's *The Band Wagon* is a Major Achievement in a Screen Genre', *New York Times*, 19 July 1953.

40 Leo Braudy, *The World in a Frame: What We See in Films* (Chicago: Chicago University Press, 1984), p. 140.

41 See Steven Cohan, *Incongruous Entertainment. Camp, Cultural Value, and the MGM Musical* (Durham NC and London: Duke University Press, 2005), ch. 4. In addition to Cohan's book, the film has received detailed analysis from Peter Wollen in his BFI Film Classics study (*Singin' in the Rain*, London: BFI, 1992). For a comprehensive account of production and reception see Earl J. Hess and Prathiba A. Dadhlkar, *'Singin' in the Rain.' The Making of an American Masterpiece* (Lawrence: University Press of Kansas, 2009).

42 The scriptwriters, Betty Comden and Adolph Green, borrowed this idea from the Broadway musical *Du Barry was a Lady* (1939), in which a blow on the head caused a night-club cloakroom attendant (Bert Lahr) to think he was Louis XV.

43 Gerald Mast, *Can't Help Singin'. The American Musical on Stage and Screen* (Woodstock, NY: The Overlook Press, 1987), p. 264.

44 Cohan, *Incongruous Entertainment*, pp. 184–185 and 228–234.

45 The participation of Edens could not be acknowledged, as he was under contract to MGM. See Ronald Haver, *A Star is Born. The Making of*

the 1954 Movie and its 1983 Restoration (New York: Applause, 2002), pp. 185–196, and Patrick McGilligan, *George Cukor. A Double Life* (New York: St Martin's Press, 1991), pp. 228–230.

46 Feuer, *The Hollywood Musical*, p. 79.

47 On the cut-throat relationships between the Shuberts and their rivals, see Foster Hirsch, *The Boys from Syracuse. The Shuberts' Theatrical Empire* (New York: Cooper Square Press, 2000).

2

Biopics, classic and revisionist

CHARACTERISTIC elements of the fictional backstager's optimism are absorbed in the quasi-documentary mode affected if not fully adopted in Hollywood biographies of stage stars, 'biopics'. Because the careers of stage stars were imagined – often by the subjects themselves – in the same terms, these tend to confirm familiar patterns of individual achievement, with obstacles overcome, personal crises weathered and great ideas brought to fruition. The tug-of-war between innovation (young as yet unacknowledged talent, new ideas) and orthodoxy (established players, routine or formulaic techniques) is usually given a narrative framework that includes – as with the backstager – a love affair. History, of course, is on the side of the theatre's hard-working lovers.

Robert Rosenstone, in *History on Film/Film on History* (2006) argues that historical films, including the biopic, participate in the discourses of history rather than being an excrescence on the discipline as it is constructed in academia. The mainstream feature film, 'much like written history, ... tells the past as a story with a beginning, a middle and an end'. It is 'a tale that leaves you with a moral message and (usually) a feeling of uplift'. The other markers of the mainstream history film are: insistence on history as the story of individuals; presentation of a 'unitary, closed, and completed past' that 'personalizes, dramatizes and emotionalizes'; an attention to the 'look' of the earlier periods; and a teleological version of history as process.[1] Regarding 'biofilms' (his preferred term), Rosenstone insists that they, too, 'like all works that deal with the past, are entities with unstable meanings that shift over the years'.

> Less than full-blown portraits, they should be seen and understood as slices of lives, interventions into particular discourses, extended metaphors that suggest more than their limited timeframes can convey.[2]

The classic theatrical biopics from the Hollywood studios were conceived both as sources of profit and as contributions to a more or less national mythology. At the same time, Hollywood – though it has not been alone in this – drew on the expertise of academic historians to support what David Eldridge has described as the impression of 'a definitive account of "how it really was."'[3] Against this validating background of more or less convincing detail in the historical environment and dress, the biopics invariably include what George F. Custen calls 'the breakthrough moment': the invention, discovery or achievement of recognition that constitutes personal and professional achievement.[4] In the context of United States history, approval by the public is, as Custen notes, a key element. Performers are by definition the people's choice, a factor whose political signif-icance is unmistakable. However, the same model can be found in the context of other nations and their cultural heroes and heroines. So can the tendency described by Manny Farber in a review of the George Gershwin biopic *Rhapsody in Blue* (1945): 'Most of the scenes are written in the standard biographical-movie way, so that each has its joke, each shows the hero scoring one more victory, and each uses the people round Gershwin ... as though everything they ever said or did in their lives was concerned in helping, praising, or explaining the composer.'[5]

Adjustments made in the interests of conformity to a narrative model or as the result of legal pressure (often a combination of the two) have to be accounted for. Sometimes these were extreme: *The Dolly Sisters* (1945) glosses over the subjects' rackety life-style and omits any reference to the suicide of one member of the sister act. The concluding credits of *The Story of Vernon and Irene Castle* (1939), which was closely monitored by the surviving partner, Irene, offer a typical disclaimer:

> This photoplay is based generally upon events in the lives of the principal characters and other persons whose true names are used. With the exception of these persons and actual events depicted, the characters and events are fictitious. Any similarity to other persons, living or dead, is coincidental.

'Based generally' is accurate: most of the film's plot points differ considerably from the real events.[6] Among the many divergences from documented fact, the film's final sequence stands out as exemplary in contriving a sentimental closure. Irene (Ginger Rogers) has arranged to meet Vernon (Fred Astaire) in a hotel near the base where he is now stationed and has engaged an orchestra to play their favourite music: when news of his death in a flying accident is brought to her

by the faithful servant Walter, she fights back her tears and insists that
the orchestra play as requested – the finals shots show a vision of the
couple dancing to the familiar music. In fact, Irene was in New York
and received the news in a telephone call. As well as this would-be
transcendent moment, the film also has to make room for such inspirational statements as the reassurance after Vernon's death that 'There's
got to be something of [Vernon] in every boy and girl that get up and
dance together'. It is hard to imagine the Astaire and Rogers of *Swing
Time*, *Top Hat* or *The Gay Divorcée* being tired of touring because 'We
want to live like simple married people – with our clothes in closets,
not in trunks'.

Theatrical biopics of the 1930s and 1940s often looked back to the
allegedly idyllic world before the 1914–1918 war. In opening titles and
the images that support them, films commonly remind the viewer of a
glamorous past. *The Story of Vernon and Irene Castle* returns us to
'a fabulous and beloved era, near enough to be warmly remembered,
[when] two bright and shining stars, Vernon and Irene Castle, whirled
across the horizon into the hearts of all who loved to dance'. *Show
Business* (1944), effectively a fictionalized (auto)biopic of its star and
producer Eddie Cantor, invokes 'the colourful era of belles – bloomers
– and beer in buckets' when there 'trouped ambitious groups of lovable
hams known as show folks, all dreaming of the Big Time'. Nostalgia is
blended with recognition that life for most troupers in the earlier period
was hard but character-building.

Al Jolson's iconic career
and the religion of show business

Although technically fictional, *The Jazz Singer* (1927) is a virtual
biopic, retailing elements of its leading performer's career. In many
respects it is a poor film, and its sentimental characterizations and
situations are complemented by Jolson's stiff acting. When he sings
and in his few moments of dialogue, his charisma takes over, but in
silent scenes – which account for most of the film – too often he is
left to look awkwardly cheerful or soulful as the situation demands.
Despite this, the film holds up through the power of its archetypal
situations. *The Jazz Singer* is *about* a great deal, speaking clearly
to and from the experiences of its star performer and – it has been
convincingly argued – the situation of the Warner Brothers themselves.[7]
The jazz singer's rise to fame asserts by implication the dignity of the
newly enhanced Hollywood entertainment film. As a melodrama it
expresses the division of identity experienced by a second generation

in immigrant communities, combining forward-looking espousal of the new American values with an acknowledgement of the cultural divide between generations.

The Jazz Singer also functions as a backstage musical, although without being wholly given over to the genre's defining fantasy of musical performance as a metaphor for courtship and emotional success. Jakie Rabinowitz, the cantor's son who becomes Jack Robin the jazz singer, does 'get his girl' in the end, but when in the final moments he pours out his feelings his singing is directed towards his mother rather than his sweetheart. The script is based on a play by Samson Raphaelson, adapted from his own short story, 'The Day of Atonement' (1922), inspired by a performance by Jolson in Champaign, Illinois in 1917. After reading the story, Jolson himself proposed it without success to D.W. Griffith and other producers as a film subject. Approached by Jolson with a view to making a musical comedy from the material, Raphaelson declined the offer and made it into a 'straight' play. Its success on the New York stage in 1925 led Warner Bros to buy it. George Jessel was originally to be cast in the leading role he had played on Broadway, but he was replaced with Jolson, a bigger star and – it has been suggested – a more fully assimilated Jewish performer.[8]

As a backstage story, the film presents the familiar territorial divisions between the world behind the scenes and the 'civilian' world in the auditorium and the city beyond it. There are dressing-room and rehearsal scenes, together with such familiar elements of theatrical life as an audition and a railway call for a company on tour. Set against these, though, are not merely the usual private spaces. The Rabinowitz home is an apartment overlooking the synagogue, providing yet another liminal situation: Jakie has to cross the threshold between the room where his father is dying and the sanctified realm where on the year's most solemn festival, Yom Kippur (the Day of Atonement) he must sing Kol Nidre. The cantor's singing lessons are conducted in the apartment, and so is his wife's role-defining cooking. The synagogue and its rituals are made vivid to Jakie and to the spectator in three 'visionary' episodes. In the first, Jakie goes to hear the famous cantor Josef Rosenblatt give a recital in a concert hall whose platform has been set up to resemble a synagogue. During the singing, in an image faded in over a shot of the cantor on stage, he 'sees' his father officiating in his own synagogue.

In a later scene, Jakie is in his dressing-room preparing for the dress rehearsal of the revue that will make him a Broadway star. His father is dangerously ill and his mother has begged him to take his place at Yom Kippur. In his blackface make-up he gazes into a mirror, where he sees a vision of his father singing in the synagogue. Subsequently, when he has finally taken his father's place, as Jakie sings we see the 'ghost' of his father – dying even as the service continues – lay his hand in approval and benediction on Jakie's shoulder. Jakie is wholly engrossed in his rendition of Kol Nidre, which he performs with expressive gestures resembling those of his theatre act. Here his mannerisms read as being genuinely from the heart, much as on stage (and especially in blackface) he habitually performs emotions so deep that his whole body is taken over by them and he has to break into his singing to recite a verse as though his feelings went beyond 'art'. In the synagogue he does not go so far, but his vocal style and physicality are distinct from those of Cantor Rosenblatt or his father.

Raphaelson recalled his first experience of Jolson's performance as a revelation. 'This grotesque figure in blackface, kneeling at the end of a runway which projected him into the heart of his audience', was 'embracing his audience with a prayer – an evangelical moan. ... The words didn't matter, the melody didn't matter. It was the emotion – the emotion of a cantor.'[9] This identification of 'jazz' with liturgical singing is emphasized repeatedly in story, play and film. As Jakie's career begins to take off, a seasoned professional remarks to him that 'There are lots of jazz singers, but you have a tear in your voice'. When his mother hears him rehearsing a number in the theatre, she cannot help being moved, even though he has just refused to come to sing in the service: 'Just like his papa, with the cry in his voice'. In the apartment where the old cantor is dying, Mary, the dancer who loves Jakie, comments that his off-screen voice is that of 'a jazz singer – singing to his God'. That both Jews and gentiles in the film should recognize the special quality of the singing effectively asserts the benefits of assimilation.

The conflicting calls on the singer's loyalty are emphasized repeatedly. Jakie tells his mother 'I'd love to sing for my people – but I belong here', even though 'the songs of Israel are tearing at my heart'. His mother acknowledges that '[his] career is the place God has put [him]' and recognizes that he 'belongs' in the theatre. Some expressions of the conflict are crudely melodramatic. Jakie agonizes: 'It's a choice between giving up the biggest chance of my life – and breaking my mother's heart.' The cantor insists that he 'taught [Jakie] the songs of Israel' and a love of the 'old world', but his son's reply amounts to rebuke from the new, forward-looking American generation: 'If you were born here, you'd feel the same as I do.' In another riposte, he exclaims 'You taught me that music is the voice of God. It is as honourable to sing in the theatre as in the synagogue.' When the family friend Yudelson comes to find Jakie in the theatre, he appeals to his sense of familial obligations, which combine tradition with piety. Jakie replies: 'We in show business have our religion too – on every day – the show must go on!' Allied with this assertion of the stage's dignity is the reiterated emphasis on the new country's commitment to progress. The film endorses this when a title card heralding a return to the cantor's apartment declares: 'For those whose faces are turned toward the past, the years roll by unheeded – their lives unchanged.'

Hardly mentioned but implicit is the racial and ethnic dimension of the 'jazz' itself. The worldly Yudelson discovers that the boy is singing 'Waitin' for the Robert E. Lee' in a bar room, with appropriate imitation of the 'shuffle' associated with 'coon' performers. (In the 'final' script – but not in the film's intertitles – the music is identified more crudely as 'nigger' songs.[10]) The verbal and physical caricatures of blackface have been recognized as providing Jewish artists with a disguise and an expressive vocabulary that permitted the articulation of emotions and conflicts less easily encompassed by their own traditions of performance.[11] The racist clichés about African Americans also allow for sentimental evocations of an old country (for 'plantation', read *shtetl*) and yearning for the security of family bonds. From his rendition – not in black makeup – of 'Dirty hands, dirty face' in the café to the climactic performance of 'Mammy', the mature Jakie/Jolson progresses from a parent's expression of love for his scamp of a son to the grown man's assumption of a child's yearning for his mother. 'I'd walk a million miles/ For one of those smiles' represents the journey away from and back to home that the character has taken in the course of the film. (The lyric's 'speaker' is a black southerner living in the north.) Jakie is making a public declaration of private feeling that also validates Jolson's own choice of material and performance style.

At another level, only fleetingly alluded to in the film, Jakie is transgressing his family's and religion's traditions by becoming involved with a gentile. The allusion to this is in a comic context. Yudelson reads Jakie's mother the letter in which he refers to Mary, whom he has met on the road and who gets him his break on Broadway. Jakie's mother exclaims 'Maybe he's fallen in love with a shiksa'. Thus reads the title card, but the actress's expression shows that the Yiddish word is not spoken with contempt. She doesn't seem unduly fazed by the thought, and it never surfaces again. (The issue is dealt with more explicitly in the short story and the play.) Dressed fashionably and moving gracefully both off stage and on, and encoded in performance in terms of high art (ballet) and Anglo-Saxon girlhood, Mary stands apart from her peers – the gossipy but not malicious chorines – and also from the upwardly mobile and eager Jakie (Figure 4). The film treats any

4. *The Jazz Singer* (1927):
Mary in Jakie's dressing
room (production still)

potential conflict as if it were somehow already dealt with: there is no
confrontation between his doting mother and the woman in whom she
must recognize the potential for her son's 'marrying out'.

When Jakie returns home he is able to sing and speak his feelings,
joking with his doting mother and showing off his new-found modern
and thoroughly American art. Speech has been heard breaking into the
recorded music and song spliced into the otherwise silent action in the
café scene where Jakie is discovered by the vaudeville manager: he sings
'Dirty Hands, Dirty Face' and speaks to the audience and the band
before launching into 'Bye-Bye Blackbird'. However, the most famous
use of spoken dialogue occurs in the scene with his mother. He draws
her over to an armchair by the piano and sings to her. The move from
silent mode, with title cards for dialogue, into recorded song takes
place as Jakie segues into semi-improvized recorded dialogue before
demonstrating the syncopated 'jazz' version of 'Blue Skies' he will be
performing in the Broadway revue. The performance is interrupted by
his father's sudden arrival, and his call for 'Silence!' which is heard on
the soundtrack before the film reverts to silent action and title cards.
His father's return reinforces the patriarchal refusal to speak to his son
by the literal refusal of the film itself to utter dialogue, and diegetic jazz
is replaced by non-diegetic Tchaikovsky [12] 'Silence' is in fact the one
word of speech heard from the father in the film, and it is a title card
that conveys his dying acceptance – 'Mama, we have our son again' –
as he hears Kol Nidre.

Early scenes in *The Jazz Singer* offer its documentary credentials:
location shots of the crowded Lower East Side establish the milieu of
the Rabinowitz' home, and later the backstage sequences, as always,
suggests a 'real' world behind the shows on stage. Details of touring life
are sketched in to indicate Jakie's rise from café performance to the Big

Time. In a vivid railroad depot scene, he progresses rapidly from the arduous 'split weeks' of the road company to the prospect of *very* Big Time, a chance to prove himself on Broadway. Informed bluntly that his contract with the tour has been terminated, he is ordered to not board the train with the rest of the company, then told that he has been offered a part in a revue in New York. Jubilantly, he crosses the track to board a train in the opposite direction. A rapid succession of title cards expresses his elation: 'NEW YORK! – BROADWAY! – HOME! – MOTHER!' Having started in New York, done his time in the sticks, met the second woman in his life (after mother, of course), and shown his potential, he is heading on a journey that is both upwards and back. As he follows the traditional geographical route of the show business career, culminating in an appearance on Broadway, Jakie is also returning to the place where he has been in emotional terms since the moment when he sneaked back to the Hester Street apartment and purloined a photograph of his mother. The American freedom to roam and to move upwards is magically combined with the affirmation that home, where the heart is, will still be available. The conclusion of the film, with Jakie in blackface singing a declaration of love to a fictional black 'Mammy' to his own *yiddische momma*, is arrived at by a sleight of hand not anticipated in the 'final' script. Up to the cantor's death, Jakie had to choose between Broadway and conscience. Suddenly, the first-night audience is being told that the performance has been postponed. We might expect this to be the end – as it is in the play – of Jakie's show business career. An intertitle announces: 'The season passes and time heals – the show goes on.' Something (presumably) in the manager's experience of the deathbed scene seems to have taken the dilemma away, and at an unspecified later date the show does go on with Jakie's name in lights as top billing on the theatre marquee.

The Jazz Singer dramatizes elements of Al Jolson's own life, but two biopics made some twenty years later claim to deliver the 'real' story. Paradoxically, whereas *The Jazz Singer* had delivered his voice to an otherwise silent medium, in the musical numbers of *The Jolson Story* (1946) and *Jolson Sings Again* (1948), Jolson voices the skilful impersonation of him by Larry Parks. The second film encompasses a fictional account of the production of the first, with Jolson (played by Parks) encountering Parks (playing himself) in a studio viewing suite where he has been astonished by the effectiveness of the younger man's performance in a screen test. The impersonated Jolson is seen coaching his impersonator, and vouching for the authenticity of the result, which is also endorsed within *Jolson Sings Again* by the Hollywood producer, a long-time Jolson fan. Quite apart from its psychological implications, this extraordinary *mise en abyme* cuts clean through the usual obstacles attendant on impersonation of performers in biopics. There is even a scene in which Jolson briefs the scriptwriters, dictating a mass of facts about his life to them but insisting that they should feel free to select and shape their story as they think fit.

Throughout the two biopics, Jolson's mother is more sophisticated than Jakie's, but still fulfils traditional roles, as a nurturing and supportive companion to her husband, always proffering food for her son and her guests (notably gefilte fish with an overpowering horseradish sauce) and ready with seemingly naïve but very acute questions. The singer's father is a kindly and humorous man, who would prefer his son to follow his calling but soon comes to accept the situation. (Jolson's father, like the figure in *The Jazz Singer*, objected sternly to his career: he was reconciled to it only after many years.) Even Asa's changing of his given name to Al is accepted with good-humoured resignation. By the end of the first film, the couple's pride in their son is unalloyed, and he brings home his intended bride, 'Julie Benson' – Jolson's (third) ex-wife Ruby Keeler was paid for permission to make the film, presumably to forestall any possible lawsuit, but would not allow her name to be used. No reference is made to her not being Jewish: in this film, the mother would never think of referring to her son's girlfriend as a *shiksa*.

In *The Jolson Story* religious divisions are glossed over and the social milieu of the Yoelsons, who live in Washington DC, is more securely bourgeois than that of the Lower East Side Rabinowitz family. Jakie had been caught doing ragtime and 'coon' songs, but young Asa sings safely sentimental songs at first: he is 'discovered' by the vaudevillian Steve Martin when he joins in 'On the Banks of the Wabash' from the gallery of Kernan's Burlesque House in Washington. (This simplifies and sanitizes the early days of Jolson's theatre life, with their quota of down-market burlesque houses.) Early on he evinces a desire to communicate more directly with his audience by raising the houselights so he can see them clearly from the stage. He discovers blackface by standing in for a drunken colleague when Lew Dockstader, leader of a famous minstrel troupe, is in the house, drawn there by Oscar Hammerstein. (Hammerstein had no part in the discovery of Jolson by Dockstader, but this is the familiar biopic trope in which show business luminaries preside like godfathers over the emerging 'showbiz legend'.) Soon Jolson is a featured singer in Dockstader's show, but as he rises through the ranks from chorus to soloist he grows weary of an old-fashioned sentimental repertoire (we see repeated variations on 'I want a gal/ Just like the gal/ That married dear old dad') and wants to introduce the new, jazz-inspired music. The film dramatizes Jolson's epiphany in true biopic style. After performing in blackface, he wanders through New Orleans and comes across an impromptu jazz performance in a courtyard. The singer who has faked black identity suddenly experiences genuine black music, and is, so to speak, converted. This is 'music nobody heard of before', with 'the feeling in prayers' that (as in *The Jazz Singer*) implies a kinship between Jewish and black culture.

Jolson's next step is an engagement in a Broadway revue with Gaby Delys, but he is almost deprived of his chance (he is last on the bill, a poor position in itself) when the show is running over time. Forcing his way to the front of the stage and pushing through the curtains, Jolson collars the audience, and delights them to the point where they cannot get enough of his singing. By now he has developed fully his characteristic style: the expressive and expansive gestures, leaning back (his head often at a 45-degree angle across the frame) as if to invite the audience into his confidence, and breaking from song into speech. Soon he is having a runway built to bring him into the centre of the orchestra stalls. As Jolson's performances become bigger and more confident, his embrace of the audience thus becomes paradoxically more personal and intimate. This is celebrated in a cinematic apotheosis: when he has the houselights turned up at the Winter Garden (he finally has the authority for this) we see his face superimposed in close up over a shot that pans across the enthusiastic spectators.

So far, *The Jolson Story* has presented Jolson's rise to fame though familiar tropes: the discovery of the talent by others; the crucial moments when managers and other powerful personalities recognize his potential; the successful negotiation between show business and personal or familial demands. In contrast to *The Jazz Singer*, the religious dimension is dealt with smoothly: a minor element rather than the central source of conflict. Now the problem is that 'there's only one thing wrong with Al – he's got to sing'. This compulsion, a key element of his success, is also the cause of division between him and Julie. Unsurprisingly, there is no mention of the real Jolson's gambling and unfaithfulness, or his previous marriages. His wooing of Julie is seen in three public/private spaces. First, he singles her out in the audience of a late-night benefit where he is performing. Then he finds her imitating him at a party, and takes her out onto the terrace to make an astonishingly direct proposal of marriage. Finally, when as the star of a Ziegfeld spectacular she gets dizzy on the flight of stairs down which she must sing and dance, he stands up in his orchestra seat and sings the number for her. This adapts two incidents, one in which he annoyed Keeler by rushing down the aisle to sing along – repeating the offence at subsequent performances – and the other in which she fell off a spiral staircase and broke her ankle.[13] The impulsive exhibition of private feeling in a very public arena is supposed to be endearing, but in reality romance flourished despite rather than because of it. After a montage depicting Julie's Hollywood career, Jolson agrees to retire from singing in public, but his inner life slumps. He is not made for domestic life. The crisis that precipitates the separation is foreshadowed by the private performance of 'The Night We Were Wed' he has given over the family dinner to celebrate his parents' wedding anniversary. The decisive moment comes later that evening at a night-club, where a celebrity in the audience would often be invited to give an impromptu performance. He is there because his mother has insisted on seeing what a night-club is like, and the old demand of filial loyalty has now conspired with Jolson's suppressed yearning for the charge he gets from public performance. When his vow is broken, it is the audience's physical pressure – they crowd round him urging him to sing again – that makes the rupture inevitable: 'Baby, it looks like I'm not getting out of this.' Julie quietly leaves the club while he is still singing: the second film takes up the story from this point.

A list of the films' departures from the 'real' biography would be long, but the chief deviations are the omission of any whiff of scandalous behaviour (transmuted into ebullience and love of public performance), simplification of the family's life (ignoring Jolson's stormy relationship with his brother Harry) and creation of one fictional helper ('Steve Martin') to replace Jolson's successive managers and acolytes. The first film, ending with his return to performance, presents a standardized version of the trajectory of the star's career, in which retirement has merely been an interruption. In the second film, any doubts about Larry Parks' credentials as an impersonator are swept aside: there is no indication of the difficulty the studio had in finding an appropriate actor and (of course) no hint of Jolson's tense relationship with his double. In *Jolson Sings Again*, his fourth (and final) wife Erle Galbraith is discovered as a nurse attending the sick and exhausted Jolson, providing a combination of 'meeting cute' and pathos: in fact he met her on a hospital tour *after* his recovery.

Despite these and their many other freedoms, the two biopics possess a strange authenticity, not only in the use of Jolson's own singing voice, but through the correspondence between the conventional situations and structures of the show business biopic and Jolson's understanding of his story and its significance. This was how both the singer and his public perceived his career and his talents. Even those who disliked

Jolson – including a good number of his fellow artists – agreed with his estimate of himself as 'the world's greatest entertainer'. With varying degrees of emphasis the three films convey Jolson's ambivalent attitude to his Jewish identity, his acute need to be applauded and his presentation of a potent mixture of 'new' American values and nostalgia for the old world under the guise of a 'South' he was never part of. In the introduction to the published edition of his play Samuelson had framed it in epic terms: 'He who wishes to picture today's America must do it kaleidoscopically; he must show you a vivid contrast of surfaces, raucous, sentimental, egoistical, vulgar, ineffably busy – surfaces whirling in a dance which sometimes is a dance to Aphrodite and more frequently a dance to Jehovah.'[14] *The Jazz Singer* has a good deal to do with Jehovah and only a passing interest in Aphrodite, and the subsequent Jolson biopics carefully minimize the influence of the goddess over their subject. Seven years later, in its celebration of Florenz Ziegfeld, Jr, MGM would be more exercised in its dealings with Aphrodite. It would also have to present a show-business legend whose career ended in financial failure rather than the achievement of happiness through stardom, and find a way of celebrating managerial rather than performing skill.

Glorifying the American impresario: *The Great Ziegfeld*

Florenz Ziegfeld's career began on the Midway at the 1893 Columbian Exposition in Chicago, with the promotion of the strong man Eugene Sandow; matured in the presentation of the 'French' singer Anna Held; and found its greatest successes in the series of *Follies* that began in 1907. It encompassed a refined version of vaudeville, sophisticated and fashionable revue and several notable musical comedies, including *Sally* (1920) and *Show Boat* (1927). Its phases were punctuated by financial and artistic failures and a series of more or less serious liaisons, which continued during his relationship with Held and even after his marriage to Billie Burke in 1914. An inveterate gambler, he had little real financial acumen and was bankrupt when he died. However, in show business, in the words of his earliest posthumous biographers, his version of the Midas touch 'turned gold into dreams'.[15] Ziegfeld died in Los Angeles in July 1932, and many of the tributes to him are summed up in Percy Hammond's observation in the *Los Angeles Times* that 'his career was characterized by a sort of magnificent bravura, in which the showman's cunning, the gambler's willingness to take a chance were combined with the florid instincts of a maharajah' (30 July 1932). The anonymous Associated Press report published in the *New York Times* on 24 July suggested a connection between his success as a showman at the 1893 Exposition and the successive editions of the *Follies*: 'Perhaps, beneath the surface, the same idea underlay the two; that of exhibiting something so nearly perfect that people were attracted by their own desire to admire.' Billie Burke's autobiography, *With a Feather on My Nose* (1950), is remarkably compassionate and forgiving of her inspiring but wayward partner: 'Could there be a prouder boast in the theatre than "I worked for Ziegfeld"? And "Ziegfeldian" and "Glorified" are words that Flo left as on a banner above his accomplishments.'[16]

The MGM film biography, a masterpiece of celebration and emulation, translates the onstage evidence of the 'Ziegfeld Touch' into spectacles characteristic of the studio's style. *The Great Ziegfeld* (1936), 'suggested by romances and incidents in the life of America's greatest showman, Florenz Ziegfeld, Jr.', has outstanding performances by William Powell in the title role and Luise Rainer as Anna Held, his first female 'discovery' and marriage partner. The spectacular musical numbers, beyond the capability of Ziegfeld's own theatres, are effective as cinematic expressions of values present in the impresario's own work and inherited by the film's makers. Design, choreography and staging are informed by a careful study of the theatrical originals and the active participation of one of his designers, John Harkrider. The script is by William Anthony Maguire, who had written the book for Ziegfeld musicals. As in other biographical films, the protagonist's career is shaped as a trajectory through hardships endured, emotional conflicts resolved and vital innovations suddenly achieved. Ziegfeld's escape from a benign but conservative artistic family background, forsaking 'high' culture in favour of 'low', provides the requisite element of early struggle, but it is soon left behind. The project of 'Glorifying the American Girl' that Ziegfeld cannily adopted as a combination of patriotic duty and business acumen helps to legitimize him as a force for the good.

In her study of the Ziegfeld Girl phenomenon, Linda Mizejewski points out that many eulogies of Ziegfeld bracket him with such representative figures as the captains of industry Henry Ford, J.P. Morgan and William Randolph Hearst – the last of whom found his long-time lover Marion Davies in the *Follies* and bankrolled the lavish Ziegfeld Theatre that opened on Sixth Avenue in 1927.[17] Eddie Cantor's first volume of autobiography, *Take My Life* (1957), insists on the image of knighthood: 'he has made many girls and girls have made him, and on that principle is based his chivalry, theatrical display and success.'[18] ('Made' unconsciously reflects an aspect of Ziegfeld's life that the film would have to work round carefully.) A striking analysis of the glorifying process is offered in Edmund Wilson's 1923 essay on the *Follies*:

> In general, Ziegfeld's girls have not only the Anglo-Saxon straightness – straight backs, straight brows and straight noses – but also the peculiar frigidity and purity, the frank high-school-girlishness which Americans like. He does not aim to make them, from the moment they appear, as sexually attractive as possible, as the Folies Bergères, for example, does. He appeals to American idealism, and then, when the male is intent on his chaste and dewy-eyed vision, he gratifies him on this plane by discreetly disrobing his goddess.

This variety of erotic appeal does not suggest 'the movement of abandon and emotion' but plays to the American male's tendency find beauty in 'the efficiency of mechanical movement'.[19] Gilbert Seldes, in *The Seven Lively Arts* (1924), endorsed Wilson's account but insisted that 'it happens to be the function of the Ziegfeld Follies to be Appolonic, not Dionysian; the leap and cry of the bacchanale give way to the song and dance, and when we want the true frenzy we have to go elsewhere'.[20] For that quality, he suggests, one must turn to recent innovation on midtown stages of the 'negro shows' that had recently come down from Harlem to Broadway.

The commoditization of femininity and its packaging were common to other Ziegfeld revues and other similar entertainments. As Susan Glenn notes, discussing 'Laceland' in the 1922 *Follies*, 'the scene both exaggerates feminine material excess and disciplines it with the visual language of geometry and engineering'.[21] Mizejewski examines Ziegfeld's construction of 'the stage as department store', which she suggests is 'perhaps the apotheosis of modern entertainment as consumerism'.[22] Dance routines, in which coordinated patterns of colour and movement were more important than footwork, led up to the appearance of the stately showgirls (distinct from the dancers) typically processing down staircases with the famous 'Ziegfeld strut'. The costuming of the showgirls often went beyond couture into fantastic effects with no parallel in the salons, so that movement – even the 'strut' – was barely possible.[23] However, even the least practical costumes alluded to high-end fashion in the use of costly fabrics and real jewels. The same traits are present in many of the backstage musicals of the 1930s which, as Patricia Mellencamp has argued, 'proclaim then contain' female sexuality while transforming women into fetishist objects.[24] In a vivid account of a *Follies* dress rehearsal, Wilson described how formations in colour and light were achieved by using girls and their dresses as material for abstract patterns, but he

5. *The Great Ziegfeld*
(1936): 'A Pretty Girl'

also noted the presence of a woman of a kind not allowed to benefit from Ziegfeld's glorifying. As the girls crowd the wings, 'Behind them waits the Negro wardrobe woman, patient with a shade of sullenness – knowing herself handsome in another kind, she bides there, blinking at all that white beauty, those open-eyed confident white girls in their paradise of bright dresses, turquoise skirts and canary cloaks, pink bodies hung with dark green leaves, tall white flowerlike stalks that burst into purple and orange'.[25]

In *The Great Ziegfeld* the full theatrical extravagance of this girl-glorifying is represented at the end of the film's first part by a long number, 'A Pretty Girl is Like a Melody', whose relentless upward movement symbolizes the impresario's aspirations. Even in black-and-white it gives a sense of variation in colour and elaboration in design, with contrasting groups of static and dancing figures. After a first chorus sung on the shallow forestage by a tenor in tails, curtains part and the audience is taken through a series of dignified 'classical' and modern variations on the song. As a massive central tower revolves, we pass dancers in eighteenth-century costume executing a minuet, Viennese waltzing couples, singers rendering snatches of *Madama Butterfly* and *I Pagliacci*, and a phalanx of pianists 'playing' Gershwin's 'Rhapsody in Blue' with fantastically exaggerated gestures. Curtains lift to reveal yet more stairs, and a male chorus in top hat and tails frame a frenetic ballet of masked vamps in glittering black tights, whose performance to the Gershwin tune is succeeded by a more staid tableau of girls in flowing ball gowns who sit on the uppermost steps, framing the male singer who had begun the number at stage level. At the very summit of this extraordinary structure is Audrey Dane (Virginia Bruce), the girl chosen for glorification (Figure 5). As the enveloping drapes begin to fall again, hiding the towering structure and its occupants, the curtains slowly draw together as the screen is taken over by the title card 'Intermission'.

'A Pretty Girl' shows what MGM's designers and technicians are capable of, and the cinema audience sees it as no theatre audience ever could have. The last 3 minutes 19 seconds of the number's total running time of 7 minutes 49 seconds are in a single continuous shot, with the camera crane pulling back at the climax to a full-frame view of the whole edifice at the conclusion. The extravagant *kitsch* may seem hard to reconcile with the repeated claims of contemporary commentators that Ziegfeld brought high art and exceptionally good taste to his work. However, the presence of 'high' cultural markers alongside jazz, and the general sense of overabundant display are authentic. What is 'low' gains from its association with 'high' art, and the consumption of the 'high' is made palatable by being mingled with less austere pleasures. The 'Ziegfeld touch' has been administered, the effect summed up as 'transforming popular but plebeian dramatic forms into art without losing their mass appeal'.[26]

Ethan Mordden, Ziegfeld's most recent biographer, suggests shrewdly that 'he was a salesman, and his product was not just song and dance but the unnameable feelings of pleasure and stimulation that musical theatre creates in us'. He 'created a community of playgoers who knew what to expect yet kept getting surprised'.[27] These descriptions, which echo the contemporary comments already quoted, might be applied with equal justice to the Hollywood cinema in general, and to the MGM of the 1930s and 40s in particular. A more personal interpretation of Ziegfeld's showmanship, identified by Richard and Paulette Ziegfeld in their 1993 biography and implicit in much written in his own time, is congruent both with the film's version of him and with MGM's corporate self-image: 'He had a vision of what he wanted, and the passion that drove him would not let him rest. At times, he seemed to take on new responsibilities simply because he welcomed the challenges.'[28] This is the Ziegfeld played by William Powell, who dies repeating the words with which he once urged his stage crew to build ever taller versions of his trademark staircase: 'I've got to have more steps. I need more steps. I've got to get higher.'[29] The process by which MGM managed to turn his career into an acceptable fable of show-business success, can be documented in detail from script materials in the Flo Ziegfeld-Billie Burke Papers in the Billy Rose Theater Collection at New York Public Library, which take us into the workshop of theatre historiography, Hollywood style.

The Great Ziegfeld began as a Universal project, but before any filming could take place and after an expenditure of between $225,000 and $250,000, it had proved beyond the studio's means, and it was sold on to MGM. (Studio records show the eventual cost of the film as $2,183,000: it brought in $4,673,000 world-wide.) Maguire, initially engaged as both producer and script writer, retained screenplay credit in exchange for the offer of a producer–writer–director role on a subsequent MGM film: Hunt Stromberg took over as producer. The property was officially MGM's as of 13 March 1935. Principal photography for the non-musical sections of the film began in September 1935, with Robert Z. Leonard as director – reportedly, among the other candidates considered was George Cukor.[30]

The three drafts of Maguire's script illustrate the problems of managing a biopic when embarrassing personal details had to be omitted. A structure had to be found for a life story that – deprived of the insights these might afford – lacked dramatic shape. Ziegfeld's career, once he had arrived on Broadway, consisted essentially of a series of more or less successful shows. Other major developments in his professional life were his losses in the 1929 stock-market crash and the reverses he suffered and then overcame in his last years. His emotional life, far more interesting material, had to be rendered blander and its crises had to be sketchier. His extra-marital affairs and the ambiguous status of his relationship with Anna Held had to be glossed over or represented indirectly. At the same time, some basic elements of the Ziegfeld personality had to be presented: risk taking (but not compulsive gambling), love of women (but not womanizing) and artistic adventurousness (but not infuriating capriciousness in rehearsals). A great deal depended on William Powell in the title role, while the production team had the task of emulating productions still fresh in the memory of many theatregoers and (if only by report) cinemagoers in general.

Maguire's first version, 'The Great Ziegfeld. He Lived to Glorify Beautiful Womanhood', is dated 27 December 1934 and bears the Universal Pictures imprint.[31] In overall design it corresponds to subsequent drafts, with several episodes and transitions that are seen in the completed film. Ziegfeld's career and private life are dealt with tentatively in all three pre-production versions. In the December 1934 draft the title and credits are accompanied by a montage evocation of famous Ziegfeld stars: 'This dissolves into a Foreword by Billie Burke – as the strains of music continue softly. In this Foreword she will say "That Flo Ziegfeld lived for the public – therefore his memory belonged to the public; hence her willingness to tell the story of his life. She can tell it truthfully – for even though he had many loves, his real love was for her. She can tell his faults because his virtues were so many."' This seems to deal with the problematic aspects of his private life, but in fact makes the mistake of indicating that they existed at all. In the second script (16 July 1935) the wording of the 'Foreword' is anxiously pedantic, as Maguire struggles to get it right: 'Naturally, in presenting an extended career of this adventurous nature, it has been necessary to take certain liberties, and to make certain transpositions in Time, Date and Place. That it would be virtually impossible, in the limited time of an evening's entertainment, to at all times be accurate in the chronological order of events – but that, nevertheless, the incidents recorded in the Screen Play are actual occurrences in this notable career'.[32]

The third script, dated 31 September 1935, makes further adjustments, including instructions (now that this is the second version for MGM and the production team is lining up) for Adrian, the studio's chief designer of 'gowns'.[33] After the initial montage:

> All these impressions overlap in a veritable rush of Music and Figures, and finally the impressions disappear and BILLIE BURKE is seen to come forward to the camera. (Background for her scene to be decided). She is dressed in lovely organdie, in character with the femininity and loveliness that have always been hers. (Adrian, give particular creation to this as the effect of Miss Burke's presence must be soft, pastel, beautifully simple and sweet.) Miss Burke addresses our screen audience. Miss Burke's Foreword, will not indicate that we are telling the actual facts in their proper sequence, but rather have we used incidents in Ziegfeld's career to base our story on.[34]

By now, Maguire seems to have given up finding words for Billie Burke to speak, but the finished film goes further, dispensing with her altogether. It opens with credits displayed as if on lighted theatre marquees, and the title card that claims it has been 'suggested by romances and incidents' in Ziegfeld's life.

In all the pre-production versions, and in the film as released, two showmen, Jack Billings and Florenz Ziegfeld Jr (the script refers to him as 'Ziggy') meet in the fairground on the Midway at the Chicago exposition as rivals in love as well as business. Billings, an invented character, functions as a substitute for several real figures, including the impresario Charles Dillingham, whose name could not be used. He serves as a foil for Ziegfeld, a friendly rival who will hold the film's episodes together. Ziegfeld is promoting the strong man Eugene Sandow, whom he has brought from New York as a sideshow attraction. He is no match for Billings' star, the gyrating 'cooch' dancer Little Egypt, but Ziegfeld has a brainwave: he invites the ladies of Chicago to feel Sandow's muscles. Other scenes in this section show Ziegfeld's success with women, and we also give an early example of his habit of advising them on their choice of clothes and accessories.

Ziegfeld experiences one of his many financial setbacks, but embarks for Europe in search of talent. Having found themselves – to Billings' annoyance – on the same Europe-bound liner, the managers go together to Monte Carlo, where a scene in the casino establishes Ziegfeld's love of gambling. The overall scheme of his thwarting Billings with a pre-emptive 'wooing' of his discovery Anna Held corresponds in most respects to the subsequent script drafts and the film's final version. Back in New York, after Anna's less than spectacular debut, we see Ziegfeld thinking up the famous milk-bath publicity ploy, in which he arranged to have a dairyman sue him for failure to pay for milk that Anna allegedly bathed in – a sensational fact that court proceedings would oblige the newspapers to report.[35] In the first draft this scene is followed by an elaborate montage sequence, including bathing girls and a moment of routine 1930s racist humour with a 'pickaninny' being washed in the hope of changing her colour ('Is I white yet?'). The December 1934 draft notes that 'If Colbert's milk bath was sensational in De Mille's picture [Cleopatra, 1934], this sequence should be many times as sensational, filled with beautiful girls and based on a true press story in the life of Ziegfeld and Anna Held'. A version of the sequence figures in all three of the draft scripts but not in the completed film.

An invented character, Mary Lou, connects Ziegfeld to his Chicago origins, and establishes his generosity and his essentially chivalrous (rather than exploitative) attitude to women. In the first version she also provides a substitute for the 'drunken actress' episode later devised to reflect his affair with Lillian Loraine without naming her. In all versions, Mary Lou is first seen as a little girl taking piano lessons from Ziegfeld's father. She has a crush on the young man – who lets her down gently when she insists he is to be her fiancé. Years later she visits the impresario in New York, and he agrees to employ her: no casting couch is involved, though its availability for other cases is hinted at. In due course, her indignant boyfriend arrives from back home and accuses Ziegfeld of 'glorifying' women – a euphemism that gives him the phrase he needs for publicity. In a subsequent scene Mary Lou is drunk in the dressing room, and while Ziegfeld is giving her a talking-to and *refusing* to kiss her, Anna interrupts them. As a consequence of this, the couple divorce.

By this point in the story Maguire's first draft has reached page 133 out of its total of 166, and events have to move very fast. In the middle of the Mary Lou episode Ziegfeld has already 'discovered' Fanny Brice singing in burlesque, and heard (and redirected) her performance of the torch song 'My Man'. Now he sees theatre marquees advertising Billie Burke in the musical comedy *Jerry*, and 'poaches' her from Billings at a New Year's costume ball. (In fact they did meet on such an occasion, but she was with her agent, and the element of rivalry was absent.) Rather than proceed directly to the wooing, the December 1934 script introduces Daniel Frohman, the impresario who has brought Billie over from London. Frohman, angry with his rival, embarks hurriedly for England, leaving his hat on the table. In the very next scene Ziegfeld proposes to Billie during a carriage ride in Central Park (he is wearing Frohman's hat), after which we dissolve to the scene in which their '3 or 4 year old' daughter Patricia is playing by the Christmas tree. In this way the film distinguishes between the wooing of Burke and his other amours: he has not stolen her from Frohman to bring her out in a show of his own then bed her, but has marriage in mind. (She is also, of course, a great acquisition for the theatre.) After a series of successes, by page 151 Ziegfeld's career is going through a bad patch again.

As in the finished film, a scene in a barber's shop, where Ziegfeld is being talked about as a has-been, provokes him to issue the defiant announcement that he will have four Broadway successes. These are represented by a montage of titles, songs and glimpses of performance. The script moves towards its finale with the news of the Wall Street Crash arriving while Ziegfeld is at a party in Palm Beach. The 'Pretty Girl' number takes place at this point, simpler here than in its eventual version. The script ends with Ziegfeld's death – not in Los Angeles, but in his New York hotel room with a view of the electric sign on the roof of the theatre with his name.

Maguire's second draft refines and simplifies many aspects of the first. Now the idea for Anna's milk-bath comes as he is feeding toast to his poodle in a milk bowl. The cynical and ultimately dissolute 'Audrey Lane' character now replaces the innocent Mary Lou as a stand-in for Lillian Lorraine, who occasioned Held's divorce from Ziegfeld. To give a clearer sense of Anna's erotic appeal (and possibly in the light of the casting of Luise Rainer), Ziegfeld's intimacy with her is emphasized in a scene where he takes off her stocking. Two notable 'lightbulb' moments are now included: he arrives at the title 'Ziegfeld Follies' for a new kind of show with 'personalities – but mostly blondes and brunettes', and hits on the word 'glorify'. At this point the script gives a sense of the greater scale of what has by now become a major MGM production:

MUSICAL PROGRESSION OF TIME (SYMBOLICAL)

Money – distribution- costumes – scenery –girls – FOLLIES! – A Seymour Felix-Reis futuristic conception, beginning with the first Follies of 1907 and progressing to the Modern Period (Note: At this point in the construction our backgrounds, costumes, details, etc., become STRICTLY MODERN). This time-lapse is a study of white against black, fantastically we see just the hands – the famous cigar – and the famous gardenia of Ziegfeld (no face or body in the movement) as the hands reach out and miraculously transform Girls into forms of loveliness; costumes and scenery into works of Art; finally emerging in a succession of the heads of glorious girls, each singing snatches of the hit-tunes from well-remembered early Follies – AND THEN CLIMAXING IN A GREAT BURST OF MODERN MUSIC AND CRACKING THROUGH TO: HUGE ELECTRIC SIGN – ZIEGFELD FOLLIES'.

The 'Pretty Girl' number is also introduced, but it is not yet the spectacle of the final film, and is cut into for dialogue scenes establishing Ziegfeld's relationship with Audrey and shots towards the audience that would have shown Anna perceiving what is going on between them.

By page 119 (of 187) the second script is proceeding rapidly to the discovery of Fanny Brice and the signing of Marilyn Miller. When Audrey is found drunk in her dressing room, Anna thinks Ziegfeld has come to the room for a tryst rather than to rebuke her. The script briskly announces the consequent divorce. Audrey, sacked for unprofessional behaviour, confronts Ziegfeld and smashes one of his 'lucky' china elephants. After a montage establishing the openings of the successful musical comedies *Sally* and *Kid Boots*, the script moves to the masked ball and Billie Burke. Grant's Tomb now replaces Central Park as the location for the proposal, and a new scene (pages 169–171) shows Anna receiving news of the marriage from Ziegfeld by telephone. In the film it occasions an acting *tour de force* for Rainer, fighting back the tears and heroically wishing her erstwhile lover well. She falls on the bed: 'I'm too tired to go anywhere and to do anything.' (This suggests a quasi-operatic death through noble but thwarted love: in real life it was an unexpected but far from fatal blow.) This is followed directly by the scene of Ziegfeld and Billie with their daughter Patricia, at home at Christmas, opening the presents under the tree. As Ziegfeld examines a model of his new theatre, he is told that he is bankrupt. The subsequent 'barbershop' sequence and his access of optimistic resolve then lead to a montage of Broadway successes. He is still losing money: Billie gives him her jewels, but the future remains bleak. In his office in the Ziegfeld Theatre, Ziegfeld is in his private box watching a performance of *Showboat* when he gets news of the Wall Street Crash. In the final scene (two pages later) he is sitting in his chair in a suite in the hotel across from the theatre – the last sign to go out is that for *Showboat*, 'the dying lights of the sign [are] reflected in his face' as he expires.

The third draft makes many minor adjustments, adding 'Billy' (Ray Bolger), a stage hand who wants to be a dancer, replacing the other would-be performers who vie for Ziegfeld's attention in earlier drafts. The most notable innovation is in the final sequence. Ziegfeld, in his hotel room, wires Eddie Cantor and W.C. Fields, telling them to quit movies: to Fields he writes 'Wouldn't you rather tour the country again as real artists than be shipped all over the world in a tin can like a lot of tomatoes?' To comfort Ziegfeld, his valet Sidney reminds him of his great successes. Left alone, Ziegfeld gazes towards the theatre he has built, and as he dies, we see his spirit leave his body and ascend the 'golden steps to heaven'.

> This apparition-like figure is seen to walk up steps – steps – STEPS! Golden steps – into clouds – into the Heavens! As this is occurring, we hear a BURST OF MUSIC, and down the steps – meeting him – joining him – are figures and characters representing the memories Sidney had so eloquently spoken of'.
>
> As the figure of Ziggy continues UP the steps, these characters continue DOWN the steps – until finally we have a veritable riot of colour, design and music, all fantastically arranged in a glorious blaze of music and rhythm. Through this, AS WE COME IN CLOSER, Ziggy's voice is heard to say: 'I've got to have more steps. I need more steps. I've got to get higher'. And on this musical Finale, which, by the way, should top everything previously staged in the picture, we are FADING OUT.

The line survives (with an additional 'higher') in the film's final sequence, as do the images of figures from his shows. Although the 'ghost' performers are moving down steps in this montage, Ziegfeld himself is not shown ascending.

The final three-hour version of *The Great Ziegfeld* was widely accepted as having achieved its goal. Ziegfeld emerges as a painstaking supervisor of shows, a canny manager and audacious showman. Above all, he is credible as a charming and desirable person. Many of his famous quirks are worked in: the compulsive sending of telegrams (even to recipients in the same building); the cultivation of a mystique around his ability to select and groom his protégées; his lavishness with gifts of jewellery; and even his superstitious collection of china elephants. The gambling is glanced at, and the Mary Lou plot line softens the effect of his philandering by allowing us to see him as generous and principled where he might have seemed profligate and exploitative. The impression is reinforced by Anna's initial rueful acceptance of his affair with Audrey – she is loyal to him until he seems to be making it public – and the omission of any extra-marital affairs after his marriage to Billie Burke (Myrna Loy). The film emphasizes the admiration and affection in which he is held even by his business rivals.

As Mizejewski points out, Ziegfeld's fastidious dressing, love of luxury and sharp eye for the details of female attire and ornament might easily be read as queer. But the show business context, his patriotic glorifying mission and the relentless heterosexual wooing confirm him as acceptably straight. His father's European (high) culture is treated respectfully, but Florenz Ziegfeld, Jr discovers a passion for extravert, energetic showmanship that cannot be satisfied by the Academy of Music. None of Maguire's scripts includes the story of young Ziggy running away to follow Buffalo Bill's Wild West show, but the episodes on the Midway serve the same purpose as that perhaps legendary episode. In Held he finds and promotes a singer whose Parisian naughtiness is a revelation for the American public, and Rainer gives a charming performance of the song 'I Wish You'd Come and Play with Me'. Sophie Tucker commented that the shows 'offered Americans something Americans used to think they could only get in Paris, and at prices that lifted this form of variety way out the vaudeville class'.[36] In the 1936 film Ziegfeld passes on seamlessly from his 'Anna Held' period to the invention of the *Follies*, and his fastidiousness and connoisseurship do not get in the way of his essentially masculine and American obsession with progress. To Glorify the American Girl is to glorify America itself. As might be expected, the ethnic dimension of Ziegfeld's shows goes unremarked: that the showgirls and chorus dancers chosen for stardom should all be white is quite simply assumed as normal. The comedian Bert Williams is referred to, but there is no sequence to represent the incident in which Ziegfeld insisted that this African-American performer should be accepted by his company. Fanny Brice's scenes – she appears as herself – provide an element of traditional Jewish humour. No reference is made to Held's Jewish ancestry or her career on the Yiddish stage before she transformed herself into a 'French' *chanteuse*.

Frank S. Nugent of the *New York Times* was representative of the critics who identified the hero's own methods in the 1936 film: 'the picture has the opulence, the lavishness, the expansiveness and the color of the old Follies; it has the general indifference to humor which was one of Ziegfeld's characteristics; and it has the reverential approach with which, we suspect, Mr Ziegfeld himself might have handled his own life story.'[37] Several reviewers thought the film too long. In *Life* Don Herold admitted a strong desire during the first part to go home to bed, but his final recommendation was 'Stick through to the middle of this and you won't be sorry'. Ziegfeld was 'probably doing his best to send M-G-M three-page telegrams of congratulations from the other world'.[38] Graham Greene was appalled by the duration as well as the ethos of 'the silliest, vulgarest, dullest novelty of the season', one of the films 'which belong to the history of publicity rather than to the history of the cinema'.[39] The 'Ziegfeld Touch' had been emulated at the biopic's premiere, reportedly the first on a lavish scale since the early years of the Depression. In the words of the *Los Angeles Times*:

> Beauty has the world at its feet! Ten glorified girls from the cast of Metro-Goldwyn-Mayer's *The Great Ziegfeld* will be literally placed on pedestals for the premiere at the Carthay Circle Theater, Wednesday night.
>
> The pedestal adornments will wear the lavish costumes in which they appear in the picture. They were personally selected by Seymour Felix, who created and directed the dance sequences for *The Great Ziegfeld*.[40]

So successful was this 'pleasaunce of pulchritude' that it was announced that the girls on their pedestals would remain a feature of the approach to the cinema throughout the film's initial run.

In *Ziegfeld Girl* (1941), the studio returned to the exploitation of the rights it had bought from Ziegfeld's estate, but freed itself from the responsibility of characterizing Ziegfeld himself: he is an off-screen presence, unseen and unheard. Now the moral hazards of being glorified could be exploited as melodrama. The film's opening titles announce that it will take place in 'That Fabulous Era – when Florenz Ziegfeld Glorified the American Girl, and New York wore her over its heart like an orchid – while she lasted'. Of the three girls chosen for the Ziegfeld Touch, one (Hedy Lamarr) ends up renouncing show business and returns to her concert violinist husband; another (Judy Garland) achieves stardom but retains her shining innocence: a shot of her on top of the great staircase is spliced into re-used footage from the earlier film's 'Pretty Girl' scene. Audrey (Lana Turner), a department store elevator operator 'discovered' by a Ziegfeld aide, starts her new career promisingly but goes to the bad, takes to drink and literally falls off her pedestal during a performance. Excluded from the show, she watches from the gallery but leaves when she can take no more and has an apparently fatal collapse on the theatre lobby's staircase. *The Great Ziegfeld* had suggested only in passing, through the example of Audrey and almost as a routine health and safety warning, that being selected for celebrity might be dangerous.

The Great Ziegfeld had stopped short of the literal ascent to heaven of its hero indicated in the script drafts. That would be accomplished jokily in the prologue to *Ziegfeld Follies* (1946), in which the camera seems to float upwards through the clouds – past a toy half-timbered theatre labelled 'Shakespeare' and a circus tent with P.T. Barnum's name – to find Powell once again playing Ziegfeld, this time in heaven and sipping nectar from a champagne bottle in a luxuriously appointed suite. There he contemplates his glamorous past, lovingly holding a 'Ziegfeld Girl' doll and gazing at animated displays representing the shows of his heyday. 'What would I give to be able to put on one more *Follies*?' he wonders, as he contemplates the 'great shows that were part of the dream of America' in that 'innocent world believing in a golden future'. Dipping a quill in ink, sure sign of a high-class artist at work, he drafts a programme for new *Follies*, of the kind only MGM can deliver. As he leans over the bar of heaven we follow his gaze into a dissolve that brings us Fred Astaire introducing 'Here's to the Girls'. The celestial boudoir provided for Ziegfeld is camp enough in itself, but Steve Cohan has aptly described the 'unforgettable camp' of the number that follows as 'push[ing] Ziegfeld's own imagery of Anglo-American beauty past the point of excess, if that can be possible, juxtaposing straight and queer perspectives of the Follies' idealized vision of femininity in a dialectic vision of female spectacle which elevates "the Girls" to a camp apotheosis'.[41] (After a ride on a pink carousel, Lucille Ball cracks a whip to 'tame' a squad of cat-women in fishnets.) With prodigality worthy of Ziegfeld himself, the film, first planned in 1939, began production in April 1944 and accumulated a catalogue of sequences so long that its running time at previews was 273 minutes.[42] The studio's appropriation of the theatrical revue is finally accomplished, and now the great man can be shown to endorse it from on high.

Yankee Doodle Dandy:
George M. Cohan and 'the mainspring in the Yankee clock'

George M. Cohan (1878–1956), an irrepressible force on Broadway and in American popular musical theatre for more than three decades, would seem to be a natural subject for a celebration on film: he certainly thought so himself. The scripting of Warner Bros' *Yankee Doodle Dandy* (1942) makes an interesting comparison with that of *The Great Ziegfeld*. Patrick McGilligan's meticulous edition of the screenplay shows how the material was drafted and redrafted in the preparation and production phases.[43] The task was complicated not merely by the need to work round aspects of Cohan's personal life that would have been unacceptable in a patriotic biopic governed by the Production Code, but by the existence of a treatment by the subject himself. Cohan's permission was conditional on the omission of all reference to his troubled private life. This was in itself a major problem for a narrative that, as with Ziegfeld, threatened to become a summary of his on-stage *curriculum vitae*. Eventually, the script writers managed to create a 'safe' fictional love interest to replace the reality Cohan embargoed and provide the requisite element of romance. Cohan was aware of the effect of his self-assertive behaviour. In *Twenty Years on Broadway (And the Years It Took to Get There)* he is unsparing in describing his unbearable cockiness as a youth, and reports the answer he gave his sister Josie when she accused him of bragging: 'Listen, sis. Between you and me, I don't care about what they say about me, so long as they keep mentioning my name.'[44]

The film's most effective strategy for coping with these un-amiable traits lies in James Cagney's dynamism and the quality of vulnerability underneath bluster that he had brought even to his gangster roles. A fictionalized version of the award to Cohan of the Congressional Medal brings him to the White House from Broadway, where he has been mimicking Franklin D. Roosevelt in *I'd Rather be Right*. The President elicits the reminiscences that the film enacts, and Cohan's life story is romanticized in an appealing manner, with many elisions of characters and incidents. The opening titles announce the story as beginning in 1878, 'at the beginning of the Horatio Alger era' – evoking, in other words, the spirit of that author's fables of upward mobility achieved against the odds by pluck and hard work. As with many film biographies of stage personalities, the Horatio Alger dimension – now theatrical lodgings rather than log cabin to White House – fits neatly with the customary biopic pattern: early hardships bravely endured, lessons in the school of hard knocks, and so on. In the first part of the film Cohan's domestic dimension (not in real life his strongest suit) is represented by his affection for the family act, allowing neat superimposition of show business and wholesome family feeling. ('It's a lucky family that dances together every day.') Even the early touring is given a patriotic twist, in a montage sequence as George's voice announces that 'they kept putting new stars in the flag and the Cohans kept rushing out to meet them'. George makes it to New York ('Things were tough, but at least I was in New York') but he needs to call the family – out touring in the sticks – to join him.

One invented episode stands out as a skilful promotion of the hero's standing as a representative American. This follows the success of *Little Johnnie Jones*, itself a fable of the American pluck of a jockey prevailing over the old-world skulduggery of criminals trying to 'fix' an English race, the Derby. Scenes from this 1904 production are re-enacted with a fair degree of accuracy, with Cagney as Cohan giving an energetic performance of 'I'm a Yankee Doodle Dandy' on the racecourse and singing 'Give My Regards to Broadway' as a ship pulls away from the quayside. This is a considerable achievement on the part of the film-makers and the star, convincingly marking the show's significance in Cohan's career. Subsequently Cohan and his associate Sam Harris visit the up-market star Fay Templeton in her dressing room, to enlist her as the lead in George's next show.[45] It is made clear that this will be not so much a simple chat as an audience with the singer, whose refined accent and lavishly appointed dressing room (with the customary black maid) suggest a new level of sophistication for the pair. Before they arrive she and the impresario Abe Erlanger are arguing about the proposition, and Templeton expresses her contempt for the 'loud, vulgar flag-waving' of *Little Johnnie Jones*. A few minutes with the pushy, wise-cracking Cohan convince her that she was right, but as she leaves to go on stage she tells him that far from relishing life on the Great White Way, she looks forward to her nightly return to New Rochelle: 'It's only forty-five minutes from Broadway, but thank heaven it's a thousand miles from all the noisy, neurotic people one has to associate with in our profession.' George and Sam are left in the dressing-room, and George 'musingly' repeats 'forty-five minutes from Broadway'. In the next shot we see Fay finishing her number and coming off stage. Erlanger pleads with her as she stalks towards her dressing-room, but she is not impressed by his eulogy of Cohan's 'magic': 'I know his formula – a fresh young sprout gets rich between 8.30 and 11.00 pm.' Erlanger persists:

> That's just it! George M. Cohan has invented the success story, Fay. And every American loves it because it happens to be his own private dream. He's found the mainspring in the Yankee clock – ambition, pride, and patriotism. That's why they call him the Yankee Doodle Boy.[46]

The door to Fay's room is locked, and to her further indignation when she gets in she finds Sam and George still there. However, as soon as George has played her 'Forty-Five Minutes from Broadway', the song he has written while she was doing her turn, she begins to soften. By the end of the scene, after Sam has insisted George allow her to play through 'Mary' (which he had composed for his girlfriend) and agree that she should sing it in the new show, she has been won over.

Almost every detail of the scene is fiction. 'Forty-five Minutes from Broadway' was suggested by a remark made by an actor friend who lived in New Rochelle, 'Mary' was not written for Cohan's future wife, and – most important – Templeton was not a stuck-up 'high-class' performer.

Cohan's biographer John McCabe describes her as 'something of a multi-talented Sophie Tucker' who 'could sing almost any kind of song in a resonantly warm contralto and ... was cheery, jolly'.[47] However, the invented scene allows the film to set up important tensions. Any bad impressions made by Cohan's flag-waving brashness and his cocky, assertive personality have already been sufficiently qualified for the film's audience by the preceding sequence, a tender domestic scene between him and Mary in her modest apartment. Templeton's contrasting prima-donna behaviour and luxurious dressing-room represent a new world he will be able to conquer. Erlanger, here a warm, enthusiastic friend rather than the cold manipulator he was justly renowned for being in real life, voices a central 'truth' about the film's Cohan: he embodies the American Dream. By resisting him, Templeton would be going in the face of history. In reality, not every observer was convinced that Cohan represented positive values. James Metcalfe, drama critic of *Life*, launched an outspoken attack after the opening of *George Washington, Jr* (1906), which featured 'She's a Grand Old Flag': the 'ideal of young American manhood' Cohan created was 'a vulgar, cheap, blatant, ill-mannered, flashily dressed, insolent, smart Aleck, who for some reason unexplainable, on any basis of common sense, good taste, or even ordinary decency, appeals to the imagination and approval of large American audiences'.[48] In effect, the film uses Templeton as an easily dismissed mouthpiece for a not uncommon reaction to Cohan.

After this episode, as if to set aside such objections, the film again asserts the hero's essential goodness of heart as Cohan (with chocolates and a bouquet) returns to Mary's apartment to explain the situation and make his apologies. To his delight she not only insists that the song should be Templeton's, but accepts his proposal of marriage: 'Listen, darling – how would you like to make it a lifetime job? Leading lady, no options. There may be a little heartache in the show at times, but I'll guarantee you a million laughs, too ... How does it sound?'[49] The show-business metaphor comes irresistibly to Cohan and is understood by Mary: the couple met when she came backstage to see him when he was appearing in stock. On that occasion she symbolized the mixture of pride and pluck represented by a trouper's hardiness and desire to make the Big Time: 'I know I have talent', she insisted, 'even if I am from Buffalo'. As George's career progresses through the film, the Big Time is of course achieved. The status of his theatres and audiences is steadily enhanced. When he appears for Ziegfeld at the New Amsterdam on 42nd Street, our first glimpse of the stage is past a fashionably dressed woman sitting in a box. Outside the theatre his encounter with the

6. *Yankee Doodle Dandy*
(1942): dancing down the
White House stairs

famous comedian Eddie Foy confirms Cohan's new standing but also
reassures us that he is still an amiable man of the people and can crack
wise with the best of them. This is entirely consistent with the film's
combination of New Deal populism and wartime spirit. On New Year's
Eve, 1912, he and Mary are sitting in a diner, looking through the
window – 'Front row center – the greatest show on earth – the people'.
Cohan warns about the consequences that would ensue 'whenever we
get too high hat – too sophisticated for flag-waving'.

By the end of the film, Cohan and Mary have achieved a happy rural
retirement from which he is summoned to appear again on Broadway
in *I'd Rather be Right*. In the first scene in the family's newly acquired
farm house George is chopping wood when his sister comes to tell him
she has decided to marry and leave the stage, a decision he accepts with
good grace. Since his mother and father have already decided to retire,
the end of the family act has become inevitable. Through Cohan's
father Jerry (Walter Huston), the film is able to maintain contact with
an old and warm-hearted trouping ethos while celebrating the more
modern, forward-looking spirit of the son. Jerry's career supports and
parallels that of George and allows for two moving episodes of filial
affection: the birthday gift to Jerry of partnership in all his real estate
and copyrighted properties; and a death-bed scene in which the rest
of the family watch from the other side of the room through an arch
resembling a theatre's proscenium while father and son take leave of
each other. This superimposition of theatricality and 'heart' is carried
through into the final shots of the film. After his talk with the president,
Cohan tap-dances down the grand flight of stairs in the White House
(Figure 6). Arriving at the gate, he encounters a company of soldiers
singing 'Over There'. The crowd on the sidewalk joins in, and a soldier
asks Cohan 'What's the matter, old timer? Don't you remember this

song?' George replies 'It seems to me I do', and the soldier remarks 'Well, I don't hear anything'. Cohan answers by stepping into the column and joins in the lusty performance of his own composition. Public, patriotic sentiment, personal pride and a sense of arrival are combined as the film's closing shot fades out on a full-frame close-up of the singing performer.

In *Yankee Doodle Dandy* none of the staged numbers are impossible to conceive as being staged in a theatre, and, although the camera is granted its usual freedom of movement, each sequence is established so as to emphasize the theatre spectators' viewpoint as definitive. One of the film's strengths is its assertion that the cinema should and can convey the theatre's vitality rather than treating it as something to be improved on by enlarging the fictional scenic space. Cohan, by contrast with Ziegfeld, shares with Jolson the honour of being a man of the people, most alive when in direct contact with his audience. The overwhelming effect is more Dickens than Zola: the world of show business, for all its hardships, is ultimately life-affirming and benevolent. In *Yankee Doodle Dandy* the Warners stake their claim to be considered 'real live nephews of Uncle Sam's', even if they were born not born on the fourth of July.

The revisionist biopic: Shakespeare and Molière in love, Gilbert and Sullivan in difficulties

In the decades since these Hollywood films were produced, attitudes to the depiction of the private lives of exemplary historical figures have changed, and intimate aspects of private life are not only treated with greater frankness but are expected to be shown or at least alluded to. A wayward love life is now a badge of honour and a guarantee of human sensibility. With Shakespeare, Molière, and Gilbert and Sullivan there is no question of legal action on the part of any individuals who feel their good name or that of their ancestors has been impugned. In *Shakespeare in Love* (1999) and Laurent Tirard's *Molière* (2006) amatory exploits humanize authors who have become cultural icons. Whereas Jolson, Ziegfeld and Cohan needed careful handling to qualify as exemplary national figures and satisfy the demands of the Production Code, at the turn of the millennium Shakespeare and Molière are brought nearer to the audience by a demonstration of their amiable flaws. They are men of the theatre and of the people, appealingly unaware of the dignity to be conferred on them by posterity. However, neither film is radical in relation either to its subject or to the biographical genre. Mike Leigh's

Topsy-Turvy (1999), by contrast, is truly innovative with respect to both.

In Madden's film, Shakespeare (Joseph Fiennes) is near the beginning of his career. Inspiration does not come easily and is bound up with the vagaries of his energetic love life. He is not served well either by the real-life 'muse' he shares with the actor Burbage or the more ethereal presence he tries to summon up when he sits down to write, a process attended with a brief ritual (turning round, spitting, rubbing his hands) and explained in amusingly proto-Freudian terms to the quack doctor (Dr Moth): 'It's as if my quill is broken...'. During the opening credits he is trying to find a spelling for his own signature, as though this basic element of authorial identity were still in flux. Dissatisfied with his progress, Shakespeare has little regard for *The Two Gentlemen of Verona* and is struggling towards a more romantic, less formal kind of writing. In the old-established terms of Shakespearean biography, he is trying to get from 'early Shakespeare' to something resembling maturity. For the time being he is stuck over the title (*Romeo and Ethel, the Pirate's Daughter*) and the plot. Meeting Christopher Marlowe (Rupert Everett) in a bar, Shakespeare is offered an escape from the bathos of the title – Marlowe is working on *The Massacre at Paris*, acknowledged as a 'good title' – and given pointers for the plot of his tragedy. The film takes advantage of the many gaps in biographical information to good effect, but in this case Shakespeare's evident reliance on literary sources makes it less than likely that he would need Marlowe's help with such basic elements of what will become *Romeo and Juliet*. As Michael Anderegg points out, in Madden's film we never see Shakespeare reading.[50]

Adherence to the facts would ruin the film: Shakespeare would not need to experience an illicit affair with a young noblewoman (abetted by her nurse) after meeting her at a ball and climbing her balcony (and falling off it), or find inspiration in love-making and its glowing aftermath for the lyrical speeches of his play. Having him settle down with a good book would hardly make an exciting or engaging storyline. It would also shackle the film to a pedantic construction of play writing, excluding happenstance and the fervour of the moment. The jokes about inspiration range from directly parallel situations (climbing the balcony, etc.) to stray phrases picked up as Shakespeare walks the streets of the bustling, muddy London that the art department has created. Along the way, the film encompasses the potentially oppressive nature of arranged – or enforced – marriage, anti-theatrical prejudice, and the tension between governmental control and popular entertainment. It even contrives to anticipate the development of colonies in America. Knowledge of the story's circumstances enhances some of the humour, so that there is a moment of comic anticipation when Marlowe delivers *The Massacre at Paris* and announces that he is off to Deptford. But such references are always followed through in terms of plot (Shakespeare thinks he has caused his rival's death) and humour at another level: Henslowe thinks that Marlowe was killed in a brawl over the billing rather than the bill, and (rather less sophisticated) Shakespeare laments the loss of a friend whose 'hand was in my *Titus*'.

Shakespeare in Love presents Shakespeare as a writer immersed in the world of the theatre, impatient with himself rather than the conditions he works in or the colleagues he serves as author and actor. The concluding scenes see him confirmed as a sharer in the company and projected towards new achievements by the hurtful but necessary thwarting of his love for Viola de Lesseps (Gwyneth Paltrow). The theatre is subject to the hazards of finance, the power of government officials, professional rivalry and plague. The intimate relationships and workaday tensions are represented in terms not only of show business in general, but specifically of Hollywood and the film business: the tavern is staffed as well as patronized by actors, and even the waterman who takes Shakespeare to the de Lesseps mansion has a play he asks Shakespeare to read. Henslowe explains the subtleties of finance to the threatening moneylender he persuades to become a backer: as in modern Hollywood a sleight of accounting means that the playwright's or actor's percentage points from the profits hold no threat to the 'money' – there are no profits. ('It's a mystery.') The conventional opposition between commerce (the business of putting on plays or films) and the creative talent, which has been challenged convincingly as a model for understanding the Elizabethan theatre, is perhaps inevitable in a popular fiction of this kind, and it corresponds to the generic expectations audiences bring to the backstage movie.[51] At the same time, the script's sophisticated self-consciousness may prompt a corresponding degree of sceptical awareness on the spectators' part. Clichés are wittily parodied: Henslowe begins a sentence with 'The show must' and Shakespeare impatiently prompts him to 'go on'; and a street-corner preacher inveighs against the business of shows. These are touches of the kind associated with at least one of the authors of the screenplay, Tom Stoppard. (The other is Marc Norman.) The effect is a cross between the juxtaposition of present and past (*Arcadia*) and a historical fiction burlesquing the manner in which 'history' has represented its events and personalities (*Travesties*.) The film superimposes on these the device of a fictional plot intersecting with another fiction, alluded to or shown in brief excerpts, as in *Rosencrantz and Guildenstern Are Dead.* Fictions created in the past and those invented in the present day thus have a degree of equivalence.

This Shakespeare *has* to be in love in order to write effectively, and in the film's terms that experience must be one of unqualified (or only temporarily disturbed) heterosexual attraction, discounting the gender conventions of his theatre. Sam, the boy cast as Juliet, is by no means inadequate, but we are to believe that the presence of a genuine woman (Viola) behind the disguise of 'Thomas Kent' produces the answer to the wager – proposed foolishly by Lord Wessex, the impoverished aristocrat to whom her rich bourgeois father insists on marrying her – that 'the very truth and nature of love' could not be represented in the theatre. The authenticity of Juliet as played by Viola/Thomas is supported by cruder portrayals of the play's Nurse and Lady Capulet and, for good measure, Shakespeare's own impersonation of Viola's nurse at Greenwich. It is not qualified by any sense of the differences between constructions of gender and sexuality in the sixteenth and twentieth centuries or the possible homoerotic appeal of the Elizabethan boy player, except in the moment when 'Thomas' kisses Shakespeare in the boat – a surprise for Shakespeare, whose puzzlement is cut short by the waterman's revelation that he has known who 'he' was all along. More important, though, is the clear suggestion that dressing as a man is a liberating experience for Viola de Lesseps: somewhere in the cross-dressing is located the passionate self-assertion that goes with the *un*dressing. Shakespeare and Viola 'rehearse' lines in private in her bedroom and he even takes some of her (Romeo's) lines, a scene intercut with a stage rehearsal where she appears as Thomas Kent playing Romeo to Sam's Juliet. In Elizabethan drama, as Juliet Dusinberre observes, 'disguise makes a woman not a man but a more developed woman'.[52] Nevertheless, in the first performance of *Romeo and Juliet* Shakespeare goes on in place of the injured Burbage and she takes over from the boy actor whose voice has cracked. The classic backstager situation of real, private love being voiced in public is achieved, and the gender roles are returned to their 'normal' ownership.

This is a theatre of transformations, some of them puzzling even to the actors themselves, but expressing truths that the Lord Wessexes of this world cannot perceive but which the theatre people and their queen intuit. Elizabeth's unhistorical visit to the theatre is essential not only to the plot but to its demonstration that (theatrical) art has access to mysteries that it takes a great spirit – Shakespeare or his queen – to appreciate. Her understanding of a woman in a man's role is informed by political and emotional experience, his by a corresponding artistic and erotic insight. The path to theatrical success is represented in terms familiar from backstage movies – the imperatives of a deadline, problems with money, impatience with the rehearsal that is going nowhere, the last-minute crisis solved by the emergence of another actor to substitute for the one who is suddenly unavailable. Within a framework of carefully researched but modified period detail, the show does go on. Although there is no conventional happy ending to their affair – that can only happen in the theatre, as Queen Elizabeth points out – Shakespeare's and Viola's relationship is no less bound up with the success of the performance than it would be in a 1930s backstage musical. That it also releases the inspiration for the subsequent works of Shakespeare is an added bonus, and for it to be figured in terms of heterosexual romance as 'the very truth and nature of love' as encoded in *Romeo and Juliet* has made for untroubled acceptance in the international box-office. Although the film presents Shakespeare (in Douglas Lanier's words) 'as a genuine artist whose authority springs from his ability to transcend the ephemeral fads and fame of the pop market place' (Henslowe's repeated insistence on 'love and a bit with a dog') it does so while conforming – pleasingly enough – to the very equivalent of such demands in the contemporary movie industry.[53]

Shakespeare faces writer's block but the theatres he works in thrive, albeit under some pressure. In Laurent Tirard's *Molière* the actor-dramatist and his troupe are in an artistic quandary, following the (for him) false gods of classical tragedy. He works in a theatre world that is more strictly polarized by neoclassical discriminations between comedy and tragedy and the techniques they call for. As the film begins, Molière's company in their new theatre and under the patronage of the king's brother, Monsieur, have reached a stalemate. Their patron wants comedy, but the playwright cannot see his way to writing it. He receives a summons to the deathbed of a mysterious woman, and before we learn more about their relationship a flashback takes us back thirteen years to much less prosperous times. The troupe is performing in a barn, presenting the tragedies Molière misguidedly insists on before an uncomprehending and unappreciative audience. As the actor-playwright struts and declaims, two sheriff's officers arrive to arrest him for debt. The performance turns into an impromptu farce of the kind that reflects his true talent for comedy. Thrown into the local lock-up, he is liberated by the enigmatic agent of a local grandee and offered the proposition of work as a tutor. Monsieur Jourdain, a bourgeois elevated through industry and marriage beyond his intellectual accomplishments and social class, needs lessons in deportment, etiquette and all the arts. A married man, he is nevertheless paying court to an artistically obsessed neighbour, one of the *précieuses* notorious for their pretensions to advanced taste. Molière will be passing as a man of the cloth and his daughter's tutor in order to allay the suspicions of his employer's elegant wife, Elmire. He is to take the name of Tartuffe.

For an audience familiar with Molière's career and plays it will by now be evident that a notorious thirteen-year gap in the record is going to be filled, and that the narrative will include his exposure to the themes and situations of his plays.[54] Characters bear names from them – Dorante, Célimène, Elmire, M. Jourdain – and famous scenes are anticipated. These include the 'table' scene in *Tartuffe*; the lessons given to the social climber in *Le Bourgeois gentilhomme*; and the literary salons of *Les Précieuses ridicules* and *Les Femmes savantes*. Familiar lines are spoken in everyday situations, with an effect similar to that of the quotations in *Shakespeare in Love*.[55] Beyond this level of reference, Tirard's script uses organizing principles borrowed from Molière: the obsessive head of the household who eventually sees his errors; the young lovers threatened as a result of father's fads; the unmasking of those who exploit his obsessions; and the revelation of greed and social status as the true motivation of lawyers, doctors, pretentious intellectuals and other self-important authority figures. Among the plays' familiar character types, the sensible friend or *raisonneur* is represented in the film by Elmire, who provides not only wise counsel but erotic fulfilment. In dress and coiffure she is contrasted with the pretentious and insincere Célimène, and in one sequence of shots we cut from a close up on her natural hair and complexion to the elaborately ringletted and farded *précieuse*. (In fact Célimène's appearance is historically correct, and Elmire's a romantic variation on the look of the period.) Sincerity in feeling and manners is one of the goals to be achieved, a necessary discrimination alongside the playwright's progress towards serious comic drama. As in the film itself, in the new kind of comedy the pleasures of farce are not so much to be discounted as put to new purposes.

In the Jourdain household Molière acquires the raw materials for subsequent plays, but it is his relationship with Elmire that gives him the insight to make use of them. The germ of *Tartuffe*, though, would take a long time to come to fruition: the first, banned, version was performed in 1664, and there is neither time nor place in the film for the author's indignant opposition to the pious Société du Saint-Sacrement and its adherents. Despite this, and the simplifications of the little that is known of his travels and travails, Tirard frames the development of the playwright/actor in terms of dramatic principle. Unlike Madden's Shakespeare, who seems not to read and may not have a theoretical thought in his head – fulfilling a cliché about the playwright's 'natural' gifts – Molière has to break away from an outmoded notion of the dignity of neoclassical drama. He starts the film as a failing tragedian who wants to outgrow the simpler pleasures of farce, and has to learn that he can bring a different kind of feeling to farcical situations. This conversion takes place in a bedroom scene between the youthful playwright and the stylish and accomplished older woman, a situation more complex than that of two young people discovering sexual pleasure and affection, and incidentally reanimating Shakespeare's drooping pen. Molière finds the comic mode that will make people laugh at matters that could otherwise be the basis of tragedy.

Tirard gives a sense of salient aspects of Molière's theatre: its dependence on a combination of box office receipts and royal or at least aristocratic patronage; the threat of bankruptcy; the 'outsider' status of actors; and touring as a training ground. No account is taken of the possible implication of his affair with Elmire for the playwright's relationship with his colleague and lover Madeleine Béjart.[56] Tirard's film is far from sharing the historical and ideological self-consciousness of Ariane Mnouchkine's two-part *Molière* (1979), informed by the communitarian spirit of the Théâtre du Soleil and in some measure a response to issues that had arisen within the company. This is not a film in which – as in Mnouchkine's – the actors will be told that René Descartes has arrived in Paris and rush off to sit at his feet while he reads them his *Discours de la méthode*, a scene very much in the spirit of 1968. Mnouchkine contrasts the formal but by no means unloving household of Molière's father and the chaotic, affectionate *milieu* of the players the youth joins after giving up his legal studies. Her film offers vivid re-enactments of different kinds of theatre in the playwright's life, from the *commedia* troupe's booth to the palace of Versailles and, finally, the newly adopted hall at the Petit-Bourbon. The vulnerability of actors to religious prejudice and their dependence on the protection of royal and aristocratic patrons play a considerable part in Mnouchkine's approach: hers is a film enmeshed in debates about the cultural politics of its own time, expressed through the lively depiction of the historical period.

Like *Shakespeare in Love*, Tirard's film features theatrical performances in both private and public contexts, but the private occasions of acting are more numerous and are integrated with the scenes anticipating plays not yet written. In terms of public performance, after an initial scene establishing the film's 'present', the flashback occupies most of the film's running time, and when we return to the 'present' the dying woman is identified as Elmire, who urges the playwright to carry out the plan for serious comedy that she proposed to him some years ago. In the final sequence the company has its fully equipped stage and theatre, and has progressed from an audience of uninterested country people to royal (and fashionable) approval for the new style of comedy.

The private performances occur for the most part in the Jourdain house. Molière's first unconvincing performance there is his first lesson for the Jourdains' youngest child, watched by Elmire. As well as the anticipation of the 'table' scene from *Tartuffe* – this time with the wife using the occasion to prompt 'Tartuffe' to woo her in earnest – the performance sites include the bedroom where Molière and Elmire make love and he shows her his improvisatory as well as amorous skills. In the attic where he coaches his employer for an appearance at Céliméne's salon, Molière seems to work on principles drawn from twentieth-century acting techniques, but his pupil shows little aptitude, making a fool of himself when he accosts Céliméne in the garden and when he recites a eulogy to her in her salon – an episode we do not see. The plot moves towards two triumphant performances in which both employer and actor have a part. In the salon Molière appears as a 'rival poet' flamboyantly reciting his nonsensical opuscule 'Au voleur!' (from *Les Précieuses ridicules*) and prompts Céliméne to reveal her contempt for M. Jourdain, who in his first convincing impersonation has disguised himself as a woman to infiltrate the company and who rebukes her publicly for her bad faith. Within his own house, M. Jourdain, Elmire and even M. Bonnefoy (his lawyer) 'act' in the scene that unmasks a fraudulent fortune hunter by pretending that the Jourdains' daughter has been captured and held to ransom by pirates. The first of these sequences brings the husband to his senses, while the second unites the family as if they were a troupe of actors. After his adventures in the Jourdain household Molière is not to be rewarded with a continuing liaison, because the Jourdains have come to understand themselves and each other through acting. Tirard thus locates the inspiration for the playwright outside the playhouse, while bringing the playhouse into the domestic sphere. Nevertheless, Molière's future does not lie with Elmire but with his company and the future of the drama, a destiny implied but not enunciated in the script. *Molière*, advertised in the United States as 'the French *Shakespeare in Love*', is more urbane and polished than Madden's film, with no desire to make its hero an unthreateningly unsophisticated 'natural' poet – still less 'one of the lads' – but it remains a qualified rather than wholly revisionist approach to its genre.

In *Topsy-Turvy* Mike Leigh offers a more effective challenge to the conventional theatrical biopic. The film creates a detailed picture of the Victorian theatre's working conditions, qualifying expectations that a biographical film would focus primarily if not exclusively on the emotional lives and professional careers of its central characters. Private and public lives coincide not only in the composer and librettist, but in the whole company, and the financing, casting and rehearsal of *The Mikado* is dramatized with rare thoroughness and regard for authenticity. Whereas *Shakespeare in Love* picks and chooses among scholarly evidence and represents sixteenth-century rehearsal techniques as more or less those of the present day (exploration, discovering 'depth' and 'finding' the characters), *Topsy-Turvy* discards nothing of the research its director and cast have conducted.[57] Leigh, a Gilbert and Sullivan enthusiast since boyhood, had long been interested in such a project but had put it off as inconsistent with the 'voice and style' he had found in plays and films, 'with [his] neutral commitment to character-driven, contemporary tragic-comic social observation'. Moreover, he was aware that historical subjects seemed incompatible with his working methods, 'creating contemporary original drama without scripts, through extensive discussion, research and improvisation, working with [his] actors over long periods of preparation'.[58] The film, developed and shot during 1998, was grounded in the same kind of improvisatory rehearsal as Leigh's other films, but with the difference that research materials included documents of nineteenth-century society and, in particular, its theatrical and musical worlds.

Although it includes carefully recreated extracts from three of the Gilbert and Sullivan operas, there is no suggestion (until the final scene) of a direct correspondence between these and the personal lives of the characters. In the closing sequence the actress Lenora Braham speaks lines from the second act of *The Mikado* as, glass in hand, she examines her face in the dressing-room mirror:

> Yes, I am indeed beautiful! Sometimes I sit and wonder, in my artless Japanese way, why it is that I am so much more attractive than anybody else in the whole world. Can this be vanity? No! Nature is lovely and rejoices in her loveliness. I am a child of Nature, and take after my mother.[59]

In the next shot she is on stage alone, singing the lyric that follows this, 'The Sun Whose Rays', and the camera moves up and back from a close-up to reveal the whole of the stage, the orchestra pit and the front of the stalls. Sullivan's music pulls against the gentle but cynical humour underlying Gilbert's lyric, and the shot both celebrates Braham, and expresses the pathos of the situation. The narrative has already moved through the opening night – with Gilbert enduring his habitual first-night nerves – to its triumphal finale. The curtain-call has been followed by scenes turning first to Sullivan's, then Gilbert's private lives. Now the sequence with Braham is a coda detached from the performance rather than a part of it recalled. Whenever it takes place – some time after the opening, as Sullivan's assistant is conducting – it brings an unexpected and moving element of pathos. The music also, as Leigh points out in his DVD commentary, returns the film to Gilbert and Sullivan.

In this respect, the sequence is a final touch in the overall strategy of subverting the genre, concentrating on a limited period in the collaboration – the artistic and managerial difficulties of 1884–1885 and the genesis of *The Mikado* – and striving (as Leigh puts it) 'to make us look at Gilbert and Sullivan's work within the context of their personal and professional lives, stripping it of its accumulated baggage of coy whimsy, instead revealing its true spirit – bold, clear and robust'.[60] He was determined to subvert the conventions of the biopic by using them only when his strategy was served by them: there is no attempt (as in the 1953 *Story of Gilbert and Sullivan*) to cover the span of their careers. The final scene is followed by laconic announcements in captions that the pair write three more operas, and that Sullivan's only grand opera, *Ivanhoe*, although moderately successful in its time, 'isn't as much fun as the Mikado'. Rather than direct attention towards future successes, all three of the concluding scenes have addressed the underlying personal problems of characters. Gilbert's wife Lucy (addressed by him as Kitty), sitting up in bed, suggests a fantastic idea for a new piece that expresses with painful clarity her frustration at the childless state of their marriage and goes far beyond anything that Gilbert would write or the theatre of his time attempt to stage. Gilbert is clearly affected but is unable to respond except by saying 'I shouldn't imagine Sullivan'd much care for that'. In the second scene Sullivan, exhilarated but exhausted – and evidently suffering from his kidney complaint – is told by his mistress Fanny Ronalds that she is pregnant but has 'made [her] own arrangements' to deal with the situation. She leaves her lover with a tender kiss on the cheek and the assurance 'You light up the world. You can't help it', and Sullivan is left 'pondering'.[61] By ending with Braham, Leigh returns the film – unconventionally – to the cast members she represents. Her addiction to alcohol and uncertainty about the future – her child by a deceased husband is an obstacle to her chances of an appropriate marriage – parallel the insecurities of other actors. George Grossmith, who plays Ko-Ko, suffers agonies of stage fright and fortifies himself with morphine injections; Richard Temple, in the title role of the Mikado, has his professional insecurity intensified when his one song is taken from him after the

7. *Topsy-Turvy* (1999):
Temple and Lely in their
dressing room

dress rehearsal; Durward Lely, the tenor who sings Nanki-Poo, is anxious about his figure and his voice; Jessie Bond struggles with a varicose vein and has to use a walking stick when she is not on stage. In costume fittings the female principals are worried about not being able to wear corsets, and so is Lely, who insists that he needs his to support his vocal delivery (Figure 7): the scenes also give a sense of the tensions between costumiers and actors, particularly the social distinctions that the male actors try to defend.

When Temple loses the Mikado's song – 'My Object All Sublime' – the chorus is almost unanimous in agitating for its restoration, and a delegation from them prevails on Gilbert to restore it. (In a typically realistic touch, there is dissent among their ranks from two choristers anxious not to jeopardize their position in the company.) The episode 'appealed to [Leigh's] basic sense of grassroots politics'.[62] Leigh shows the manner in which Gilbert (decisive, trenchant) and Sullivan (suave, ironic) exercise control in rehearsal, and we even see the author at work in his study with the set model and little blocks of wood with which he plotted every move of chorus and principals.[63] All this, even down to Sullivan's manner of conducting (seated, and with sparse movements) and Gilbert's habit of demonstrating business to actors, is backed up by research. Scenes in the office of the owner and manager of the Savoy, Richard D'Oyly Carte, dramatize the business relationship between Carte and his assistant Helen Lenoir, and their handling of the crisis when Sullivan, anxious to devote himself to more dignified tasks (a grand opera, a symphony) rejects the proposal of yet another libretto in which a magic potion, lozenge or similar trick turns the characters' lives upside down – 'topsy-turvy'. All these elements, grounded in character through the director's working methods, have dramatic shape and point: there is no sense of the kind of striving to accommodate every available (and permitted) aspect of the characters' lives in the manner of such scripts as *The Great Ziegfeld*. Only one relationship seems slightly undeveloped, that between Lenoir and Carte, and a scene removed through considerations of time from the final cut would have made that clearer. (After their difficult interview with the recalcitrant collaborators, it would have shown Carte and Lenoir frustrated by his married status.)[64]

Leigh and his cast immersed themselves in the language of the period, so that his habitual procedure of creating a script by improvisation would result in authentic dialogue that remained true to their perception of the characters. The result is a sense of absolute ease in the dialogue, a clear but unfussy adoption of Victorian speech and behaviour, and – consequently – of the social structure of the company. Some incidents are invented, but are in the spirit of the anecdotes that lie behind them, notably the business of Temple's song and the moment of inspiration when a Japanese sword falls from the wall of Gilbert's study. Accounts of this alleged incident vary, but the film treats it with great comic skill. Gilbert picks up the sword and toys with it, imitating for a few moments the swordplay he has seen in a Kabuki performance at the 'Japanese Village' exhibition his wife has taken him to. He lays the sword on his desk, but then pauses. In a frame-filling close-up we see the idea germinate and then grow, a gleam in Gilbert's eye leading to a vision of the fully staged performance (it has yet to be written and composed, let alone produced) of the arrival of Ko-Ko, the Lord High Executioner. Sullivan is delighted by the new work, which fulfils his desire for something 'in the realms of human emotion and probability', rather than his 'familiar world of topsy-turvydom'.[65] Rehearsal scenes show Gilbert's meticulous insistence on the manner in which his dialogue should be delivered, and his determination to replace conventional 'oriental' mannerisms with authentic gestures and body language based on those shown the company by visitors from the 'Japanese Village'.

In a note on the performance of *The Sorcerer*, Leigh writes: 'I did not want this sequence to be merely an extract from the show. It is important that it is about work – the theatre as a factory. Thus we see the activity on stage, backstage, in the pit and in the auditorium.'[66] In this he sums up the approach that confirms the film's break with established biopic convention. Other biographical films approach this quality, notably *Mrs Henderson Presents* (2005), with its depiction of London's Windmill Theatre, and *Me and Orson Welles* (2009), set in the context of Welles' 1937 Mercury Theatre production of *Julius Caesar* in New York. Both show the 'theatre as factory' but use a fictional (or semi-fictional) love interest as the armature of their plot. *Topsy-Turvy* encompasses relationships of this kind, but does not resolve them or imply a resolution beyond the script's limits.

Professional and artistic success is no longer depicted as the inevitable and mysterious result of devotion to show business, and getting the show on does not bring all-encompassing joy. The film celebrates the collaborative art that is its subject, and gives a vivid impression of all involved. It does not offer its principal characters as exemplary or inspirational, but their humanity is respected and enjoyed. Nor does it depend on setting up an opposition between creativity and commerce or depend – as Madden's film does – on an imagined or dramatized rivalry between personalities: the problems for Gilbert, Sullivan and Carte derive from divergent artistic aims rather than rivalry or hostility. The whole artistic community is celebrated along with the work it produces, and the theatre of a past time is treated with documentary respect without being deprived of a sense of wonder at what it can achieve.

Notes

1 Robert A. Rosenstone, *History on Film/Film on History* (Harlow: Pearson Education, 2006), pp. 47–48.
2 Ibid., p. 109.
3 David Eldridge, *Hollywood's History Films* (London: I.B. Tauris, 2006), p. 197.
4 George F. Custen, *Bio/Pics. How Hollywood Constructed Public History* (New Brunswick, NJ: Rutgers University Press, 1992), pp. 206–207.
5 Manny Farber, *Farber on Film. The Complete Film Writings of Manny Farber* (New York: Library of America, 2009), p. 245.
6 This summary is based on Eve Golden's biography, *Vernon and Irene Castle's Ragtime Revolution* (Lexington: University Press of Kentucky, 2007).
7 See Neal Gabler, *An Empire of Their Own. How the Jews Invented Hollywood* (New York: Doubleday, 1988), pp. 139–145. On the Jolson films and the significance of blackface for Jewish performers see Michael Rogin, *Blackface, White Noise. Jewish Immigrants in the Hollywood Melting Pot* (Berkeley, Los Angeles and London: University of California Press, 1996).
8 The principal sources for details of Jolson's life are Herbert C. Goldman, *Jolson. The Legend Comes to Life* (New York: Oxford University Press, 1988) and Michael Freedland, *Jolie. The Story of Al Jolson*, 2nd edition (London: W.H. Allen, 1985). On the genesis of *The Jazz Singer*, see Goldman, *Jolson*, and the 'final' script in Alfred A. Cohn, *The Jazz Singer*, edited by Robert L. Carringer (Madison: University of Wisconsin Press, 1979). This edition includes Raphaelson's short story as an appendix.
9 Cohn, *The Jazz Singer*, p. 11: quoted from *American Hebrew*, 14 October 1927.

10 On 'nigger songs' see Carringer, in Cohn, *The Jazz Singer*, p. 61. In the film's intertitles, Yudelson refers to 'raggy-time songs'.

11 The range of interpretations is considered by Bruce Kirle, *Unfinished Show Business. Broadway Musicals as Works-in-Progress* (Carbondale: Southern Illinois University Press, 2005), pp. 51–53.

12 Carrington, in Cohn, *The Jazz Singer* (pp. 182–183) provides a list of the film's 85 musical cues and their composers.

13 Goldman, *Jolson*, pp. 143–144.

14 Quoted from Cohn, *The Jazz Singer*, p. 23.

15 Eddie Cantor with David Freedman and Jane Kenser Ardmore, *'My Life is in Your Hands' and 'Take My Life': The Autobiographies of Eddie Cantor* (New York: Cooper Square Press, 2000), p. 35.

16 Billie Burke (with Cameron Shipp), *With a Feather on My Nose. With a Foreword by Ivor Novello* (London: Peter Davies, 1950), p. 207.

17 Linda Mizejewski, *Ziegfeld Girl. Image and Icon in Culture and Cinema* (Durham, NC and London: Duke University Press, 1999), p. 157.

18 Cantor, *Take my Life*, p. 193.

19 Edmund Wilson, 'The Follies as an Institution' (1923), reprinted in *The American Earthquake. A Documentary of the Twenties and Thirties* (New York: Farrar, Strauss and Giroux, 1958), pp. 50–51.

20 Gilbert Seldes, *The 7 Lively Arts* (New York: Harper and Brothers, 1924), pp. 131–132.

21 Susan A. Glenn, *Female Spectacle. The Theatrical Roots of Modern Feminism* (Cambridge, MA and London: Harvard University Press, 2000), p. 177.

22 Mizejewski, *Ziegfeld Girl*, p. 91.

23 See Barbara Stratyner, *Ned Wayburn and the Dance Routine. From Vaudeville to the 'Ziegfeld Follies'*, Studies in Dance History, no. 13 (New York: Society of Dance History Scholars, 1996).

24 Patricia Mellencamp, *A Fine Romance. Five Ages of Film Feminism* (Philadelphia, PA: Temple University Press, 1995), pp. 50–73.

25 Edmund Wilson, 'The Finale at the Follies', (March 1925) in *The American Earthquake*, pp. 45–46 (March 1925).

26 Richard and Paulette Ziegfeld, *The Ziegfeld Touch. The Life and Times of Florenz Ziegfeld, Jr* (New York: Abrams, 1993), p. 12.

27 Ethan Mordden, *Ziegfeld. The Man who Invented Show Business* (New York: St Martin's Press, 2008), pp. 74, 182.

28 Ziegfeld and Ziegfeld, *The Ziegfeld Touch*, p. 12.

29 Ibid., p. 79.

30 American Film Institute Catalogue (www.afi.com.members/catalog).

31 NYPL Flo Ziegfeld-Billie Burke Papers, Box 12, Folder 1. 'The Great Ziegfeld. He Lived to Glorify Beautiful Womanhood.' By William Anthony Maguire, 166 pp., blue covers. Dated 27 December 1934.

32 Box 125 folder 2. 'Incomplete' 'From: Mr Stromberg'. 16 July 1935, 187 pp., yellow covers.

33 On the costume designs, see Howard Gutner, *Gowns by Adrian. The MGM Years, 1928–1941* (New York: Abrams, 2001), pp. 56–62.

34 Box 125 folder 3. 'Incomplete' 'Script okayed by Mr Stromberg'. 21 September 1935, 196 pp., yellow covers. Revisions on pink pages (undated).

35 On the milk-bath episode see Eve Golden, *Anna Held and the Birth of Ziegfeld's Broadway* (Lexington: University Press of Kentucky, 2000), p. 31.

36 Sophie Tucker, *Some of These Days* (New York, 1948; London: Hammond, Hammond & Co., 1957), p. 67.

37 Frank S. Nugent, 'The Great Ziegfeld, Metro's Lavish Biography of a Showman, Opens at the Astor', *New York Times*, 9 April 1936.

38 'Going to the Movies with Don Herold', *Life*, June 1936.

39 Graham Greene, *Spectator*, 18 September 1936, in *The Graham Greene Film Reader: Mornings in the Dark*, edited by David Parkinson (Manchester: Carcanet, 1993), pp. 138–139.

40 'Beauties to be on Pedestals at Film's Premiere', *Los Angeles Times*, 13 April 1936.

41 Steven Cohan, *Incongruous Entertainment. Camp, Cultural Value, and the MGM Musical* (Durham, NC and London: Duke University Press, 2005), p. 53.

42 The troubled progress of *Ziegfeld Follies* is chronicled in detail by Hugh Fordin, *MGM's Greatest Musicals. The Arthur Freed Unit* (New York: Da Capo, 1995), pp. 119–146: the impetus for the production was the studio's possession of rights to material from Ziegfeld's estate.

43 Robert Buckner and Edmund Joseph, *Yankee Doodle Dandy*, edited by Patrick McGilligan (Madison, WI: Warner Bros / University of Wisconsin, 1981).

44 George M. Cohan, *Twenty Years on Broadway (And the Years It Took to Get There. The True Story of a Trouper's Life from the Cradle to the Closed Shop* (New York: Harper and Brothers, 1925), p. 178.

45 Ibid., pp. 152–160. Dialogue is quoted from the soundtrack of the film, which differs in many respects from that in the script.

46 Ibid., p. 157. (Here the film's final version follows the script.)

47 John McCabe, *George M. Cohan. The Man who Owned Broadway* (New York: Doubleday, 1973), p. 68.

48 Ibid, p. 77.

49 Buckner and Joseph, *Yankee Doodle Dandy*, p. 162.

50 Michael Anderegg, 'James Dean Meets the Pirate's Daughter. Passion and Parody in *William Shakespeare's Romeo+Juliet* and Shakespeare in Love', in Richard Burt and Lynda E. Boose, eds, *Shakespeare, the Movie, II. Popularizing the Plays on Film, TV, Video and DVD* (London and New York: Routledge, 2003), pp. 56–71; p. 66.

51 The commerce/creativity dichotomy in the historiography of Shakespeare's theatre has been challenged by – among others – Rosalyn Knutson: see her

Playing Companies and Commerce in Shakespeare's Time (Cambridge: Cambridge University Press, 2001).

52 Juliet Dusinberre, *Shakespeare and the Nature of Women*, 3rd edition (Basingstoke: Palgrave Macmillan, 2003), p. 233.

53 Douglas Lanier, *Shakespeare and Modern Popular Culture* (Oxford: Oxford University Press, 2002), p. 124. On the fictional representation of Shakespeare as a 'man among men', see also Jill Levenson, 'Shakespeare in Drama Since 1990: Vanishing Act', *Shakespeare Survey 58: Writing about Shakespeare* (Cambridge: Cambridge University Press, 2005), pp. 148–159.

54 The events of this period are more fully documented than the 'years of exile' myth suggests: see Virginia Scott, *Molière. A Theatrical Life* (Cambridge: Cambridge University Press, 2000), pp. 56–65. The failure of the Illustre Théâtre and its financial and consequently legal difficulties reached a crisis during its tenancy of a converted tennis court on the left bank of the Seine rather than a provincial barn. Alfred Simon, in *Molière*, 2nd edition (Paris: Seuil, 1996) notes that the complete absence of letters in the playwright's hand allowed biography to be ambushed by legend from an early stage (p. 8).

55 Notable examples are 'Le Petit chat est mort' – from *L'École des femmes*; 'Que diable allait-il faire dans cette galère?' from *Les Fourberies de Scapin*; and the poetic parody 'Au voleur...', from *Les Précieuses ridicules*.

56 After the death of Madeleine Béjart (1618–1672) Molière married her sister – or, possibly, daughter – Armande (1642–1700).

57 On rehearsal in Madden's film and its relationship with the film's anachronistic construction of romantic heterosexual love, see Anna Kamaralli, 'Rehearsal in Films of Early Modern Theatre. The Erotic Art of Making Shakespeare', *Shakespeare Bulletin* 29/1 (Spring 2011), pp. 27–42.

58 Mike Leigh, 'Topsy-Turvy. A Personal Journey', in David Eden and Meinhard Saremba, eds, *The Cambridge Companion to Gilbert and Sullivan* (Cambridge: Cambridge University Press, 2009), pp. 153–176; here p. 160.

59 W.S. Gilbert, *The Savoy Operas, being the Complete Text of the Gilbert and Sullivan operas as Originally produced in the Years 1875–1896* (London: Macmillan: 1926), p. 345.

60 Leigh, 'Topsy-Turvy. A Personal Journey', p. 156.

61 Mike Leigh, *Topsy-Turvy* (London: Faber, 1999), pp. 134–135 (hereafter 'Topsy-Turvy script').

62 Comment in Criterion DVD commentary. (This audio commentary was available on the British DVD released in 1999, but not on its Region 1 counterpart.)

63 On Gilbert's preparations and rehearsal procedures see Jane W. Stedman, *W.S. Gilbert. A Classic Victorian and his Theatre* (Oxford: Oxford University Press, 1996), chapter 13, and William Cox-Ife, *W.S. Gilbert. Stage Director* (London: Dennis Dobson, 1977).

64 The scene is among the supplementary materials in the Criterion DVD edition. Carte and Lenoir (Helen Cowper-Black) were married in 1888, after the death of Carte's first wife.
65 *Topsy-Turvy* script, p. 51. Discussions between Gilbert and Sullivan are based on letters between them: see Arthur Jacobs, *Arthur Sullivan. A Victorian Musician* (Oxford: Oxford University Press, 1996), pp. 282–285.
66 Leigh, '*Topsy-Turvy.* A Personal Journey', p. 168.

3

All about the actress

FASCINATION with the performer's personality in its various historically contingent definitions is intensified in the case of actresses.
The term itself, although no longer in favour, focuses complex attitudes
to gender and status and questions of authenticity in life as in art.
In *Gender Trouble* (1990), Judith Butler argues in terms that have
particular relevance in the theatrical context: 'Gender ought not to be
construed as a stable identity or locus of agency from which various
acts follow; rather, gender is an identity tenuously constituted in time,
instituted in an exterior space through a stylized repetition of acts.'[1] In
film studies, study of the representation of women has been energized
by Laura Mulvey's article 'Visual Pleasure and the Narrative Cinema',
with its establishment of the concept of the 'male gaze'. Subsequent
adjustments and qualification, specifically to reassert the existence of a
female gaze, have not diminished the term's usefulness in considering
both the roles and the nature of women's performance on screen: it has
a double application in the case of films dealing with performance in
another medium, where the cinema watches women acting in all senses
of the word.[2]

In recent years feminist historians have effectively challenged
assumptions regarding the work of women in the theatre: in particular
Tracy C. Davis's *Actresses as Working Women. Their Social Identity
in Victorian Culture* (1991) has been a key text not only with regard
to its specific topic but as a model for work on other periods.[3] Two
recent films reflect a shift in representations of women in the theatre
in Restoration England, a period central to the more or less discredited
conflation of actress and whore. Colley Cibber (1671–1757), in his
autobiographical *Apology*, first published in 1740, finds a gallant way
of putting the case: the appearance of 'real, beautiful Women, could
not but draw a proportion of new Admirers to the Theatre', especially
as 'we may imagine … that these Actresses were not ill chosen, when
it is well known, that more than one of them had Charms sufficient in

their Leisure Hours, to calm and mollify the Cares of Empire'.[4] The situation is encapsulated in the title of John Harold Wilson's 1951 study *All the King's Ladies*.[5] Revision in the light of feminist studies was to be expected and has been persuasive and effective. Kirsten Pullen has noted that 'In general, histories of Restoration theatre assume that actresses embarked on stage careers primarily to entice audience members into liaisons and even marriage, ignoring their theatrical skills and professional status as well as the economic conditions that might drive some women to seek paid labour of all kinds.'[6] Her own work redresses the balance by examining performance in the light of such factors rather than simply in aesthetic, formal terms or purely as historical gossip.

The advent of the professional actress on the English stage after 1660 is represented in two films, *Stage Beauty* (2004) and *The Libertine* (2005), in terms of authenticity in acting and gender politics. In the former the approach of the first actress to the role of Desdemona reveals both an alleged 'truth' about the part and the falsity of the old style of gendered gestural and vocal behaviour which constitutes the artistic accomplishment of the pre-eminent female impersonator Edward Kynaston, whom she supplants.[7] Kynaston's performance of gender on stage is complemented by that in his private life, and his lover the Duke of Buckingham even prefers to sodomize him while he is still wearing Desdemona's wig – and that, ideally, on the on-stage bed after the play is over. In this construction of theatre history, the actress represents a new honesty in performance, corresponding to the alleged shift from an outmoded gestural code – fixed, hierarchical and informed by assumptions – by a new spontaneity that is presented as the forerunner of 'modern' psychological truthfulness.[8] At the same time, the shadow of the myth of Pygmalion and Galatea still falls across these *fin-de-siècle* European films. Kynaston and (in *The Libertine*) Rochester are both seen shaping the artistic techniques that will bring the artistic personality of the actresses to light. Rachel M. Brownstein observes in her study of Rachel that 'The thing to remember about Pygmalion's story is that it is not Galatea's. It is a myth about a man whose ideal becomes real in a beautiful woman's form.'[9] In the case of Rachel, a flock of would-be Pygmalions vied with each other for the credit of finding and shaping her talent.

In many Hollywood films the peril of female spectacle and the attractions and dangers of the theatre cause heartache to the actress, and her friends and family. Linked to this is anxiety about ageing, perceived as specific to the woman performer, committed to a profession that has traditionally prized youth. *All About Eve* (1950) and *All About*

My Mother (1999) draw in different ways on the 'strong' women in Hollywood melodramas exemplified by the heroines of Douglas Sirk's *All I Desire* (1953) and *Imitation of Life* (1959), actresses who come to the realization that 'imitation' is not enough. Sirkian melodrama is especially powerful when performance is a topic within the story (or stories) it has to tell. Characters conflict with each other because their desires have competing trajectories, as though they are battling for control of the dramatic structure. Who will get to act out the feelings that will dominate a situation? Performance *within* the narrative complements performance *of* the narrative. For the fictional stage actress on screen, acting encompasses the dual consciousness of the impersonating performer and rival definitions of womanhood.

In *Imitation of Life*, the widowed actress Lora Meredith (Lana Turner) endures some years of frustration, during which she copes with being a lone parent, and finally makes a hit in a Broadway play. In a scene resembling Satan's temptation of Christ played in a minor key, Lora has resisted the advances of the agent ('a man of very few principles, and they're all open to revision') who takes her to the window of his apartment, and gestures towards the Great White Way: 'There's your empire – not big, it stretches from 42nd to 52nd Street, but it's the heart of the world.' Although she defies him with a determination worthy of Richardson's Clarissa Harlowe, managing the conquest without sacrificing virtue or integrity, it takes Lora many reels of postponement and much grief to herself and those around her to arrive at the resolution she and the film require. (The pleasure of the genre also resides, of course, in the prolongation of that grief.) She marries the photographer who has been waiting for more than a decade after taking her photograph at Coney Island. The security that Lora achieves is expressed by a palatial ranch-style home that (as she finally sees) lacks only a husband to complete it. Sirk aligns Lora's story with that of a black mother whose daughter passes as white and – until her mother's funeral – disowns her and runs away to become a night-club singer.

Imitation of Life includes tragedy but promises life beyond it: the earlier *All I Desire* makes even fuller use of theatre as a symbolic discourse through which the female condition can be encoded. Years ago Naomi Marshall (Barbara Stanwyck) deserted her family in the little town of Riverdale, Wisconsin to shield them from the scandal caused by her affair with a local sporting-goods merchant. Now she receives a letter from her daughter begging her to come home to see her in a high-school play. Naomi, now a vaudeville singer, has been representing herself as a big-time actress ('I'm supposed to be in

Europe, doing Shakespeare'). She returns to Riverdale to satisfy the long-suppressed desire to see her family. As soon as she arrives at the railroad depot she is on display and is eyed with appreciation by the male population, but when she reaches the old home she stands outside watching the activity in the lighted rooms – a familiar motif in film melodramas. Her situation is not an easy one, as she discovers that her younger daughter had written to her without informing any of the others. They do not all want her back. She is an object of curiosity not only in the small town but, most important, among the audience at the play. Already the actress's dual function as an object of admiration and reproach has been thoroughly established.

Before the play Naomi's daughter and her friends look at her through the peephole in the curtain, reversing the relationship of spectator and domestic scene suggested by Naomi's initial approach to the family home. The play itself, *Baroness Barclay's Secret*, seems to live up to its title as a stock 'woman with a past' melodrama. Lily speaks the curtain line, 'If loving you is a crime, then I'm willing to pay the penalty', and kisses the young man playing the hero, but after the curtain falls she rebukes him with 'Haven't I told you it was just a stage kiss?' and flounces away. She is not the sophisticated aristocratic woman she has been playing but an adolescent girl in small-town America. By invoking humorously the theatrical precursors of his own dramaturgy, Sirk adeptly places a degree of distance between himself and the material without forfeiting any of the emotional commitment this movie genre requires.

The amateur theatricals are thus part of the wider strategy common to screen melodramas, in which characters constantly make dramatic entrances and exits, invariably underlined by music. At the party after the play Sirk makes effective use of the stair and landing built into the side of the parlour. Naomi is prevailed on to act a scene from a play, but professes (accurately) that she does not know anything. Lily rushes over to the bookcase and gets a book, one of her father's favourites, with the leaf turned down. Naomi has the lights lowered, climbs to the landing and recites the sonnet 'How Do I Love Thee?' directing it to her husband. For the parlour Naomi's reading is a display of skill, but for her and her husband it tells an uncomfortable truth. Performance as a professional in the private domestic space lends her the opportunity to act out an emotion she feels in reality. All this leads, unsurprisingly, to the conclusion that home is where the heart belongs.

By the final scene she is about to leave, but her husband has learned the truth about an alleged tryst with her former lover, and that she resisted rather than encouraged his advances. She is soon in the arms of the man who was not strong enough to keep her years ago, and crosses the threshold into the family home once again. Naomi prevents Lily from following in her footsteps – the prospect of going on the stage has turned the girl's head – and wins back the respect of the elder daughter, who resented being left responsible for the care of the family. Naomi is now in the home she never should have left, and which her spectatorship when she arrived and the director's *mise en scène* throughout have made into a theatre of domesticity. Like Lora in *Imitation of Life*, Naomi's career has been an interlude of avoidance and she has come back full circle, a point of arrival Sirk tends to provide for his characters. Naomi earnestly insists: 'You don't know how unimportant success is until you've had it – or what a home means until you've lost it.'

Not quite *All About Eve*

In *All About Eve* the actress Margo Channing (Bette Davis) finds happiness in marriage and in the acceptance that she no longer needs to play women half her age, but this is not a choice between a conventional womanly role and a career. The script derives from a short story, 'The Wisdom of Eve', based on an incident that occurred to the actress Elisabeth Bergner.[10] In some respects Joseph L. Mankiewicz' film may invite comparison with the conventional dilemmas of such melodramas as *Imitation of Life*, but the view of the theatre that it presents is more complex than the success-at-a-price career the Sirkian genre required. Although the question of 'a woman's career' is discussed in a crucial scene, this is a more sophisticated work. Emotional displays are framed as part and parcel of the histrionic temperament. Comedy is the predominant mode, with space for ruefulness but not pathos. The film is also tantalizing: even when it is over, it is doubtful that the audience or any of the characters have in fact learned 'all' about Eve Harrington.

The opening sequences place the theatre at the forefront, together with the intimation that its hidden histories and concealed emotions are to be brought to light. Replacing even the trademark MGM fanfare (which he had also composed) over the studio's identification and sweeping through the title and opening credits, Alfred Newman's triumphal score brings the viewer into the Sarah Siddons Society, where an old actor (the very senior Walter Hampden) is about to present its annual award to a young actress – no previous recipient has been younger. While he drones on, covering the whole of theatrical history 'since Thespis first stepped out of the chorus', the critic Addison De Witt (George Sanders) identifies in a suave and acidulous voice-over the principal players in the drama that is to unfold. The film's actors are familiar and at least one of them is unmistakable: Bette Davis as Margo Channing. With the exception of the producer Max Fabian, who is busy taking a dose of bicarbonate of soda, all those identified (the director of the play the newcomer has starred in, its author Lloyd Richards and his wife, Karen, and Margo) hardly seem enthused by the occasion. Margo looks distinctly jaded, smokes determinedly, and, after pouring a stiff shot of hard liquor, waves away the hand of the unseen waiter who offers to dilute it with tonic or soda. The room is festooned with portraits, in the manner of the Players' Club, and the award itself is a statuette modelled on Sir Joshua Reynolds' portrait of Siddons as the Tragic Muse, but there is no doubt that the star here is Bette Davis. Margo is already performing in the manner which is her forte: private or social occasions are turned into theatres in which she enacts her special brand of barely polite behaviour that expresses her scorn, frustration or aggression (often all three) more emphatically than out-and-out rudeness could achieve. The action freezes as Eve Harrington (Anne Baxter) reaches out to take the statuette, and the film moves into the flashback that will occupy most of its narrative.

Although De Witt promises to reveal everything about Eve Harrington, to a significant extent the film is really *All About Margo*, with the teasing suggestion that it may even be *All About Bette*. In Margo's case, the salient fact we know about her is that she is forty years old, and that underneath the bravado she is anxious about keeping the man she loves – eight years her junior – and no longer trusts in her ability to go on playing younger women. The presence of her dresser Birdie (Thelma Ritter), a former vaudevillian, reinforces this effect: Ritter was forty-six when the film was released, but did not have the tense relationship with glamour and its maintenance that caused Davis (and Margo) so much anxiety. An outstanding representative of the long line of real and fictional dressers, Birdie has the type's characteristic access to the wisdom of the theatrical ages, the confidence and cynicism provided by a school of hard knocks, and a kindly but sardonically expressed clarity of vision. As for Margo's place in Broadway history, Lloyd's old-fashioned melodrama *Aged in Wood* – even the title seems significant – suggests that she has yet to find a place in the post-war renewal of American theatre associated with Arthur Miller and Tennessee Williams. *A Streetcar Named Desire* premièred in 1947, and Margo's choice of parts seems uncomfortably close to the self-aggrandizing fantasies of Blanche du Bois.[11] When Margo stands in the theatre foyer in front of a blown-up caricature of her as a pistol-toting belle, the sly evocation of Davis' popular persona

8. *All About Eve* (1950):
Eve, Bill, Karen, Margo
and Lloyd in Margo's
dressing room
(production still)

and the pre-war melodrama *Jezebel* (1938) offers an image far removed from the dignity of the Siddons statuette or the original painting – a reproduction of which hangs on the staircase of Margo's apartment and presides over a pivotal scene of self-pitying theatrics in the dying minutes of her party. In the scene between Eve and Bill in the dressing room after she has replaced Margo at a performance, a smaller version of the caricature hangs on the wall behind them, juxtaposed now with Eve in the 'southern belle' disguise with its ringletted wig. The Siddons image and the caricature balance one another as icons of the theatre. The career of the actress, they imply, exists in an uneasy equilibrium between these poles of dignity and public notoriety.

When she learns that Eve has become her official understudy, Margo literally takes the stage in the empty theatre for a full-scale confrontation with Bill, which begins in the presence of others but becomes an on-stage bedroom scene. Apart from curtain calls, almost all the performing we see in the film goes on away from the theatre as well as out of sight of its patrons. In her dressing room Margo at first plays the great actress (to Birdie's disgust) then drops the pretence as Eve delivers her mendacious story to a rapt audience; at the party Margo acts an exaggerated version of her own persona; and in the New Haven hotel room before the out-of-town opening of the new play, Eve's performance of victory over Margo is savagely undercut by De Witt's revelation that he knows her true identity. For a film about the theatre, *All About Eve* gives surprisingly little sense of a public, theatrical performance. The first encounter with Eve is in the alley leading to the stage door, and the theatre exteriors are seen outside performance hours or (in the first scene) just after them. The apparent glamour of the on-stage world is contrasted with the backstage effect of a lumber room, and the dressing room when we first see it is dowdy and very much a workplace (Figure 8).

What we see of Margo's private (or semi-private) performance suggests that her career depends on repetitions of a well-polished set of mannerisms, emotionally charged and expertly delivered. We do not need to see her on stage to perceive that Margo belongs to an old-fashioned star-driven theatre, not at all extinct in 1950 but already challenged by new dramaturgy and innovative approaches to acting. Eve, by contrast, is a skilful underplayer. When she delivers her monologue in the dressing room, and on similar occasions during the film, her physicality combines timidity and earnestness: her upper body holds back while her head is carried forwards as if by the force of the sincerity she projects, and her verbal delivery is clear, incisive and modulated. It is as if she cannot help herself and is abashed at her own access of candour. There are moments when her rapt idealism does seem involuntary, for example when the actors' life is being discussed on the staircase at the end of the party and she looks into the distance (that is, beyond the camera and not catching any established eyeline) and murmurs 'if there's nothing else, there's applause ... it's like waves of love coming across the footlights'. In the scene's staging Eve is here opposite Miss Caswell (Marilyn Monroe), who eyes her carefully: Monroe's soft voice and determined gaze suggest an equivalence of ambition if not of tactics. However, when Eve does not have to perform this persona her posture is less contained and her voice has a harder tone. Mankiewicz places these moments carefully, enhancing the effect of the film's exceptional – if ultimately limited – access to the 'real' Eve.

In public as in private performance, Eve seems not to aspire to the trenchant theatricality of Margo's style, but to be more attuned to the new dispensation in the theatre. Margo is constructed by Davis out of exaggerated aspects of her own career and performing style, with a dash (arguably) of Tallulah Bankhead, but at crucial moments she shows a normally hidden vulnerability. The revelation of 'strong' and (in the prevailing ideology) almost unwomanly self-assertion struggling with the dictates of the heart and demands of decorum is a common feature in many of Davis' most successful performances. In some films, such as *Jezebel* and *The Little Foxes* (1941), the Davis character is less conflicted and much tougher, and it is hard to believe in the conventional insistence of the scripts that in the end crime and/or lack of feminine compassion do not pay. Part of the appeal of Margo Channing is the way the role's comedy, signalled from the very first sequence, is in a pleasurable tension with the suspicion of three threats: that Margo might become an embittered and destructive element in the terms of her own world; that her relationship with friends and lover will be fatally compromised; and that she will remain the prisoner of what might turn out to be fatal flaws. Given Mankiewicz's penchant for the self-conscious use of Aristotelian concepts – they are referred to directly in the opening narration of *The Barefoot Contessa* (1954) where the speaker is himself a writer/director – it is not unreasonable to regard *All About Eve* as a lesson in comedy's formal status as the avoidance of tragedy.

Together with the 'bedroom' confrontation that follows it in the post-audition sequence discussed above, the party Margo throws to welcome Bill back from Hollywood is one of the film's two most explicitly theatrical sequences. It begins with Margo before her dressing-table mirror, and for the first time we hear her in voice-over as narrator. Told by Birdie that Bill arrived twenty minutes ago but is talking with Eve instead of coming up to see her first, Margo makes a dignified exit from the room, rushes down the narrow staircase, then collects herself to make an entrance at the bottom as she hears Bill's voice telling Eve a Hollywood story. The dressing room/wings/on-stage equivalents of the apartment's spaces are firmly established. As Margo ostentatiously acts the dutiful hostess, checking the cigarette supply and opening and closing a covered dish of chocolates, she makes her annoyance clear to Bill: he accuses her of speaking what sound like lines from a Clyde Fitch play, and when she ripostes that the playwright was before her time he ill-advisedly cracks that he has 'always denied the rumour that [she was] in *Our American Cousin* the night Lincoln was shot'. Margo complains that Eve has been 'studying me as though I were a play or a blueprint'. Karen, Lloyd and Max arrive; Lloyd observes that the atmosphere is 'very Macbethish' and Margo issues her famous warning that they should fasten their seatbelts, because 'it's going to be a bumpy night', before sweeping up the stair and into the lobby to greet more guests.

The party wears on, with the hostess fuelling herself with Martinis, and reaches a comic display of maudlin self-pity, as the drunken Margo insists on repeated performances of *Liebestraum* by the pianist, preventing his attempts to break into a jaunty rendition of 'How about You?' ('I like New York in June...') Although she turns the apartment into a theatre, she is capable of accusing Bill of doing exactly that, in a speech that amounts to an assertion of her control: 'This is my house, not a theatre. And in my house you're a guest, not a director', to which he replies 'Then stop being a star.' Addison greets her behaviour with a critic's appraisal: 'You're maudlin and full of self-pity – you're magnificent.' Margo has a few moments in a 'backstage' space when she takes the dyspeptic Max to find bicarbonate of soda in the pantry. When Max leaves, Lloyd comes into the pantry, and Margo tells him about her anxiety over the disparity in ages between her and Bill. The sense of the public's demands and more private imperatives is emphasized when Lloyd tells her she can be 'as young as [she] want[s]' and she snaps back with 'As young as *they* want' – that is, the fans she has told us she despises in the first dressing-room scene, when Karen told her about Eve. The vulnerability expressed here is all the more touching for being exposed in a break in the 'on-stage' performance. At the end of the party, as Margo trudges up the staircase, Addison remarks 'Too bad. We'll miss the third act. They're going to play it off stage.'

The private Margo is more fully displayed in the aftermath of the understudy audition, after her tirade from the stage. Bill pitches her onto the property bed and the camera remains above her as she registers the truth about the effect her 'performing' has on others and on him. What could now become a scene of erotic passion is nothing of the kind. Bill holds her down as if restraining the victim of a fit, in an embrace that seems more that of protective restraint than amorous assault. His insistence that she is 'a great actress' marks a turning point in her mood. Margo cannot resist a parting shot, in which she asks whether he is going to Eve. This astonishes Bill, who replies: 'There isn't a playwright in the world who could make me believe this would happen between two adult people.' As a further confirmation of Addison's observation in the party's final scene that 'theatre folk' are 'a breed apart from the rest of humanity', the scene thus ends with a restatement of the difficulty of identifying and experiencing true emotions in the theatre.

Karen devises a stratagem to give Margo a 'boot in the rear' to avenge her treatment of Lloyd, Bill, Max and others. 'Heaven knows she had one coming', she reflects in a voice-over. To prevent Margo reaching New York, she drains gasoline from the tank of the car that should deliver her to the station after a weekend with Karen and Bill in the country. There is no indication that she realizes what the consequences of her missing the performance might be. Margo and Karen are left alone together, huddled in their fur coats, while Lloyd goes to find help. Margo turns on the radio but is dismayed to hear an orchestral version of *Liebestraum*. Her eyes register what may well be annoyance at her behaviour at the party, but she characteristically modulates this into an imperious generalization: 'I *detest* cheap sentiment.' Here the dialogue has the fullest indication so far of her anxieties about her age, her love life and her career, and although the uneasiness of Karen (who has emptied the fuel tank) is comic in effect, it is also a moment when she, like us, can perceive the sadness underneath the behaviour she is trying to correct. When Karen says that her friends pardon her behaviour because she is Margo, she muses on what that means: 'so many people – *know* me. I wish I did. I wish someone would tell me – about me.' The emphases and pauses, and even the use of a cigarette as a prop connect this with the 'public' displays of temperament, but here the same modulations and idiosyncrasies register as real. Compared with Eve's contrasting performances of public sincerity and private hardness, there is a genuine continuity between public and private Margo, which is probably behind Karen's rather weak claim that she is 'just Margo'. Margo compares herself to a child having a tantrum when she can't get what she wants, 'When they feel unwanted, or insecure, or – unloved'. She talks about her love for Bill, the vulnerability that it brings out, and the wider issue of 'a woman's career'. Success is achieved at the expense of the real career of simply being a woman, and 'sooner or later we've got to work at it', and it includes having someone to wake up with. This reflects much in Davis's own career and its dilemmas, and the film is tactful enough to end the speech by pushing it back into the framework of metatheatrical discourse with Margo's self-deprecating line 'Slow Curtain – the end'.[12] The car's running out of petrol is 'one of Destiny's merry pranks', she adds, but Karen's face reminds us that this is Karen's work, her attempt to construct a plot, and not that of the gods. It isn't going too far to imagine that, like Mankiewicz, Karen knows Aristotle's *Poetics*: she met her playwright husband when he lectured at Radcliffe, then a prestigious liberal arts college for women, affiliated with Harvard.

We never discover whether Margo, Karen and the others know the full extent of Eve's duplicity: Margo's decision not to insist on appearing in Lloyd's new play pre-empts Eve's attempt in the scene at the Stork Club's Cub Room (the 'sancta sanctorum' of Broadway gossip in the 1930s and after) to blackmail Karen into getting her the role by threatening to reveal the truth about the car running out of gasoline.[13] Karen returns to the table, and is about to admit her guilt when Margo announces that she no longer wants the part and is going to marry Bill. So Margo never learns about Karen's benevolent deception. Eve's perfidy is also unrevealed because nothing suggests that De Witt shares his knowledge of Eve's lies with her former friends. Mankiewicz plays a trick on his principal narrator, though, because his and the film's promise to tell 'all' is still unfulfilled by the final scene. This takes place after the award ceremony, which has begun with De Witt's commentary and is interrupted so that the main diegesis can be related in flashback. The final moments of the film are witnessed only by the camera, and take place after De

Witt has left the apartment. Moreover, the last moment of all is not seen by Eve herself. A new 'Eve' ('I call myself Phoebe', she tells De Witt) has moved into Eve Harrington's life. As the film's celebratory music reaches a climax we see her don the new star's cape, take the statuette in her hands and bow gracefully to the multiplied reflections in the dressing-room mirror. The final shot was intended as 'the full realization, dramatically and musically, that the world is filled with Eves and that they will be with us always'.[14] The self-styled Phoebe's action duplicates Eve's in an early scene when she took Margo's costume and practised curtain calls in front of a mirror. After giving a brief and probably false account of herself and claiming to be the chair of her high school's Eve Harrington Society, Phoebe has moved even more rapidly than Eve into the role of protector. There are already hints that Eve is seeking ways to resist De Witt's control of her, and with Phoebe as gatekeeper she may well succeed. Whether she will manage to deal with Phoebe is another story, unwritten and unfilmed.

In the film's skilful manipulation of exegesis and diegesis, Addison seems at first to be in charge: his voice opens the film and he is its chief repository of knowledge – or so it seems. Although he is able to suspend the action in the opening sequence, the film itself remains the only all-knowing witness. Mankiewicz himself would go much further in 1954 in *The Barefoot Contessa*, which has three narrators, the principal one being like Mankiewicz a writer/director. *A Letter to Three Wives* (1949), for which he won an Oscar as writer and director, sets up three flashback narratives which build to the resolution to the overarching story in which the husband of one of the three wives will be revealed to have 'run away' with the never-seen Addie Ross. The critic Vincent Amiel suggests that 'from his very first films, over twenty or twenty-five years, [Mankiewicz] insistently juxtaposed two directional lines: that of the primary plot, constructed rigorously according to classical conventions; and that of the ironic commentary, more or less explicit, more or less destructive, applied to the very act of narration, putting a story together, and constructing a mechanism designed to seduce the spectators.'[15] In *All About Eve* Mankiewicz intended to have at least one scene shown in differing versions from the point of view of more than one character, but this was vetoed by the producer Darryl F. Zanuck.[16] Even the music, with its emotionally charged support for the apparent sincerity of Eve's dressing-room story, is deceptive, manipulating the first-time audience's response so that until Addison's revelations in New Haven we are a few steps behind the other principals but not yet the step ahead we will take when we (and not Addison) see the final sequence. Within the narrative, although Eve,

Margo, Addison and (less culpably) Karen are in their different ways actively manipulative, the film itself trumps them all.

Margo's career will not end with Eve's ascendancy. She does not dwindle into a wife, but moves into another category of personal and professional life. She is allowed to leave the film on a note of triumph with her comically cynical attitude to Eve's apparent apotheosis and her scathing parting shot: 'Nice speech, Eve. But I wouldn't worry too much about your heart. You can always put that award where your heart ought to be.' This is also effectively the final section of the interrupted opening scene, so that we are reassured that the Margo we saw in the first sequence has in fact come through not merely unscathed but rewarded by the betrayals we have witnessed in between.

All About Eve is not *only* about Eve, and Mankiewicz insisted that it was not even mainly about her but about the effect she and those like her have on other people, specifically in the theatrical world. It is certainly unable to deliver everything about her. This self-referential work of fiction about a performing art directs its audience towards a familiar paradox, that of truthful lying. Eve invests her lies about herself with an idealism and skill that make it hard for her audience to reject her in the first dressing-room scene, but the fiction she creates is a sentimental tear-jerker, a 'soldier's (non) return' tale that sounds like a hackneyed screen melodrama. As she does this, she reveals herself as a consummate actress/liar. The theatre can be a transforming element in which a privately manipulative and dishonest woman (the gender is significant) can be a star. In *Twentieth Century* (1934) the star made by the director Oscar Jaffe out of Mildred Plotkin is a comic caricature, but under it Carole Lombard's playing establishes that she maintains contact with real life and good-heartedness. Eve Harrington, when all is said and done, is all about herself and her desire to 'be something, be somebody' and escape her sordid existence as Gertrude Slescynski, the brewery worker caught in an affair with her boss.

In 1972 Mankiewicz observed that the film was about 'every woman for whom acting was identical with existence', and elaborated his theory that the intimate relationship between the two did not exist in the same way for men – partly because of the pitiless demand of the theatre and the film studios for youthful glamour.[17] Viewed from this perspective, *All About Eve* is an exploration of the strategies by which women make their way and survive in the theatre. Although 'psychology' as such is not referred to at any point, the psyche of both Margo and Eve is revealed as something quite different from that of Karen, the well-bred and educated outsider married to the theatre through Lloyd. In *More About 'All About Eve'*, Mankiwiecz does not specify a school of psychology, but his terms have distinct Jungian elements: the film dramatizes his concept of the actress experiencing the 'traumatic re-emergence of that inner Self she had decided so long ago was inadequate to attain even acceptance', and which had been hidden 'behind those magical protean masks'.[18] In Margo and Eve – much as in the figures of Ava Gardner as Maria Vargas in *The Barefoot Contessa* and Elizabeth Taylor as Cleopatra (in the 1960 film that he ended up directing) – Mankiewicz is fascinated by the mysteries of female stardom as a corollary to the exercise of his own abilities to seduce an audience and – when appropriate – mislead them enjoyably. Molly Haskell, in a discussion of *All About Eve* and other films, identifies the director with a tendency she suggests is shared with homosexual artists (such as Tennessee Williams), and concludes that he 'declares his love for women while denying or disguising his affinity with them'. The subtext of Haskell's account – its implication that Mankiewicz is himself homosexual – is, to say the least, questionable, but her expression of a duality in his work seems appropriate: 'sometimes he speaks through his women, sometimes against them, and sometimes the two are confused.'[19] In any case, his approach brings him closer than might be expected in a mainstream Hollywood director to the serio-comic genre/gender games of Pedro Almodóvar's comic melodramas. The Spanish director's predilections parallel those of his American colleague: it would not have been surprising if it had been Almodóvar rather than Mankiewicz who declared in an interview 'I'm besotted by women and the problems of women. They offer so much more to a writer, to a director: they're more complicated, more exciting than men.'[20]

All About My Mother:
performing (as) women

Pedro Almodóvar's *All About My Mother* (*Todo sobre mi madre*) is permeated by performance and the theatre. Stage performance is viewed in it through the frame of *All About Eve*, and this filmic representation of the stage medium is also placed alongside writing and photography as the means through which characters find the sometimes onerous ability to deal with and describe their past, and to create a future in the face of death and desertion.[21] Mankiewicz's film provides one of the basic patterns of the plot – a woman enters the life of a famous actress and becomes her confidant – but there is no malicious intent involved, and no plot to take over the actress's roles on stage or in life. The final moments of the film suggest the primacy of theatre in its scheme of representations, but do so in a way that simultaneously asserts the cinema's equal if not greater ability to absorb and embody the older medium. In this respect, *All About My Mother* is firmly in the tradition it invokes through *All About Eve*, of theatre as a metaphor peculiarly adaptable to the purposes of film. Compared with Mankiewicz, though, Almodóvar displays a much greater exuberance in generating patterns and analogies between the experiences of the characters among themselves, their means of expression, and the options available to the film's viewers and director for story-telling. *All About Eve* evokes a more stable regime of theatrical performance – that of the fashionable Broadway star and the well-made play – than the volatile, edgy closeness to subcultures favoured by the Spanish director. Almodóvar moves among the more extreme cultural styles of the 1990s, even teasing the audience with the possibility that the young writer at the centre of his film, Esteban, may be a gay man on the verge of coming out. A penchant for Truman Capote, Bette Davis films, Tennessee Williams, life at home with a single mother and a burning ambition to turn his experience into writing all identify him with the director, never shy of offering but not quite delivering 'all' about Almodóvar.

As well as *All About Eve* Almodóvar's film alludes directly to John Cassavetes' *Opening Night* (1977), in which Gina Rowlands gives a bravura performance as an actress, Myrtle Gordon, racked by self-doubt, anxiety about ageing and fear in the face of a role that is too close to her own situation. Playing the title role of a Broadway-bound drama, *The Second Woman*, she is refusing to accept her loss of youth and struggling to assert herself as an independent, desirable woman. Her descent into alcoholism in a milieu where heavy drinking is normal – the drinking on stage corresponds to the impulse she and others have to open a bottle as soon as they enter a room – takes her in the final sequence to the gravest of 'will the show go on?' situations. Drunk to the point of being unable to walk, she drags herself into the dressing room while the first-night audience is already giving the slow handclap on the other side of the curtain. Propped up as she staggers backstage for her first entrance, fuelled with black coffee and shame, she manages to get through the first act and gradually revives to the point where she is able to turn a potential disaster into professional triumph.

Myrtle keeps finding images of herself in the play's situations – compounded by having to perform opposite an ex-lover – and, more alarmingly, in the ghost (or hallucination) of a young fan killed in the attempt to secure her autograph. 'Nancy Stein' has to be exorcized, not by the spiritualists Myrtle is taken to by the play's author, but by confronting the inner demon that she represents: the violent physical attacks of the girl are self-inflicted, as is the 'spectre's' claim that she has dedicated herself to the theatre as well as to Myrtle in terms that suggest the actress's secret anxiety about the link between her sexuality and her profession: 'I devoted my life to you ... I never bothered you. You want to kill me. I devoted my life to you. To movies. To music. To theater. I'm 17 years old. I like sex. I like to turn people on. And that's what the theater is: sex. It's like getting laid.' Seen first in a dressing-room mirror, then in the eerily spacious hotel apartment Myrtle occupies in New Haven, 'Nancy' recalls Eve Harrington as a reminder of the youth Myrtle, like Margo, no longer possesses. As she descends into the despair from which she finally recovers, the wife of her director, going through a less histrionic or public crisis, also finds stability and clarity. Cassavetes' film is rawer than *All About Eve*, and the director's technique goes against the highly polished Hollywood norms in the framing of shots, editing and dialogue. Margo fuelled wit with alcohol, but Myrtle uses it to stumble into incoherence. The indeterminate sentences, half-expressed thoughts and overlapped dialogue are in sharp contrast to Mankiewicz's highly literate script and his actors' crisp quasi-theatrical delivery. However, *Opening Night* revisits the earlier film's theme of the ageing actress – here addressed specifically in terms of the menopause (which Myrtle rejects). In 'Nancy', Myrtle Gordon has an Eve Harrington of the mind.

Almodóvar's central character is an actress in her own way. Manuela (Cecilia Roth) is a nurse in a transplant unit at a Madrid hospital, who specializes in role-playing sessions for doctors who have to learn how to obtain permission from bereaved relatives to use the organs of their loved ones. Her son, Esteban, is celebrating his 18th birthday: she has bought him a book he wanted, Truman Capote's *Music for Chameleons*, and they are going to see a performance of *A Streetcar Named Desire* with his favourite actress, Huma Rojo (Marisa Paredes) as Blanche. The night before his birthday they settle down to watch *All About Eve* on television. Esteban is an aspiring writer, and has asked permission to sit in on one of the training sessions where his mother, once an amateur actress, will be 'performing' on video. The following night, after the performance, they wait for Huma to leave the stage door, because Esteban wants her autograph. It is raining heavily when Huma finally appears, together with the actress who has played Stella. Ignoring Esteban, who has dashed across the street, they get into a taxi and drive off. We see his face behind the window, and the notebook he is pressing against it, from Huma's point of view. Pursuing them, he is knocked down by another car and killed. The scene, including some of its most arresting shots – especially those from within the car – is modelled directly on the sequence in Cassavetes' film when Myrtle is mobbed by fans outside the stage door, struggles to her waiting car and sees the face and hands of the doomed teenager through the rain-streaked window.

Manuela now has to go through the process she has been simulating – and with the same pair of doctors. After a period of intense grief, during which she goes to the hospital in La Coruña to catch a sight of the man who received her son's heart, she travels to Barcelona in search of Esteban's father, now a transsexual going by the name of Lola, a quest motivated by her son's request to know about him. In the course of the next few scenes, the truth about the father emerges. The production of Williams' play has now moved to Barcelona, and Manuela does not immediately find Lola, but becomes involved in the life of Huma, as well as that of another transsexual prostitute, La Agrado (Antonia San Juan) and a young nun, Sister Rosa (Penélope Cruz). For a while Manuela becomes the dresser and personal assistant of Huma.

At a crucial juncture in the film, two members of the cast of *A Streetcar* fail to turn up. La Agrado, who has succeeded Manuela as Huma's dresser, entertains the audience with an account of how she came to be the way she is. She concludes her monologue with the insistence that 'a woman is more authentic the more she resembles what she dreams herself to be'. La Agrado has chosen her name to denote her desire to give pleasure (*agrado*) to others, and she has in fact taken steps to 'resemble' her dream with expensive radical cosmetic surgery, whose costs she enumerates for the audience's benefit. Gwynne Edwards notes that La Agrado's 'entire life is a kind of dramatic spectacle, the locations in which she happens to find herself her stage'.[22] Here, for the first time, she is performing on a 'real' stage and describing her own life – unlike the actors who normally perform Williams' play there – as a series of alterations, mainly of addition to rather than subtraction from her body, that have created the 'authentic' person the audience see before them. Earlier, La Agrado had declared her contempt for ordinary cross-dressers who are spoiling the trade for transsexual prostitutes: 'I can't stand drag queens! They've confused circus with transvestism – what am I saying, circus? Theatre!'[23]

Almodóvar's films, with their heady and entertaining confusions of gender roles, and polymorphous sexual and emotional situations, often acted out flamboyantly, include a fair number of transsexual or transvestite characters. As Paul Julian Smith points out in his discussion of *The Law of Desire* (1987), 'It seems unlikely that

Almodóvar has a great interest in transsexuals per se; rather he is concerned with suspending that distinction between artifice and truth which has so oppressed sexual dissidents of all kinds.'[24] No false pathos attaches itself to them: they are expressing themselves as women and participate in the female solidarity that marks many of his narratives. The emphasis is on what they have gained, not what has been taken from them. Both La Agrado and Lola, the father of Manuela's son, have kept their male genitals. With their figure suitably enhanced, they cater mainly for men whose desires are channelled towards active or passive fellatio. They are capable, as Lola has proved, of intercourse with a woman and fathering a child, but they also embrace womanhood with enthusiasm. One of the most celebrated scenes in *All About My Mother* is an impromptu party, with cava and ice cream, at which Sister Rosa (impregnated by Lola, it turns out), Manuela, Huma Rojo and La Agrado celebrate the experiences and outlook they have in common.

The specifically theatrical context of *All About My Mother* provides an additional dimension for the director's exploration of this distinction and its consequences: *All About Eve*, *Opening Night*, *A Streetcar Named Desire* and texts from Lorca are quoted and (re)enacted, becoming means for the characters to express what would otherwise not be articulated. In fact the texts converge with one another and with the major narratives of the film: Manuela's search for Lola; Sister Rosa's pregnancy; childbirth and death; and the resolution of Huma's troubled lesbian relationship with her fellow actress, Nina. When Manuela appears as the pregnant Stella in place of Nina she is enabling the show to go on and repeating a stage role she first assumed years before in an amateur production where Lola (then Esteban) played Stanley Kowalski. Huma in her own persona twice repeats off stage Blanche's line about having always depended on the kindness of strangers, but she is only half in jest: her relationship with the wayward and drug-addicted Nina is that of parent and child, and the arrival of two strangers, first Manuela and then La Agrado, brings order to her life. Manuela, a stranger, befriends Sister Rosa and temporarily takes over her mother's functions, and by the end of the film she has effectively become the mother of Rosa's child. There are in fact three Estebans: Lola in her/his original guise and name, the son whom Manuela loses, and Rosa's child. The kinship between Williams' play and film melodramas strengthens the effect of Almodóvar's appropriations from the screen tradition of the genre, with its characteristic reversals of fortune, complex plotting, use of flashbacks and exploitation of coincidences, and the centrality of the moral and emotional dilemmas of women.[25]

None of the relationships and parental roles in *All About My Mother* are in strict accord with 'normal' heterosexual templates or sanctioned by direct biological connections: are they all 'performed' in the sense of being assumed and inauthentic? Or do they simply exemplify the performative nature of gender roles? Here, as often in Almodóvar's films, the polarity of such normative notions of performance and authenticity is reversed. La Agrado is a triumphant and comically resilient artist, on stage and off, but the film includes two tragic female figures, one off and one on stage, one a transsexual and the other a transformed woman – an actress. The tragic transsexual, Lola, is dying of AIDS. Her first appearance, on the steep stone steps of the graveyard looking down on Rosa's funeral, is staged as a dramatic entrance, and in dark glasses, propped up against a walking stick, she is both a symbol of death –Almodóvar thought of the white-faced Death in Bergman's *The Seventh Seal* (1957) – and a (self-)stylized 'theatrical' figure, 'a death that is grand and elegant, disguised'.[26] Subsequently, Manuela takes Rosa's child to a café so that its father can see and hold it, if only for a few moments. Lola has bequeathed a deadly illness to the child – subsequently its immune system miraculously defeats the infection – and as she sits in the café, a melodramatic figure of a tragic queen (so to speak), the grief is genuine and dismaying. Less direct, but no less powerful, is the image of the other tragic queen, this time 'authentically' female, seen when Huma as Blanche emerges from her bathroom and asks for her jewel box (significantly heart-shaped) and later is overpowered by the nurse in the play's final scene. In both scenes her wig has been removed and her hair held under a skull cap, a detail absent in Williams' stage directions but clearly inserted to resonate with the laying bare of Huma's emotions in her off-stage life. Without her wig Marisa Paredes as Huma resembles a drag queen without her makeup, an effect strengthened by her gaunt features and her tall stature: like the singing star, Becky, she plays in *High Heels* (1991) she seems ripe for imitation by cross-dressing men or transsexuals. Appearing as Blanche, she is already impersonating one of the more celebrated camp icons, and she has modelled herself on another, Bette Davis, to the extent of smoking so much that she has adopted the stage name 'Huma' – 'smoke'.

In this context of shifting perspectives, calling into question the stability of gender and other identities, Almodóvar's habitual play of transgressive dramatic and non-dramatic spaces can thrive. From an early stage he forged for himself an authorial identity that, in Marvin D'Lugo's words, 'privileges performance as one of the marks of identity, breaking down the traditional borders between public and private'.[27] The varying and border-crossing expressive behaviour of the characters is accommodated by a corresponding fluidity in the spaces they inhabit, to the point where Almodóvar treats his sets, almost on reflex, as theatrical and patently devised environments, as in Pepa's apartment in *Women on the Verge of a Nervous Breakdown* (1988), expressly designed for bed- and living-room farce. He also evokes voyeurism in quotations from Hitchcock's *Rear Window* (1954) in more than one film and, in *Kika* (1993) and *Broken Embraces* (2009), Michael Powell's *Peeping Tom* (1959).[28] In *All About My Mother* there are several points at which public and private are disturbingly reversed, such as the open-air 'carousel' of cars in the waste ground where prostitutes wait for clients, or the false privacy of the video in which Manuela is initially imitating a grieving parent, then (in the film, not on video within it) assuming the identity she previously imitated for a training seminar. The most significant liminal space of this kind is, unsurprisingly, the theatre's dressing room. Here the wall-length mirror above the dressing table features prominently in several scenes, with the familiar effect of destabilizing the audience's sense of its point-of-view while offering rivals to it within the diegesis when characters (specifically Huma, making herself up) peer into it – simultaneously away from and towards the camera. The featuring of the mirrors in this way, common in films about the theatre, here seems a specific imitation of *Opening Night*: Myrtle sees 'Nancy' for the first time in her dressing-room mirror and in other scenes is placed before her dressing-table with characters in the room reflected in front of her.

When Esteban and his mother settle down on the sofa, the scene from *All About Eve* shown on the television is the dressing-room sequence when Eve tells her tale, so that Almodóvar has us watch his two characters watch Eve as she turns the dressing room into her stage and Margo and her friends into an audience. Manuela's subsequent entrance into Huma's life, and assumption of the role of assistant, have obvious parallels with Eve's career, but her presence is benign, not destructive or an attempted takeover. La Agrado becomes Thelma Ritter (Birdie) rather than Eve when she takes over Manuela's job with Nina and Huma, more of a sardonic mother confessor or nurse than a predator.[29] In his script Almodóvar indicates that as he watches this scene from Mankiewicz' film Esteban has the sensation of witnessing 'the origin of performance and of story-telling in general: a woman telling her story to a chorus of women.'[30] In two superimposed images, the first achieved by association and point-of-view, the second in a dissolve, Esteban sees his mother standing against the giant image of Huma as Blanche, her raincoat suggesting Eve in the film, and in a cross-fade to the theatre performance, the same image of Huma is briefly superimposed on the actress herself on stage as Blanche.[31] Manuela, the mother who has not yet told her secret, resembles – at least in Esteban's mind – both Eve about to tell her false secret and Huma whose public persona is about to be blended with Blanche, the fictional character whose secret will be betrayed by the end of Williams' play.

The size of the poster, effectively taking over the whole façade, turns the theatre into Blanche/Huma: the fair-haired Manuela, in her red coat and black stockings and holding an umbrella, matches but does not disappear into the dominant and strident red of the design. In comparison with Eve Harrington in her dowdy mackintosh, lurking in the unglamorous alley leading to the stage door in *All About Eve*, Manuela cuts a stylish figure in a striking environment. Later, when in Barcelona she enters the backstage realm and finds Huma's dressing room, the environment is altogether unlike the junk-room effect of Mankiewicz' film. This is a clean, well-appointed space in a modern theatre. Similarly, the stage setting for *Streetcar* is modern – even post-modern – in its simplicity. (Almodóvar compares it in a script direction to the work of Robert Wilson). However, it shares with Joe Mielzener's original design for the play and Williams' stage directions the sense of permeable boundaries between rooms within the apartment and between the apartment and the world beyond.

Within the story-telling that at once reveals and conceals, the writing of Esteban is especially significant. He asked to be told everything about his father, 'todo sobre mi padre' and one might assume that the notebook might reveal 'todo sobre Esteban'. Just as his mother has concealed from him the truth about his father by ripping off 'his' half of the photos that once showed the couple together, Esteban's journal becomes an icon of the story-teller as well as a quasi-sacred object in itself. It is held back from others, until Manuela gives it to Lola in the café, and the father learns 'all about' the son who never learned 'all about' him. At the very beginning of the film, after a credit sequence establishing the transplant unit, the film's title has still been withheld. It is 'announced' in the first scene of the main narrative. Manuela arrives home and prepares a meal for her son and herself. They settle on the sofa as *All About Eve* begins, and he remarks that the Spanish title, spoken by the TV station's announcer as *Eva al desnudo* – Eve 'uncovered' or 'laid bare' – is inaccurate. It should be *Todo sobre Eva*. Manuela replies that this sounds odd (*rara*), and Esteban writes in his notebook, 'Todo sobre ....' The writing appears on the page but is completed on Almodóvar's screen with the full title of his film.[32] It is after all a film about 'mi madre', and Esteban is the only candidate for ownership of the possessive pronoun.

Because Esteban is killed Manuela is not able to grant him his wish to know about his father. By the end of the film the notebook has been read, the two halves of a photo have been brought back together, and both image and word have been brought to completion. At the same time, resolution has been reached by unorthodox means in family life: Manuela is adoptive mother to Rosa's child; La Agrado is with Huma; Nina has gone back to her native village and married, with what La Agrado calls 'a fat, ugly child'. But as for Esteban, has the promised knowledge in fact been granted? His death is shown from his point of view, as the camera somersaults with him when he is knocked over, and shares his view of his grieving mother as she crouches by him. Words from Esteban's notebook are heard spoken by him in voice-over as Manuela waits at the Intensive Care Unit, clutching the book as though holding on tightly to the hand that had written in it. The screenplay suggests that 'It is as though the words of Esteban slipped out from between her fingers.'[33] After her visit to La Coruña, Manuela comes back to her apartment and goes straight to Esteban's room, and we hear him in voice-over: 'Tonight mother showed me a photo of her when she was young, half of it was missing. I didn't like to tell her, but my life was missing the same piece.'[34] The book's precious nature as a relic and a source of information is emphasized by Manuela's protective attitude. In a later scene she warns Nina not to open it, and as the camera tilts down to view its cover, the book's image is superimposed over what turn out to be the lights under the marquee of the theatre where *Streetcar* is now being performed: in a virtuoso editing stroke, the new shot continues the tilt down to the figure of Manuela as she enters the foyer.

Images of Esteban as a writer and observer also recur after his death. In the continuation of this sequence of shots, Manuela imagines that she sees him waiting in the café across the road from the Madrid theatre, writing in his notebook.[35] When she explains the story of her son to Huma and Nina in the dressing room, Huma looks across to her left and 'sees' the image of Esteban pressing his notebook against the car window on the rainy night in Madrid. Esteban's photo watches over his mother's bed, and is later given by her to Lola when she brings the baby to the café. Lola reads out the same lines, 'Tonight, mother showed me a photo...', heard in Esteban's voice in an earlier scene. Manuela tells him to read on. Then, as Lola reads the page Esteban wrote shortly before his death, the book is placed on the table on top of the photo, with Esteban's eyes gazing at the reader

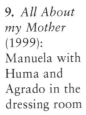

9. *All About my Mother* (1999): Manuela with Huma and Agrado in the dressing room

and – as this is Lola's point of view – the audience. The camera approaches closer and closer to the lips of the image, then fades to black for a few moments – one of the film's few fades of this kind, the most remarkable of which occurs as the boy dies. (The effect is not anticipated in the published script, in which Lola simply holds the book to his heart as the scene ends.) In the final scene, two years later, Manuela returns to Barcelona and brings the child to Huma's dressing room, where she notices the photo tucked into the mirror along with one of Nina: Lola had given it to Huma, but now Manuela declines her offer to return it. The mirror allows for the presence of absent (or even dead) characters as well as uniting in its reflection and for the camera's benefit all those within the room. As well as these pictures, the set-up also includes the reflected image of Elizabeth Taylor as Cleopatra, framed on the dressing-room wall (Figure 9). The multiple reflections in the mirrors, in this and other scenes, allow the juxtaposition of figures within the scene, extending the camera's field of vision. Mirrors also allow Almodóvar, as so often in his films, to let the camera hold actors – especially actresses – in long close-ups that favour the intensely expressive acting he elicits from them. His framing often recalls that of the photographs that permeate his work. In the final dressing-room scene the mirror with photographs attached to it and the reflected image of the women underline the dressing-room's status as a private space for preparation of the persona, and complement the use of film and theatre throughout.

Performance is represented as offering a release but sometimes demanding a heavy emotional price. In this respect both Esteban's writing and the acting of Manuela and Huma are alike. (La Agrado's price list for the alterations to her body is a comic variation on the theme, as are the Chagalls that Sister Rosa's mother forges.) Esteban's birthday gifts included Truman Capote's book, whose preface includes a clue to the director's own attitude to the responsibilities and rewards of writing:

One day I started writing, not knowing that I had chained myself to a noble but merciless master. When God hands you a gift, he also hands you a whip, and the whip is intended solely for self-flagellation.[36]

He asks his mother to read to him from the book, but after reaching the end of the second of these sentences from its preface she pulls a face and observes that it is enough to put one off writing: something about the masochistic suggestion clearly disturbs her. Self-expression through writing or the interpretation of real-life situations in art is set up here as a source of anxiety. Later, when Manuela finds herself reliving her video simulation in real life, and later when she plays the role of Stella, the experience overwhelms her. In the performance her cries of grief are taken by the theatre audience as an achievement of acting: in fact, she has been overcome by the play's painful associations and the experience of speaking Stella's lines opposite an actor in the part once taken by her husband. We have previously seen Nina, equipped with a cushioned 'bulge' imitating pregnancy and motherhood, but here Manuela, a 'genuine' mother is having to perform as one within a fiction that is itself too close to the reality of her life with the former Esteban who behaved with aggressive *machismo* (she tells Rosa earlier in the film) even after becoming Lola: 'How can you be a male chauvinist with a pair of tits like that!'[37] Almodóvar has suggested that Manuela differs from Eve Harrington not only in telling the truth rather than lies, but in being 'a character who has everything except ambition'.

> She is not the kind of ambitious actress who wants to make it on stage: she is a born actress, who knows what to do, but who doesn't have the least bit of interest in acting ... It's the opposite of Eva [sic] who is nothing but fiction, unlimited ambition.[38]

In a film about – or drawing on – theatre, it is remarkable to find as a central figure a gifted actress who wants nothing to do with the profession.

Self-expression, particularly theatrical performance, may be cathartic and therapeutic, as it seems to be for Huma in her rehearsal of an excerpt from Lluis Pascal's *Haciendo Lorca* where she performs lines from *Blood Wedding* with an added passage from *Yerma*. In the speech from *Blood Wedding*, Huma takes on the responsibility of speaking for mothers who have seen a son dead. The full passage connects directly with Manuela's experience:

> That's why it's so terrible to see your own blood spilled on the ground. A fountain that flows for a minute – and takes years out of our lives! When I got to see my son, he was lying in the middle of the street. I wet my hands with blood, and I licked them with my tongue. Because it was

mine! You don't know what that is! I would place the earth soaked with
his blood in an urn of crystal and topaz![39]

As always in Almodóvar, the telling of stories from the past has a
political dimension, a reflection of the retelling of Spain's history in the
post-Franco years. Moreover, the use of Lorca's texts brings together
the themes of bereaved motherhood, the lost son and the death of the
playwright himself at the hands of the fascist regime.[40]

Thus within the film a theatre piece is rehearsed which reaches out
beyond the personal experience of the actress but is at the same time
informed by the past she has by now shared with the other women.
It is in the semi-private space of the dressing room that Manuela and
others connected with the theatre but not on stage are able to find
resolution through relating their stories. Ernesto Acevedo-Muñoz notes
that, in contrast to corresponding sequences of performance in other
Almodóvar films, here 'the theatrical space is appropriated by Manuela
and Agrado as the locus of authenticity and relief not of performance
or the "hysterical" symptoms of crisis.'[41] It can also be observed that
the dressing room, conventionally an off-stage site of emotional stress,
is similarly converted into a 'therapeutic' space, where truths are told
and realizations occur.

In the narrative itself the manipulation of melodramatic situations
allows Almodóvar to grant or avoid deathbed scenes or moments of
postponed revelation: often the specifically 'theatrical' scene is held
back from the viewer. Esteban is denied 'last words' but these are in fact
conveyed after his death; Rosa's death is not shown, and after Manuela's
promise to take care of the child the camera pans to a wide view of the
sea, seen between the cross-like bars of the window frame; Manuela
is not present at Lola's deathbed but is told about it by Huma. Each
of these 'endings' is carefully styled to remove the scene from conventional melodramatic gestures, but at the same time they include their
potential. Williams' play embraces melodrama but distances itself from
it. The violent emotional crises and oppositions of temperament and
outlook are vivid in a degree familiar from the stage and screen genre.
The play also has much in common with what Thomas Elsaesser has
identified as a 'recurrent melodrama plot' of 'the woman who, having
failed to make it in the big city, comes back to the small-town home in
the hope of finding her true place at last, but who is made miserable
by mean-mindedness and bigotry and then suffocated by the sheer
weight of the none-too-glorious, still-raw-in-the memory past.'[42] In the
performance we see in the film this quality is intact, but Almodóvar
alters the conclusion, partly following Elia Kazan's 1951 movie version,

but giving it his own spin. After Blanche's departure, Stella walks off sobbing and holding her child: Stanley calls out her name, leaving a question mark in the air as the curtain falls.[43] As if to connect the film decisively with theatrical representation, Almodóvar gives the final line of his script to Huma, who is leaving the dressing room to go on stage for the Lorca performance. She turns to face the camera and says 'I'll see you.' In the script she adds, 'after the performance' and we hear a stage-manager calling beginners, but the simpler version lends Huma's words the force of a more numinous and general farewell: she almost resembles Lola as Death.

Michael Sofair suggested in a review that the film is seen as if by the dead Esteban, interpreting the instances of his 'appearance' as an indication that 'we we cannot be sure whether or not Esteban is actually dead, whether he writes all about his mother, or whether she finds new life in and for his memory'.[44] A more persuasive inflection of this aspect of the film is Marsha Kinder's alignment of this continuing authorial presence with the transplant theme: 'Manuela carries these voice-overs inside her as vital organs for a trans-subjective collaboration, a merging of voices that cannot save him ... but that does extend his life story.'[45] Seen from another perspective, Esteban can be identified with the society of women and their privileges. Among the film's men, he stands out as unique. Both La Agrado and Manuela's husband have chosen to become women, albeit with the retention of some vital physiological elements of manhood. Mario, the actor who plays Stanley Kowalski, lacks the alpha male charisma of a Brando (Almodóvar insisted on this) and cuts an abject figure in the scene where he begs La Agrado to fellate him. Sister Rosa's father is a sad, senile and bewildered presence, a child whom his wife must care for. In this film only Esteban seems truly worthy of the company of women, and he is the only fully male presence in the film to rival Manuela as a channel for the audience's perceptions. In this respect, metaphorically, he is indeed alive. His ambition to develop as a writer and the thoughts Almodóvar ascribes to him – the perception of women talking as the origin of story-telling – align him with the director and grant him membership of this sisterhood. In effect, the film elides mother and son, so that 'everything' about Manuela is in the last analysis also 'everything about Esteban' and something about Almodóvar. Huma's final words are followed by a cut to a screen-filling shot of patterned red cloth, and the camera pulls back to reveal it as the theatre's curtain against which, before, the final credits are displayed, we see Almodóvar's dedication of his film: 'To Bette Davis, Gina Rowland, Romy Schneider... To all women who have played actresses. To all women who act. To all men who act and transform themselves into women. To all those who love their mothers. To my mother.' Esteban, without undergoing surgery or establishing himself definitively as gay, has been one of these 'men who act and transform themselves into women'.

Notes

1 Judith Butler, *Gender Trouble. Feminism and the Subversion of Reality* (London: Routledge, 1990; new edition, 2006), p. 191.

2 Mulvey's article, first published in *Screen* in 1975, is included along with subsequent adjustments to and applications of its conceptual framework in E. Ann Kaplan's anthology *Feminism and Film* (Oxford: Oxford University Press, 2000).

3 Tracy C. Davis, *Actresses as Working Women. Their Social Identity in Victorian Culture* (London and New York: Routledge, 1991).

4 B.R.S. Fone, ed., *An Apology for the Life of Colley Cibber, with an Historical View of the Stage During his Own Time, Written by Himself* (Ann Arbor: University of Michigan Press, 1968), p. 55.

5 John Harold Wilson, *All the King's Ladies. Actresses of the Restoration* (Chicago, IL: University of Chicago Press, 1958).

6 Kirsten Pullen, *Actresses and Whores. On Stage and in Society* (Cambridge: Cambridge University Press, 2005), p. 23.

7 The film's scheme calls for the defeat of the 'old school' in personal and aesthetic terms. Elizabeth Howe points out that although 'by the middle of 1661 actresses were an established feature of the English stage', Kynaston's career in female roles ended with the arrival of the actress; he continued as a successful tragic actor for many years: *The First English Actresses. Women and Drama, 1660–1700* (Cambridge: Cambridge University Press, 1992), pp. 24–25.

8 The notion that the 'codes' of gesture of the kind represented here inhibited the expression of 'real' feeling has been challenged by many scholars, including Joseph Roach, in *The Player's Passion. Studies in the Science of Acting* (Newark, NJ: University of Delaware Press / Associated University Presses, 1985), and Evelyn B. Tribble in *Cognition in the Globe. Attention and Memory in Shakespeare's Theatre* (Basingstoke: Palgrave Macmillan, 2011).

9 Rachel M. Brownstein, *Tragic Muse. Rachel of the Comédie Française* (Durham, NC and London: Duke University Press, 1995), p. 91.

10 The most recent biography is Ed Skirov, *Dark Victory. The Life of Bette Davis* (New York: Henry Holt and Company, 2007). The screenplay was published by Random House in 1951. Two important sources on the film are *More About 'All About Eve'*, a colloquy by Gary Carey with Joseph L. Mankiewicz, together with his Screenplay 'All About Eve' (New York: Random House, 1972) – which also reprints the screenplay – and Sam Staggs, *All About All About Eve. The Complete Behind-the-Scenes Story*

of the Bitchiest Film Ever Made (New York: St Martin's Press, 2001). Rudy Behlmer gives a more concise account in *Behind the Scenes. The Making of...* (New York: Ungar, 1982; repr. New York: Samuel French, 1990), pp. 200–218. On Mankiewicz, see Kenneth L. Geist, *Pictures Will Talk. The Life and Films of Jospeh L. Mankiewicz* (New York: Scribner's, 1978); Cheryl Bary Lower and R. Burton Palmer, *Joseph L. Mankiewicz. Critical Essays with an Annotated Bibliography and a Filmography* (Jefferson, NC and London: McFarland, 2001); and Brian Dauth, ed., *Joseph L. Mankiewicz Interviews* (Jackson: University of Mississippi Press, 2008).

11 On the models for Lloyd see Mankiewicz, *More About 'All About Eve'*, p. 53.

12 On this aspect of the sequence, see Skirov, *Dark Victory*, pp. 294–295.

13 On the Stork Club, see Neal Gabler, *Walter Winchell. Gossip, Power and the Culture of Celebrity* (London: Picador, 1995), pp. 265–266. An earlier scene takes place in the lobby of '21', another centre of Broadway 'café society'.

14 Mankiewicz, *More About 'All About Eve'*, p. 98.

15 Vincent Amiel, *Joseph L. Mankiewicz et son double* (Paris: Presses Universitaires de France, 2010), p. 28.

16 Behlmer, *Behind the Scenes*, p. 209; Dauth, *Mankiewicz Interviews*, pp. 84–86: Eve's speech in the end-of-party staircase scene about 'waves of applause' would have been shown twice, through the eyes of both Margo and Karen.

17 Dauth, *Mankiewicz Interviews*, p. 96.

18 Mankiewicz, *More About 'All About Eve'*, pp. 22–23.

19 Molly Haskell, *From Reverence to Rape. The Treatment of Women in the Movies*, 2nd edition (Chicago, IL and London: University of Chicago Press, 1987), p. 245.

20 Mankiewicz, interview with David Shipman, 1982: Dauth, *Mankiewicz Interviews*, p. 147.

21 References to the script of the film are to Pedro Almodóvar, *Todo sobre mi madre, edición definitiva del Guión de la Pellicula* (Madrid: El Deseo, 1999).

22 Gwynne Edwards, *Almodóvar. Labyrinths of Passion* (London and Chester Springs, PA: Peter Owen, 2001), p. 192.

23 Almodóvar, *Todo sobre mi madre*, p. 49: '¡No puedo con los drags! Han confundo circo con travestismo, ¡qué digo circo, mimo!' In *The Law of Desire* (1987) Carmen Maura appears as a transsexual, while Bibi Anderson, a 'genuine' transsexual, plays the mother of a little girl. Almodóvar had always known Anderson as a woman, and wanted an actress as Maura to show 'the exaggerated, tense, and highly exhibitionist femininity of a transsexual' (Frederic Strauss, ed., *Almodóvar on Almodóvar*, revised edition [London: Faber and Faber, 2006], p. 71).

24 Paul Julian Smith, *Desire Unlimited. The Cinema of Pedro Almodóvar* (London and New York: Verso, 1994), p. 87.

25 On the genre's role in Almodóvar's work, see Mark Allinson, 'Mimesis and Diegesis. Almodóvar and the Limits of Melodrama', in Brad Epps and Despina Kakoudaki, eds, *All About Almodóvar. A Passion for Cinema* (Minneapolis and London: University of Minnesota Press, 2009), pp. 143–165.

26 Strauss, *Almodóvar on Almodóvar*, p. 185.

27 Marvin D'Lugo, *Pedro Almodóvar* (Urbana and Chicago: University of Illinois Press, 2006), p. 19.

28 In *Women on the Verge of a Nervous Breakdown* Pepa watches scenes behind apartment windows, including a direct imitation of 'Miss Torso' in *Rear Window*; in *Kika*, a film preoccupied with voyeurism, a poster from Michael Powell's *Peeping Tom* features on the wall in Ramón's flat. *Broken Embraces* is in many respects an anthology of Almodóvar's favourite themes, including multiple ways of seeing and representing people and occurrences; the psychology of the actress; a family secret laid bare (a son discovering his father's identity); torn photographs pieced together; and even the revisiting of *Women on the Verge of a Nervous Breakdown* as a film-within-a film. There are two references in the dialogue to *Peeping Tom*.

29 Almodóvar, *Todo sobre mi madre*, p. 96: the directions note that Agrado acts as a friend, intimate and confidant in the best Thelma Ritter style ('amiga-íntima-respondonda en el mejor estilo Thelma Ritter').

30 Ibid., p. 20. 'A Esteban, el escritor adolescente, le invade la sensación de hallarse ante el origin del espectáculo, y de la narración, en general: Una mujer contándole su historia a un coro de mujeres.' Almodóvar suggests that the reminiscence is specific, with the dressing room a '*sancta sanctorum* of the feminine universe', comparable to the patio of his aunts' house, and the women sitting there (p. 171).

31 Ibid., pp. 25, 26.

32 Ibid., p. 19. 'Anoche mamá me enseño una foto de cuando era joven, le faltaba la mitad. No quise decírselo, pero a mi vida también le falta ese mismo trozo...' The question of the titles of both films is discussed at length by Leo Bersani and Ulysse Dutout, 'Almodóvar's Girls', in Epps and Kakoudaki, *All About Almodóvar*, pp. 242–266; pp. 242–246.

33 Almodóvar, *Todo sobre mi madre*, p. 32: 'Es como si le tuviera agarrado de la mano con que escribia esas notas. Las palabras de Esteban se le escurren entre los dedos.'

34 Ibid., p. 36.

35 The script (Almodóvar, *Todo sobre mi madre*, p. 80) develops the idea more fully than the finished film.

36 Truman Capote, *Music for Chameleons. New Writing* (London: Hamish Hamilton, 1981), p. 1.

37 Almodóvar, *Todo sobre mi madre*, pp. 70–71: '¡Cómo se puede ser machista con semejante par de tetas!'

38 Quoted by Guillermo Alatres, 'An Act of Love Towards Oneself' (*Positif*,

1999), translated in Paula Willoquet-Maricondi, ed., *Pedro Almodóvar Interviews* (Jackson: University of Mississippi Press, 2004), pp. 139–153; p. 146.

39 Federico García Lorca, *Three Plays*, translated by Michael Dewell and Carmen Zapata (New York: Farrar, Straus and Giroux, 1993), p. 61.

40 The film's various intertextualities are examined in Vilma Navarro-Daniels, 'Tejiendo nuevas identidades: la red metaficional e intertextual en *Todo sobre mi madre* de Pedro Almodóvar', *Ciberletras*, 7 (2002), pp. 1–13.

41 Ernesto R. Acevedo-Muñoz, *Pedro Almodóvar* (London: BFI, 2007), p. 236.

42 Thomas Elsaesser, 'Tales of Sound and Fury: Observations on the Family Melodrama', in Barry Keith Grant, ed., *Film Genre Reader III* (Austin: University of Texas Press, 2003), pp. 366–395; p. 378.

43 On the ending of *Streetcar*, see Stephen Maddison, 'All about Women: Pedro Almodóvar and the Heterosexual Dynamic', *Textual Practice*, 14/2 (2000), pp. 265–284.

44 Michael Sofair, '*All About My Mother*' [review], *Film Quarterly*, 55/2 (Winter 2001–2002), pp. 40–47; p. 43.

45 Marsha Kinder, 'Reinventing the Motherland: Almodóvar's Brain-Dead Trilogy', *Film Quarterly* 58/2 (Winter 2004–2005), pp. 9–25; p. 17.

4

The uncanny theatre

IN an essay published in 1919 Sigmund Freud developed a theory of 'das Unheimliche', the uncanny, in which mundane (*heimlich*) circumstances surround fantastic and often terrifying supernatural events. In *Caligari's Children. The Film as Tale of Terror* (1980) S.S. Prawer identifies the characteristic of the uncanny as that which arouses 'feelings of uneasiness and apprehension, but an uneasiness and apprehension that seem necessary, fruitful and true'.[1] Freud proposes two sources of the sensation: 'the uncanny element we know from experience arises either when repressed childhood experiences are revived by some impression, or when primitive beliefs that have been surmounted appear to be once again confirmed.' Fiction, Freud argues, provides especially rich examples of the uncanny, because the assent it commands from the reader – one might add, audience – permits the simultaneous operation of both factors. 'Surmounted' beliefs are no longer subjected to the 'reality test.' For Freud, E.T.A. Hoffmann (1776–1822) was 'the unrivalled master of the uncanny in literature'.[2]

Several features characteristic of Hoffmann's tales lend themselves to the medium of film: startling shifts in visual (and moral) perspective; figures whose 'daytime' persona belies their demonic status; the sense of confinement within a magically transformed world; and the crossing of boundaries between the real and the imagined, so that the subject's disorientation is shared with the reader. *Der Sandmann* (1836–37), which furnishes Freud with his principal literary example, is particularly relevant to the uncanny in film on account of its shifts of point of view and emphasis on vision and illusion. The narration is initially carried by the student Nathaniel, who describes in a letter his childhood fear of the mysterious visitor identified by a nurse as the Sandman who preys on children's eyes; the identification of him as the sinister Dr Coppélius, who visited his father to engage in alchemical experiments; and an episode in which he hid in his father's room and spied on the pair. Coppélius, having begun the story as an unwelcome but 'real' visitor to the narrator's rooms, peddling barometers and spectacles, is remembered (in flashback, so to speak) as an imagined bogeyman who was shown to be 'real', but then – once the story has passed out of the narrator's hands – emerges again as a supernatural being. Moreover, Coppélius deals in vision, both through the sale of spectacles and the procurement of eyes for Olimpia, the automaton made by the inventor Professor Spalanzani. In this, as in other of Hoffmann's tales and in works influenced by them (such as F.W. Murnau's 1922 film *Nosferatu*), the uncanny elements are enclosed within a world that is familiar, the comfortable milieu of Biedermeier middle-class life.

Although *Der Sandmann* does not engage with the theatre – as other works by Hoffmann do – it has particular significance on account of the prominence in it of vision and spectatorship and the presence of 'normality' represented by Clara, Nathaniel's beloved, who lacks his dangerous and ultimately fatal perceptive insight. The cinema of the uncanny depends for many of its effects on the inclusion alongside characters whose disturbing visions are shown of others who do not perceive what is plainly visible to the cinema audience. Moreover, films commonly play on our willingness to suspend our rational rejection of 'surmounted' beliefs, so that we accept that graves might give up their dead, and werewolves and vampires exercise their unavoidable tendencies, analogous to the commonplace sexual and other appetites we control in ourselves. Alongside the Freudian theory of the uncanny, films have often alluded to – or assumed – the validity of his distinctions between id, ego and superego. In addition, and directly relevant to the theme of the actor's divided self, is Jung's theory of the persona, as 'that which in reality one is not, but which oneself as well as others think one is', and of the shadow, which 'personifies everything the subject refuses to acknowledge about himself' and 'that hidden, repressed, for the most part inferior and guilt-laden personality whose ultimate ramifications reach back into the realm of our animal ancestors'.[3] In the case of *A Double Life* (1948), this concept of the personality, the persona/mask and the shadow, is at least as relevant as Freudian theories of the repression. *The Phantom of the Opera* (1925) is not so susceptible to sophisticated psychological interpretation, but does share the element of the uncanny with many horror films. *The Red Shoes* (1948) and *Fanny and Alexander* (1982) move into areas of greater uncertainty, less susceptible to rational explanation in psychological terms but still profiting from the theatre's combination of mundane labours and inexplicable inspirations and motivations. Vicky in *The Red Shoes* is arguably at a somewhat delayed formative and therefore vulnerable stage in the development of her psyche: she has a formidable

Coppélius figure to cope with in the form of the impresario Lermontov. Bergman's film also encompasses childhood experience, a dimension of major significance in both Freudian and Jungian theory.

Beneath the scenes, behind the walls:
The Phantom of the Opera

The Phantom who haunts the Paris Opéra in Gaston Leroux' 1910 novel and the films (and musicals) derived from it is not a real ghost. In the opening paragraphs of his preface the novel's narrator announces that the famous Phantom did exist, and was not a figment of imagination or superstition, but a being of flesh and blood.[4] We are told that the true mystery is that various tragic and inexplicable incidents that took place some twenty years ago, including the abduction of the singer Christine Daaé, have not hitherto been connected with the legend of the Phantom. Now, after diligent research, the story can be told. Leroux provides much more background for the characters than Universal's 1925 film accommodates or needs, particularly regarding the earlier career of Erik the phantom, the longstanding love affair of Christine and Raoul de Chagny and the superstition and chicanery that surround the directorate of the opera house and their staff. Erik, hideously deformed from birth, was shunned by his family, though he was trained as a stonemason by his cruel father. He ran away with gypsies, becoming a skilled illusionist and ventriloquist. In Persia he served the Shah, creating secret passageways, trapdoors and murderous devices to protect the tyrant's palaces. For a sadistically inclined 'little Sultana' he created a torture chamber with a window through which she could enjoy the agony of her victims.

Forced to escape the monarch's decree that those who knew his secrets must be murdered, he made his way to Paris, where he was employed in the construction of the Opéra. He learned the secrets of the building at first hand, including the caverns far below its stage and the passageways used by the Communards during the siege of 1870–71. Meanwhile, his talents as a musician were developing, and he toiled at his masterwork, 'Don Juan Triumphant'. Gifted not only as a composer but as a singer with an 'angelic' voice, Erik has been engaged in a campaign to school a young Swedish singer and force the directors to give her leading roles. He has also been extorting money from them. Erik's impressive theatrical and artistic qualifications are thus placed at the service of a deep-seated grudge against the directorate of the Opéra, any suitor of Christine, and the world in general. He has protected his lavishly appointed subterranean lair with devices of the kind he prepared for the Shah, and is able to roam at will throughout the enormous building. He is also a prankster, given to leaving snide, politely phrased ultimatums on the desk of the directors, charmingly signing himself as 'Le F. de l'O'. Leroux combines traits common among the leading characters in stories of suspense and the semi-supernatural. Erik is not a 'real' spirit, but in his own way he is in a state of suspense between redemption and damnation, as represented by the 'angelic' music he creates and the Inferno-like depths of the Opéra cellars. His habitual formal attire, with his felt hat, suggests the suavity of a man of the world, with a touch of Bohemianism befitting an artist. The insistence that his mask should not be lifted and the secrets of his underground apartments should not be investigated places Christine in the position of Bluebeard's brides: when she purloins his keys, he exclaims 'I do not like curious women! ... and you ought to be wary after the story of Blue Beard'.[5]

More sinister is the reminiscence of the novels of the Marquis de Sade in the situations engineered by Erik: both Raoul and the mysterious 'Persian' who comes to his aid are confined in a way that combines cruel illusory effects with acute physical danger, and Christine's imprisonment recalls the misfortunes inflicted on his heroines. In the novel her escape is permitted because she shows pity for Erik and goes so far as to kiss his repulsive, parchment-like face. He is not transformed into a handsome prince – this is not *Beauty and the Beast* – but it does precipitate an ending in which his relenting allows the lovers to disappear into happy obscurity in a distant country and Erik dies of a broken heart. It is important to distinguish Erik from other figures that made the successful and lucrative transition into the cinema from the romantic literature and theatre of the macabre. Unlike Frankenstein or Dr Jekyll, the Phantom is not ambitious to discover more than natural law allows; he does not suffer from the compulsion to prey on innocent humankind and convert them to a relentless career of infamy, as do Dracula and other un-dead victim/villains; and unlike werewolves he lacks the inherited or acquired tendency to transform himself into a murderous beast. For much of the narrative it seems as though his principal ambition, to which all other motives are subordinate, is to run an opera house.

The opera house in question, of course, has great symbolic value, and control of it is linked to the need for some kind of redemption through love. Christine must star as Marguerite in Gounod's *Faust*, a heroine redeemed by the purity of her love in one of the most highly prized works in the French lyric repertoire – and this in a theatre designed to celebrate opera and ballet as national treasures. Work on the new Opéra had begun in 1861. Despite the immense cost, and the political difficulties of its association with the Empire, the project survived the vicissitudes of the war with Prussia, the Commune and the change of regime, and the house opened with great pomp in 1875.[6] The size and complexity of the building (the architect Charles Garnier formally handed over 1,942 keys when it was delivered) made it a magnet for sight-seers as well as operagoers, and the grand staircases lent themselves to ceremonial display. It was predicted that the warren of corridors, alcoves and smaller foyers in front-of-house would soon be notorious as a trysting place:

> Here and there are deep recesses, dark passageways, and mysterious grottoes. ... Before very long promenading in the Italian manner will become the fashion. On the pretext of looking round, people will wander. There will be a lot of wandering. There is definitely no need for masks: the pale light that falls from the lamp standards is exceedingly favourable to romance.

Another journalist suggested that the monumental Opéra was shocking to the highest degree ('du dernier choquant'), a brothel ('maison close') on a grand scale, that might have been designed for 'us men' with all its mirrors, hidden recesses and open spaces'.[7] Among the many depictions of the Opéra in the illustrated papers, the longitudinal cross-section by Théodore de Lajarte in *Le Monde Illustré* for 6 February 1875 gives the most striking impression of its scale and also – importantly for its place in the popular imagination – the height and depth of the construction. Like the large-scale cross-sectional model now in the Musée d'Orsay, it suggests the potential for concealment and mystery latent in an edifice devoted to scenic and social display, qualities exploited by both Leroux and the production designers at Universal Pictures. When Raoul first visits the substage levels of the theatre, he glimpses only a part of the 'extravagant abyss, sublime and childish, as amusing as a Punch-and-Judy booth [*Guignol*] and as terrifying as a chasm'.[8]

Leroux refers to the historical circumstances of the Opéra's construction in terms that suggest that the Communards employed it not only as a refuge but also as a place where they could torture their enemies: Erik makes use of a passage created by them to bring prisoners into the depths of the cellars. For Universal, this specific reference has no significance. Instead, a vague atmosphere of old-time cruelties is conjured up. After brief opening credits over a shadowy green background, red-tinted shots show a figure with a lantern in the cellars, while a lurking shadow is cast on a wall in the background. The title accompanying an establishing shot of the building's exterior identifies the Opéra as the 'Sanctuary of Song Lovers … Rising Nobly Over Medieval Torture Chambers, Hidden Dungeons, Long Forgotten'. The film conducts the viewer from the façade to the grand staircase and into the auditorium, showing the audience from the stage and then looking at the performance from the conductor's perspective and from a high tier of boxes. The ballet in progress exhibits the spaciousness of the stage itself, as well as associating it with the artistic display of female bodies – an image that will recur in the film. The next scene takes us to the executive offices, as 'melody floats through hall and corridor'. In the first few minutes, the scale of the Opéra and its distinct public and backstage realms has been established, with an ominous intimation that below the surface are sinister shadowy depths. The designer of the sets for the underground scenes, Ben Carré, had studied in Paris in the early 1900s and knew both the building and the novel well.[9]

Apart from a few brief scenes the action remains confined to the Opéra. The Phantom stays within his domain until his attempted flight in the final sequence, but is able to penetrate its public and private spaces, including some not known to the holders of the 1,942 keys, and has adapted some of these to his own use. The film shows stage sets from in front and behind, and has enough of the machinery (windlasses, traps) to suggest the mechanisms by which they are manipulated. Erik, though, has constructed a backstage within the backstage itself, extending it into the walls of the theatre's other areas. He has installed trapdoors in the floor of the scene dock and in the subterranean passages that lead to his lair, moves in the spaces behind the dressing-room and office walls, projecting his voice by ventriloquism and through hidden ducts, and has installed a trick mirror in the room used by Christine.[10] The Phantom is employing the standard techniques of theatrical illusion, familiar from *féeries* and British pantomimes, but the magic is not being performed where it should be, on the stage itself.

The skills that in the novel made Erik so valuable to his Persian employers, as the trapdoor enthusiast ('amateur des trappes'), also create the cruel illusions of the 'torture chamber'. Its walls are made of mirrors, with scenic elements that can be rotated to give the illusion of a tropical forest which is then transformed to a desert, complete with a projected effect of a mirage. Prisoners in this room can be subjected to sensory deprivation, disorientation and extreme discomfort, and may be driven to madness: a rope is provided for their convenience should they be tempted to suicide. The theatre's own scenery is good enough in its own way, but compared to the sophistication of Erik's work the effect of Marguerite's ascent to heaven, seen on the stage, is crude and unconvincing. Together with the technical knowledge that enables him to detach the chandelier from its restraining cables and send it plummeting into the orchestra stalls, Erik's theatrical skills give him a degree of command over the Opéra that its directors cannot achieve.[11] The effect of mystery is supported in the film by the theatre's stock-in-trade. As the mysterious Persian, Virgil to Raoul's Dante, explains in Leroux' novel, the depths of the Opéra, 'the very land of phantas-magoria', are the appropriate setting for a man of Erik's talents and disposition.[12]

When the tableau curtains are brought in after the fall of the chandelier the singer playing Mephistopheles is stranded on the forestage – he is later glimpsed in the dressing-room passage. Erik can outdo any such conventional effect of devilry: at the *bal masqué* his costume and skull mask as the 'Red Death' are awe-inspiring, and the other revellers shrink from him. The scene is in two-strip Technicolor, giving it a richness and theatrical impact beyond anything shown in the performances on the stage. In the impressively staged and shot sequence that follows, where he stands on the roof of the theatre, holding onto the giant statue of Apollo as the lovers plot, the romantic majesty of his demeanour – the cloak billowing in the wind, the expansive gestures – expresses a degree of nobility in the private grief beneath all this display and histrionic skill.

Lon Chaney gives the Phantom an expressively stylized body language that seems appropriate to the character's romantic view of himself as an artist and a hero/victim – he is, after all, the Phantom of the *Opera*. When Christine removes his mask she recoils from him in a way that would be entirely appropriate to the operatic stage, and his admonitory stances and gestures, particularly in a pose chosen for a familiar production still in which he is leaning back with his right arm extended, recall the iconography of nineteenth-century melodrama and opera (Figure 10). The makeup largely immobilizes Chaney's face, although in moments of pathos the discrepancy between Erik's feelings and the threatening grimace is still evident. 'Feast your eyes, glut your soul', he exclaims, 'on my accursed ugliness!' Camera angles and lighting help to make the distorted contours more grotesque and threatening. With Chaney, we know that choices have been made by an actor capable of more realistic acting, but with the lovers, there is room for doubt. Mary Philbin as Christine has many such moments, in which she portrays a woman in peril within the conventions considered appropriate to film without spoken dialogue. Raoul (Norman Kerry), in the film a pugnacious, stiff-backed officer rather than the youthful and impetuous boy of the novel, adopts hackneyed poses of defiance

10. *The Phantom of the Opera* (1925): Christine has unmasked Erik (production still)

and astonishment as necessary. Although it is fair to assume that Erik is carried away by real emotion in this scene, there are others in which he seems to be self-consciously performing his adopted role. As the Red Death he achieves a thrilling and haughty dignity as he admonishes the revellers: 'Beneath your dancing feet are the tombs of tortured men – thus does the Red Death rebuke your merriment.'

The cumulative effect is to make Erik's performance as the Phantom more theatrical than anything seen on stage – even in *Faust*. He crosses boundaries of all kinds, physical and moral, while besting the theatre in the exercise of its own craft. In other scenes Chaney's mime is subtle and restrained, commanding attention with stillness of body and simple, eloquent hand gestures and achieving an almost balletic grace when he falls to his knees to declare his love for Christine. Jeanine Basinger, surveying his film roles, describes the actor's ability to 'use his whole body as an expressive force, and eliminate the need for titles with a single gesture, an eloquent movement, or a cruel half-smile'.[13] The smile is out of the question here, with his mouth either veiled or revealed as frozen in a skull-like grimace, but the mimetic skill is always impressive. Masked, Erik is a mime artist, but unmasked he becomes a terrifying melodramatic villain with extreme gestures to match, a duality reflecting the division in his character between the 'angelic voice' and the potential for demonic cruelty. Thwarted in his hopes that the gift of her love would redeem him by bringing out the goodness suppressed in his heart, he cries to Christine 'Now you shall see the evil spirit that makes my evil face'. This famous moment of revelation is shot and edited so as to situate the cinema audience rather than Christine as the recipients of the horrific sight, as she is behind him, horror-struck even before his face is visible to her: as Gaylyn Studlar observes, it is a function of the exploitation of the actor's persona as a one-man spectacle, a 'star-as-freak exhibition'.[14] Christine is a surrogate for the audience, confirming and expressing its responses within the diegesis, a model that would become familiar in the horror genre.

The 'angelic' voice described in the novel can only be rendered in the film through the written word of the intertitles, and Erik's organ playing – which a cinema organ could convincingly double – has to stand in for it. The fact that his composition is 'Don Juan Triumphant' suggests an erotic threat that both novel and film leave largely to the imagination of reader and viewer – in the common-sense world even of the novel's more sentimental Raoul, beautiful women are hardly going to be abducted merely for their vocal abilities – but it is also paralleled by the notorious erotic world of the Opéra itself. Behind the scenes the Opéra offered the fascination of privileged admission for their 'protectors' and others to the spectacle of scantily clad and very possibly available women. In the film this element is represented directly by the ballet dancers who fill the stage in the film's opening sequence, the striking contrast between these girlish figures and the menacing shadows of the scene dock, and the blatant eroticism of the goings-on at the masked ball. Confined in the Phantom's suite of rooms, Christine is first shown his own bedroom, with the coffin in which (à la Sarah Bernhardt) he usually sleeps, and then the room prepared for her, which is decorated elaborately and has a bed shaped like a gondola, a reminder of Erik's own conveyance on the underground canal.[15]

In the film Erik's motivation is reduced to an undefined record of unfocused terrorism: 'If I am the Phantom, it is because man's hatred has made me so!' In a change that may have been made at a late stage of the film's production, the novel's exotic 'Persian' has been transmuted into the routine stock figure of Ledoux, of the 'Secret Police'. He shows the minister of justice a file card identifying Erik as an escapee from Devil's Island ('for the criminal insane') and a self-taught adept in music and the 'black arts'.[16] The script's need for Erik to expiate his crimes takes precedence over the romantic and solitary death he endures in the novel. There has to be a climactic chase and he must be killed.[17] His final performance takes place immediately before his death, flung into the Seine by a vengeful torch-bearing mob of the kind soon familiar in Hollywood horror films. The crowd advances towards him from both sides as he stands on the towpath: with a grand and defiant gesture he flings back his arm with his fist clenched round what must surely be some devilish device – a vial of acid, perhaps, or nitro-glycerine. Then, with a mocking grin that shows glee not previously visible in his skull-like face, he opens his hand to show – nothing. Erik's last theatrical gesture is the ultimate sleight of hand: there really was nothing there, just as there was in fact no phantom, except for that created by the Erik.

A Double Life:
mean streets, shadows and noir Shakespeare

Erik wears a mask to hide his hideously damaged face, significant as a notable example of the horror-film trope whose later manifestations include Mystery of the Wax Museum (1933) and its 1953 remake House of Wax. In such films the masked face affects the audience at several levels, invoking deep-rooted anxieties about identity and personality of the kind associated with theatrical masks in many cultures as well as in folk legend and ritual. In George Cukor's A Double Life the physical disguise is superficial – Ronald Colman is not heavily obscured by his Othello makeup – the theme of the actor's mask and/or face meets the cinematic vocabulary of film noir. As so often in the tale of terror – and in classic noir detective stories – the (Jungian) shadow within or alongside the central character is complemented by expressionistic elements in lighting, camerawork and design.

A Double Life, a tragedy with little place for humour or hope, is unusual in Cukor's work. Variety's ebullient verdict seems to ignore the darkness at its heart: 'There's murder, suspense, psychology, Shakespeare and romance all wrapped up into one polished package of screen entertainment' (31 December 1947). It did, however, return both director and principal actor to their theatrical roots and provided Colman – in a role originally conceived for Laurence Olivier – with the opportunity for a psychologically intense performance that won him an Academy Award. Patrick McGilligan suggests that the double life of Tony reflects Cukor's own situation as a homosexual, accepted within the business of film and theatre but passing as straight in the world outside.[18] However, the association of Tony's double existence with criminality hardly seems to chime with Cukor's perception of himself, so far as that can be judged.[19] Although not every late-1940s film with dark corners, off-kilter camera angles and conflicted (or morally ambiguous) heroes is necessarily a *film noir*, the genre's pervasive sense of anxiety and – often vague – 'psychological' exploration is powerfully present in *A Double Life*. In many scenes the *mise en scène* and lighting achieve the 'visually unstable environment' identified by Janey Price and Lowell Peterson as a distinguishing feature of the *noir* style, although it is not the case here that 'no character has a firm moral base from which he can operate'.[20] The film combines these elements with a Shakespearean actor's fear of a 'dark' and conflicted role. 'Not I' is dangerously close to the real 'I'.[21]

The mysterious qualities of the theatre are complemented by the darkness that lies in the streets outside: apart from the opening scenes on and around Broadway and a few subsequent establishing shots of the Empire Theatre, almost all the exteriors take place at night, many in shadowy and threatening Lower East Side streets. Hitherto suppressed psychological stresses and the work of Shakespeare are the lethal combination of forces Tony must cope with alone in these mean streets. He is also his own *Doppelgänger*, frequently seen in mirrors and reflected in windows, doubled visibly as his personality is divided mentally. Jung's concept of the persona suggests a way of understanding this, although the film makes no reference to it. In generalized Freudian terms, this can be described as a story of repression, the release of subconscious desires that are revealed as specifically violent and sexual, although again there is no analysis in such terms within the film. That it is triggered by *Othello* suggests that art can give access to the id, by-passing the ego and the superego. Intimations of Tony's self-regard are scattered through the film – there are images of him in the theatre and in the apartment he used to share with Brita – but there is little to suggest that this goes beyond the self-confident and self-promoting mentality acceptable in a leading actor in his kind of commercial theatre. Maybe that in itself is the problem, and the film reflects an underlying apprehension about acting, which might well in itself have been a warning to steer clear of plays where his character would murder the woman he loves.

In the opening sequence, Tony arrives at the theatre as a foyer placard is delivered announcing the critical plaudits for the comedy he is starring in: *A Gentleman's Gentleman*. Admiring female fans notice him when a door is opened and he is seen gazing at paintings of himself in juvenile lead roles. His face is not seen until he turns from an image of his younger self to face the camera. His raincoat and tilted derby contrast with the dashing, immaculately clad figure behind him as he lights a cigarette, his expression suggesting a degree of dissatisfaction.

This is the first of several shots juxtaposing two images of the actor: subsequent examples include his reflection in mirrors, or in a shop window. Tony's ruminations take place in the half-light at the back of the orchestra stalls in daytime, so that contemplation of the pictures occurs in a marginal territory between the sunlit streets and the dark void of the theatre. He moves away, then pauses before a bust of himself, and as he strides towards a lighted door the camera stays with the bust, keeping it in profile at the right of the frame. He leaves and goes to meet his producer, Max Lasky. On the way he greets three male acquaintances whose opinion of him is divided: 'Good actor' –'He's no good'. He then meets two actresses who to their surprise have similarly divergent opinions: 'What a darling' – 'Stinker'. It has been established that there might be more than one view of him, as well as his own discontent with his current situation and, implicitly, his ageing.

In Lasky's office Tony is reminded of a long-cherished project for a production of *Othello* which will return him as 'a great actor' to the roles he should be playing. Tony's ideas for the play included the strangling of Desdemona 'with a kiss'. In the dialogue that follows we learn that marriage to Brita (Signe Hasso), from whom he is now divorced, spurred his ambition to be 'an actor, a real actor', a process that involved the refashioning of himself: 'I had to teach myself to talk, remember? And move, and think. I had to tear myself apart, and put myself together again and again. And the left-over pieces are scattered somewhere between here and a thousand one-night stands.' After Tony has left, Lasky and Victor, the director, discuss the *Othello* problem. Lasky's matter-of-fact view of acting is countered by the director. Tony's acting is on a deeper level: 'the way he has of becoming someone else every night, for just a few hours, so – completely. Now don't tell me that his whole system isn't affected by it.'

What is shown of the comedy bears out Max's grounds for being dissatisfied with the waste of his talent. As Brita explains to Bill, Tony's press agent, he is buoyed up by playing in a comedy, 'but when he gets going on one of those deep numbers...' She explains the difficulty of living with Tony's shifting moods: 'We were engaged during Oscar Wilde, broke it off during O'Neill, we were married during Kaufman and Hart and divorced during Chekhov.' Brita's dressing room is cosy, chic and intimate, with an elegant lighted mirror. Tony's is a darkly furnished old-fashioned actor-manager's room, whose clutter includes a phrenological bust, which stands on a table next to the portfolio of *Othello* sketches that Victor brought to Lasky's office. After Brita has left, Tony leafs through it and contemplates a sketch for his makeup. This transformed image is echoed again soon after. He wanders aimlessly downtown, pausing before a travel agent's window with advertisements for Venice. As lines from the play run through his head, the soundtrack music moves to a 'renaissance' mode, and his reflection dissolves into that of the madeup face and 'Moorish' hood of the character. Eventually he arrives at (where else?) the Venezia Restaurant, where he encounters Pat (Shelley Winters), the waitress who will become his murder victim. Her come-hither, wise-cracking manners and frankly sensual demeanour contrast with the elegance of Brita and the world Tony normally inhabits.

When later that night he takes up the invitation to come to her flat, Tony enters once again the shadowy world of the streets, now made more sinister by the rattle and roar of an elevated railway train as he walks (seen from a low angle) below its track. The same tracks run past the window of Pat's room, and she has to yell from the kitchen alcove to tell him to sit down. The room has its own shadows as well as a bed and a mirror (the two items of furnishing on which the camera lingers). When Tony says he will tell her his name 'when I know it myself', her rebuke – 'Don't give me that … I've handled lines all my life' – unwittingly associates her position (a waitress looking out for some kind of opportunity in the city) with that of the actor. His inability to tell her who he is makes no sense to her, being expressed in terms of a list of identities in the form of dramatic characters, temperaments and nationalities. He stands before a mirror, with the 'renaissance' music on the soundtrack and (as it were) in his head, and holds an earring against his cheek, as if trying out props. Quite reasonably, Pat wonders whether she is mixed up with 'some kind of nut'. When she asks 'What's the matter fella?' he seems to hear Brita as Desdemona asking 'What's the matter Othello?' Later, the setting and atmosphere in Pat's room will be recalled by the stage set and lighting for the *Othello* production. For the time being the juxtaposition of an actor and his double and the 'doubling' of Brita/Desdemona by Pat have been set up. The scene ends with a kiss, after Pat has insisted 'Don't talk funny no more'. To her the play's eloquence is barely comprehensible and implicitly threatening.

A fade returns Tony to the sunnier world of Brita's apartment. Discussion of *Othello* leads to an impassioned account by Tony of what lies ahead, in which his voice-over accompanies a virtuoso montage of episodes from the play's first reading to its final rehearsal. Tony describes how, in order to master a role, 'you dig for it in yourself', so that it 'begins to seep into your soul'. Eventually the character takes over, but the struggle is always there: 'You're two men now, grappling for control. You – and Othello.' With these lines the script melodramatizes elements of Stanislavski and Diderot, in a necessary fusion of theatrical theory and vaguely defined 'psychology' that provides, more starkly than previous hints, the assumption on which the story is based. The montage segues into the first night. The performance, with its stately (and, for the late 1940s, authentic) diction and elaborate stage compositions, presents yet another *milieu* distinct from Brita's apartment and the tenebrous Lower East Side. Othello's murder of Desdemona 'with a kiss' startles the theatre audience and, for a moment, Brita. A close-up of his face from her point of view, seeming to show Tony's emotions behind those of Othello, is doubly disturbing on account of the chiaroscuro provided by the stage lights. Now the theatre is offering him its own dark space, as tenebrous as the streets outside. Lasky, the director and Bill are in a bar across the street, assuaging first-night nerves. Bill's witticism about reviews, 'tonight he murders the girl, tomorrow they'll murder him', does not seem welcome. They go to stand at the back of the orchestra: Tony has given the performance of a lifetime, the investment will be safe. After the curtain-call, the falling drop leaves him in darkness for a moment until the working lights come on amid the routine bustle of the backstage.

Tony's isolation has begun in earnest. At the first-night party in Brita's apartment his mind is invaded by lines from the play, and he sees Brita and Bill as if they were Desdemona and Cassio. He bumps into an ornament, whose tinkling chimes take over in his head from the diegetic piano music, and the guests' chatter is overwhelmed by inner voices intoning 'Farewell the tranquil mind' and warning against 'the green-eyed monster'. Voices repeat 'Let us hide our loves' repeatedly, in a chorus underlined by Miklós Rósza's score, and the repeated 'Fool! Fool! Fool!' is heard as the music climaxes and Tony's face, in left of frame, is balanced by its double in a mirror to the right.

The production flourishes, reaching its second year, and the strain is beginning to tell. In a terrifying moment Tony as Othello seems about to strangle Brita, to the dismay of all concerned. As he strides towards her, his figure framed by the stage lights in the wings facing her, a tight close-up of her face registers her dismay. She pleads with him *sotto voce* to be careful but his hands grip her throat more powerfully, until finally he grasps her in his arms and for about thirty seconds, as the audience's anxiety and that of the backstage staff become palpable, the scene's thunder effect is all that can be heard. Emilia's knocking at the chamber door, urgently needed as an interruption in the play's fiction, has now become a disturbing reality. In the dressing room as she recovers, Tony – still in his costume and make-up – tries to reassure Brita (Figure 11). Some months or weeks later, when Tony visits Brita's apartment to celebrate their 200th performance, his suppressed

11. *A Double Life* (1948):
Brita and Tony after the
performance (production
still)

emotions again take over. She has ordered a cake, with figures of them
as Othello and Desdemona. His jealousy erupts when she refuses to
consider remarriage – they are standing by a 'life mask' sculpture of
him, which adorns the apartment wall. Enraged, he pursues her up
the darkened staircase, but she slams and locks her bedroom door as
he lurches after. The sound of the door is heard as darkness envelops
Tony's figure and the score suddenly breaks in with assertive, ominous
chords. The apartment has become a shadowy, threatening place in
a shot that harks back to many horror-film images of the predatory
demonic pursuit. Tony in his 'real' voice mutters 'No, don't hurt Brita'
but in his head (as voice-over) his sonorous 'Othello' voice counters
with 'Yet she must die, else she'll betray more men'. The two voices
of the actor are superimposed, a distinction supported by the stylized
stage diction of the period.

From now on, as he makes his way down the street, the voices of real
and imaginary impulses struggle with each other, strongly suggesting
that paranoid schizophrenia has taken over. He pauses in front of
a road sign which he does not see: 'Stop. Dead End.' Compelled to
carry out the harm his better self knows he must not do to Brita, Tony
seeks out Pat in her dowdy lodgings, where her bed, still balanced
by the mirror on the other side of the room, is lit and curtained as
if in imitation of the stage scene she will never see but must act out.
'Woman, put out the light', leads inevitably to his extinction of her as
the substitute for Brita as Desdemona. Tony is in the foreground, with
Pat by the bed behind him. His voice in 'Othello' mode, he asks 'Seen
Bill lately?' before proceeding with 'Had all his hairs...' as he turns
towards her and the back of his head fills the frame. Desdemona's voice
seems to answer him, and he clutches Pat's throat and leans in to kiss
her with 'Nay, an you strive'. In a move recalling the stage scene, she

clutches at a curtain, but he forces her backwards. The elevated railway provides thunder that replicates the sound effect heard in the theatre. He seems to hear Emilia's voice, and draws the curtains across the bed before leaving: in the centre of the frame the body is seen lying against the white sheets. A single very brief shot of Tony walking away from the building is followed by one of Brita lying in bed, waking as if from a nightmare. Curtains cast a shadow across her, and as she gets up and walks to the bedroom door, they wave between the camera and the room, recalling those prominent in Pat's apartment and on stage. Still in shadows, she makes her way down the staircase, and finds that Tony, whom she expected to be asleep on her sofa, is not there. As she climbs slowly back upstairs, the screen fades to black and the cadences of the ominous music are suddenly interrupted by a sharp cut to the inverted face of Pat seen through her bed rails and a giant close up of her landlady, who screams as a flashbulb goes off.

The film now moves into its final, investigative, mode, as the police and the press – in particular one sharp reporter who is a friend of Bill's – move to solve the crime. This is effected in the nick of time, and the final sequence, in which Tony kills not Brita but himself, gives a third view of the play's last scene as staged in the theatre, now including for the first time a shot from immediately behind the bed, looking towards the audience and with the bright stage lights across the top of the frame. Tony's death is preceded by a few moments in which as an actor he appears to have lost his way, wavering and missing cues and failing to respond to prompts. Afterwards, as he lies dying in the wings, curtain calls are taken by the rest of the company, including the distraught Brita. She comes backstage and takes off his wig, and he peels off his beard and moustache, so that his own face is revealed again. He effectively gives Brita and Bill his blessing and tells them that they are 'all, all right'. His last words are 'don't let them say I was a bad actor', but his attempt to speak to Brita gets no further than his repetition of her name three times before his features stiffen in death. The camera is placed alongside Brita's shoulder, in left of frame. The soundtrack mixes applause, Brita's sobbing and a plangent violin solo, as a shadow advances across Tony's face before Bill leans forward to close his eyes. The final images, seen as if from the balcony of the theatre, show the curtain call taking place without Tony. The tableau curtains close, and on the forestage is an empty circle of spotlight. In a faded-over shot from the side of auditorium the descending house curtain closes off the light as the music reaches its final crescendo. Both the actor and his double have been vanquished, and the darkness has taken over.

The Red Shoes:
glamour, ambition and retribution

Michael Powell and Emeric Pressburger's *The Red Shoes* may well have inspired many a young dancer, but it represents performance as mysterious and hazardous. The film had its origins in the 1930s as a proposal for a biopic about Vaslav Nijinsky, subsequently modified to become a vehicle for Sir Alexander Korda's protégée Merle Oberon.[22] Bought back from Korda and developed further, it metamorphosed into a plan to combine dance, music, visual art and narrative on film, with the infusion of the theme of Hans Christian Andersen's story 'The Red Shoes', and the performance of a ballet inspired by it. The figure of Boris Lermontov, modelled on Sergei Diaghilev, epitomizes the romantic image of the artistic director as a ruthless but vulnerable creative genius.[23]

Powell and Pressburger, jointly credited for writing, production and direction as 'The Archers', established a reputation for adventurousness in technique and romantic eccentricity in subject matter. 'Reality' and 'fantasy' – for once the quotation marks are unavoidable – are fused in what is often a surrealistic exploration of the unconscious sources of the supposedly 'real' world, inheriting the expressionistic and realistic legacy that has been identified in early cinema with Méliès and Lumière. A line in *Black Narcissus* (1947) sums up a dominant tendency of the Archers: 'There's something in the atmosphere that makes everything seem exaggerated.' In 'The Shape of Films to Come', published in 1948, Powell insisted that 'sets and sound should become a backdrop to the story and actors; not an entangled aura of supposed-reality', and declared that 'Pseudo-reality reduces the actors merely to men in fancy-dress, and anti-magical-climax'.[24]

Writing from the perspective of the 1960s, Raymond Durgnat suggested that if Powell, the cinema and Technicolor had 'flourished in the first half of the nineteenth century instead of the twentieth, the period, in fact, of Romanticism encountering Victorian realism', the director 'might have been working with the cultural grain rather than against it'.[25] A backstage film by this team, set in the world of ballet, could hardly be less than spectacular and mysterious.

Accounts of the development of the project suggest that the ballet sequence dominated their thinking, almost to the point of making the lengthy surrounding narrative a pretext for it. The sequence is justly famous for its combination of Robert Helpmann's choreography, Hein Heckroth's fantastic designs and Jack Cardiff's Technicolor cinematography. The technical difficulties of creating a ballet-by-film rather than simply a filmed ballet were discussed in detail with the team in a valuable account of the work by Monk Gibbon, which goes far beyond the customary purposes of a studio-sanctioned 'making of' publication.[26] It is in the 'Red Shoes' ballet that the film's element of cruelty becomes manifest, for even without its religious dimension and the crudity of its heroine's physical punishment, the story it inherits from Andersen is relentlessly retributive. In Andersen's story pride and vanity, into which the young Karen falls inadvertently, are punished savagely before her abject repentance is responded to. Having acquired the red shoes through her susceptibility to the attractions of the eye and aided by the failing sight of her guardian, the little girl is led from one unthinking iniquity (red shoes worn at confirmation) to another (dancing when she should be tending her mortally ill patron) until she finds herself unable to take off the shoes that force her to dance, day and night. She hopes to achieve some respite by prevailing on an executioner to take drastic action by chopping off her feet: 'Then she confessed her sin, and the executioner chopped off her feet with the red shoes. But the shoes kept dancing with the little feet across the fields and into the deep forest.'[27] Even with her shoes (and feet) gone, and provided with wooden feet and crutches, Karen is still barred from entering the church until an angel appears before her and, accepting her heartfelt repentance, brings the church into her room with a wave of his 'lovely green bough ... covered with roses'. Filled with the joy of her redemption, Karen's heart bursts. 'Her soul flew on the sunlight to God, and no one asked about the red shoes.'[28]

The film loses coherence through the imperfect fit between its main narrative and this story, an adaptation of which is acted out in the fifteen-minute 'Ballet of the Red Shoes'. The imbalance in screen time makes itself felt. As Adrienne McLean points out, 'The ballet tells a fairy tale in minutes; the film, in two hours.'[29] Pressburger outlined the story to Monk Gibbon in deceptively simple terms:

> A girl gets the red shoes – a girl decides to go in the limelight – wishing for the red shoes – ambition – and to be in the limelight had much more consequence than the girl ever realized. The red shoes and the limelight will lead to the destruction of the girl.[30]

In the usual run of backstagers something less admirable than ambition would have been responsible for the heroine's downfall – thoughtless self-indulgence fuelled by drink, perhaps, as in the melodramatic storyline of *Ziegfeld Girl*. Despite general admiration for the producers' achievements, several reviewers agreed with *Variety* in finding the story 'trite' and the basic premise hackneyed: 'For the first 60 minutes, this is a commonplace backstage melodrama, in which temperamental ballerinas replace the more conventional showgirls.'[31]

Experts in the dance journals agreed on the inappropriate effect of the ending. 'The producers', wrote John K. Newman in *Dancing Times*, 'have strangled themselves in their own story, and have been guilty of the most distasteful ending ever tacked onto a picture'. *Dance* (New York) used more sophisticated language to a similar effect, suggesting that 'the programmatic insistence on the parallelization of real-life and fairly tale allegory ... paradoxically enough, induces the directors to finish the picture with a brutal passage of unnecessary realism'.[32] Andersen's cruel fable has at least the coherence of its piety, but nothing justifies Vicky's fate. In the final sequence the sight of her mangled body, with the shoes taken from her torn legs as she lies beside the railway track, seems to satisfy an urge for picturesque punishment on the part of the filmmakers rather than intellectual or emotional logic. What was the offence that merits this treatment? The laws she contravenes are those of art as defined by her employer, Boris Lermontov, not the commandments of any god. *The Red Shoes* is a romantic melodrama in which art is an inevitable force and a cruel taskmaster. The personification of this in the 'Red Shoes' ballet is the shoemaker, a truly Hoffmannesque figure danced with demonic energy by Léonide Massine. In the film's main narrative it is Lermontov, an autocrat played by Anton Walbrook with subtlety and humanity that carry the role beyond the crudity of the script's conception. Lermontov's privacy in the public space of the opera house is established when he hides behind the curtain in his box, a benign or at least less melodramatic version of the Phantom of the Opera, and in scenes with Vicky close-ups of his face suggest a steady, mesmeric gaze.

The memoirs of his associates testify to Diaghilev's uncanny, quasi-hypnotic effect on them. The ballerina Tamara Karsavina described the moment when she first saw him, at a rehearsal of *The Nutcracker* in 1900: 'He walked into the almost deserted auditorium [of the Maryinsky Theatre] and soon left. A casual act, seemingly unconnected with anything that was going on, but to me strangely appropriate, like another trick of magic by Dr Drosselmayer.' This moment during a ballet inspired by Hoffmann was a presage of the influence she was to see at work on others.[33] Massine, recalling the moment when he accepted Diaghilev's offer of a contract, despite having resolved to turn it down, attributed his change of mind to 'some unknown power, some emanation from the subconscious', that 'took control' of him as it did at other junctures in his career.[34] Diaghilev's emotional attachments and his unwavering insistence on his artistic principles, especially when they were united in his intimate relationships with Michel Fokine, Nijinsky and Massine, made him acutely susceptible to a sense of betrayal, producing a combination of anger and depression – masked for the most part by the mystique with which he surrounded himself.

At the beginning Vicky Page (Moira Shearer) is an outsider hoping to get into the world of ballet. She is already a princess, as we see her in her aunt's box at Covent Garden, watching the new ballet, *Heart of Fire*, being performed by Lermontov's company. The child of an aristocratic family, she is robed in blue and even has a dainty crown on top of her flaming red hair. Her attention is wholly focussed on the stage, and a frame-filling close-up establishes her as an emotional barometer, a set-up the film returns to repeatedly. In another box, Lermontov hides behind a curtain, avoiding the gaze of the audience – including Vicky's socialite aunt, Lady Neston. Backstage we see the dancers warming up and final preparations being made by stage hands. The choreographer Grischa Liubov (Massine) peers through the curtain peep-hole, a moment Ian Christie has identified as signalling the film's 'fundamentally Hoffmannesque supernatural quality'.[35] The stalls audience are sketched in, mainly in this moment from the dancer's point of view, but the occupants of the gallery are more fully realized. The film's opening scenes include a rush up the gallery stair of the students who have been clamouring to be admitted. In the gallery they provide an enthusiastic audience of music students and 'balletomanes' vehement in their partisanship for the musical and choreographic aspects of the performance respectively. The score is by the music students' professor, and they have come to support him. The balletomanes are priggish, but the music students affect a more rebellious manner: on the way up the stairs one of them is heard to yell 'Down with tyrants'. The young composer Julian Craster (Marius Goring), enraged to discover that his professor has stolen some of his ideas, pushes his way out of the gallery, intent on a confrontation.

So far, the theatre's different areas have been established in a manner common to the backstage genre, but they have also been associated with distinct artistic and social ambitions, setting up the tensions that will be developed subsequently: Lermontov's imperious reticence; Julian's bumptiousness as a young genius; the diligent professionalism of the performers; the social ambitions of Vicky's aunt; and, of course, as a focus for all this, the image of the girl herself, as yet only a wondering, engrossed spectator. Soon we discover that she is also committed and determined. At the reception Lermontov learns about the proposed show of Vicky's dancing and makes clear his feelings about the unwarranted crossing of boundaries: 'If I accept an invitation

I do not expect to find myself at an audition.' Vicky has meanwhile been told by her aunt that there will no longer be an exhibition of her dancing. Presently she finds herself beside Lermontov. Not knowing who she is, he comments 'now I understand we're to be spared that horror'.[36] For him, dance is 'a religion' which, he has told Lady Neston, should not be 'practised in an atmosphere such as this'. Vicky's gentle but firm admission that she was to be that 'horror' non-plusses him for a moment. The occasion furnishes an insight into the girl's mind that no display of talent could give, when she answers his question 'Why do you want to dance?' with one of her own, 'Why do you want to live?' Soon she is at the stage door, braving the traditional hostility towards outsiders and observing the ease with which those already on the inside are accepted. She discovers that she is merely one of several hopefuls who have been summoned to the theatre. When the company leaves for Paris, she is one of the few who are chosen to stay with it.

In a parallel strand of the plot, Julian is making his way through the same kind of obstacles, his aggressive self-regard contrasting with her winning naïveté and determination. He has come to Lermontov's mansion-block apartment, intending to retrieve the letter he has written protesting about the plagiarism. Lermontov has read it, but sets this aside suavely, asking him to play something of his own. Julian responds enthusiastically but stops playing when he realizes that Lermontov is busy with his breakfast. He begins to make a rude and hasty exit, but is stopped in his tracks by the offer of employment. Lermontov goes to the Mercury Theatre to watch Vicky dancing in Marie Rambert's company, and Vicky sees him as she pirouettes. The shot is a technical tour de force that, like many of Powell and Pressburger's effects, draws attention to its own artfulness. Theirs is not an art that conceals art, but then neither is that of the ballet as they depict it. As Vicky and Julian make their way into the world of dance, the camera asserts its ability to move into the dancers' subjectivity. Both the characters in the narrative and the film itself are crossing boundaries.

Vicky progresses from the tiny stage of the Mercury Theatre to Covent Garden, the Paris Opéra and ultimately the opera house in Monte Carlo. Along the way she receives important lessons, the first of which comes when, to Lermontov's disgust, the *prima ballerina* Boronskaya announces her marriage. The other dancers crowd round to congratulate her, but when she turns to find him, she discovers that the angry director has left the room. Later, as Vicky is in the wings about to go on stage in the *corps de ballet*, Lermontov remarks, clearly intending to be overheard, that 'the dancer who relies upon the doubtful comfort of human love will never be a great dancer – never'.

To Grischa's insistence that 'you can't alter human nature' he answers 'No? I think you can do something better than that, you can ignore it'. The mask-like makeup of the dancers emphasizes the alteration that inevitably does take place in 'human nature' in this world of art. (The effect will be repeated at critical moments.) Lermontov has already told Julian about the plan for a 'Red Shoes' ballet, so that Vicky's fate is being prepared without her realizing it. In his office, as he talks to Julian, Lermontov runs his hand over a cast or life-size marble carving of a dancer's ankle and foot in a pointe shoe, with the air of a Pygmalion whose craft reverses the usual transformation of marble to flesh. His business makes art from the human body, taking and giving life at one and the same time. As he outlines the plan for the ballet, the music that will become Julian's score is heard on the soundtrack, as though Lermontov were exercising his 'magic' inspirational powers on the composer.

Vicky's rise to stardom is represented hauntingly in a sequence where, dressed again as a fairy-tale princess, she is driven in a chauffeured limousine around the winding cliff-side roads to a villa where Lermontov is lodging during the Monte Carlo season. She then ascends a steep overgrown flight of steps up to the villa. In this celebrated series of shots the fairy-tale element of the film's main narrative is firmly asserted. The soundtrack music emphasizes the sense of fantasy as a gate slowly swings open as if she is to enter a magic kingdom, but she finds herself at a conference where a new ballet is being planned. No one is dressed formally, and she has not been admitted into the private life of Lermontov. Moreover, the all-important decisions have already been made, and Vicky is simply issued with an edict. Successive scenes show Vicky and Julian working hard, losing their temper with each other as she tries to fit her dancing to music he refuses to alter. The process brings them closer together, with the romantic consequences inevitable in more commonplace backstage films. Just before the performance Vicky has a last-minute attack of stage fright, but it is Lermontov who reassures her. As he hums the first bars of the music to which she will make her entrance, he adjusts the shoulder strap of her costume in a gesture that shows more tenderness than he permits himself anywhere else in the film, but also reasserts and reinforces his Svengali-like influence. Typically, Vicky's face seems open and vulnerable in close-up, while Lermontov's gaze is hard, narrow and mesmeric.

The cinema audience sees – as the theatre audience cannot – the imagination of the dancer. From a performance in itself barely conceivable on a theatre's stage the ballet shifts to a series of images and developing scenes that use filmic technique to represent the psychological state of the dancer rather than that of the character she is impersonating. Or perhaps this is Vicky Page as transformed by the character? The story of 'The Red Shoes' is told in a mixture of romantic fantasy and the kind of balletic realism represented by Helpmann's *Miracle in the Gorbals* (Sadler's Wells, 1944), in which a symbolic narrative centres on a figure identified as 'the Stranger' and unfolds in a stylized urban setting that – in the ballet world of the time – passed as 'realistic' and 'squalid' with choreography that, compared even with Kurt Jooss' *The Big City*, was 'brutally real'.[37]

When Vicky passes beyond the fantastic but identifiably theatrical stage setting into the even more extravagant realm of her own mind, we are shown the conductor (Julian) emerging from the orchestra pit to metamorphose into a male dancer. Throughout the sequence the few shots establishing the auditorium show a stylized rendering in grisaille, so that when it turns into a tempestuous seascape with waves breaking against the 'stage' space there is no violent contradiction between the two scenic realms. After the extended fantasy scenes of the girl's journey through what is at first a carnivalesque town but soon becomes a city of dreadful night, there is a brief episode in which Vicky dashes into the wings to make her costume change. Otherwise, even when it might be expected that the action could be played in a theatre, there are trick effects possible only on film, such as the image of the red shoes on a dancer in the shop window, the 'magical' placing of them on the girl's feet (the ribbons tie themselves) and, in the final section, the transformation of a knife into a branch of foliage and back again. Scenic transitions within the stage performance, including that from the shoemaker's shop to the front cloth representing it, are elided in a manner impossible on this stage.

Because what we see in the ballet is Vicky dancing in her mind, we are admitted to an enhanced private world within the public performance, not accessible to any of those in the theatre and not so much a backstage view as one from beyond the stage. In the original storyboard, there would have been a moment when the shoemaker leapt through a brick wall. In the words of the synopsis – possibly derived from an earlier draft or rough cut – included with the continuity script, the image 'grows vaguer and becomes a broken wall, the wall between her and her subconscious'.

> She dances through the wall into a dream world of fantastic shapes and sounds. It is the recapitulation of her life. Ambitions, loves and hatred; fears, triumphs and failures; beauty and ugliness; envy and generosity,

all take some living form before her eyes and are personified by the same dancers, the shoemaker and the lover.[38]

The synopsis identifies the grotesque apparitions that menace her as 'The Dead City of Failure' and 'the Monsters of Malice and Envy'. But who is 'she' in this account, or for that matter in the sequence as edited and shown? If this is Vicky's subconscious, how has it come to be in this state? Powell and Pressburger are creating a psychological gloss on their version of Andersen's story that connects with their heroine only on a superficial level – she has been ambitious and has endured some relatively minor hardships and uncertainties, but so far she has not had to cope with any real setbacks or conflicts in private or professional life.

Perhaps the ballet is really about Lermontov, who has waited for a dancer to wear the red shoes, but he would seem to be represented more obviously by the shoemaker than the girl herself. The whole conception of the ballet is attributed to him, and he already has a set design and a score – discarded in favour of Julian's – before he broaches the idea of entrusting it to Vicky and Julian. Vicky's performance, however, contravenes the artist's personal life as defined by her master, in which the only acceptable privacy is that required for the creation of art, to the exclusion of commonplace notions of the private sphere reserved for love. In dismissing the very idea of 'a dancer who relies upon the doubtful comforts of human love', Lermontov seems to assert the superhuman (and religious) dimension of the art that is his passion.

He is a solitary eminence. No one has invited him to the company's party in honour of Grischa's birthday, and when he arrives at the waterfront restaurant he remarks that it 'seems a long time since I sat down to supper with my entire family'. Unfortunately this leads to his discovery that Vicky and Julian have left the party already, and his sense of betrayal is manifest. He sees his dancers as raw material that should be entirely at his disposal: 'I want to create – to make something big out of something little.' Vicky compounds the offence of lèse-majesté by responding as she dances to Julian's presence in the pit as conductor: 'She was dreaming – and dreaming is a luxury I've never allowed in my company.' (At least, not on stage or by his dancers: he is the one to do the dreaming.) In his eyes, though not those of his colleagues, Vicky has regressed to the status she had at her aunt's reception, dancing 'like a debutante at a charity matinée'. Pygmalion ('I could make you one of the greatest dancers the world has ever known') is betrayed by his Galatea, and Julian does not help by pettishly dismissing ballet as 'a second rate means of expression' in a confrontation with Lermontov.

The final sequence, when Vicky, having returned to Monte Carlo,

12. *The Red Shoes* (1948): Vicky between Julian and Lermontov (production still)

has responded to Lermontov's plea – 'Put on the red shoes, Vicky, and dance for us again' – lurches into melodrama. In her dressing room she hears the radio announcement from Covent Garden that Julian has not been able to conduct the premiere of his new opera. Deserting his post, he has rushed to Monte Carlo, not to support but to reproach her: she has been unfaithful to him and returned to her other love, which can be defined as ballet in the person of Lermontov. On her dressing table a double photo frame holds a photograph of Julian and a caricature of Lermontov. Now, as she sits at her dressing table, the two men face each other across her, confining her by the force of their opposing wills (Figure 12). The catastrophe is precipitated by this trite 'women's picture' situation ('Nobody can have two lives and your life is dancing') in which only the woman can lose and the woman can only lose. A cruelly unflattering close-up from a high angle emphasizes the heavy makeup on Vicky's face as she declares 'I love you Julian'. This is to no avail: she will still go on in the ballet, and Julian storms out to catch the express back to Paris.

Vicky sets off for the stage, but suddenly it seems that the red shoes are taking possession of her feet. She dashes down the corridor towards the French windows that open onto the terrace and hurtles down the steps outside the theatre towards the balustrade overlooking the railway station. She flings herself onto the tracks before the arriving train in a moment that combines ballet technique with a trick of editing. The synopsis quoted above suggests that she overbalances, but in the film the leap is no accident. Is Vicky's subconscious telling her she is on stage? In a final gesture of love and contrition, Julian unties the ribbons of her red shoes and places his cheek against her leg: the moment suggests Prince Albrecht placing lilies on the grave of Giselle – a scene not shown in the film, although we do see Helpmann partnering Shearer in a brief sequence from the ballet's second act. This is the ballet in which the tragic death of a thoughtless but repentant young man is averted by the intercession of a beautiful (and dead) young woman. As McLean points out, given the examples of Giselle and her other tragic roles, Odette and the Sylphide, Vicky's death seems preordained by the fictions enacted in her chosen vocation: 'She is doomed merely because she is a ballerina.'[39]

The presentation of the relationship between art, love and death is powerful but incoherent. If the red shoes are taking control of Vicky, are they doing so to punish her, to bring her back to Julian, or simply to provide the occasion for a neatly symbolic final scene? Vicky's guilt seems minimal compared to that of Julian (the selfish genius) or Lermontov (the obsessive Pygmalion). Her admission to the ballet was secured when she answered Lermontov's question with 'Why do you want to live?' but in the end that also prepared for her death. A perverse romantic sentimentality haunts much of the work of Powell and Pressburger, alongside the simultaneous cultivation of eroticism and admonition. There is a strong sense of a creative patriarchy at work, simultaneously exploiting and punishing the woman as an erotic object without whom its artistic goals cannot be attained. Both the sexual politics of *The Red Shoes* and its attitude to the theatre are at once questionable and hard to fathom. The film anchors its fantasies as well as its romantic realism in what is in fact a partial understanding of the 'real life' of the theatrical world. It skimps on information about the collaborative creative processes – a scene showing the designer and choreographer discussing plans at a café table was shot but eventually cut – and we see only glimpses of the rehearsals and the choreographer's working practices.[40] All is subordinated to the proposition that wanting to dance just as others might want to live is likely to be achieved at too great a price. Art is celebrated and at the same time surrounded with warning placards. Moreover, as McLean observes, the film is one of the 'long line' of British and American films 'in which ballet is linked with excess and deviance, disaster and doom, as well as beauty and glamour'.[41]

Comparison with *Black Swan* (2010), the latest in this not always distinguished catalogue, suggests how powerful and effective *The Red Shoes* remains as an expression of the danger and glamour of the art. In *Black Swan* the ballet company's artistic director tells his ballerina 'I have to see you lose yourself' if she is to be able to perform both Odette and Odile in *Swan Lake*. Undaunted by the fact that even in the fraught world of ballet this has not so far involved a fight to the death between ballerinas in a dressing room, the film labours through the emoting of the leading actress (Natalie Portman) towards a conclusion in which on-stage hallucination (she seems to sprout the wings of the black swan) leads to backstage death. Bleeding from a wound inflicted by a shard of glass embedded in the white tutu, she falls as planned onto a mattress then, as colleagues crowd round with their congratulations on the performance of a lifetime, she is discovered to be *in extremis*, the final shot being the stage lights seen from her point of view. For all its horror-film trappings and the pains taken by the makers to achieve a mixture of fantasy and pseudo-documentary elements, *Black Swan* signals its heroine's – and its own – frail hold on reality from the first moments, with a prologue that takes the audience directly into the dancer's nightmare of being possessed by the ballet's evil sorcerer Rothbart.

The Red Shoes is effectively a murder mystery, with the ballet and theatre as the joint culprits. Grounded in the imperatives of performance and production but at the same time romantic and with the darkness of the fairy tale fully achieved, it has a range of imagination far beyond that of the 2010 would-be shocker – rated 'R' in the USA for 'strong sexual content, disturbing violent images, language and some drug use'. The retributive fable in *The Red Shoes* arises from sources beyond the troubled psyche of an individual dancer; its implicit sexual politics are more disturbing than the banal sexism of the artistic director in *Black Swan* who asks a dancer whether he would want to fuck (his word) the young ballerina he is partnering – a rebuke to her for holding back on the eroticism. The visions of the 'Red Shoes' ballet range further than those resulting from the choreographer's desire to 'strip [*Swan Lake*] down – make it visceral – and real'. The theatrical world in *The Red Shoes* is equivocal and threatening, while that in the newer film fits all too easily into the horror genre its makers wanted to fuse with documentary. Powell and Pressburger let *angst* insinuate itself, while the makers of the recent film push it in the audience's face. The exchange 'Why do you want to dance? – Why do you want to live?' is a more potent expression of the imperatives and mystery of performance than 'I have to see you lose yourself'.

Theatre and the haunted childhood:
Bergman's *Fanny and Alexander*

Although it is more stylish and intelligent than *Black Swan*, *The Red Shoes* is nevertheless a lurid warning to the stage-struck. Ingmar Bergman's cinematic dealings with the theatre summon up some of the same familiar demons, but with a sense that they are ultimately beneficial elements of the healthy artistic imagination. Alexander in

Fanny and Alexander is his most fully developed and directly autobiographical representative of the theatrical visionary.

Between 1945 and 2003, Bergman directed some fifty feature-length films. Together with a rich and varied theatrical career, several television scripts and autobiographical writings, these constitute a lifelong meditation on a large number of interrelated themes, in which personal experiences and anxieties are mediated through a variety of filmic, theatrical and literary genres. Late in his career, after his farewell to directing for the cinema, he published works that are half-novel, half-screenplay, and which move in and out of autobiography, with Bergman occasionally speaking directly to the reader to comment on the shifts as he makes them. *The Best Intentions* (1989) and *Sunday's Children* (1993) complement his memoirs *The Magic Lantern* (1987) and *Images* (1990) as accounts of his career and, in the case of the novels, childhood, although none of them is a formal, chronologically organized autobiography. The recurring images, symbols, narrative patterns, character names and even casting of actors in Bergman's films, and the weaving in and out of them of identifiable autobiographical elements, invite critics to arrange them as if they were pieces of a jigsaw puzzle that when assembled correctly would produce a single, unified image or system. But the life and works resist this. As Irving Singer points out in *Ingmar Bergman, Cinematic Philosopher*, the director creates philosophically but does not build a system or method that can be identified as such. Singer observes that, in his TV film of *The Magic Flute* (*Trollflöjten*, 1974), 'Bergman's basic approach ... emanates, as in all his movies, from themes out of his own life whose realistic details he transmutes into strands of imagination that become fictional entities comprehensible through his art'.[42]

The multifarious influences on Bergman's work include cinema, in particular the pioneering work of the directors Carl Theodor Dreyer, Victor Sjøstrom and Mauritz Stiller, and a variety of literary and dramatic works. He repeatedly stressed the importance of music in his creative life, making eloquent use of it in several films. Throughout a theatrical career that encompassed an extraordinary range of playwrights and genres, including notable productions of Shakespeare, Molière and Ibsen, he engaged in a continuing dialogue with the plays of August Strindberg. Bergman returned repeatedly to the relentless analysis of mutually destructive marital relationships in such plays as *The Dance of Death* and *The Father*, and the visionary, symbolist mode of *The Ghost Sonata* and *A Dream Play*. Shifts of perspective in his films move us back and forth between 'visions' and meticulously rendered realistic domestic detail, and are often shocking and sometimes lyrical. In cinematic terms, an influential example was set by Sjøstrom's *The Phantom Carriage* (1921), with its combination of social realism and the supernatural. Among literary influences, E.T.A. Hoffmann was acknowledged by Bergman as an important source of inspiration.[43]

There are traces of Hoffmann in Bergman's films when there is no specific theatrical context, for example in *Wild Strawberries* (1957), *Through a Glass Darkly* (1961) and *Cries and Whispers* (1973). When a theatrical dimension figures in the narrative, the Hoffmannesque seems to be developed more fully. In *Hour of the Wolf* (1968) the leading character's visionary ordeal at the hands of his 'demons' is ushered in by a toy-theatre performance in which the tiny figure of Tamino in *The Magic Flute* is apparently a 'real' actor uncannily miniaturized. When the theatre is central to the plot's *heimlich* mundane reality, its potential as a vehicle for the unreal is – as might be expected – even more fully exploited. In *Summer Interlude* (1951) the theatrical life of the central character, a ballerina, frames the flashbacks to a summer love affair that culminated in tragedy. The film's final sequence marks her return to happiness (or the possibility of achieving it) by way of a dressing-room scene in which her scrutiny of her made-up face and the advice of a grotesque figure – the ballet master in his get-up as Dr Coppélius – bring her to a new understanding and the release from the melancholy that threatens to overwhelm her. *The Seventh Seal* (1957) and *The Magician* (1958) play on the potential for both sinister and comic effect in theatrical performance, the former as a grimmer allegory in which Death appears, in more human form than the conventional skull mask from medieval theatre. Typically for Bergman, these early films play on the boundaries between generic distinctions, using cinematic magic and sleight of hand to direct and deceive the spectator. In *The Magician* – whose Swedish title, *Ansiktet*, translates as *The Face* – the tricks by which the mesmerist and illusionist Dr Vogler terrorizes his enemy, the aggressively rationalistic Dr Vergérus, are only just credible as within the powers of a magician who works without the technical resources of the cinema – except for its precursor, the magic lantern. The comic evocation of small-town life in *The Magician* is balanced by a hint that the seemingly macabre may well be either an illusion or a reality.

Among Bergman's darker works, including the so-called 'chamber' films tightly focussed on the mental and spiritual life of a small group of characters, *Persona* (1966) stands out as an exploration of the kind of divided and conflicted personality that might be attracted to or intensified by the theatre. (Oddly, none of Bergman's translated writings refer to Jung.) The actress Elisabet Vogler (Liv Ullmann) is recovering from a breakdown during a performance in *Electra*, and her emergence from her abject mental state is accomplished – or possibly compromised – by the merging of her personality with that of the apparently commonsensical nurse (Harriet Andersson) in whose charge she is placed. Dream sequences, reveries or flashbacks are frequent in the films. Both *Summer Interlude* and *Sawdust and Tinsel* (1953), set in a context of ballet and circus respectively, employ flashbacks. Near the opening of the latter a flashback, rendered with the jerky action and flickering degraded film stock associated with silent comedy, illustrates the story of the clown's humiliation when his wife paraded herself naked in front of a company of artillerymen. At the end of the film the circus leaves town and the show must go on, but there is no triumph in this resolution, and it seems like a depressive counterpart to the optimism of the final sequence of *The Seventh Seal*, in which the little family of players have been spared for the time being from joining in the dance of death, and we see their wagon begin to trundle on to the next stage of their journey.

Bergman's engagement with the theatre forms a major part of the imaginative world of his characters and contributes significantly to the way of seeing proposed through images created in the comedy *Smiles of a Summer Night* (1955). Compared with the films discussed above, this is effectively a holiday from the darkness of vision with which the director habitually responds to questions of identity and its metaphysical and psychological dimensions. In retrospect (for example, in *Images*) Bergman refused to regard it as one of his major works: he appeared embarrassed by the international success of this accessible movie. The narrative is delivered without flashbacks or visionary sequences in clear linear progression and with strictly observed classic continuity. Although such episodes as the drinking of the 'magically' fortified wine at dinner and the folkloric theme of the 'smiles' evoked in the summer night itself suggest a less down-to-earth perspective, the milieu remains firmly fixed in the convincingly realized worlds of the small town and the country house. The actress Desirée Armfeldt effectively directs the comedy in which her erstwhile lover, his son and wife and an absurd martinet and his restive partner come to what will pass – in the final analysis – as their senses. The theatre, in particular as represented by Desirée Armfeldt, functions as a pervasive metaphor for life and the identification and performance of the self. It does so without solemnity, but with full consciousness that a comic sense of fulfilment always exists in defiance of a serious if not tragic alternative.

Fanny and Alexander, announced prematurely as the director's farewell to the cinema, engages with the theatre in different but related ways, with an emphasis on the child's vision of the grown-up world that interested him increasingly towards the end of his career. 'Even in those days', he writes of his childhood self in *Sunday's Children*, 'I had difficulties with reality, its limits unclear and dictated by adult outsiders. I saw and heard: yes, indeed, that's dangerous, that's not dangerous'.[44] Childhood was no matter of comfortable nostalgia to Bergman, but the gifted child's ability to see visions, combined with a sense of what the theatre can achieve and foster, appears as a key element in his engagement with the two media that dominated his life. *Fanny and Alexander*, Bergman's most explicitly theatrical film, apart from his TV version of the *Magic Flute* and the TV play *After The Rehearsal* (1984), revisits his childhood in an imaginative construction that is partly autobiography, partly ghost story and wholly theatrical in context. A five-hour version was made for TV and edited for theatrical release to a running time of 2 hours 45 minutes, the fuller version being divided into a prologue, a series of acts and an epilogue.[45]

The storyline is simple: the widow of the actor-manager Oscar Ekdahl seeks love and security in marriage to the Bishop of the diocese, and takes the children, Fanny and her elder brother Alexander, to live in the Bishop's place. The Bishop's cruelty to the children and the oppressive atmosphere of his household dismay her, but she seems trapped and it is only through the intervention of a family friend, the Jewish antique dealer Isak, that the children are rescued. This is achieved by the apparently supernatural powers of Isak's nephew Ismael, who helps Alexander to will the destruction of the Bishop in a fire. The narrative is framed by a prologue and an epilogue, within which it is also bracketed by two feasts: the Ekdahls' Christmas party and the christening of two children. One of these is the daughter of a servant who has been made pregnant by Alexander's uncle Gustav Adolf, the other is Emilie's child by the late Bishop. Within this 'family saga' framework Bergman unfolds the increasingly fraught visions of the young Alexander, who seems to have the faculty of one of 'Sunday's children' (the title of the later novel) to see the spirit world – or who may be no more than an imaginative artist and daydreamer, both honourable occupations in the Bergman view of the world.

Bergman denied that the film was autobiographical, and it is set some twenty years before 1918, the year of his birth, but both incidental details and some larger elements of the plot, in particular the religiously motivated cruelty of a (step)father, can be identified as reflections of his life. In particular, a leading motif is the magic lantern which Alexander receives as a Christmas present, much as the

13. *Fanny and Alexander*
(1982): Alexander gazes
across his toy stage

young Bergman acquired a primitive film projector. It seems as though
retrospective wish-fulfilment makes Alexander's father an actor and
theatre manager (the artist Bergman might wish had engendered him)
while the stepfather takes responsibility for the spiritual oppression and
physical punishment Bergman endured at the hands of his clergyman
father. Although the film ends before Alexander's formal career as an
artist begins, the audience is aware that it has seen an account of the
artistic temperament informed by childhood experiences. Although
there is no evidence of direct influence, the narrative of a critical
period in the boy's moral, spiritual and imaginative development
corresponds in some respects with that of another son of a Lutheran
pastor, C.G. Jung, whose *Memories, Dreams, Reflections* was first
published in 1961. Bergman's film shares with Jung's book the child's
sense of living simultaneously in two worlds, and the difficulty of
understanding the concept of God in relation to experience and the
opinions and precepts pronounced by adults. Some of Alexander's
visions, notably the appearance of an outsize puppet he at first takes
for the authentic image of God, resonate with Jung's experiences.

Throughout the film, visions and tableaux embody the theatricalized imagination. In the opening shot the camera tilts down from
the inscription above the proscenium arch of a toy theatre, 'Not For
Joy Alone' ('Ei Blot Tyl List'), to the face of a boy (Alexander Ekdahl)
peering across the stage where scenery and characters for a romantic
play are set up (Figure 13). Subsequent episodes include performances
and rehearsals in the theatre owned by the Ekdahl clan. Acting and the
adoption of a persona recur as symbols for the experience of life itself,
while the first sight of the town's theatre, with the cathedral spires
looming behind it, suggests the opposition between religion and the
theatre. In the event, the two realms are not as mutually exclusive as
they may seem: role-playing, the working-out of emotional crises and
a carefully contrived aesthetic (even down to furnishings) characterize

both the Bishop's palace and the Ekdahl apartments. Once again, the theatre represents a liminal space, in which the real and unreal (or apparently unreal) collide and change places. In this it provides an analogy for both seemingly opposed households. The sense of the stage itself as being halfway between two realities, backstage dowdiness and front-of-house bourgeois comfort, also corresponds to the film medium's more fluid ability to move through a real world or shift the viewer into one of dream, reverie and remembrance. Laura Hubner, in an analysis of the film and its relationship with earlier, more astringent treatments of identity by Bergman, describes the manner in which its 'fluidity' in advocating 'a sense of life as a series of illusions' contrasts with the 'binary oppositions of good and evil' represented by the Ekdahls and the Bishop and his household.[46]

In *The Magic Lantern*, Bergman describes an early experience of the backstage world, during a performance of Strindberg's *A Dream Play*. This was the first time he had encountered 'the magic of acting', and he was particularly struck by the moment when the actor playing the Advocate held up a hairpin: 'There was no hairpin, but I saw it.' He also witnessed a moment of transformation of the kind that is commonplace during a performance.

> The Officer was backstage waiting for his entrance, leaning forward looking at his shoes, his hands behind his back. He cleared his throat soundlessly, a perfect ordinary person. Then he opened the door and stepped into the limelight. He was changed, transformed: he *was* the Officer.[47]

The resonance of both epiphanies can be felt throughout Bergman's films: the imagining of scenes or objects that are not really present, and the moment in which a person steps across a threshold – real or imagined – to take on another's identity. In a production of Strindberg's play at the Dramaten in 1970, Bergman sought to reproduce a sensation he recalled from his childhood:

> The front room, achieved by extending the stage, opened on to a magical back room. As a child, I had often stood in the dark dining room at home, peeping into the salon through the half-open sliding doors. The sun lit up furniture and objects, glittered in the chandelier and cast moving shadows on to the carpet. Everything was green, as in an aquarium. Inside people moved, disappeared, reappeared, stood quite still and spoke in low voices. The flowers in the window glowed, the clocks ticked and struck, a magical room.[48]

The vision is recalled in the prologue of *Fanny and Alexander*. This is not the first of Bergman's films to evoke this experience of distanced spectatorship. Commenting on his work with the cameraman Sven Nykvist for *Cries and Whispers*, Bergman describes 'an idea that was new and seductive: the motionless camera':

> I decided I would place the camera in one particular position in the room, and it would only be allowed to take one step forward or one step back. It would be the characters who would have to move in relation to the lens. ... It should remain coldly objective even when the action was moving toward emotional heights.[49]

After several attempts at a solution to the problems this created 'the whole thing became too complicated and [they] finally gave up on it', but the strategic use of stillness and distance on the camera's part remained an element of the techniques adopted by cinematographer and director.

In *Fanny and Alexander* similar camera placements are frequent, punctuating sequences of shots and sometimes bracketing entire scenes with tableaux that suggest the relationship of an audience (the camera) to a stage (the space occupied by the action). The opening shot of Alexander peering towards the camera through the framing proscenium of his toy theatre announces this recurring device by way of a close-up that positions him as a 'director' (of the toy stage) and as both spectator in the film and object of our spectatorship. He is looking directly at the camera lens, a gaze Bergman frequently allows his actors. This is followed by his exploration of his grandmother's apartment, access to which is gained through a 'secret' door in the party wall shared with his parents' rooms. They are modern, light and airy: his grandmother's has dark red walls and its furnishings are darker and old-fashioned. Alexander explores the bedroom and – in the TV version – the lavatory, where he sits on the 'throne' and declaims as if playing a king, until the sound of a rat being caught in a trap distracts him. Finally he settles under a table, from which he looks towards another room where the light gradually changes and a white marble statue seems to move its arm. The only sounds, magnified as if from his aural perspective are the ticking of a clock and his breathing. A clock's chimes are synchronized with the movement of gilded figurines, the chandelier's crystals seem to be moved by a current of air, and in the TV version he hears the scraping of a scythe across the carpet and glimpses Death as he approaches the statue. The spell is broken by the sound of coal being shot into a stove by one of the maids. The camera holds the boy's point of view as his grandmother, Helena Ekdahl, comes in and sees him under the table. Expressing no surprise, she greets him, walks into the next room and asks 'Would you like to play cards before dinner?' In a film where others will chastize him for his indulgence in imaginative reverie, Helena, formerly an actress, understands.

This is the first of several scenes in which an enhancement or partial transformation of reality is accompanied by shift in spatial perspective, the distant camera placement often emphasized by the sliding doors between rooms that frame the half-distant and magical scene. These shots commonly correspond to Alexander's point of view as the film's leading visionary but, as will be seen, there are other occasions when the camera adopts this kind of perspective without his participation. The list of such scenes is a long one, and for present purposes it is sufficient to note the range of effects. In the prologue, when the enfilade of his grandmother's rooms is seen from the point of view of Alexander, crouching under the table, the hangings at each doorway (where the sliding doors have presumably been drawn back) suggest a series of proscenium arches. In the second part, woken in the night by howls of grief, the children move through the apartment's rooms towards the bedroom. There, again as if through a proscenium partially closed in by doors open only in the centre, they see their father's body laid out on the bed as their mother paces across in and out of this theatrical frame within the film's frame. Her cries are 'noises off' at first, uttered after she reaches the 'wings' of this theatre. (The sequence echoes the earlier scene of Alexander's magic-lantern show in which he provided the 'Oh's of the terrified 'Beautiful Arabella' haunted by her mother's ghost.)

Such glimpses of real or unreal visions are private counterparts of the carefully composed tableaux attendant on death and marriage. These are sights Alexander finds repugnant and does not wish to witness. He tries to hide himself from the sight of his dying father; holds back from the assemblage of mourning actors around the body lying in state; and breaks away from the ceremony in which his mother marries the Bishop. The staging of such events is made explicit: people compose tableaux for them, much as they assemble round the head of the household reading from the Christmas gospel story or group themselves for a photograph. (The first of these is seen by us almost as if it were a nineteenth-century genre painting, the second more directly as a photo, which fades from colour into black and white.) Sometimes the tableau effect is especially pronounced, with the camera in a position that could not be occupied by anyone in or near the room. When the camera discovers Helena dozing in the sunlit room of the summer house at the opening of the TV version's third part – after shots of the coastline and the rain pouring on the garden – she is framed in a long shot composed as if the room were on a small stage viewed from an auditorium. Here the set was on a platform raised from the studio floor, achieving a distancing not possible with 'break-away' walls normally used to give the camera access.[50] Whereas the visions associated with the Ekdahl homes, in town and country, are occasionally disturbing but predominantly benign, those experienced in the Bishop's palace and Isak's curiosity shop are more sinister, and they are not 'framed' as tableaux in the same manner.

At a press conference in 1980 Bergman described the film as 'a huge tapestry filled with masses of colour and people, houses and forests, mysterious haunts of caves and grottoes, secrets and nights skies'. This evocation of the fairy-tale dimension is in part metaphorical – there are no actual forests, caves or grottoes – but it reflects the suggestive quality of the film.[51] In *Images* Dickens and E.T.A. Hoffmann are identified as its 'godfathers'. Specific elements of the narrative are attributed to Dickens: 'the bishop and his home, the Jew in his boutique of fantasies, the children as victims; the contrast between flourishing outside life and a closed world in black and white'.[52] The debt to Hoffmann is acknowledged as the product of Bergman's plans in the 1970s for a production of Offenbach's *The Tales of Hoffmann*, but, as has been noted, the German author's influence seems to go further in his work. Such characters as Nathaniel in *Der Sandmann* embody the kind of confusion that makes Bergman's Alexander a visionary when viewed from one perspective and a liar from another. To spiritual authorities like the Bishop, such persons are more than a threat to proper family discipline: they challenge his authority more deeply.

Compared to the Ekdahl apartments the Bishop's palace is bleak – Bergman recalled that when the unit first moved into the set he remarked 'Now I feel as though I'm in a Bergman film'. – but for all the thunder and lightening outside the windows it is not a place of threatening shadows.[53] Until Alexander is locked in the attic after his beating, there is no sign of haunting and apparitions. The image of Emilie sitting in the window embrasure while the Bishop plays his flute, seen at first as a tableau with the children sleeping on a chair in the foreground, identifies the couple's union in aesthetic terms. The soigné asceticism of the Bishop's dress and manners contrasts with the more threatening appearance of his sister and mother. The servants, including the 'rat-like' cook and the treacherous maid Justina are more identifiably 'gothic', but the Bishop is not like Mr Murdstone, the grim stepfather of David Copperfield. He delights in music, smokes a pipe and has an impressive library. There is an implicit suggestion that his attraction for Emilie is strongly sexual, and the scenes immediately before the catastrophe are reminiscent of the anguish and the mutual attraction and destructiveness of the couple in *Scenes from a Marriage* (1973).

However, the spaciousness and light of the Bishop's palace belie the oppression it supports. The sister and mother and Justina – named perhaps with a glance towards de Sade – are the prevailing spirits of the house. Or perhaps they are its demons, for like all of Bergman's clergy (and not a few of his laity), the Bishop has demons, spiritual terrors that lurk in wait for him and impulses that can betray him. At his most triumphant, especially in the scene of negotiations with Emilie's brothers-in-law, he can pass himself off as an imperturbably smiling controller of circumstances. But earlier, after Justina has told him about Alexander's fantasy concerning his dead wife and children, he is seen in a moment of private despair, prompted perhaps by the realization that the boy is beyond his influence. When Isak arrives with his offer of money for a chest and performs the trick that enables him to abduct Fanny and Alexander by hiding them in it, the Bishop loses his composure for the first time. He at first maintains a calm, almost affable demeanour, but suddenly seizes Isak, insults him in violently anti-Semitic terms, flings him to the ground and rushes upstairs. It is at this point that Isak's moment of 'magic' takes place. The Bishop and his sister burst into the nursery to find the children apparently lying on the floor, and as he takes a step towards them Emilie, wraith-like and threatening, forbids him to touch them. In the hallway, Isak, who has been shattered by the effort that has produced this illusion, gathers himself together and has his workmen remove the trunk in which the children are hidden. The film offers no explanation for this: the image of the children is seen by both the Bishop and his sister and is shown by an 'objective' camera, rather than from the bishop's point of view. Isak seems to exercise the kind of power which will later be associated with the sequestered and dangerous Ismael, a more sinister figure than his other nephew, the puppet-maker Aron. Jesse Kalin, in his 2003 study *The Films of Ingmar Bergman*, suggests that the inexplicable nature of the rescue makes it part of the film's pattern of story-telling, and that acceptance of it by the audience affirms the narrative's affinity with fairy tale: belief in what (morally) should rather than what (literally) can happen.[54]

It is in Isak's old curiosity shop that Alexander encounters a truly weird and perplexing environment, crowded with sinister and grotesque images: there are life-size nodding oriental figures in the dark passageways, as well as the puppet theatre and the mysteriously animated 'mummy' – perhaps with a glance at Strindberg's *The Ghost*

Sonata – that he is shown before his visit to Ismael. After their meal, the rescued children are installed in a bedroom whose walls are painted a vivid red, the colour used in *Cries and Whispers* as part of the director's personal imagery of the unconscious. There, as Isak reads to him from a book of ancient allegorical lore, Alexander imagines a complex scene of religious extremism (seen only in the TV version) with a procession of flagellants, Justina exhibiting her stigmata, Death with his scythe and (glimpsed briefly) a couple out of the *commedia dell'arte*. In the climax of the vision he sees his mother, who offers him a bowl of cooling water as Isak looks on. (The sequence is dangerously like a parodic assemblage of Bergman motifs.) At least a day seems to elapse before the subsequent night scene at Isak's house. Alexander wakes up and, failing to find a chamber pot, goes in search of a lavatory. Eventually he compromises, and urinates into a potted plant.

Like his grandmother's apartment with its damasked walls and the 'moving' statue, Isak's is a transforming and transformational space. In this respect it shares some of the qualities associated with the theatre. It is here that Alexander has his most matter-of-fact conversation with his father's ghost, who admits he has not had an opportunity to confront God with Alexander's pressing questions. At this point Alexander hears a door-handle being rattled, and a voice behind the partition claims to be that of God. Alexander cowers under a table, genuinely scared, as the apparition makes itself manifest, first a huge sandaled foot, then the whole of what turns out to be a bearded puppet, which almost immediately collapses in a heap on the floor. Aron appears, explains that he has made this puppet to order for a theatre in England and taunts the boy with having been frightened. Alexander strikes him, but Aron brushes this attack off, and presently they are in his workshop, drinking coffee.

This apparition is an illusionist's trick, abetted by the boy's propensity for imagining such things, but it is followed by the genuine mystery of the mummy. Aron does not reveal whatever makes this figure breathe, glow and turn its head towards Alexander and the camera. Instead, he describes an incident which places his family (presumably that of his father, Isak's brother) in a theatrical context reminiscent of Vogler and his assistants in *The Magician*:

> Anything unintelligible makes people angry. It's much better to blame the apparatus and the mirrors and the projections. The people start laughing and that's healthier from all points of view – particularly the financial one. My father and mother ran a conjuror's theatre in Petersburg. That's why I know what I'm talking about. One evening, in the middle of

the performance, a real ghost appeared, an aunt of my father's. She had died two days earlier. The ghost lost her way among the machines and the projectors. It was a fiasco and Papa had to refund the admission.[55]

The anecdote also connects with the magic lantern owned by Alexander, as well as that employed by the illusionist and hypnotist of the earlier film. Alexander is in the same business as Aron.

Ismael is locked behind a set of doors and an inner cage in a room which the children have been warned not to try to enter. They are also told not to be alarmed if they hear the sound of his singing during the night. The danger represented by this androgynous youth – played in the film by an actress speaking with a Finnish-inflected dialect – takes the uncanny a stage further. Whereas Alexander and his sister might try without avail to destroy the Bishop simply by thinking hard about him ('Die, you devil!') Ismael can carry Alexander's vision into the realm of action, partly by a laying on of hands, partly by a form of mind-reading. What he claims Alexander imagines is in fact true, though it is couched in quasi-Biblical language ('The doors are thrown open' and the burning, screaming figure is seen), but the most frightening aspect of all this is the notion that Alexander has somehow fused with Ismael, who is speaking his thoughts. Absorption of one person by another may hark back to *Persona*, and the relationship between the actress Elisabet Vogler and her nurse, but here it seems like an extreme version of a magician's act, as though Ismael may have to be restrained because the magic is all too real. Recalling his work on the initial screenplay, Bergman commented 'It is dangerous to invoke the infernal powers ... [Ismael] is like a membrane that quivers with the slightest touch'.[56]

In the lavishly realized material world of *Fanny and Alexander*, lovingly recreated by the sets and costumes, the theatre is at first sight not especially mysterious. Bergman's published script describes it in great detail, leading the reader through all its backstage and front-of-house areas, and the film reproduces this meticulously. On the audience's side of the curtain all is spick and span, but behind the scenes the theatre is 'dirty, dusty and dilapidated'. Two performances are seen on the stage, together with two rehearsals. In the first, which follows the film's Prologue, the Ekdahl company performs its annual nativity play, a naïve production in rhymed verse and with stylized gestures, sets, makeup and costumes. Angels appear behind the tableau of Joseph, Mary and the child, and warn of Herod's wrath, Oscar Ekdahl as Joseph declares his intention take his family away from this danger, and everyone joins in a short hymn that ends with Emilie, the principal angel, wishing the audience Happy Christmas. After a single curtain call, the curtain descends. Backstage a buffet table is brought on and Oscar's brother Gustav Adolf, the theatre's restaurateur, carries in a flaming punch bowl at the head of the theatre's band, his staff and other members of the company. Now behind the curtain the on-stage Holy Family becomes once again the theatrical family.

The second play is *Hamlet*, in a rehearsal interrupted by the seizure that leads to Oscar's death. Alexander watches from beside the stage-manager's chair as his father declaims the Ghost's lines urging Hamlet to revenge. Just after 'But soft, methinks I scent the morning air', he goes to make his exit but falters and falls. Bewildered, as the actors crowd round him he asks Emilie what he was doing: 'You were acting – I was acting? Why was I acting?' On his deathbed he remarks that he will now be better as the ghost than he was when was alive – a prophecy his subsequent appearances bear out. (We later find that Emilie is all too aware of the Hamlet-like resentment her son bears towards her new husband. After their arrival at the Bishop's palace she warns him not to think of himself as Hamlet and of her and the Bishop as Gertrude and Claudius.)

At the beginning of the TV film's third part – but not in the cinema version – we see a performance of the final scene of *Twelfth Night*, with Feste's valedictory song. Both *Hamlet* and *Twelfth Night* present situations that rhyme with the off-stage life of the characters: Oscar's passage into death had begun as he rehearsed the ghost's insistence that his son should revenge his murder, and Emilie is cast as Olivia. Although she wears the vivid red of a character liberated from her grief by love, the patent falsity of her makeup and costume underline her detachment from the joy she is performing. After the play she announces to the company that she has lost her faith in the theatre – a statement that suggests the equivalence (and conflict) between theatrical and religious belief. She is ashamed of the comforting shelter the theatre affords ('We draw the theatre over us...'), contradicting a declaration made haltingly and movingly by Oscar in a speech at Christmas about the value of the 'little world'. The last on-stage scene is a brief episode of rehearsal. The dispirited actors are preparing a fusty melodrama set in the eighteenth century. Emilie, in mourning dress after the Bishop's death, arrives unexpectedly to announce that she is taking control of the theatre back from Gustav Adolf, whose inept management has run it down. All the performance sequences thus provide a setting for pivotal moments in the Ekdahl family's life. The film ends with the promise of another performance, in which Emilie and Helena will appear in *A Dream Play*: apart from any other consideration – a decisive step forward in the theatre's repertory – this will effectively bring into the theatre the other world of illusion that has been played out beyond its walls since she left the stage.

In this respect, in *Fanny and Alexander* the theatrical mysteries are more potent outside the building itself than within it. It is explicitly offered as a place of refuge in speeches by Oscar at the Christmas Eve party and Gustav Adolf at the christening feast in the final episode. Oscar's speech has a hesitancy that presages the tensions within the family that are already becoming apparent and the fragility of his own situation:

> My only talent, if you can call it a talent in my case, is that I love this little world inside the thick walls of this playhouse. ... Our theatre is a small room of orderliness, routine, conscientiousness, and love.[57]

Gustav Adolf's long speech pleads for the recognition of the 'little, little world' as a shelter from the threats that lie outside it, insists that the Ekdahls 'have not come into the world to see through it', and appeals to the actors: 'It is you who are to give us our supernatural shudders and still more our mundane amusements.'[58]

The image of the mask recurs in the film. Emilie confesses to the Bishop that she needs the spiritual certainty and stable identity he seems to offer her:

> I am an actress; I am used to wearing masks. My God wears a thousand masks. He has never shown me his real face, just as I am incapable of showing you or God my real face. Through you I shall learn to know God's being. Kiss me now and hold me in your arms, quite still, as only you can, my darling.[59]

Helena, reflecting on her career in conversation with Oscar's ghost, is more philosophical about these matters, acknowledging (as Emilie never does) that her off-stage life has been a succession of roles: 'As an artist', she suggests, 'I had a right to be emotional', and the roles had their satisfaction.

> I enjoyed being a mother. I enjoyed being an actress too, but I liked being pregnant and I didn't care tuppence for the theatre then. For that matter everything is acting. Some parts are nice, some not so nice. I played a mother. I played Juliet. Ophelia. Suddenly, I am playing the part of a widow. Or a grandmother. One part follows the other. The thing is not to scamp. Not to shirk.[60]

When she visits her in the country house, Emilie admits to Helena that as an actress she should have been able to understand his pretence, but failed to see the true nature of the Bishop. The Bishop is accused of hypocrisy (by the philandering Gustav Adolf), but nothing is shown to indicate that he does not believe in the God-given justice of his behaviour. However, the haunted spirit already hinted at after Justina's tale-bearing is evident in his final conversation with Emilie: 'You once said you were changing masks – I have only one, burned on my face.' His abject, despairing collapse after he has taken the drugged broth she has prepared is all the more shocking.

The film's first theatre is the toy theatre across whose stage Alexander gazes back at us, as though his perception of the world, like ours, is mediated by it. Although he is the principal seer of visions, Fanny is capable of seeing ghostly visitations – she is the first to see Oscar as he sits at the spinet – but is sceptical of Alexander's fantasies. Unlike him she does not hesitate to approach her dying father's bedside, and watches with sympathetic but implicitly objective determination when Alexander is beaten by the Bishop for telling his invented story about the 'ghosts' of his first wife and his children. After sending Alexander to his confinement in the attic, the Bishop goes to place his hand at the back of Fanny's head, but as his hand enters the frame she turns abruptly away. This recurring gesture of patronizing benevolence has been seen to turn into aggression in his interviews with her brother: now she refuses to accept its benign version. In such moments Fanny more than justifies her name's first place in the film's title. She is a 'Bergman woman' in the making: wise, loving, aware of the men's faults and adept at managing them: the film ends with two such women, Helena and Emilie, happily in charge and making plans. Without his sister's critical (and female) appraisal and support, Alexander the visionary would lack a vital connection both with the real world and the film's own observers, the audience.

Notes

1 S.S. Prawer, *Caligari's Children. The Film as Tale of Terror* (Oxford: Oxford University Press, 1980), p. 112.

2 Sigmund Freud, *The Uncanny*, translated by David McLintock with an introduction by Hugh Houghton (London: Penguin Books, 2003), pp. 141, 155.

3 C.G. Jung, *Collected Works*, ed. Herbert Read, Michael Fordham and Gerhard Adler, 20 vols (London: Routledge & Kegan Paul, 1953–78), vol. IX.i, *The Archetypes and the Collective Unconscious*, 2nd edition, translated by R.F.C. Hull, para. 221; p. 122.

4 Gaston Leroux, *Le Fantôme de l'Opéra* (1910; Paris: Le Livre de Poche, 1981), p. 9. Universal's film underwent considerable altertation between previewing and the 1925 release, and again before the 1929 re-release

with added sound: reference is made here to the 'special collector's edition' published by Eureka! Video (2002): EKA40052.

5 Leroux, *Le Fantôme de l'Opéra*, p. 422.

6 Martine Kahane, ed., *L'Ouverture du nouvel Opéra, 5 Janvier 1875* (Paris: Musée d'Orsay/ Bibliothèque Nationale, 1986), p. 5.

7 Ibid., p. 9.

8 Leroux, *Le Fantôme de l'Opéra*, pp. 361–362.

9 On Carré's work, see John Hambly and Patrick Downing, *The Art of Hollywood. A Thames Television Exhibition at the Victoria and Albert Museum* (London: Thames Television, 1979), pp. 20–27. Four of his sketches for the film are reproduced in colour on pp. 74–75.

10 Leroux (and Erik) would have found descriptions of this and other trick effects in Moynet's *L'Envers du théâtre* (1873): see the edition translated and augmented by Allan S. Jackson and M. Glen Wilson, *French Theatrical Production in the Nineteenth Century* (Binghamton: SUNY Press, 1976).

11 Leroux may recall an incident in 1896, when one of counterweights to a cable broke free and crashed through an interior wall of the auditorium, killing one spectator and causing panic: *Annales du Théâtre, Académie Nationale de Musique, Année 1896*, quoted in the section 'Lustre' (chandelier) in *Petite Encyclopédie illustrée de l'Opéra de Paris* (Paris: Théâtre National de l'Opéra, 1974; 2nd edn, 1978), unnumbered pages.

12 Leroux, *Le Fantôme de l'Opéra*, p. 402.

13 Jeanine Basinger, *Silent Stars* (Hanover, NH and London: Wesleyan University Press, 1999), p. 342.

14 Gaylyn Studlar, *This Mad Masquerade. Stardom and Masculinity in the Jazz Age* (New York: Columbia University Press, 1996), p. 223.

15 In the version of the film currently available, the quality of the scenes in Christine's bedroom is poor, which may indicate that they have been restored from a print inferior to that used for most of the film.

16 The available print, as well as being subject to alterations made for the re-release in 1929, must also represent a reduction of the film's length (to ten reels) after the previewing of a longer version. The fact that Ledoux is identified only in this short scene, and the absence of any explanation of his exotic disguise, suggest that in earlier cuts the film made clear the identity of the Persian.

17 Andrew Lloyd Webber's successful stage musical *The Phantom of the Opera* (1986) was followed by *Love Never Dies*, which opened to largely negative reviews in London in 2010. Set in 1907, it brings Christine to New York's Coney Island at the invitation of a mysterious impresario, unsurprisingly Erik. Other film versions of Leroux's novel include a more romantic 1943 remake with Claude Rains in the title role and a 2004 film based on the musical.

18 Patrick McGilligan, *George Cukor. A Double Life* (New York: St Martin's Press, 1991), pp. 196–197.

19 Gavin Lambert, *On Cukor*, edited by Robert Trachtenberg, revised edition (New York: Rizzoli, 2000), p. 146.

20 Janey Place and Lowell Peterson, 'Some Visual Motifs of Film Noir', in Alain Silver and James Ursini, eds, *Film Noir Reader* (New York: Limelight Editions, 1996), pp. 65–75; p. 67.

21 The Shakespeare quotations in this chapter are taken from William Shakespeare, *The Complete Works*, edited by Stanley Wells and Gary Taylor, 2nd edition (Oxford: Clarendon Press, 2005).

22 On Pressburger and the film's origins with Korda, see Kevin McDonald, *Emeric Pressburger. The Life and Death of a Screenwriter* (London and Boston: Faber and Faber, 1994), pp. 272–273. On the Powell and Pressburger *oeuvre*, see Ian Christie, *Arrows of Desire. The Films of Michael Powell and Emeric Pressburger* (London: Waterstone and Co., 1985), and the meticulous study by Natacha Thiéry, *Photogénie du désir. Michael Powell et Emeric Pressburger, 1945–1950* (Rennes: Presses Universitaires de Rennes, 2009). Powell's account of the production is in his *A Life in Movies. An Autobiography* (London: Heinemann, 1986). The fullest account of the film's production and reception, and its relation to the real life of the ballet world, is Adrienne L. McLean, '*The Red Shoes* Revisited', *Dance Chronicle*, 11/1 (1988), pp. 31–83. In *Dying Swans and Madmen. Ballet, the Body and Narrative Cinema* (New Brunswick, NJ and London: Rutgers University Press, 2008), McLean places the film in its broader context. The Criterion Collection DVD edition includes an audio commentary by Ian Christie. References to the film's script are to the continuity script deposited in New York Public Library: see bibliography, p. 277). In 1978 Powell and Pressburger published a paperback novelization of their own film, which incorporates sequences not in the final cut and elaborates details, possibly with reference to earlier script drafts: this is cited below from the subsequent reprint (New York: St Martin's Press, 1996).

23 Powell writes in his autobiography that 'Lermontov was based upon an impresario like Diaghilev, but more like Alex [Korda]' (*A Life in Movies*, p. 614). In the novelization the action takes place in the 1920s, and explicit reference is made to Diaghilev.

24 Michael Powell, 'The Shape of Films to Come', in Peter Noble, ed., *British Film Yearbook, 1947–48* (London: Skelton Robinson, n.d.), pp. 102–105; p. 104.

25 Raymond Durgnat, *A Mirror for England. British Movies from Austerity to Affluence* (London: Faber and Faber, 1970), pp. 208–209.

26 Monk Gibbon, *The Red Shoes Ballet* (London: Saturn Press, 1948).

27 Hans Christian Andersen, *Fairy Tales*, translated by Tiina Nunnaly, edited and introduced by Jackie Wullschalger (New York: Penguin Books, 2004), pp. 210–211.

28 Ibid., p. 212.

29 McLean, '*The Red Shoes* Revisited', p. 39.

30 Gibbon, *Red Shoes Ballet*, p. 53.

31 *Variety*, 4 August 1948.

32 John K. Newnham, 'Dance Film Notes: *Red Shoes* and *The Unfinished Dance*', *Dancing Times* (May 1948), pp. 647–648; 653; p. 648. *Dance* New York (November 1948), pp. 28–29, 36–37; p. 37. In a 1981 interview, Powell insisted on the need for 'brutal realism' as a contrast to the 'almost fairytale angle of the magic red shoes': David Lazar, ed., *Michael Powell Interviews* (Jackson: University of Mississippi Press, 2003), pp. 93–94.

33 Tamara Karsavina, *Theatre Street* (London: Constable, 1950), p. 220.

34 Léonide Massine, *My Life in Ballet* (London: Macmillan, 1968), pp. 43–44.

35 Christie, *Arrows of Desire*, p. 84.

36 A scene showing Lady Neston telling Vicky about the change of plan was filmed but not included in the final cut: the novelization includes this element of the storyline.

37 Arnold Haskell, 'Ballet Since 1939', in *Since 1939. Ballet, Films, Music, Painting* (London: Readers' Union / British Council, 1949), pp. 11–55; pp. 34–35. Heckroth had worked as designer with Jooss' troupe in Essen before their (and his) exile from Germany. Thiéry (*Photogénie du désir*, p. 68) observes that Vicky appears within the sequence as if seen by herself in her dream, and draws attention to the defining moment when she imagines the shoemaker transformed into Lermontov and Julian, marked by a close-up of her startled face, with her hands holding the sides of her head.

38 NYPL script, page 4 (synopsis). An animated montage of Heckroth's storyboards for the ballet is among the Criterion DVD's extras.

39 McLean, '*The Red Shoes* Revisited', p. 63.

40 The script of the omitted scene is printed by Powell, *A Life in Movies*, pp. 614–616. He notes that it reflects his way of working with Pressburger.

41 McLean, *Dying Swans and Madmen*, p. 153.

42 Irving Singer, *Ingmar Bergman, Cinematic Philosopher. Reflections on his Creativity* (Cambridge, MA; MIT Press, 2007), p. 72.

43 Interviewed by John Simon in 1975, Bergman acknowledged indebtedness to Hoffmann (someone he liked 'very much') in *The Magician* and, more particularly, *Hour of the Wolf*: Raphael Shargel, ed., *Ingmar Bergman Interviews* (Jackson: University of Mississippi Press, 2007), p. 75.

44 Ingmar Bergman, *Sunday's Children*, translated by Joan Tate (New York: Arcade Publishing, 1994), p. 8.

45 References to the screenplay are to Ingmar Bergman, *Fanny and Alexander*, translated by Alan Blair (London: Penguin Books, 1989). References to the film are to the Criterion Collection edition of the full-length (TV) cut.

46 Laura Hubner, *The Films of Ingmar Bergman. Illusions of Light and Darkness* (Basingstoke and New York: Palgrave Macmillan, 2007), p. 118.

47 Ingmar Bergman, *The Magic Lantern. An Autobiography*, translated by Joan Tate (Chicago: University of Chicago Press, 1988), p. 33. The passage appears almost verbatim in *After the Rehearsal* (1984), a three-handed TV

play that takes place on the stage of a theatre. As the director describes his experience, he looks across the stage and we see his younger self (Bertil Guve, who played Alexander) watching from the wings.

48 Bergman, *The Magic Lantern*, p. 37.

49 Ingmar Bergman, *Images. My Life in Film*, translated by Marianne Ruuth, introduction by Woody Allen (New York: Arcade Publishing, 2007), p. 86.

50 Images of the set designs are included among the extras in the Criterion Collection DVD of the TV version.

51 Quoted in Peter Cowie, *Ingmar Bergman. A Critical Biography*, 2nd edition (New York: Limelight Editions, 1992), p. 338.

52 Bergman, *Images*, pp. 361–362.

53 The remark is made in a 'making of' documentary included in the Criterion DVD set.

54 Jesse Kalin, *The Films of Ingmar Bergman* (Cambridge: Cambridge University Press, 2003), pp. 172–173.

55 Bergman, *Fanny and Alexander*, p. 94.

56 Bergman, *Images*, p. 373. For other accounts of the filming, see Paul Duncan and Bengt Wanselius, eds, *The Ingmar Bergman Archives* (Cologne: Taschen, 2008), pp. 482–498.

57 Bergman, *Fanny and Alexander*, p. 26.

58 Ibid., p. 207.

59 Ibid., p. 101.

60 Ibid., p. 129.

5

Theatricality and politics: *Mephisto, The Lives of Others* and *The Last Métro*

THE previous chapter has discussed films whose main emphasis was on aspects of the mystery of theatre. In each of these the elements of danger and the uncanny were paramount. This chapter examines the treatment of theatre and performance in three films whose action is situated in repressive political regimes, where the control of artistic expression is part of a more general restriction on personal freedom in the service of ideology and (alleged) state security or the subordination of a conquered nation. In these circumstances, both the mystery of the theatre and the actor's mask may be urgently needed as defensive – or, more dangerously, offensive – measures. At the same time, the mystique of the individual creative temperament or the institution itself comes up against the insistently prosaic demands of 'real life' in a brutally direct form. The personal life and even the subconscious of the individual subject are not merely set against their performing personalities: both are subject to outside controls more complex and threatening than the imperatives of putting on a show or even surviving the hazards of the artist's emotional career. In each story the theatre worker's fundamental need for public performance is subjected to stringent supervision and – in the case of one actor – exploitation for the propagandistic aims of the regime. Two of the films deal with the politics of Germany before and after the Second World War. The other takes place during the German occupation of France. Each deals in its own way with the interplay between private and public performance, the transgressive potential of theatre, and the ways in which personal and national integrity are (literally) played out on and off stage in a society whose ambition is total control. The Third Reich openly employs theatrical display, mystery and mystification as tools of the state. In the German Democratic Republic a Marxist regime proclaims the virtues of clarity of vision in art and society, while concealing its operations by methods more secretive than those of the theatre. In occupied Paris, the theatre's deceptions are aids to survival.

The three films are singled out as explicitly dealing with political circumstances of theatre, but similar elements can be found in many others. There are representations of the creation of theatre as a political intervention, notably *The Cradle Will Rock* (1999), Tim Robbins' account of the 1936 production of Marc Blitzstein's musical play, and the fraught relationship of the Federal Theater project with its opponents on Capitol Hill. As Chapter 2 has shown, both *Yankee Doodle Dandy* and *The Jolson Story* dwell on their subjects' patriotic wartime performance. Beyond this – as an important dimension of the Hollywood biopics – the element of 'can-do' initiative-taking, pluck and determination associated with the show-business career is offered as a specifically American characteristic. Even Florenz Ziegfeld's career could be represented as patriotic service by dwelling on his efforts to 'Glorify the American girl' and playing down his enthusiasm for bedding the same archetype of beauty and spirited femininity.

These specifically American constructions of show business as an expression of political and social mobility contrast with a different strain in many English films, especially those made or set in the years before or during the Second World War, where the performer's career is characteristically presented as a symbol of stoicism, especially in the context of war (*Mrs Henderson Presents*, *The Dresser* [1983]); nostalgia for good-humoured 'getting along' in better times (the British music-hall theme of the wartime film *Champagne Charlie* [1944]); and the miraculous 'survival' of an Edwardian star (Victor Savile's *Evergreen* [1934]). The resilience and good-heartedness of the music hall are central to the film adaptation of Priestley's *The Good Companions* (1933) and the novelist's script for *Sing as We Go!* (1934), where a plucky mill girl (Gracie Fields) turns success in a talent competition in Blackpool to advantage in the survival strategy for the cotton mill she works in. The final shots, with Gracie leading the entire workforce back through the factory gates in a joyous rendition of the title song, is a peculiarly English version of a socialist dream of triumphant civic virtue. The film's treatment of what was known locally as the Slump is an intriguing and informative counterpart to the individualistic response to the Great Depression in the Hollywood musicals of the 1930s. British theatre folk are also depicted as opposing the stuffiness of bureaucracy and entrenched social prejudice: both *Star!* and *Mrs Henderson Presents* show the formidable protagonists (Gertrude Lawrence and Noel Coward in the former, Judi Dench as the eponymous force behind London's Windmill Theatre in the latter) defeating the Lord Chamberlain's office.

Both 'Sir' – the actor-manager in *The Dresser* – and Mrs Henderson are 'doing their bit', bringing respectively the solace of high culture and the harmless indulgence of erotic enthusiasm to a threatened community. These acts take place in a country that was bombed and threatened but never occupied or turned into a totalitarian state. In the far less congenial films by Szabó, Truffaut and von Donnersmarck examined here, actors, directors and their theatrical institutions, state-supported or commercial, exist in an uneasy and far from comforting relationship with the wider realm of politics.

A double life in a fascist regime:
Mephisto

> Mephisto: You are just what you are. Do what you will;
> Wear wigs, full-bottomed each with a million locks,
> Stand up yards high on stilts or actor's socks –
> You're what you are, you'll be the same man still.
> (Goethe, *Faust*, Part One, lines 1806–1809)[1]

In *Mephisto*, István Szabó's 1981 film based on Klaus Mann's 1936 'novel of a career', Hendrik Höfgen makes his way to stardom and power in the artistic realm by way of a riveting performance of Mephisto in Goethe's *Faust* and what is effectively a pact with the devil, in the shape of a high-ranking Nazi based on Hermann Göring.[2] He ascends an artistic and social ladder, from Hamburg to Berlin, making and shedding an alliance with left-liberal society and embracing the good fortune offered to him by the Nazi regime. His progress towards a pact with the devil is, paradoxically, spurred on by his success as Faust's seducer. In the end, Mephisto's observation to Faust, quoted above and spoken in a scene in the film – 'You are just what you are' – is true of the protagonist. His arrival is no more than a confirmation of the point from which he began, and the freeing of his artistic spirit is an illusion. The promises made to him, like those made to the German people, are illusory. The novel's prologue brings together 'four rulers, four play actors' (*vier Machthaber, vier Komödianten*) at a grand reception: the General (i.e. Göring) who holds the political rank of *Ministerpresidänt*, his actress wife Lotte Lindenthal (representing Emmy Sonnemann), the club-footed 'head of advertising' (Goebbels) and the actor who is director of the State Theatre.[3] Szabó moves the scene to the end of his film, and omits Goebbels from the cast, but the effect is as clear as in Mann's novel. The actor is a thinly disguised version of Mann's former friend and brother-in-law Gustaf Gründgens, one of the leading German actors of his generation. His rise to power, to Mann a betrayal of all that he previously had stood for, is assured by his appointment as artistic director (*Intendant*) of the State Theatre, which is under the minister's direct patronage. Gründgens' career embodies the division in personality identified more generally in German society during the 1930s and 40s, the 'Jekyll and Hyde' quality described vividly by the exiled journalist Sebastian Haffner in a book published in London in 1940. Haffner discusses the difficulty many outside Germany have in reconciling their sense of the population as including 'several million normal civilized Europeans, as private individuals often decent and sympathetic' with the 'atrocities committed in their name, often with their connivance, generally with their consent, always without their expressed disapproval'. Both perceptions are in fact right, he insists, and 'these Germans are living a double life like Dr Jekyll and Mr Hyde'.[4]

Novel and film both follow carefully the outlines of Gründgens' career up to the mid-1930s, giving a more or less accurate (albeit jaundiced) picture of his performance style and personality. But his aesthetic principles are barely hinted at. As a director, administrator and actor, he favoured clarity, restraint and attention to the text as a guide to production. He also regarded the theatre as a distinct realm, whose purity was to be maintained. Society would be served by excellence in this special and protected space. However, as Peter Michalzik points out in a study of the actor's relationship with power, the Nazi state's reliance on theatricality made Gründgens' work complicit with its broader aims. During the regime and after its downfall Gründgens promoted the idea that the Staatstheater in the centre of Berlin had been an 'island' in which the integrity of the art and – in some cases directly – the safety of its workers was protected. To those looking from the outside, Michalzik suggests, it must have seemed that here was someone who had worked out a mutually beneficial arrangement with the regime 'because an unequivocal dividing line could no longer be drawn between the State Theatre and the State'.[5] In 1944, with the downfall of the regime in sight and after ten years of dealing with the Nazi demand for a repertoire consistent with its policies and – most critically – artistic enterprises free of hostile elements, including Jews, Gründgens admitted privately to having had to 'swallow more than one ought to take without damage to his soul'. Michalzik comments that Gründgens indirectly admits that during the Third Reich he attained the summit of his potential and at the same time was corrupted by the process.[6]

Gründgens was one of many who profited directly from the astonishing opulence of the German theatre during the period, and the resources, rewards and honours lavished on compliant artists: in contrast to the Weimar Republic, this was a time of full employment in the profession, grants and building projects, film contracts, welfare schemes and other benefits undreamt of before. In a sense, artistic standards were maintained, although for the most part this was within the conservative directorial and scenographic styles favoured by the regime and its leaders. Expressionism and non-representational approaches identified with the 'decadent' Weimar innovators were considered as manifestations of *Kulturbolschevismus* and 'Jewish' tendencies. It was also a time of brutal and comprehensive persecution, enforced exile or worse for Jewish and left-leaning artists, the drastic reduction of the range of repertoire in theatres aiming to present serious work, and the vigorous enforcement of censorship. As in the film industry, openly propagandistic works were a relatively minor element in the programmes, but theatres found themselves obliged to stage more 'light' plays, operettas and revues than before. After the seizure of power in 1933 and more insistently with the outbreak of war in 1939 the plays of Shaw – conveniently Irish – and Shakespeare remained acceptable, but others from hostile countries could not be staged: Chekhov reappeared on Berlin stages, but only during the brief period of the pact with Russia.[7] Directors trod a narrow path, and speeches from otherwise reliable classics might be seized on, so that Schiller's *Don Carlos* was suspect because of Posa's demand to King Philip, 'Sire, give us freedom of thought', while *Wilhelm Tell* and some scenes from *Die Räuber* were unplayable.[8]

In the 1950s, when he was preparing to write the memoir he never completed on power and the artist during the Third Reich, Gründgens himself insisted that although he would not be able to avoid speaking a good deal about himself, he would do so only when he considered his behaviour typical: 'I have little interest in putting my individual attitudes on show, but I regard a good deal of what I did as typical of what many people had to do.'[9] At least he did not actively participate in the production or performance of anti-Semitic works: compared to Werner Krauss with his appearance in multiple roles in *Jud Süss* (1941), his record was clear. (Veit Harlan, the director of this notorious film, was unable to fully redeem his name after the war.)[10] The exiled author Carl Zuckmayer, in a series of 'secret reports' for the American secret service (OSS) on Germans who stayed in Germany, placed both Gründgens and Krauss in the group of 'special cases – partly positive, partly negative – not to be classified without further consideration'. He describes Gründgens as a typical example on account of 'his way of tightrope walking on a razor's edge and juggling with danger'.[11] He slides – without visible skates – on smooth ice, but on ground that was not as smooth, and less dangerous, he would be likely to stumble and trip. Zuckmayer also refers to the cover-up necessary to hide his sexuality, and alludes to dangerous situations this occasioned even before the Nazi seizure of power. A sense of this personal and artistic duality, and of the actor's mesmerizing personality as well as his less acceptable side, permeates Mann's fictional account of him. He insisted in his autobiography that the novel had not been conceived as a *roman à clef* and admitted that 'he might even have been better than many another dignitary of the Third Reich'.[12] At the same time Mann could not deny the bitterness of his feelings about this particular actor, once an intimate friend with whom he had shared so much.

Mann identifies the actor with the role that made Gründgens famous, as the devil's fascinating agent rather than his deluded victim. He is characterized, through Hendrik Höfgen, as both proposer and subscriber in a Faustian bargain. The conversation between the General and the actor during the interval of *Faust* brings together two claimants to the role of Mephisto. Szabó commented to Annette Insdorf that 'these are two actors in love, speaking about their craft. The General even tells Hendrik that he learned a lot from him, especially the element of surprise.' The comment reflects the director's careful study of the novel, in which the General's wife reflects that this is 'love at first sight' and that it is Höfgen's doing, and that 'with his diabolical Pierrot make-up he seems even more irresistible than before'.[13] The fascination, though, is mutual, and Höfgen is as much the seducer as the seduced, an impression reinforced by the strong erotic – indeed homoerotic – element in his performances in rehearsal and on stage. This Mephisto's dance-like physicality allows him to command the stage in a manner not available to his colleagues, and he seems to inhabit another realm from them in which inhibition is beside the point. The mask of white makeup, the shaved head and the heavily made-up eyes (Mann specifies a rainbow-like eye makeup and brilliant red lips) both conceal the actor and allow the expression of hidden and possibly forbidden energies. This figure does not correspond exactly to the play's indication that he appears as a fashionable young aristocrat. His white face, which connects Mephisto with the comedian in Goethe's 'Prologue in the Theatre', marks Höfgen as the trickster Harlequin in the gentler Pierrot's mask.

In showing Höfgen as both Mephisto and Faust, Mann and the film-maker draw on a duality expressed in Goethe's play and its sources, which explore the tension between abandon and control, identifying material desire with erotic and intellectual ambition. In

Höfgen they are further identified with the conflict (or balance) between Dionysian and Apollonian impulses as they exist in the actor's personality. Höfgen/Gründgens finds himself divided between the theatre director's control of his human and material resources and the control exercised over him by his paymasters and protectors. The dilemma parallels the impetus to self-gratification that fuels Faust's desire for knowledge, power and sensual delight and the subjection of this liberation to the controlling personality of his seducer. The film characterizes Höfgen's acting as both sensual – notably in the erotic dance training he receives from his mistress Juliette – and intellectually incisive, as evidenced in the sharp, domineering delivery of his speeches. (Gründgens' feline and razor-sharp style, preserved on film and sound recordings, is reproduced by Klaus Maria Brandauer in the film's *Faust* scenes.) That Höfgen should have acquired his physical technique from a black woman makes this element of his art – and his past – a threat in the 'new' Germany: it represents in artistic terms the real-life hazards of Gründgens' homosexuality.[14]

The film's opening sequence, with Höfgen unable to bear the sound of applause for the visiting operetta star Dora Martin and then donning a dinner jacket and attempting to ingratiate himself with her, demonstrates his need to overcome social discomfiture in the theatrical world. Subsequently, in the days of his first successes, but before his engagement with the new regime's cultural politics that overshadow his own power as *Intendant*, Höfgen has to make an uneasy and ultimately unsuccessful attempt to accommodate himself to the social style of the family of Barbara Bruckner, his first wife. Following the novel, Szabó makes the actor's lack of social confidence clear: in scene after scene he hovers on the edge of a gathering before launching himself into it and his uneasy smile, although not as off-putting as in Mann's characterization – it is repeatedly qualified as *aasig*, which translates as 'diabolical' or 'repulsive' – conveys a disturbing mixture of unease and effortful self-presentation. The Bruckners – like the real-life Mann family – represent the cultural high bourgeoisie (the *Bildungsbürgertum*) to which neither Höfgen nor most of the Nazi hierarchy belong. The nervous strain under which he repeatedly labours produces (as was the case with Gründgens) migraines, explosive displays of anger that go beyond 'temperament', and a series of more or less serious nervous breakdowns. During the rehearsal of a production of *Orpheus in the Underworld* Höfgen loses patience with the can-can dancers and leaps into a furious solo dance at the front of the line, clicking his fingers in ecstasy and reproducing the 'jazz' steps he has learned with Juliette. At the same time his tyrannical behaviour in this and other rehearsals suggests a desire for control, exercised unashamedly at the expense of others. In front of his dressing-room mirror Höfgen can reveal his insecurities, and he can act them out in the masochistic fantasies – even the film's less extreme ones – of his relationship with Juliette. The fetishism is a fantasy of control and enslavement, foreshadowing what is to come elsewhere in his life: Juliette wisely observes that he is 'a good boy who knows how to behave', speaking sincerely rather than in her assumed role as dominatrix. Höfgen's soliloquies, a number of them spoken to his dressing-room mirror, do not break through the film's realistic mode, simply because he the kind of person who *would* talk out loud to himself, as if rehearsing alone.

In the early stages of his career Höfgen's ability to control and dominate are under threat from his temperament (when we first see him in the dressing room, in self-harming agony over Martin's success) and his social standing. The change of name from the commonplace Heinz to Hendrik is an attempt to cut free from his lower middle-class background. Actors have often made this kind of change, usually in order to differentiate themselves from a colleague with the same name, but with Hendrik (as with Gustav/Gustaf Gründgens) the alteration is a step towards asserting a new identity rather than a professional convenience. As director of the Staatstheater he inhabits a new but hollow version of high society, represented on a grand scale by the celebration of his patron's birthday. At a private view of pompously idealized 'Aryan' sculptures modelled on those of Arno Breker, the Nazis' sculptor laureate, Höfgen encounters the poisonous mixture of political, social and artistic power – and bad taste – to which he has committed himself. The sculptor says she would like to make a bust of him, but is puzzled by his ability to transform himself (*Verwandlung-skraft*). Should she render the private or the public face? 'A mixture', he suggests. His subsequent speech at a public ceremony parrots the language of the regime in praising the works as representing 'new' (or rediscovered) 'German' ideals. Höfgen derives energy from the rhetoric and attitudinizing of his early espousal of communism: his lack of sincere commitment to the cause permits the transference of this aspect of his temperament from left-wing revolutionary politics to the exercise of power in the theatre and beyond. We had seen him rehearsing the 'revolutionary theatre' troupe he and the communist actor Otto Ulrichs planned in Hamburg. In Brecht's *Der Brotladen* (*The Bread Shop*), he had thrown away the realistic designs and insisted on breaking down the barrier between stage and audience and making the actors perform in an anti-realistic 'Brechtian' manner. (The dramatist's name is never mentioned.) This, he announced, would be 'total theatre' – a phrase he later uses with equal emphasis when as *Intendant* he is briefing the press on his new interpretation of Hamlet as a man of action rather than a thinker: 'We must make a total theatre – a theatre that shatters – and mobilizes.' By this point he has absorbed a new vocabulary, that of the Nazis, which he speaks with greater poise but comparable vehemence. Hamlet is a work of the people, 'ein *völkisches* Werk' (using an adjective central to Nazi ideology) comparable to Greek tragedy, the hero a 'Nordic man' whose story 'shows us the way to the future'. From what we see of the production, with his new wife as a conventionally nordic Ophelia with blond tresses, it is clear that his social and artistic arrival is paid for by art as kitschy as the operetta with which the film began.

After the film's opening sequence with the trite operetta (Mollöcker's *Gräfin Dubarry*) on stage, the tortured Hendrik in the dressing room, and his embarrassing attempts in the bar to curry favour with the visiting star, the actor was absorbed again into the family of his colleagues, but his attempt to rise above them and the situation had been noted as commonplace if irksome. The phenomena of stardom, anxiety, applause and the separateness of the theatre world were established, but so was Höfgen's need to be different. In Juliette's apartment, stripping down to briefs for a lesson in 'jazz' dancing that turned into a sexual encounter, Hendrik was immersed in a potentially dangerous but energizing alternative world. Juliette's room, an even more ambiguous space than that of the theatre, is part bedroom, part rehearsal studio. Paradoxically, what he learns in this Dionysian place will help to propel him towards the Apollonian element he aspires to. The film and the novel trace the actor's rise to eminence with the customary geographical and social signs of the theatrical biography: from Hamburg to the capital city, through a range of dramatic and theatrical modes that take in cabaret, Wedekind, Brecht, Goethe and Shakespeare – and even more that are shown in a montage of his Berlin successes. The social settings progress from the actors' bar of the Hamburg theatre to the pomp of the penultimate scene in the monumental entrance hall of the Staatstheater. From the comfortable high-bourgeois home of the Bruckners he progresses to a spacious apartment in Berlin and finally to a grand villa in the leafy and fashionable suburban Grünewald. The novel makes it clear that this has been acquired (as Gründgens' own estate was) by being 'Ayranized' and purchased at a fraction of its true value from a departing Jewish owner, although in the film this is not explicitly stated. The fact that it comes copiously and luxuriously furnished may suggest this: it certainly intimates that he is living beyond his deserts, if not his means. He has made the Nazi version of the Big Time.

14. *Mephisto* (1981):
Höfgen in the
Ministerpräsident's box

In the first phase of his relationship with his patron, when the actor was summoned to the 'imperial' box during the interval of *Faust*, their conversation was watched from the stalls by admiring audience members, as though stage and auditorium had been reversed, but even here one suspects that Höfgen failed to perceive that this was theatre staged by the General, though as the actor became more self-confident he appeared to be in charge. His final humorous gesture, spreading his cape as if to envelope them both, was an expression of power but, as in the contract between actor and audience, this dominance had been granted to him only provisionally by the conventions of the theatre, and his costume and makeup (Figure 14). Just as the actor's life takes him – and the audience – backstage and into the dressing room, the General is revealed to have two spheres, one relaxed and genial (he is literally in his shirt sleeves at home with Lotte Lindenthal and Höfgen) and the other grand and architecturally 'staged'. But which is real? Höfgen makes his way twice to an imposing official building and is ushered through echoing halls towards the vast office occupied by the General. The first time he moves quickly towards the desk, and is treated with 'man-of-the-world' geniality when he asks for Juliette to be given an exit visa. The second time, after the same walk through the building, he is made to stay nervously at the doorway, and his attempt to intervene on behalf of an imprisoned colleague is dismissed rudely. The last phase of the film demonstrates how the real power, both theatrical and political, lies with the Nazi.

It is the birthday that provides the ultimate setting for what seems to be the climax of his ascendancy.[15] Höfgen is at first the centre of it, welcoming the General and his consort Lotte Lindenthal with a fawning speech, but here his eloquence and the incisive clarity of his elocution are functioning in an irony-free zone. Earlier, in one of their 'domestic' chats, the General has told him that he now knows his secret, 'surprise'. Höfgen has insisted that sharp diction, unexpected pauses and unpredictable movements are the key to his style, but his invocation of *Kultur* – suggesting aesthetic sensibility – is dismissed as bourgeois nonsense by his interlocutor, who continues with a line indelibly associated with Göring: 'when I hear the word culture I reach for my revolver'. The General muses on the fact that the actor has 'a German face', but despite that one that can change as the actor wishes. He replies that what he has described is acting technique (*Schauspielerei*) and the rest is humility and hard work. Höfgen does not perceive that it is not so much the acting style as the motivating personality that fascinates the General. There has always been a suggestion that the Nazi sees through 'his' Mephisto. Now, in the birthday celebration and its aftermath, Höfgen is no longer in the commanding role of Faust's mentor.

Like any actor, the General loves costumes (Göring's mania for new styles of uniform was notorious) and knows how to make an entrance – his arrivals at the receptions marking Höfgen's second marriage and his own birthday are notable examples of this. In Szabó's final scene he brings the actor to the empty Olympic stadium to demonstrate his directorial control. Forced into the middle of the arena, blinded with searchlights, Höfgen is made to perform in an exhibition of the General's directorial power: 'This is theatre. Here *I* will stage a show.' As he calls out Höfgen's name and bids him to enjoy the sound of it echoing round the arena, he insists that he should take the stage – 'right in the centre'. This should be the gratification of an egotistical actor's dream of supremacy, with a vast stage devoted to him alone and more limelight than he could ever have allowed himself in the theatre. However, seen from high above – not the General's point of view, but that of an all-seeing camera (or god) – Höfgen becomes a tiny figure pursued pitilessly by searchlight beams. In the final image of the film their glare turns Höfgen's face white, recalling his white makeup for Mephisto. To himself he mutters, 'What do they want from me? What do they want? After all I'm only an actor', and the image freezes on a close-up of his perplexed face.[16] As the General promises a political and social order that will last for a thousand years, Höfgen is dwarfed and victimized by an epic, 'total' theatre beyond his own imagining.

Subsequently, in *Colonel Redl* (1984) and *Sunshine* (1999), Szabó has explored the dilemmas faced by men who subscribe wholeheartedly to a regime – in *Sunshine* a succession of them – that ultimately destroys them. *Taking Sides* (2001), adapted from a play by Ronald Harwood, deals with the post-war interrogation of the conductor Wilhelm

Furtwängler and the ethics of another artist's complicity with the Nazi state. Furtwängler, acknowledged as a great interpreter of the classical repertoire, presents a case devoid of the glamour and mystery of the theatre but equally disturbing in its implications: his performances of Beethoven could be considered to transcend their political circumstances, and it is difficult to locate in them the kind of deception that may well have infected his personal, social life during the regime. The career of Hendrik Höfgen, by contrast, allows Szabó to dig deeper into the psychology of a creative artist, through a fable in which the familiar figure of the actor as a liar who tells the truth is projected into the criminal political and social situation effected by a society of liars. Unlike the protagonists of these later films, Höfgen starts from a position in which the suspect nature of his claims to integrity are bound up with the duplicity demanded by the very fact of his being an actor.

Spying and spectating:
The Lives of Others (Das Leben der Anderen)

Until its final sequences the action of Florian Henckel von Donnersmarck's film Das Leben der Anderen (The Lives of Others, 2007) unfolds in the German Democratic Republic (GDR) – the Deutsche Demokratische Republik – the Soviet-bloc society which claimed to be a systematic counter and antidote to the poisonous Nazi regime in which the anti-hero of Mephisto sacrificed his self-respect. It also defined itself in contrast to the other state of the divided Germany, commonly characterizing the Federal Republic (Bundesrepublik) as 'fascist' and inimical to the virtuous goals of socialism.[17] The Nazi and communist totalitarian states both defended themselves by a creating a culture of anxiety and surveillance, that of the GDR being arguably even more systematic though less murderous than the Nazis' reign of terror. Although the less oppressive aspects of life in the post-war East German state cannot be discounted, memory of the GDR is dominated by the repressive measures taken in defence against the 'threat' from the West by the Ministry for State Security, the Ministerium für Staatssicherheit (MfS), its operatives commonly referred to as the Stasi. Indeed, Ostalgie – nostalgia for a degree of order and the cradle-to-grave social support for the dutiful citizen – brings with it the danger of massaging memories of an oppressive and brutal regime to serve the ends of its surviving perpetrators. In his detailed examination of this revisionism, Die Täter sind unter uns ('The Culprits Are among Us') and his collection of testimonies by the Stasi's victims, Hubertus Knabe insists on the extent and sinister realities of the 'State Security' machine.[18] The Stasi organization was rigidly compartmentalized, and Wiesler, the Stasi captain at the centre of the film, would not in reality have conducted all the operations we see him perform: personal surveillance, consulting files, and so on. It has also been objected that von Donnersmarck focusses on an elite group of theatre workers and intellectuals, with relatively little to suggest the everyday life in the state. It has been suggested that a fuller sense of this is given by the comedy *Good Bye Lenin!* (2003), in which daily life before the fall of the Wall has to be reconstructed for the benefit of a woman – with a reputation as an energetic and committed party member – who has missed the event through being in a coma and must not be allowed to experience the shock of the changes it has brought.[19]

Even though the protagonist of *Das Leben der Anderen* is not an actor, he enters the world of theatre without realizing it. Both this film and Szabó's *Mephisto* explore the theatre's paradoxical world of 'lies like truth', the tensions between concealment and display and the implications of this for the actor's personality. Both films take these perceptions into the realm of political life, and then fold politics back into the theatre. Höfgen in *Mephisto* is an artist, whose life in the safe deceptions of the theatre is turned to its own benefit by a criminal regime founded on deceit. His self-deception lies in his need to construe his opportunism as freedom of spirit and to see his guilt as merely relative. The uncovering of what is hidden within Höfgen shows what underlies his spectacular success as an actor – he acts out his daemon – but it also destroys his integrity. Von Donnersmarck's hero does not consider himself an artist, still less a man of the theatre, and there is no suggestion that he has constructed a public persona for himself, but by the end of the film he has effectively become a collaborator in a kind of theatre and has paid the price for it. From skilfully uncovering deceptions in others he has progressed to participation in fiction. That fiction is life-giving and spirit-redeeming, but he does not find the benefit of it until the very last moments of the film. Meanwhile, in the penultimate sequence, in the newly unified Germany after the 'turning point' (*die Wende*) of 1989 – he lives in relative penury, while some of those he served continue to thrive. The political regime that Höfgen strove to circumvent and deny in his theatre corresponds in many respects to that which Captain Gerd Wiesler (Ulrich Mühe) at first serves. But he acts out of a belief in the essential humanity of his chosen profession and then comes to see its failings, and becomes – or is discovered to be – a 'good person'. Höfgen's hopes of being such a person are fatally undermined. Both films engage with the politics of theatricality as well as of the theatre as an institution, and with the paradoxes of the performing self whether in public or private. In such regimes, any hope for a division between the two realms is constantly threatened if not thwarted. Höfgen can protest, feebly, that he is only an actor and ask what 'they' want of him. Wiesler is confirmed by the evidence of others as a good human being, although initially in his capacity as a captain in the service of the Stasi he seems remote from any chance of that accolade.

The film opens with an unidentified man (in the script he is simply 'the prisoner') being led down forbidding, aseptic corridors in the Stasi interrogation and remand centre at Hohenschönhausen to face an interrogation.[20] He has been questioned more than once already, but is made to go over his version of events leading up to the flight of a friend to the West. The goal is to elicit the name of the person who helped his friend to escape. We are shown details of the routine procedures and the calm and insistent repetition with which the interrogator does his work. Then we cut to a close-up of a tape recorder, and a finger presses the 'stop' button. The scene is a lecture room in the Stasi's 'university' in Potsdam, and the interrogator is instructing a small group of students. Consequently, what we have so far been shown is being played to them as if it were a radio documentary, or rather a radio drama. The reality of the interrogation scene is available fully only to the cinema audience and the participants, including the instructor, Wiesler, who has conducted the interrogation. He pauses to ask for questions and to make comments. When a student questions the humanity of the procedure, which involves isolation and sleep deprivation, he receives no reply and is at once struck by the folly of his intervention. Wiesler says nothing, but unobtrusively makes a mark against his name on the seating plan of the class.

Wiesler is a model of restraint, implicitly with a tendency to inhibition that has been fostered and adapted to the needs of the state. Impassivity in the interrogation room and inscrutability in the lecture hall make him a formidable presence, despite the slight, unassuming figure he cuts. At the same time, the film's doubling of the auditory and visual renditions of the scene intimates a pattern that will recur: events will have more than one existence, private transactions will have an unseen audience, and acts of interpretation (and misinterpretation) will manipulate them so that they constitute evidence to confirm (or distort) perceptions. As the film progresses, Wiesler moves from being the audience for the 'radio play' that unfolds in the apartment he has bugged, first to wilfully misreporting what he hears, and then to intervening covertly in those events. An investigator whom his prey, the playwright Georg Dreyman, would never willingly trust with a secret becomes his victim's secret deliverer. The woman Dreyman trusted, the actress Christa-Maria Sieland, is turned into one of the 'unofficial collaborators' (*Inoffizielle Mitarbeiter*, abbreviated as IM) the Stasi recruits from the friends, family and associates of suspects, and is persuaded to betray her lover. This takes place in a society defined by Wiesler during the initial interrogation scene without any hint of sarcasm as 'our humanist state'. The foolhardy student in Wiesler's class uses the adjective *unmenschlich* ('inhumane') and *Mensch* and its cognates recur as the loyal supporters of the regime make casual but insistent play with the definition of human nature. From an oppositional standpoint the theme is given its fullest expression in the work for piano given to Dreyman in a later scene by the banned theatre director Albert Jerska shortly before his suicide: 'Die Sonate vom guten Menschen' ('the sonata of the good person'). Beyond this there is an echo of the title of Brecht's play *Der Gute Mensch von Sezuan* ('The Good Person of Sezuan') with its questioning of the relationship between humanity and gain.

The film's second major sequence, after the interrogation and its interpretation in the lecture hall, brings Wiesler and his superior officer, Grubitz, to the theatre, where they are to see a performance of one of Dreyman's plays. This is part of an initiative that has been requested by the formidable government minister Hempf, who sits in the stalls with an aide while Grubitz and Wiesler watch the play and the audience from a box. Grubitz points out Dreyman, and during the interval goes down to meet Hempf. Wiesler focuses his opera glasses alternately on the scenes played out in the stalls and in the corner where Dreyman has positioned himself, and observes an embrace between Christa-Maria and her lover that cannot be seen by the rest of the audience. At the actors' party afterwards, which Hempf and his acolyte attend, very much as outsiders in this world, Hempf delivers a fulsome but somewhat sinister speech in praise of Dreyman and Christa-Maria and makes a brief pass at her. Dreyman tries to get the minister to discuss the case of a director, Jerska, who has been banned from exercising his profession. He uses the word *Berufsverbot*, which is associated with the Nazis and which Hempf bridles at. The minister lets his anger be seen, but Dreyman persists in pleading for a second chance for Jerska. Hempf refuses to accept that he has judged too harshly, then modulates into praise for the humane quality of Dreyman's plays: 'But then that's what we all love in your plays, the love for human beings, the good humans; the belief that humans can change themselves. Even though, Dreyman, you often write in your plays that humans do not change...' Repeatedly Hempf uses the noun *Mensch* rather than the more commonplace

15. *The Lives of Others* (2007): Wiesler and the listening post

Leute ('people'). A typical representative of his regime, Hempf employs terms that are at a suitable level of abstraction. Although they are very much on the edge of the gathering – even more so than Hempf and his aide – Wiesler and Grubitz witness the scene.

The scarcely veiled threat to this well-established and 'safe' author, combined with Hempf's evident interest in the actress, is followed through by a high-level surveillance, in which their apartment is bugged comprehensively by a Stasi team under Wiesler's expert direction. At one point the observers are observed by the woman who lives across the landing, whom Wiesler silences with the threat that 'her Mascha' will lose her place to study medicine. A listening post is established in the attic directly above the apartment, where Wiesler sits facing his panoply of recording and communications equipment, like a stage-manager in a theatre (Figure 15). For the time being, though, he will not be giving cues: that will come later.

The first major event to be observed by Wiesler is the writer's 40th birthday party, which is to be attended by an array of more or less suspect associates from the world of the theatre and the arts. The 'banned' Jerska attends the party but will not join in the conversations, and it is now that he gives Dreyman the piano score, not unwrapped until the writer and the actress are alone and about to make love. Its significance is not yet apparent. When Dreyman plays the sonata he comments 'I always think of what Lenin said about [Beethoven's] *Appassionata*: "I can't listen to it, or I'll never finish the Revolution." … Can anyone who has heard this music, really heard it, still be a bad person [*ein schlechter Mensch*]?' He does not know that the music has another listener, Wiesler in his attic 'listening post'. Immediately after, when the Stasi officer goes back to his flat, he finds himself in the elevator with a little boy, whose football bounces in before the doors close. The child asks 'Are you really with the Stasi?' Wiesler asks if he knows what the Stasi are and the boy says 'They're the bad men who lock people up, my dad says.' Wiesler begins 'What's the name of…', then suddenly checks his Stasi-trained impulse, and absurdly has to continue '…your football', to the child's disgust at such a senseless question. Has the music had an effect on him?

A subsequent scene marks a further development in Wiesler's situation, in which he is moved from being an audience to taking an active – acting – role in the lives that surveillance has rendered a private performance for him. Dreyman has pleaded with Christa-Maria not to keep her appointment with Hempf, who has trapped her into an affair by playing on her addiction to prescription drugs. The confrontation occurs because Wiesler, already starting to manipulate events, had contrived in an earlier scene that the playwright should see her getting out of the minister's limousine. Christa-Maria turns Dreyman's arguments back on him with a defiant play on words: she needs Hempf the way she needs 'this whole system', and so does Dreyman:

> Don't you get in bed with them just the same way? Why do you do it then? Because they can destroy you just as well, despite the talent you never have a single doubt about. Because they decide who gets performed, who should act and who should direct. You don't want to end like Jerska, and neither do I. And that's why I'm going now.

She leaves the apartment but rather than proceed directly to her rendezvous she goes to a local bar. Wiesler, as it happens, is already there. She walks past his table, sits down and orders a brandy. He accosts her and effectively dissuades her from going to meet Hempf by reminding her of the high regard she is held in as an actress. She asks coldly 'Do we know each other?' but he insists that he does know her:

Wiesler: Many people love you … only because you are the way you are.

Christa-Maria: An actor is never the way he is.

Wiesler: But you are. *(She looks at him enquiringly)* I've seen you on stage. There you were more the way you are … than you are now.

He tells her that he is her 'audience' but she does not know that this is literally the case, and is presumably shaken when he repeats words he has heard Dreyman speak to her, insisting that she is a great artist ('Sie sind eine grosse Künstlerin'). Dreyman's use of the same words – now forming Wiesler's 'script' – did not prevent her from leaving, but now they are spoken by this stranger and prompt her to change her mind. She replies 'And you are a good person' ('Und Sie sind ein guter Mensch'). Off the public stage, though, in her attempts to deceive Dreyman, Christa-Maria is a poor actress: her story about meeting a school friend has been unconvincing and she knows it.

This pivotal scene bringing together the themes of humanity and performance is typical of the film's methods, its characters oscillating between different situations of playing and observing (viewing or listening), and with the underlying topic of 'humanity'. Christa's insecurity about her identity is the vulnerability that presumably drives her to using drugs and then into Hempf's control, and here it is placed in the context of the psychology of acting. The moment when she was seen from Wiesler's point of view during Dreyman's play seemed to be the first moment when an aesthetic experience had touched him. It now informs his confident statement about her personality. The scene in the bar thus marks a further important stage in Wiesler's development, the gradual discovery of a dormant goodness in him, and is followed by Christa's return to the apartment. The tension between the lovers has been resolved, and they make love passionately. This intimate scene is shown lyrically, superimposed over the typed report by Wiesler's assistant Udo, whose voice-over flatly describes her return, to Dreyman's (and Udo's) surprise, and then registers in the colourless prose of his report that 'vigorous intimacies follow' (*heftige Intimitäten folgen*). The playwright is reported as saying that he feels his strength has been renewed and will now be able to do something. Udo interprets this as possibly meaning he will write a new play. Wiesler surprises Udo by congratulating him on a 'good report'. In fact the film has shown the scene in a flashback and as imagined by Wiesler – the script indicates 'Rückblende/ Wieslers Vorstellung' – so that he is responding to what he has seen in his mind's eye. The close-up on the couple, naked in bed, is bathed in the warm light that characterizes their apartment and sets it apart from the bleakness of the film's other locations, most notably the immaculate but soulless apartment where we have seen the Stasi officer receiving cold comfort from a businesslike prostitute. The omniscience of the film and the interpreting mind of the surveillance officer are literally superimposed, and the sequence also indicates his understanding of the contrast between the warmth and coldness of the two worlds. Wiesler normally listens intently to discern what is going on in the apartment. In his quest for a mental picture he has even marked out the floor of the attic with a ground plan of the rooms beneath, resembling the rehearsal-room mark-up for a studio or stage set. Now, though, he is responding imaginatively not to what he hears directly but to what a third-party report tells him. Udo's report has become a script or, more accurately, a screenplay.

The relative safety and potential for self-expression of writing and theatrical performance are a vital element of the lives of the 'others', just as they gradually become essential to Wiesler in his moves towards being a truly 'good human being'. On the day of the party Dreyman goes to visit Jerska, who has been exiled to a remote suburb and inhabits a cramped room in a shared apartment. Jerska tells Dreymann, 'In the next life I'd rather be just a writer, a happy writer, who can always write, like you. No, perhaps I'd rather be a novelist than a playwright ... What does a director have if he isn't allowed to direct? Nothing more than a film-maker without film, a miller without grain.' Like Christa-Maria, who is effectively broken in her interrogation towards the end of the film with the threat of exclusion from the stage and the end of her career, Jerska as a man of the theatre needs the self-expression that only this public art can allow: internal exile is not an option. After his suicide it is at Jerska's funeral that Dreyman conceives (and 'thinks' in voice-over) the article he can write about the concealment of GDR suicide statistics whose publication in the West will satisfy his need to take action. This 'safe' playwright has been transformed by a private experience of bereavement and the realization that the state cannot accommodate free spirits. He makes the necessary arrangements with a journalist from the West German magazine *Der Spiegel*, who smuggles in a compact 'travel' size typewriter: all machines in the GDR were registered, but this will not be traceable. It is hidden under the threshold of an internal doorway.

In the film's combination of intersecting personal journeys, Dreyman's experience parallels that of Wiesler while Christa-Maria's moves in the opposite direction. Wiesler is summoned to Hohenschönhausen where interrogating her will be his last chance to redeem his blunders in the investigation. Grubitz brings him to a room where the interview can be observed through a two-way mirror. Wiesler is now performing in what is effectively a TV play for an audience of two. The actress is no longer a prisoner, but (he observes) has agreed to be an IM, and therefore should not be handcuffed. Demoralized and cynical she tells him that as he is the officer responsible for controlling her – her *Führungsoffizier* – it is up to him to 'lead' her. When he repeats the phrase from their encounter in the bar, 'I am your audience', there is glimmer of recognition. He assures her that if she tells him where the typewriter is hidden, Dreyman will never know and they will not take any action when she is with him. She agrees. However, when Grubitz and his men arrive to make their search she is in the apartment taking a shower. Grubitz ('not a good actor', observes the screenplay) moves confidently to the place where the typewriter should be hidden, prepared to feign surprise at finding it and then puzzled not to find it. Christa-Maria is dismayed when she sees Dreyman's clear understanding of her guilt and runs out of the building. She herself has failed to act in the way Wiesler advised her to when she divulged the secret: 'Playing astonishment – you'll certainly manage that.' Now Grubitz, dismayed at what he takes to be her deception of his colleague, exclaims 'Die Schauspielerin!' – she was acting, after all. She rushes out in her bathrobe, pauses at the kerbside then runs into the street where she is hit by a passing truck. (She may do this on purpose: neither the film nor the screenplay clarifies the point.) As she lies dying, Wiesler tries to reassure her:

Christa-Maria: I was too weak... Now I can't put right what I've done.

Wiesler: *(whispering urgently)* There's nothing to put right, do you understand? Nothing... I took the type–

He then stands back so that Dreyman can take her in his arms. Dreyman asks her forgiveness. She dies.

This is the climax of the film's play with concealments and subterfuges, who knows what about whom, and the placing of misleading clues. In the most elaborate of these his group of friends tests whether Dreyman's apartment is bugged – Wiesler allows them to think it is not – and then pass the article off as work on a play when Christa-Maria returns during one of their meetings. Wiesler, who has now become a hidden co-author, presents the story to his superiors as authentic. His deception is not uncovered but his mishandling of the affair earns him the demotion threatened by Grubitz. Four years and eight months later, he is in the cellar of the Stasi HQ steaming open letters when the news of the fall of the Berlin Wall breaks.

Timothy Garton Ash, in his account of tracing the Stasi's records of his visits to the GDR as a journalist and author, describes 'how a file opens the door to a vast sunken labyrinth of the forgotten past, but how, too, the very act of opening the door itself changes the buried artefacts, like an archaeologist letting in fresh air to an Egyptian tomb'.[21] One of the strengths of von Donnersmarck's film is its multi-layered Hitchockian plotting of what becomes a detective story. When, after the fall of the regime, Dreyman's play is being performed, now in a stylized symbolist staging rather than the quasi-Brechtian sparseness and realism of its original production, he has to leave the auditorium, unable to hear another actress intone lines associated with Christa-Maria. In the foyer he encounters Hempf, now a successful business man in 'the new Germany'. Hempf taunts him with his apparent writer's block:

It would be a shame if you really didn't write any more, after everything our country has invested in you. But I can understand, Dreyman, really. What could one write in this Federal Republic? Nothing more that one *can believe in, nothing more that one can rebel against. (He looks at Dreyman)* It was nice in our little republic. A lot of people are only just realizing that.

Dreyman has one question: why wasn't he being spied on? Hempf tells him his apartment was in fact bugged, and thoroughly – he should just look behind the light switches. In a scene reminiscent of the freelance surveillance expert's destruction of his own apartment in Francis Ford Coppola's *The Conversation* (1974), he rips out wires from behind the wallpaper. Subsequently Dreyman goes to look at his files, an act that requires no little courage, and which proved traumatic for thousands of citizens of the newly united Germany. He uncovers one painful truth about Christa-Maria: her signed agreement to become an IM. He also finds out that Hempf had ordered the operation to spy on him, and to his astonishment he reads Wiesler's false report of the discussion of the play that he and his co-conspirators were allegedly writing. Grubitz asked in a memorandum for more information on the content of the play, and Wiesler supplied it. ('Content of the first act: Lenin is in constant danger. Despite mounting external pressure he holds firm to his revolutionary plans…') He realizes how he has been protected, and finally discovers Wiesler's last stratagem to save him from prosecution. The West German journalist who provided the 'secret' typewriter had been able to obtain only a red ribbon for it, and when Wiesler removed it from its hiding place some of the ink stained his hands: there are red marks on his final report.

One consequence of these discoveries, which finally give Dreyman knowledge the film audience already has, is that his writer's block is resolved. He writes the novel *Die Sonate vom Guten Menschen*. Although we do not know the book's contents, we can infer that this gives some sense of resolution and closure to Dreyman, as well as freeing him from a burden of memory. In the final scene of the film Wiesler sees the novel on display in bookstore – ironically, the Karl-Marx-Buchhandlung – and goes in to buy a copy. The dedication is to him under his Stasi designation, HGW XX/7. The bookseller asks if he wants it gift-wrapped. The final line is 'No… it's for me' and the final image is of Wiesler's expression, showing a satisfaction and a sense of self-worth not seen until now.

Mephisto takes to task an actor whose absorption in his career blinds him to the common understanding and feelings of less extraordinary beings. It does not take much to separate him from whatever scruples he may have, and he is exactly the kind of servant and artistic role model the regime can use. In the GDR, artistic personalities are suspect, for all the lip service paid to them by bigwigs (*Bonzen*) like Hempf. The state is supported by such seemingly colourless and unemotional functionaries as Wiesler. In von Donnersmarck's film, the man to whom the world of the theatre seems alien is drawn into it, or at least to a private, intimate shadow of it. The invention and plotting of drama become his ethical salvation, while his role as an investigator had been a seeming search for truth in the service of a state functioning through deception and intrigue. In her study of the East German regime, *Anatomy of a Dictatorship*, Mary Fulbrook insists that it should not be construed as 'a thin layer of evil SED [i.e. the ruling communist party] and Stasi officials at the top constantly repressing a cowering population which lived in a state of terror':

> The edifice of the dictatorship was constructed with and through the vast majority of the population, who participated in its workings in a multiplicity of organisations and activities.[22]

Wiesler's forlorn ordinariness does not condone his complicity throughout a career in the Stasi, but through contrast with the crudely careerist Grubitz his lack of a sense of humour or vitality take on the semblance of integrity, which the events of the film draw out and confirm. In an essay on Wiesler's about-face, Manfred Wilke describes his progress through the film in terms of political awareness: 'the film shows convincingly the mechanisms of repression in the Communist party state and how in its final days a communist recognizes that he is not hunting enemies for the sake of a dream of humanity [*Menschenheitstraum*], but rather that, in the interest of a cynical clique at the head of the Party and state, he is persecuting people who want to shape their lives according to their own wishes.'[23] One can also trace this progress in terms of aesthetic as well as moral and political perception.

In the scene following his encounter with the prostitute – apparently the morning after it – Wiesler lets himself into Dreyman's apartment. He examines the book and papers on the desk, including the volume of Brecht's poems that Jerska had been reading at the party. He kneels down by the bed and touches the bedspread gently – almost reverently – as if trying to sense some of the human warmth and sensuality granted to its owners and denied to him. He must have taken the Brecht away with him, and we later see him lying on the sofa in his own flat reading it as Dreyman's voice recites the first stanza of 'Remembering Marie A'. The poignant but quizzical tone of the lyric, its recall of the circumstances but not the actual experience of love, commands his attention, though to what precise effect we cannot tell. As with so much of Ulrich Mühe's performance, culminating in the film's final shot, the actor's face suggests feelings the character can barely express but which go deep. The poet remembers the still pale body of his lover, but far more vivid is the image of a cloud in the sky above them: 'It was very white and immensely high/ And when I looked up, it was no longer there.'[24] We get no sense that Wiesler, preoccupied with his new surveillance task, makes much of Dreyman's play, identified on the programme as *The Faces of Love* (*Die Gesichter der Liebe*). Nevertheless, as has been noted above, the actress herself clearly made an impression on him. The action played out to him over his earphones, the apartment-sized radio play, took him further into the theatre. Brecht's poem, like the sonata itself, seems to speak directly to him. How, we are not told, but implicitly it was an important stage in the development of his qualities as a 'good person'. It also ties him to the creative artistic world – Jerska, Dreyman, Christa-Maria – that was alien to him before. His goodness has been nurtured by art without his knowing it.

Theatre in a world of shadows:
The Last Metro

'Everything we did was equivocal', Jean-Paul Sartre recalled, 'we never quite knew whether we were doing right or wrong. A subtle poison corrupted even our best actions.'[25] Ambiguity is at the heart of François Truffaut's *Le Dernier Métro* (1980), a vivid exploration of theatre and subterfuge that goes beyond the extreme political and social circumstances it reproduces. The theatrical environment of mystery and shadows complements the darkness of the outside world, but within the theatre the shadows are unthreatening and literally warmer, through the predominant reds of the stage set and other spaces. The film's stylishness and the affection with which the theatre's world is represented sit uneasily (perhaps intentionally so) with the even grimmer aspects of life in occupied France that it touches on but does not explore. In this respect the theatrical world reflects and at the same time implicitly challenges the 'reality' that surrounds it, a politically inflected adaptation of the mystery celebrated by the films discussed in Chapter 4 with a central character, Marion Steiner, who carries the mystique of the actress into this distinctive social realm.

Truffaut's film is not a documentary exposé like Marcel Ophüls' *Le Chagrin et la pitié* (*The Sorrow and the Pity*, 1969), an exploration of the fascistic mentality such as Louis Malle's *Lacombe Lucien* (1974) or a story of courageous but failed resistance like the same director's *Au revoir les enfants* (*Goodbye, Children*, 1984). It has much in common with his comedy of film-making, *La Nuit américaine* (*Day for Night*, 1973), and a good deal of its humour. To some its tone has seemed inappropriate for the situations evoked, but it is arguable that *Le Dernier Métro* is primarily a film about the theatre that gains from the nature of those circumstances as much as a contribution to the cinematic historiography of the 'dark years'. It draws on a tradition of film mystery that includes both *The Phantom of the Opera* and Alfred Hitchcock, whom Truffaut admired intensely and befriended and to whose blend of crime, suspense and humour he paid homage in *La Mariée était en noir* (*The Bride Wore Black*, 1963).

The pervasive element of ambiguity in *Le Dernier Métro* has been examined in an article by Michael B. Kline and Nancy C. Mellerski.[26] In important respects the treatment of theatre, with its codes and practices of simultaneous deception and revelation, corresponds to an unavoidable dimension of France between 1940 and 1945, in society at large as well as in the cultural sphere. This situation persisted through the processes of purification (*épuration*) that, like their equivalent in the defeated German territories, often encompassed the settling of old scores. Survival strategies shaded into opportunism, and temporizing into activity either of resistance or subservience: three classifications are commonly identified – *collaborateurs*, *attentistes* and *résistants* – but they can usefully be thought of as a series of intersecting circles, with some of the *attentistes* who tried to wait out the occupation open to accusations of collaboration while others insisted that passivity or 'business as usual' was itself a form of resistance. A case in point was Jean Cocteau, whose diaries reveal him as almost completely self-absorbed, pursuing the gratification of his artistic life and insisting that he and the intelligent Germans he encountered in *salons* constituted a true 'homeland' where like-minded people came together.[27] Many theatre directors, administrators and heads of cultural organizations stayed in post because they perceived the need for their institutions and those employed in them to survive and preserve the national culture, but ironically in doing so they were serving the occupier's strategies. The cultural self-regard of France was to be maintained as a means of pacifying the population and supporting the vision of a subordinate territory, providing rest and recreation as well as natural and human resources for the greater *Reich*.

Allowed a degree of creative independence, and carefully supervised with regard to inoffensive repertoire and diligently screened personnel (no Jews, freemasons or communists), cinema and theatre experienced a paradoxical if relative flourishing. After the armistice of 1940 Germany occupied the major industrial and strategically important regions of the north, west and east, while the zone to the south was governed as a compliant but constitutionally independent state from the spa town of

Vichy. With the allied invasion of North Africa in 1942, German and Italian troops occupied the 'free zone', but until then it was possible to take the first step towards escape from the occupied zone by crossing into Vichy territory: news of the closing of this avenue is received in Truffaut's film when Marion sees the headline on a newspaper brought into her office by the black marketeer who is peddling stockings. So far as social and cultural policies were concerned Vichy was less efficiently oppressive than the occupied zone, but the occupiers had no intention of turning France into a Nazi state, and had no equivalent of the positive ideological policy that characterized Vichy. Containment and policing rather than the promotion of values were the aims of the censorship, although there was also a campaign to promote the occupiers' culture through concerts, lectures, symposia, and guest appearances by theatre and opera companies. The government in Vichy, with Marshal Pétain as its figurehead, was presented as a 'revolution' that bore only superficial ideological resemblance to that of the Nazi regime. Its backward-gazing appeal to the notion of rural virtue, *la France profonde*, was a weak equivalent of the forceful assertion of *Blut und Boden*, the loyalty to blood and earth that claimed the German nation's allegiance. Pétain's espousal of reactionary values of work, family and motherland – *travail, famille, patrie* to replace *liberté, égalité, fraternité* – cut little ice with the Nazis, except in so far as they provided a convenient instrument of control. In any case Vichy pre-censorship of film and theatre scripts to remove elements that did not square with the promotion of work, family and homeland was cumbersome to the point of ineffectiveness, while works promoting these concepts were hard to come by and for the most part unattractive to the public when they were found. As Richard Vinen points out in *Unfree French*, 'almost all Vichy projects were subject to considerable disagreement and almost none came to fruition'.[28] The simplistic reactionary ideology was easier to announce than to apply and were it not for the more sinister aspects of the state's collusion with such policies as the persecution and deportation of Jews, its blinkered cultural vision might seem comic. The educator and author Jean Guéhenno, in his diary of the 'années noires', describes vividly the intellectual and spiritual oppression experienced by the population of both zones: 'the dreadful silence in which we have to live, knowing nothing, the mere attempt to know being almost considered a crime, deprived of the right simply to cast doubt on the lies that the newspapers seek to impose on us every morning.'[29]

In the occupied zone, supervision of the arts was divided among two principal agencies: the *Propaganda Abteilung* and its executive branch the *Propaganda Staffel*, established by Goebbels as a unit of the military command but answerable to him; and the embassy under the able and energetic leadership of Otto Abetz, a cultured Francophile whose German Institute wooed potential collaborators in the arts.[30] Beyond this structure, whose constitutive elements were often in conflict with one another, lay the personal power of the Nazi hierarchy, notably the pervasive influence of Goebbels and the greedy enthusiasm of Göring and Hitler for acquiring works of art and – in Göring's case – opportunities for influence. The strategies by which curators protected national treasures paralleled those adopted by those non-collaborating film and theatre directors who saw it as their duty to wait out what they hoped would be a temporary situation. At the same time, theatre and cinema suffered from restrictions less directly the result of ideology or greed: materials were hard to come by, personnel might be lost to forced labour if not to exile or deportation to the camps, power shortages might interrupt performances, and the curfew and black-out made theatre-going hazardous. Quite apart from the officially sanctioned censorship, a vigorously anti-Semitic and pro-fascist element of the press was a constant threat.

The most notable publication of this kind was *Je suis partout*, whose title's claim to ubiquity was parodied as *Je chie partout* ('I shit everywhere'). (After the liberation, the flight of its staff earned it yet another title, *Je suis parti*.[31]) The anti-Semite and homophobe Alain Laubreaux had already acquired notoriety by publishing a glowing review of his own ill-received play *Les Pirates de Paris*, but was able to build a formidable power base during the Occupation. One of Laubreaux' most notorious personal campaigns was waged against Cocteau and his lover, the actor Jean Marais. The revenge taken on him by Marais provided the episode in Truffaut's film where the actor Bernard beats up the critic Daxiat: like the abusive attacks of the fascist *milices*, the confrontation with Laubreaux was one of the occasions when Cocteau came face to face with the realities of life beyond the *salons* and their Francophile German officers.[32]

Born in 1932, Truffaut's first-hand experience of the Occupation was as a child: unlike many in the film and theatre world he had not lived through it as an adult professional, nor was he able to judge it in retrospect as the next generation were. He described *Le Dernier Métro* as 'the theatre and the Occupation seen by a child'.[33] His film-going in the early 1940s and subsequent critical and historical activities as young cinephile coloured his representation of the time. Allusions to other films embed *Le Dernier Métro* in the director's personal history and that of the French film industry. The early scene in which Bernard (Gérard Depardieu) tries to pick up the wardrobe mistress

Arlette (Andrea Ferreol) recalls the opening of *Les Enfants du paradis* (1945), with Frédérick's flirting with Garance (played by Arletty), and there are passing mentions of other films and other actors, including Jean Gabin, to whom Bernard is compared, specifically in the role of Lantier in Jean Renoir's version of Zola's *La Bête humaine* (1938). There are implicit references to earlier films of Catherine Deneuve (who plays Marion Steiner), specifically Buñuel's *Belle de jour* (1967) and Truffaut's own *La Sirène du Mississippi* (*Mississippi Siren*, 1969). Jean Renoir's *La Règle du jeu* (1939) is invoked through the person of Paulette Dubost, who plays Marion's dresser and appeared as the maid Lisette in Renoir's film. The 'Norwegian' play *La Disparue* (*The Woman who Disappeared*), like *La Règle du jeu*, even features a maid and a gamekeeper, recalling characters in Renoir's film. At one point Lucas, the hidden director of the theatre, compares his situation to that of the heroine of a play he and his wife saw before the war in London, in which a young woman was terrorized by the sound of footsteps in the room above after she thought her husband had left her alone in the house: this is *Gaslight*, a play by Patrick Hamilton filmed twice – in England (1940) and Hollywood (1944) – and best known through the second screen version, directed by George Cukor. (Lucas says, 'I almost bought the rights.') The cumulative effect is to establish a frame of self-conscious artistic and cultural allusion.[34]

The film features numerous incidental details of everyday life in occupied Paris, of which the most immediate is the midnight curfew referred to in its title: because the occupiers worked to Central European Time, the curfew hour was effectively 11 o'clock rather than midnight, putting a further constraint on places of entertainment. Transport is provided by the unreliable *métro*, bicycles (in short supply and liable to theft), bicycle-powered *vélotaxis* (one is visible in a shot in the street and the rotund stagehand Raymond refuses to ride in one) and, most of all, walking. Unless, that is, one accepts lifts from the Germans (like the ambitious young actress Nadine), has a position that entitles one to the privilege of a car (a sign of Daxiat's status) or is a member of the Gestapo (the men in black coats who arrest Bernard's friend in the church). The black market provides food and luxury goods for those who can afford them, but shades off into criminality and collaboration. (Martine, who does the rounds of the theatres with black-market goods, is also a thief and, it seems, engages in *collaboration horizontale*.) Without access to what it can provide, women must make do and mend, and we see a specific example of this when Martine shows that she not only paints her legs to simulate silk stockings but even draws in a seam. The intensifying of allied air raids causes an increase in the frequency of alarms and also of power cuts, and Raymond's stratagem of using car headlights powered by bicycle-pedalling is typical of the measures taken by theatres during the period. On a graver and more directly political level, Bernard's pride in his escape from a round-up of young men for forced labour squads (STO – *Service du Travail Obligatoire*) meets with the disapproval of the dresser Germaine, whose son is a prisoner of war: a common aspect of public opinion documented by Vinen. As a homosexual the director Jean-Loup Cottins (Jean Poiret) is especially vulnerable to the insinuations of Daxiat's articles – his work is described as an 'effeminate' version of Lucas Steiner's 'Jewified' (*enjuivé*) productions – and at the liberation he is arrested in his dressing gown by the 'FIFIs' (*Forces Françaises de l'Interieur*) and released 'because of his connections', then re-arrested for the same reason. The situation (but not his personality) reflects the case of the playwright, actor and *boulevardier* Sacha Guitry and is representative of the confusions and contradictions of the liberation.[35]

Truffaut took pains to show a wartime Paris that was tenebrous and claustrophobic. He was convinced that 'a film about the Occupation should take place almost exclusively at night and in confined spaces, it should recreate the epoch by darkness, a sense of confinement, frustration, the precarious nature of existence, and – as the only element of light – it should include original recordings of some of the songs that were heard then in the street and on the radio'.[36] The opening scene establishes the 'studio realism' of design and cinematography, and conveys at once the qualities Truffaut describes in the quotation above. The young actor Bernard accosts a woman as he walks along the street, using what is clearly a well-honed routine, and she rebuffs him wittily. Posters for a number of well-known movies from the period preside over the encounter.[37] We discover he is on his way to the (fictional) Théâtre de Montmartre, where he has an appointment with the director. At first he tries the front doors, which have a notice announcing that the theatre is closed for rehearsals, and he enquires at the concierge's lodge of a building across the way to discover the stage door. Raymond, the theatre's stage-manager and general factotum, guides him through the backstage area, across the stage itself, through corridors and up staircases and parks him in an office adjacent to that of the director. As they enter this room they pass a man who is waiting for a meeting with the director, and because the room where Bernard has been placed has doors that are open onto the adjacent office, he hears and partly sees an argument between the director Marion Steiner and an as yet unidentified man about the person who is waiting. It transpires that he is a Jew with a self-evidently faked certificate of Aryan identity, and Marion will not employ anyone in such a situation. The colleague with whom she has been arguing comes into the room and discovers Bernard. He introduces himself as Jean-Loup Cottins, the director of the theatre's productions, and counters Bernard's objection that he does not wish to supplant anyone in the Jew's situation by assuring him that he was not going to be cast in the role Bernard has been called for. Bernard accepts this, and when Marion comes to meet him he agrees to sign the contract. She congratulates him on his performance at the Grand Guignol in a play called *Le Squelette dans le placard* ('The Skeleton in the Cupboard'), while at the same time intimating that she 'spoke to some people who went for the first time' to this popular theatre specializing in 'horror' pieces just to see him perform. As Bernard signs the contract, we see that he has to make a legal declaration that he is not Jewish and that to the best of his knowledge none of his parents or grandparents 'are or were Jewish'.

This introductory sequence brings Bernard, like the audience, to the theatre for the first time. As well as the direct intimations of the theatre's precarious legal position, Marion's dealings with the Jewish actor indicate a certain ambiguity regarding her character. The Billancourt film studios may be lax in these matters, but 'here we follow the regulations to the letter'. She tells Jean-Loup, 'All you have to do is tell the truth. Marion Steiner doesn't want Jews in her theatre.' The Jewish actor is outraged: this is Lucas Steiner's theatre after all. Truffaut stages this scene, like many others in the administrative offices and dressing rooms, so that we are never quite clear which doors connect with which rooms. Yet more of the theatre's secret passageways will be revealed, and although the backstage geography of the Théâtre de Montmartre is no more confusing than that of most theatres when encountered for the first time, there is already a sense of a world that is not easily navigated by those not initiated into its secrets. At the same time, it is less drab than the streets outside and the warmth of lighting and decoration in the office – whose dominant colour is a rich red – suggests a privileged space. Later, when Marion goes to the hotel room where she has her official residence, there is a suggestion of opulence: this is a stylish hotel favoured by German officers, and she even has a maid to attend her. She still has her jewels and her fur coat and she is capable of dressing in the height of pre-war fashion when she goes to a night-club. Is Marion, who is never less than chic in dress, hairstyle and makeup, part of the collaboration? It is not easy to 'read' her, and Catherine Deneuve's flawless appearance seems almost anachronistic, or at least a performance set apart from the harsher world outside. Truffaut rejoiced in her ability to project passionate nature within an immaculate exterior, the ambiguity of the 'impression of a ... "double life"' conveyed by the contrast between her face and the 'severity' of her gaze.[38] Here the quality is very much to the fore, but it is also congruent with a recurrent theme in the director's work: the concealed, fugitive, or 'stolen' passion, that in its most romantic and light-hearted version runs through the cycle of films dealing with Antoine Doinel (the Truffaut avatar played by Jean-Pierre Léaud) from *Les 400 Coups* (1959) onwards. What we learn about the secret life of the theatre suggests that she needs to 'pass' in the same way that she has to bar Jews from her stage or accept the presence of a French woman's German husband at a backstage party. Marion's acceptance of privilege is as a strategic role, but the film does not yet spell this out.

As the internal geography of the theatre becomes more familiar, so do the relationships between the characters – although, as has been noted, the precise interconnections of rooms and the access to them in the administrative areas are not made clear. The most important revelation comes when, after all the lights have been turned out, Marion returns secretly and descends, oil lamp in hand, to the cellars in a shot that recalls the situation of the pursuers of the Phantom of the Opera. The person we next encounter is a relative of that hidden director. In the first shot revealing Lucas Steiner he is seen behind a row of candles resembling footlights, a moment characteristic of suspense films and appropriately emphasized by the score. The Jewish director Lucas Steiner's clandestine existence is ameliorated in the course of the film by two innovations: Marion manages to furnish his lair as if it were an apartment, and he contrives a means of participating in the production of the play by using the old heating ducts to overhear the goings-on on stage. When he first demonstrates this to Marion he seems to speak to her through the walls, much as the Phantom spoke to his protégée. During subsequent rehearsals he makes notes and conveys them through Marion to Jean-Loup, who does not know he is still in France, let alone hiding in the cellar.

There comes a point where he can no longer bear to listen, and during the on-stage jubilations after the opening night he has to stifle the sound by stuffing his scarf into the opening he has made in the duct. This is after he has tried to insist that Marion go through his director's notes rather than rejoin her colleagues at the party, and the incident emphasizes the limitations on his participation. It also indicates a division between Lucas and Marion, whose duty is to the company as much as to him, and reflects the strain that shows in her later behaviour in a one-night stand with a stranger after the scene in the night-club and, ultimately, her acceptance that she desires Bernard. This is after she has rejected Bernard's approaches to the extent of asking him not to touch her as the play's script requires. She implements an even stricter regime of refusing to exchange even the routine courtesies with him, such as holding his hand in a curtain call. In the theatre, as Bernard is told when he complains about the recalcitrance of Arlette, *everyone* kisses. ('Tout le monde s'embrasse'). Why should this customary endearment be refused? Desire is part of the hidden world of the Théâtre de Montmartre: Marion's passionate sexual relationship with her husband conducted necessarily and like his artistic life 'en clandestinité', and (more conventionally) her feelings for Bernard; Arlette's sexual preferences, only revealed to us when Marion opens 'a door that should have been locked' to discover Arlette embracing Nadine; and Raymond's admission that he allowed people to think he was having an affair with Martine when nothing of the kind took place.

On stage in *La Disparue*, when Marion is reluctant to allow Bernard (in character) to stroke her hair, Lucas insists that this should be done, effectively directing his own displacement in her affections. Although he does not know it and, judging from the film's conclusion, never will, she is herself the 'woman who disappeared', much as he is assumed by everyone except her to be the man who got away. When the Gestapo arrive and demand to see the cellars, Bernard discovers for the first time that Lucas has not escaped to South America. They stay in the cellar after the intruders have departed, in a moment of complicity between husband and lover. At moments like this Truffaut's film pays its dues to Renoir's *La Règle du jeu* and, beyond it, to the farces of Georges Feydeau. Lucas corresponds to the Grand Guignol's 'skeleton in the cupboard' (though Marion is able to keep him well fed), but there is a figurative skeleton in the cupboard in her desire for Bernard – as yet unacknowledged. In this respect, the film resembles Ernst Lubitsch's *To Be or Not to Be* (1942) in capitalizing for comic effect on a tragic political situation. Truffaut superimposes the plot lines in which Lucas is hiding from the Gestapo and Marion is hiding feelings that, for the moment, she cannot admit to herself. To convince the Gestapo (themselves pretending to be Civil Defence inspectors looking for air-raid shelter space) that the cellar is empty, Bernard and Lucas have had to effect what is in fact a rapid scene change. The space preciously made over into an appropriately furnished underground 'apartment' now has to be turned back into a lumber-room. There may be a hint here of the Phantom of the Opera's more elaborate transformation of the opera house's cellarage into a suite of luxurious but sinister rooms.

The play performed on stage is seen only in fragments of rehearsal and performance, from which it is difficult to piece together its narrative. Under mysterious circumstances the mother of a child disappeared but now has returned, with the connivance – or possibly, under the sinister influence – of a doctor. Her son is to be taught by a new tutor (played by Bernard) who is a figure from her past, probably the lover who occasioned her breakdown. At the end of the play there is moment of revelation, apparently following some kind of crisis in which she may have attempted suicide (her dress is torn and she is bedraggled). She faints, and there is a blackout on stage. After the lights come up the dialogue resumes with an enigmatic exchange between her and the tutor, partly (in a self-referential touch characteristic of Truffaut) using dialogue from the final scene of *La Sirène du Mississippi*:

> Marion: I didn't have the right to love. Do you understand that? I didn't have the right to love, nor to be loved.
>
> Bernard: And now?
>
> Marion: Now I come to love, Carl, and it is painful. Does love hurt?
>
> Bernard: Yes, love hurts. Like great birds of prey it glides above us. It stops and threatens us. But this threat may also be the promise of happiness. You are beautiful, Helena, so beautiful that to look at you is painful.
>
> Marion: Yesterday you said it was a joy.
>
> Bernard: It is a joy. And a torment.[39]

The play within *Le Dernier Métro* clearly bears on the events of the film's main story but is not wholly comprehensible in itself, as though a work of art were struggling to express the actors' feelings. It remains a mystery, even if (one assumes) by its conclusion this is not so for the audience in the theatre. It is not so much that we do not need to know it, as that we need *not* to know it.

The strategic use of the signs and symbols of the mystery film amounts at times to a homage to Hitchcock. There are moments when music and editing build suspense by cutting rapidly from one actor to another: the most notable of these are the encounter between Marion and Martine on the staircase of the Propaganda Abteilung's headquarters and the subsequent scene in which her hand is gripped by the officer who informs her that the official she has come to see has not been sent to the Eastern front, but has committed suicide. The shots flick backwards and forwards between the two actors' faces and a close-up on their hands as Marion struggles to free herself, and the situation is only resolved when another officer enters the room. In this requisitioned house each door has an inner door, and when the officer takes her into another room to tell her his news neither we nor Marion have time to notice the layout: the sense of entrapment is vivid, and the score supports it.

In a sequence in the hotel's cellar during an air-raid alarm, Daxiat suggests that Marion should get a divorce. The scene continues one in which he has admitted his frustration as a critic and his desire to be part of the theatre world: 'It's true that I am a walking paradox. I love the theatre. I live for the theatre. But I'm hated by the vast majority of theatre people.'[40] After Daxiat's proposition that she should divorce to rid herself of the name Steiner, Marion looks away from him and Truffaut cuts seamlessly to a panning shot which seems to follow her look into the next scene, travelling past a table laden with books to a bed where Lucas and Marion are together. She proposes staying with him until the morning and he turns out the light 'to consider her proposition'. Within Daxiat are places even darker than his sinister conduct suggests, just as between Marion and Lucas there may be a falling out of love at odds with a desire on her part to remain loyal to him and protect him. Daxiat wants to enter the theatre, to invade its privacy – literally, when he turns up at a rehearsal – and at the same time in a radio speech delivered from the printing works of *Je suis partout*, he insists on the need to rid it of Jews 'from the rafters to the prompter's box' (*depuis les combles jusqu'au trou du souffleur*). (The irony here is that he does not wish to go further below the stage, and does not realize that Lucas is there 'prompting'.) To be admitted to the theatre, backstage and in the audience is a privilege: it is granted to the Jewish girl who hides her yellow star with a scarf and, by an irony of the regime's need for personnel, to the Jewish fireman on duty backstage during performances. It is permitted to Daxiat, but only grudgingly, and he even has the nerve to arrive late for the first performance, pushing his way to his seat with two German female auxiliaries in tow.

These tactics situate the theatre as a place of display and secrecy, contrasting light and shadows. 'Mehr licht', says Lucas when we first see him come up from the cellar, quoting Goethe's reported last words, and he wants to breathe the air of the theatre from the stage. It is also the place where desire is experienced and, with any luck, fulfilled, and it is in itself the object of desire on the part of those who seek employment, queue for tickets or, like Daxiat, wish to possess it. (His real-life counterpart Laubreaux even wanted to direct the Comédie-Française.) In the play being rehearsed and performed the tutor Carl complains that 'since [he] came to this house [he has] heard nothing but lies'. The reply is that these are not lies but lapses in memory: 'ce ne sont pas des mensonges, ce sont des trous noirs.' At another point he is told by the doctor that in 'this house' one must never mention the name of Charles-Henri. *La Disparue* emerges as a play about an obscure case of false identity but it is also about a house, a word suggestive of the 'house' in which it is being played, which is also full of hidden motives and (literal) black holes (*trous noirs*). When it is decided that a scene is to be played with the characters in silhouette ('ombres Chinoises') the effect emphasizes the stage as a lighted box, a place of trickery and effect. Meanwhile, within their relationship, Marion has to manage Lucas as well as the company: when he learns of the invasion of the 'free zone' he decides to break cover and persuade the authorities to allow him to continue his career, and she has to restrain him and, as a last resort, knock him unconscious to prevent this. Before the first performance of the play she makes a show of appearing calm and collected, then rushes upstairs and vomits in the lavatory. Both scenes have elements of farce and tenderness, both correspond to the deceptions that must be practised to hold more sinister forces at bay. After all, Marion is an accomplished actress, and at such moments the film's kinship with *To Be or Not to Be* is most evident. Moreover, like Carole Lombard's actress she is playing a double game with her husband, although here the stakes in all the games are considerably higher than in Lubitsch's comedy.

The final sequence is remarkable for duplicity on the film-maker's part, recalling the opening of *La Nuit américaine*, where a convincing scene on a busy Parisian street is suddenly revealed as a film set. In a hospital ward, we witness what seems to be the post-liberation final parting between Marion and the gravely wounded Bernard. They talk about their love affair, and the lies necessary to sustain it:

> Bernard: ... In order to come, you would have had to invent a new lie each time.
>
> Marion: Lie? Why lie? Lie to whom? Since he's dead.
>
> Bernard: You must have taken refuge in your work.

In the following exchanges, shot in alternating close-ups, the background becomes blurred. Bernard rejects her love and tells her to go away, but she insists. A reaction shot of two nurses is followed by a close-up on Bernard, then the camera pulls back to include Marion in frame. The background is now a painted backdrop:

> Marion: Listen to me. Listen carefully. It takes two to love just as it takes two to hate. And I will love you in spite of yourself. Just the

> thought of you makes my heart beat more quickly. That's all that
> counts for me. Farewell.

She rises, crosses and exits, and Bernard buries his face in his hands,
but as he does so theatre curtains swing across between him and
the camera.[41] We are in the theatre, and this is not the conclusion of
Marion and Bernard's love affair but a play which seems uncannily
close to what might have been its circumstances. The two join hands
for the curtain call, Lucas is brought on stage from his box – definitively emerging back into the light – and the final shot is of the three
holding hands (Figure 16), with Marion moving to take the central
position between her two men. There is also a reminiscence of one of
Truffaut's earliest successes, *Jules et Jim* (1962), with its celebration
of love between the members of a threesome with a magnetic woman
(Jeanne Moreau) at its centre.[42] This moment of dislocation returns
Truffaut from the 'well made' film to the carefully constructed indeter-
minacy of narrative and *mise en scène* associated with his earlier career
and the work of more radical colleagues in the *nouvelle vague*. Lynn
A. Higgins suggests that the jolt of this *mise en abyme* can be related
to the broader questions of engagement with history: 'It is as if history
has been a dream of an illusion, part of a play that ends, much to our
relief, freeing us to go home.' Truffaut's use of newsreel footage and
voice-over has already placed the main narrative in what might be
called 'unavoidable' non-diegetic history. The sudden note of theatrical
trickery reminds us that after all theatre is theatre, and film is film,
rather than proposing that (in Higgins' words) 'theater and history [are]
indistinguishable'.[43]

Le Dernier Métro celebrates the theatre's ability to rise above
oppression through its art rather than by some strategy distinct from
it. Bernard and Marion call on their resources as actors to maintain the
theatre and – in her case, directly – to ensure the safety of Lucas. That
Lucas is able to exercise his director's skills is something of a miracle,
and enables him to survive the long confinement to which he has been
condemned. At the same time, the liberal morality of the theatre is
protected: both Jean-Loup as a gay man and Arlette as a lesbian find
a more or less safe haven in it, and Marion's love life has the kind of
variety commonly associated with the stage. Her immaculate presentation of herself and her unfailing poise and confidence – or at least
the impression she gives of them – identify her as a creature of her
profession. Truffaut's regard for Deneuve and for women in general
and actresses in particular chimes here with his admiration for Renoir,
and the trick at the end of his film recalls the complex ending of *The*

16. *The Last Metro* (1980): Marion, Bernard and Lucas in the curtain call

Golden Coach (1952; see pp. 244–245, below) and the idea, there more explicit, of the stage as the only 'reality' for the actress.

Not only did Truffaut wish to present a child's view of the Occupation; he was also anxious to give a sense of the conditions of everyday life, but insisted that it was the film's background rather than its subject.[44] At the same time, the film reflects his delight in the skill of the film-making process as well as the resourcefulness of the theatre and its people. It also accepts without solemnity or condemnation the need for theatre (and film) workers to find employment, even during the Occupation. The film was widely acclaimed, but dissentient voices suggested that the director had offered a romantic and superficial vision of wartime France. Naomi Greene summarizes this response: 'The constraints and dangers of the era become little more than a stylish backdrop of iconic images; moreover, as if to reinforce the sense of illusion that permeates the film, these iconic scenes frequently appear to have been drawn less from real life than from earlier films.'[45] Bertrand Tavernier's *Laissez-passer* (*Safe Conduct*, 2002) – set in the film industry – is arguably a more comprehensive account of the context of the creative life during the Occupation, achieved without any forfeiture of humour or warmth and without undue bitterness.

As Truffaut's biographers Antoine de Baecque and Serge Toubiana show, his film's depiction of the circumstances of the Occupation, and of a 'clandestine' world of theatre and film, corresponds to the director's experience as a child and teenager. The title of their first chapter, 'Une enfance clandestine', reflects not only the 'hidden' nature of such experiences during the Occupation but also Truffaut's situation as an unwanted and not fully acknowledged child establishing his own world.[46] Diana Holmes and Robert Ingram suggest that *Le Dernier Métro* is effectively an assertion of the dominance of the 'provisional' celebrated in his other films: totalitarianism, they point out, is 'unequivocally aligned with the definitive, with an essentialized and changeless definition of nation, gender, and personal identity'. The theatre is 'as a symbol of the right to dream, to redefine the self and relationships, to choose provisional forms of community rather than those based on blood or on an authorized social contract'.[47] Their conclusion places it in the context of *Jules et Jim* and other explorations of the 'provisional'. It has the merit of placing it in the superimposed frames of the director's own life and career, not so much an escapist film, as a film about the uses and contradictions of escapism, and of the theatre's 'lies like truth' in the society of greater lies and stifling silence chronicled by Guéhenno in his diary. In a world where the audience includes an occupying force and its willing agents, the *ombres chinoises* of the lighting are doubly necessary. In Truffaut's film the theatre's pleasurable deceptions are stratagems for survival.

Notes

1 'Du bist am Ende – was du bist./ Setz dir Perücken auf von millionen Locken,/ Setz deinen Fuss auf ellenhohe Socken,/ Du bleibst doch immer, was du bist.' The translation is that by David Luke for the Oxford *World's Classics* edition (Oxford: Oxford University Press, 1987).

2 Klaus Mann died in 1949. The novel, written in exile and published in Holland in 1936, was issued after the war in East Germany but blocked for legal reasons in the Federal Republic. The situation was not fully resolved until 1980, when Rowohlt published a paperback edition. The stage adaptation by the Théâtre du Soleil in Paris in 1979 and the release of Szabó's film in 1981 can be seen as definitively supporting the challenge to the ban. For details of this 'career of a novel', see Bodo Plachta, *Erläuterungen und Dokumente: Klaus Mann, 'Mephisto'* (Stuttgart: Philip Reclam Jr, 2008), pp. 212–239.

3 Klaus Mann, *Mephisto. Roman einer Karierre* (Reinbek bei Hamburg: Rowohlt, 1981), p. 49.

4 Sebastian Haffner, *Germany: Jekyll and Hyde. An Eyewitness Analysis of Nazi Germany*, with an introduction by Neal Acherson (London: Abacus, 2008), pp. 100, 101.

5 Peter Michalzik, *Gustaf Gründgens. Der Schauspieler und die Macht* (Munich: Ullstein Econ List Verlag, 2001), p. 24.

6 Letter to Heinz Tietjen, *Generalintendant* of the Prussian state theatres, in Rolf Bandehausen and Peter Gründgens-Gorski, eds, *Gustaf Gründgens. Briefe, Aufsätze, Reden* (Munich: Deutsche Taschenbuch Verlag, 1970), pp. 13, 40; Michalzik, *Gustaf Gründgens*, p. 185.

7 On the 'opulence' of Nazi theatre, see Gerwin Strobl, 'The Age of Mephistopheles: Theatre and Power', in *The Swastika and the Stage. German*

Theatre and Society, 1933–1945 (Cambridge: Cambridge University Press, 2007).

8 Günther Rühle, *Theater in Deutschland, 1887–1945, seine Ereignisse, seine Menschen* (Frankfurt am Main: S. Fischer, 2007), p. 860, notes that by 1939 the four 'classic theatres' in Berlin were restricted to a narrow range of works from the established repertoire. See also Mann, *Mephisto*, pp. 342–343.

9 Bandehausen and Gründgens-Gorski, *Gustaf Gründgens*, p. 13.

10 On *Jud Süss* and Harlan's partial rehabilitation in the historiography of German film, see Eric Rentschler, *The Ministry of Illusion. Nazi Cinema and its Afterlife* (Cambridge, MA: Harvard University Press, 1996), pp. 166–169.

11 Carl Zuckmayer, *Geheimreport*, edited by Gunther Nickel and Johanna Schrön (Gottingen: Wallstein Verlag, 2002), pp. 132, 153.

12 Klaus Mann, *Der Wendepunkt. Ein Lebensbericht* (Munich: Edition Spangenberg, 1989), p. 385. This is the longer version, in German, of *The Turning Point* (New York: L.B. Fischer, 1942).

13 Annette Insdorf, *Indelible Shadows. Film and the Holocaust* (New York: Vintage Books, 1983) p. 146; Mann, *Mephisto*, p. 272.

14 Gründgens' homosexuality made him vulnerable. In Mann's novel an equivalent is provided by the sadomasochistic relationship with Juliette, which the film tones down because Szabó did not want a spectator to be able to say 'This man is collaborating with the Nazis because he is a pervert and a fetishist; and since I am not a pervert and fetishist, I could not collaborate with the Nazis': John W. Hughes, '*Mephisto*: István Szabó and "the Gestapo of Suspicion"', *Film Quarterly*, 35/4 (Summer 1982), pp. 13–18; 17.

15 Mann had seen reports of Göring's marriage and in a letter to an émigré paper expressed disgust at its 'grotesque pomp', the model for the novel's birthday celebration. The text is printed in *Klaus Mann, Briefe und Antworten, Band I: 1922–1937*, edited by Martin Gregor-Dellin (Munich: Edition Spangenberg, 1975), pp. 212–215.

16 The film's line is 'Was wollen sie von mir? Was wollen sie? Ich bin doch ein Schauspieler.' The word 'doch' has the force of 'after all' or 'only'. In the novel's final pages Höfgen is in his country house, where a comrade of the dead Ulrichs seeks him out and taunts him with the retribution that the future will bring. It is 'people' whose demands perplex him in Mann's final sentence: 'What do people want of me? Why do they persecute me? Why are they so hard [on me]? After all I'm just a perfectly ordinary actor' ('Ich bin doch nur ein ganz gewöhnlicher Schauspieler' [p. 399]).

17 Characteristically, the Berlin Wall, constructed in 1961 to prevent escape to the Federal Republic, was labelled officially in the East as an 'anti-fascist defence' measure. Accounts in English of the GDR's surveillance culture include Timothy Garton Ash, *The File. A Personal History* (London:

Harper Collins, 1997) and Anna Funder, *Stasiland. Stories from behind the Berlin Wall* (London: Granta Books, 2003).

18 Hubertus Knabe, *Die Täter sind unter uns. Über das Schönreden der SED-Diktatur* Berlin: List Taschenbuch, 2009) and *Gefangenen in Hohenschönhausen. Stasi-Häftlinge berichten* (Berlin: List Taschenbuch, 2009).

19 In *Hohenschönhausen* (p. 19), Knabe notes that none of the former inmates he interviewed had discovered that a Stasi officer had secretly helped them. A useful collection of interviews and comments, including press reactions, is provided in a school study guide edited by Jörn Brüggemann, *Florian Henckel von Donnersmarck, 'Das Leben der Anderen'. Materialien und Arbeitsanregungen* (Braunschweig: Schroedel, 2010).

20 Translations of the dialogue have been checked against the published screenplay: *'Das Leben der Anderen.' Filmbuch von Florian Henckel von Donnersmarck, mit Beiträgen von Sebastian Koch, Ulrich Mühe und Manfred Wilke* (Frankfurt am Main: Suhrkamp Taschenbuch, 2007).

21 Garton Ash, *The File*, p. 96.

22 Mary Fulbrook, *Anatomy of a Dictatorship. Inside the GDR, 1949–1989* (Oxford: Oxford University Press, 1995), p. 61.

23 The article is appended to the published script, pp. 201–213. The quotation is from the final paragraph, p. 213.

24 Bertolt Brecht, 'Erinnerung an Marie A.', in *Ausgewählte Gedichte*, selected by Siegried Unseld, with an afterword by Walter Jens (Frakfurt am Main: Suhrkamp, 1964), pp. 12–13.

25 Quoted by Frederic Spotts, *The Shameful Peace. How French Artists and Intellectuals Survived the Nazi Occupation* (New Haven, CT and London: Yale University Press, 2006), p. 4. Recent studies of the arts in occupied France include Stephanie Corcy, *La Vie culturelle sous l'occupation* (Paris: Penin, 2005) and Alan Riding, *And the Show Went On. Cultural Life in Nazi-Occupied Paris* (New York: Knopf, 2010). On the theatre, see Serge Added, *Le Théâtre dans les années Vichy* (Paris: Éditions Ramsay, 1992).

26 Michael B. Kline and Nancy C. Mellerski, 'Structures of Ambiguity in Truffaut's *Le Dernier Métro*', *The French Review*, 62/1 (October 1988), pp. 88–98. The Criterion DVD edition of the film has been used for this analysis, and translations from the dialogue have been checked against the film's screenplay, Francois Truffaut and Suzanne Schiffman, *Le Dernier Métro* (Paris: Cahiers du Cinéma, 2001); and the English translation edited by Mirella Jona Affron and E. Rubinstein in the *Rutgers Films in Print* series (New Brunswick, NJ: Rutgers University Press, 1985). Accounts of the film's making and reception will be found in Antoine de Baecque and Serge Toubiana, *François Truffaut* (1996: revised edition, Paris: Gallimard, 2001) and in Truffaut's article 'Pourquoi et comment le *Dernier métro*?' from *L'Avant-scène cinèma*, 303–304 (March 1983)

reprinted in François Truffaut, *Truffaut sur Truffaut*, edited by Dominique Rabourdin (Paris: Chêne, 1985), pp. 174–178.

27 Jean Cocteau, *Journal 1942–1945*, edited by Jean Touzot (Paris: Gallimard, 1989), p. 31 (12 March 1942). There were also moments when he realized that this was a partial view: 'The little intellectual German circle in Paris. We look at this goldfish bowl and take it for the sea' (11 April 1942, p. 79).

28 Richard Vinen, *Unfree French. Life under the Occupation* (New Haven, CT and London: Yale University Press, 2008), p. 72.

29 Jean Guéhenno, *Journal des années noires, 1940–1944* (1947; Paris: Gallimard, 2002) p. 297 (3 November 1942).

30 A succinct description of the structures of propaganda and censorship is given by Riding, *And the Show Went On*, pp. 52–54.

31 The film's voice-over observes that in his flight Daxiat 'l'homme de partout' has become 'l'homme de nul part'.

32 Jean Marais' account of the incident, in *Histoires de ma vie* (Paris: Albin Michel, 1975) is translated in Affron and Rubinstein's edition of the film's screenplay, *The Last Metro*, pp. 182–184.

33 Rabourdin, *Truffaut sur Truffaut*, p. 178.

34 The 1940 version of *Gaslight*, directed by Thorold Dickinson, was 'suppressed' when MGM bought the rights and it only became available again in the 1990s.

35 On Guitry's controversial wartime career see Spotts, *The Shameful Peace*, pp. 232–246. Added (*Le Théâtre dans les années Vichy*, p. 311) notes that his case was the subject of the first post-war opinion poll held in France: 56 per cent of those polled thought he should be arrested, 12 per cent were against it, and 32 per cent registered as 'don't know'.

36 Rabourdin, *Truffaut sur Truffaut*, p. 174.

37 Affron and Rubenstein, *The Last Metro*, identify the most significant of the films: *La Symphonie fantastique* (1941) in which Jean-Louis Barrault played Hector Berlioz; the German propaganda film *Ohm Krüger* (1940) with Emil Jannings; and *Bel ami* (1939), an Austrian film based on Guy de Maupassant's novel.

38 Reprinted in Francois Truffaut, *Le Plaisir des yeux* (Paris: Flammarion, 1987), pp. 193–197; 194.

39 Affron and Rubinstein, *The Last Metro*, p. 126. A comparable effect is achieved in *La Nuit américaine* when the leading actress is given lines to learn that more or less reproduce those of a 'real' scene in which she has just dealt with a painful emotional situation.

40 Ibid., p. 96.

41 Translation and description of shots from Affron and Rubinstein, *The Last Metro*, p. 161.

42 In *Francois Truffaut*, revised edition (Cambridge: Cambridge University Press, 1994), Annette Insdorf comments that the final image resolves a formation that was threatening in earlier Truffaut films: 'If most of *The Last Metro* suggested that "everyone has his secrets" (as in Truffaut's

Hitchcockian films), the close-up of [Marion's] hand clasping Bernard's and then Lucas's implies Renoir's line from *The Rules of the Game*, "Everyone has his reasons"' (p. 239).

43 Lynn A. Higgins, *New Novel, New Wave, New Politics. Fiction and Representation of History in Postwar France* (Lincoln and London: University of Nebraska Press, 1996), p. 152.

44 Rabourdin, *Truffaut sur Truffaut*, p. 174; see also Higgins, *New Novel*, pp. 157–162, on this aspect of Truffaut's 'otohistoriography' and the continuities between the film and *Les 400 Coups*.

45 Naomi Greene, *Landscapes of Loss. The National Past in Postwar French Cinema* (Princeton, NJ: Princeton University Press, 1999), p. 81. A sampling of reviews is given by Affron and Rubinstein (*The Last Metro*, pp. 187–92). De Baecque and Toubiana (*François Truffaut*, pp. 703–715) describe the film's reception in the context of Truffaut's relationship with his colleagues.

46 De Baecque and Toubiana, *François Truffaut*, pp. 52–53.

47 Diana Holmes and Robert Ingram, *François Truffaut* (Manchester: Manchester University Press, 1998), p. 199.

Three *auteurs* and the theatre:
Carné, Renoir and Rivette

THIS chapter considers the treatment of theatre in works by three French film-makers with an indisputable claim to be classed as *auteurs*: Marcel Carné, Jean Renoir and Jacques Rivette. Previous chapters have included discussion of films by directors – including Almodóvar, Bergman, Truffaut and, arguably, Mankiewicz – who were also regarded by themselves and others as working with a strong sense of authorship, but with these three, theatre forms a consistently integral part of an identifiable and coherent *oeuvre*.

The term *auteur* might more usefully be accepted as a critical tool rather than set up as a job description. Raymond Durgnat's simple and preliminary definition of the concept is pertinent here: 'The auteur theory is the assumption that most films can be interpreted in terms of their director's artistic personality just as intensively as a novel can be interpreted in terms of its author's.'[1] The terms of this bare statement call for qualification and a reminder that, in the *politique des auteurs* shaped by the *Cahiers du cinéma* critics and film-makers, the designation of directors as *auteurs* was both descriptive (when applied to the history of film) and prescriptive.[2] The two aspects of the theory were complementary: for the *nouvelle vague*, identifying authorship in Hollywood directors (notably Ford, Hawks and Hitchcock) was a critical strategy that supported the argument that films should be judged (and made) by the director rather than the writer of the screenplay. An influential article by Andrew Sarris introduced the *auteur* into the discourse of American film criticism in 1963, providing a concise definition that complements that of Durgnat, arguing that, ultimately, 'the auteur theory is not so much a theory as an attitude, a table of values that converts film history into directorial autobiography'. The 'meaningful coherence' sought by the *auteur* critic 'is more likely when the director dominates the proceedings with skill and purpose'.[3]

Defining film history as the tracing of 'directorial autobiography' is distinct from identifying common aesthetic and philosophical tendencies or even a coherent purpose in a director's films. Irving Singer's contention that Bergman is a philosopher through cinema but not the proponent of a 'philosophy' (see p. 161) is relevant here. In the course of his work as a director Jacques Rivette became more and more convinced that there was no such thing as an author in films: 'a film is something that already exists', and the director discovers rather than creates it.[4] A further definition of auteurship, especially germane in the present context, is proposed by Singer in his study of Hitchcock, Welles and Renoir, *Three Philosophical Filmmakers*: 'directors whose mind and character retain a discernible identity throughout their output, sometimes to a greater extent, sometimes less so, but usually evident and ongoing'.[5] The films discussed here have all been related – sometimes by the directors themselves – to themes that recur throughout a body of work: performance on and off stage, the theatricality of personal relationships, the place of performance in the subject's self-image, and the common ground (as well as distinctive qualities) of cinema and theatre.

Marcel Carné's *The Children of Paradise*: the theatre as film's double

Like Carné's historical fantasy *Les Visiteurs du soir* (*The Devil's Envoys*, 1942), *Les Enfants du paradis* (*The Children of Paradise*, 1945) was produced at a time of severe constraint – scarcity of film stock and every material requirement down to wood and nails, the need to negotiate with oppressive regimes in occupied and 'free' zones of France, and the necessity for Jewish members of the team to be hidden and provided with a sympathetic 'front' as composer and designer. *Les Enfants du paradis* is a two-part film divided into two *époques*, *Le Boulevard du Crime* – the popular name of the Boulevard du Temple, reflecting the content of the melodramas played in its theatres – and *L'Homme blanc* ('The Man in White'), named for the mime Baptiste Debureau's character of Pierrot. As the Allies advanced, Carné managed to hold back release of the film until the liberation of Paris, and to insist on the showing of both feature-length parts together.[6]

There is a strong element of theatricality in many of Carné's pre-war films, most obviously in *Drôle de drame* (*A Strange Affair*, 1937), in which the household of a mild-mannered clandestine writer of detective novels (Michel Simon) is torn apart in a farce of mistaken identity, and he becomes the quarry of a psychopath who kills butchers (Jean Louis Barrault). The setting is a flagrantly studio-built version of turn-of-the-century London, and the whole affair is summed up in one of its most memorable lines, Louis Jouvet as the Bishop of Bedford murmuring 'bizarre, bizarre'. Two of his darkest films, *Le Quai des brumes* (*Port of Shadows*, 1938) and *Le Jour se lève* (*Daybreak*, 1939) combine tragic narrative with the self-conscious artificiality of atmosphere through design and cinematography that acquired the label of 'poetic realism'. The second of these relates the events that have brought the hero (Jean Gabin) to the murder with which the film begins and the deadly shoot-out with which it concludes. The final moments have a paradoxical and shocking beauty, as sunlight floods into the room where his body now lies.

In *Les Visiteurs du soir*, a fantasy of the fifteenth century with set designs based on illustrations from books of hours, two emissaries of the devil, disguised as troubadours, have been dispatched to gather souls on his behalf. One of them, Dominique (played by Arletty) is cross-dressed as a youth. By the end of the story the devil himself (Jules Berry) has arrived at the castle to make sure his commands are being obeyed. Infuriated by the attempt of one of his missionaries to escape through his love for the daughter of the lord of the manor, the devil turns the couple into stone. In the final moments, possibly to be interpreted as a sign of the persistence of the spirit of occupied France, he is dismayed to hear that the hearts of the petrified lovers are still beating. The bright, airy tone of the film with its gleaming white castle – built on the back lot of the Victorine studio – supports an overall atmosphere of lyrical escapism, but the devil's threat, however comically energetic in Berry's performance, remains real. The optimism of the conclusion is appealing but qualified: they remain stone, after all. *Les Visiteurs du soir* has a dimension of theatricality – or at least self-conscious performance – but this is located mainly in the performance of Arletty as an androgynous troubadour and Jules Berry's finely histrionic devil. In *Les Enfants du paradis* theatricality is pervasive and central.

The double significance of the title *Les Enfants du paradis*, with its reference to both the patrons who sit in 'le paradis' at the very top of the auditorium, and the special status of the film's principal characters, reflects a pervasive element of doubling within the film text. Instances range from parallelisms between characters and situations to repeated words and phrases and even puns and plays on words. Chronology is elided, events ignored and characters recreated in the interests of a general sense of period. The script announces that 'we are in 1827 or 1828' at the beginning, but adds 'it really doesn't matter'.[7] If we allow for the six-year chronological gap between the two parts, the action takes us at least as far as 1833. There is no mention of a defining cultural event, the riot at the first performance of Victor Hugo's

Hernani in 1830. More important, but hardly surprising in the circumstances of its production, is the absence of any reference to the July
Revolution of 1830. The first part establishes the central characters,
Baptiste Debureau (Jean-Louis Barrault), the actor Frédérick Lemaître
(Pierre Brasseur), the dandy and criminal Lacenaire (Marcel Herrand),
Count Éduard de Montaray (Louis Salou) and Garance (Arletty),
the woman who connects them all. The first three are adapted from
historical figures, and it was an anecdote about Debureau, related
to Carné and Jacques Prévert by Jean-Louis Barrault, that gave the
project its impetus. With the exception of de Montaray they are all
outsiders, but not political or social activists. In Edward Baron Turk's
phrase, the film 'prizes recalcitrant individuals, but gives no hint of
alternative systems of power'.[8] In many respects *Les Enfants du paradis*
adopts and celebrates the values of the popular theatre it depicts. The
film's kinship with nineteenth-century melodrama has been described
eloquently by Mirella Joan Affron: 'a cross between a tear-jerker and
a black novel, marked by grandiloquence and pathos, concerned with
historical truth, revealing a taste for the exotic, the fantastic and the
macabre, inspiring strong emotions by simple means, attention to plot
and spectacle, to décor and costume, combining finally the grotesque
and the sublime, the comic and the terrifying'.[9]

The populist, anti-aristocratic implications of Frédérick Lemaître's
performances – including not only the melodrama *L'Auberge des
adrets* (*The Brigands' Inn*) but also *Othello* by the romantic 'barbarian'
Shakespeare – connect the film with the cultural politics of its period.
The convincing effect of carefully observed detail in sets, furnishings
and costumes is qualified by a deliberate generalization in the interests
of the 'spirit of the age', which bears on the characters as well as
the plot. At the same time, the film avoids the limitations of strict
historical accuracy: Carné was anxious, for example, to keep Garance's
gowns clear of fussy decoration, achieving a 'timeless' quality of
elegance in keeping with the character's function in the drama.[10] Like
the evocation of the panoramic scope of nineteenth-century art and
literature (literally, in the establishing shot of the Boulevard du Crime),
this dimension of the film is at once promising and deceptive. Narrative
and pictorial satisfaction are never fully achieved, performances are
not seen whole and erotic desire is never fully satisfied. The careers
of both Baptiste and Frédérick move rapidly – by the end of the first
part – towards celebrity and success, so that fulfilment on that level is
achieved, but for Baptiste the film ends with distressing frustration. The
spectator is arguably encouraged to find symbolic significance beyond
the 'character' of all the principal players, none more so than Garance.

Truth is first invoked by Garance's personification in a sideshow illustrating the proverb 'la Verité est dans un puits' ('Truth is in a well'). As an erotic display it disappoints the customers: naked from the armpits upwards, she revolves slowly in water that appears to hide the rest of her body. As she turns, she gazes at herself in a mirror, the first of many with which Garance will be associated at almost every important juncture in her passage through the film: we do not see what she sees, any more than the customers do, and the film's first mirroring of on-screen spectators and the cinema audience (both voyeurs) has taken place. This job does not last long. When, after her first encounter with Frédérick amid the crowd on the Boulevard, she comes to see Lacenaire in the office where he functions as a public letter-writer, he greets her with 'Out of your well already, my angel, light of my life?'

Garance: *(smiling as always)* Oh, the well. I've finished with that, and with Truth!

Lacenaire: Already?

Garance: Yes, the audience were getting a bit difficult. You know what I mean... 'Truth, but not below the shoulders'... they were disappointed.

Lacenaire: Well, naturally, those fine fellows wanted more. Nothing but 'Truth' and 'The Whole Truth.' I understand them very well. The costume must suit you perfectly!

Garance: Perhaps... but it's always the same!

Lacenaire: How modest! And how chaste![11]

The exchange is full of double meanings, which Garance accepts rather than parries, seeming to take them as complimentary rather than disparaging. These people know more than they need to express about each other. Their complicity suggests a long acquaintance, but its nature is never made clear, either now or in the rest of the film. As for the public, Garance's observation that 'they are really too unpleasant' leads to one of Lacenaire's outbursts of misanthropic energy: 'What I'd really like to do is to get rid of as many of them as possible.' Lacenaire has been heard composing a letter for a presumably illiterate client, a middle-aged man who wants to win back a wife or lover who has run out on him. If we knew at this point what we later learn about the letter-writer himself, his words would seem ironically personal: 'My love and my life ... I have always loved you, and since you went away, time drags as heavily on my heart as chains on the legs of a convict'.[12] While he is composing the letter, Lacenaire's accomplice Avril comes in and stands listening with admiration: 'It's a mystery to me how you manage to think up all that stuff!' Lacenaire dismisses this tribute to his 'learning' and gets down to business, which involves receiving silver cutlery Avril has stolen. As the film's later scenes will show, Avril carries to an extreme his admiration for Lacenaire's style. In the scene of the Count's murder, which is shown through his reactions, he will react 'admiringly and terrified' to what 'Monsieur Lacenaire' has done; he is always 'Monsieur' to Avril. This distancing lends the character some choric aspects, but film offers other, more articulate interpreters, all with competing claims on the audience's trust.

The central section of this scene includes Lacenaire's credo as a rebel against what 'they' wanted to make of him. 'I took a serious look at myself, and I've never wanted to look at anyone else!' It also provides evidence of the contrast between Garance's ability to pass through life with impregnable equanimity and Lacenaire's scarcely suppressed anger against his enemies, the same 'they' who were disappointed by Garance's performance of Truth. After the conversation with Garance discussed above, the old clothes man Jéricho arrives. Lacenaire announces his entrance: 'Here comes the Last Trump.' Unembarrassed by Garance's presence, Lacenaire gives him the spoons, which he weighs expertly in his hand before stating his price. Lacenaire's work as a letter-writer may bring him closer to the truth than we can yet suspect (the convict's chains), but it also acts as cover for his criminal activities. Jéricho is privy to this, but seems unaware of the real nature of Lacenaire's relationship with Garance. Meanwhile the erstwhile impersonator of Truth remains enigmatically in the background, brushing her lips with the quill used by the author. Lacenaire moves to the window, looking out at the humanity he despises; Garance, looking at his desk, observes that he is still writing plays. They stand close together by the desk as he explains that his play 'A Bad Example' is not a tragedy: 'No, it's a little music hall comedy, slightly licentious ... I can't bear tragedies ... it's an inferior form – all those people who kill each other without hurting each other in the slightest – I find it depressing.'[13]

In the course of the film, it is soon apparent that Truth can only be approached by indirect routes, requiring the audience to take in a variety of perspectives and situations. Pleasurable appreciation of the film's artifice is stimulated throughout by the elaborate settings for the world outside as well as within the various specifically theatrical locations it shows. Balanced between cinema and theatre, it also evokes the romantic realism of its forbears in the nineteenth-century popular novel. In particular, Balzac's great project, La Comédie humaine, is reflected in the milieu, characters and narrative. Beyond the profane world inhabited by Carné's characters is a celestial one, represented by the stars Baptiste and Garance gaze at as they look out over Ménilmontant, and in the title of the pantomime in which the realities of their love are acted out, *Le Palais des mirages, ou l'amoureux de la lune* ('The palace of illusions, or the man who was in love with the moon'). Garance, having impersonated Truth, appears in this performance – the only one in which she is seen on stage – as the statue of Diana, with bow and quiver that signify her attributes of a huntress and the tendency to change like the phases of the Moon: her 'real' name is allegedly Claire.[14] This chaste, motionless goddess resists the advances of the lovelorn, sensitive Pierrot (Baptiste) but can be charmed off her pedestal by the skipping, grimacing Harlequin (Frédérick) and even taken by him on a boating trip. When Baptiste as Pierrot, who has been trying in vain to hang himself, sees Frédérick with Garance at the side of the stage he stops dead. His lover Nathalie (Maria Casarès), who is watching from the opposite wing, calls out his name, an offence attracting a fine from the management. The three characters are linked together across the performance space, their line of communication passing *through* it and the fiction being enacted.

The world may be, figuratively speaking, a theatre, but the actors are at the mercy of the gods in the form of their public, in particular the occupants of its highest level, 'paradise'. These gods are not the only source of power and control in the society shown by the film, but they are the most vocal. Paradoxically, they are at the highest level of direct power in the theatre, but would seem at first to be at the lowest level of society in general. The film's representations of theatrical and non-theatrical spaces suggest approaches to the performance dimensions of what both actors and non-actors in the film take as real life. The variety of theatrical spaces allows for play on the lines of demarcation between the backstage and 'in front' experiences, complementing the performing that goes on in the other private and public spheres of the action. The hierarchy of entertainments is clear: the sideshows and their barkers; the theatre companies advertising their wares; the Théâtre des Funambules itself; and the 'Grand Théâtre' – standing in for a number of actual theatres – where *L'Auberge des adrets* and *Othello* are performed. The Funambules is a popular theatre of pantomime, where legal decree forbids the use of the spoken word, while the Grand Théâtre is licensed to offer the 'higher' drama to a middle-class and aristocratic clientele. In effect the film's first theatrical performance is given on the platform where Baptiste's father Anselme (played by Barrault's teacher, the great mime artist Étienne Décroux) drums up business. Baptiste, in the role of a simpleton, sits drooping to the side of the stage while his father mocks him as 'the despair of the family – a family of artistes!'[15] Presently, though, Garance is accused of stealing a watch from a spectator. A policeman asks whether there were any witnesses to support her protestation of innocence and Baptiste suddenly breaks his silence: 'Moi!' He then mimes the incident with grace and humour, impersonating each of those involved and exonerating the young woman.

Both the theatres have backstage areas. At the Funambules the dressing room is effectively a scene dock or property room, below the stage and furnished with little for the artistes' convenience beyond a mirror and a dressing table. At the Grand Théâtre Frédérick has a spacious and elegant dressing room, richly furnished, where he is supplied with a champagne supper and entertains two girl friends ('deux jolies filles' in Prévert's script). It has a 'picturesque disorder' and a wall is hung with portraits – including some of him in his greatest roles. The Grand Théâtre is seen by day, during a rehearsal, with a makeshift version of the scenery used later in the play. In Part Two, after the performance of *Othello*, we see the privileged social space of its spacious *foyer des artistes*. In fact, the borders between the various areas of the theatres are shown to be permeable. To find Garance at the Funambules in Part One, the Count had to enter the jumbled makeshift dressing room where his formal attire and aristocratic manners were out of place. The Grand Théâtre's *foyer* is luxuriously appointed. Here the Count can behave as though he is at home in an extension of fashionable society, attempting to patronize the actor and exercising the right given by his rank – as in his own house – to have Lacenaire thrown out. (In fact, it proves impossible to patronize Frédérick with any hope of success, as the actor is more than his match in urbanity.) However, between these two scenes we have witnessed his encounters with Lacenaire and Garance in his mansion. There, the characters' roles are not so much reversed as mirrored and multiplied: the Count's house has effectively become a theatre, with Garance's boudoir and the staircase corresponding to backstage and stage. Lacenaire's dandyism is a more outré version of the Count's, while Garance is seen in a private dressing room that reinforces the sense of her continuing to be a performer. The confrontation between Lacenaire and the Count on the grand staircase is a meeting between two self-fashioned beings who both employ language that is at once polite and unambiguously hostile, and claim an amoral detachment from all considerations but their desires and impulses. When Lacenaire murders the Count it is as though he were killing a *Doppelgänger*.

In the opening sequence of Part One a recurring theme was

announced when Frédérick was denied admission to the stage door of
the Funambules: accused of trying to get in to see the performance free,
he insisted that 'It's not the show I want to see. It's the director' and
that one day his name would indeed be at the top of the bill, 'and in
giant letters too. Frédérick. Have you got it? Frédérick Lemaître.'[16] Six
years later, by the beginning of Part Two, this has been achieved, and
the actor has attained star status long before he discovers the key to
playing the comic criminal hero, Robert Macaire. Frédérick 'finds' his
costume as Macaire when he is assailed by his creditors and his clothes
are torn (an incident invented by Prévert and Carné). Lacenaire, the
would-be playwright, penetrates the sanctum of his dressing room after
the tumultuous first night of the melodrama Frédérick has turned into
a farce. Lacenaire brings with him his own melodrama, even down to
the sudden revelation of Avril lurking behind a screen – an effect the
actor applauds as worthy of *L'Auberge des adrets*.[17]

Meanwhile Baptiste has advanced at the Funambules, but there
are no obvious signs of greater prosperity. He has become a star, his
new status being reflected in the giant image of him as Pierrot that
hangs from the theatre's façade, but he is permanently situated in an
earthier theatrical world, implicitly 'purer' and less pretentious and
socially ambitious than that conquered by Frédérick. His marriage to
Nathalie and the presence of their little boy (sent to speak to Garance
in her box) suggest that a measure of private stability and prosperity
has been found by Baptiste, in contrast to the rakishly insouciant life
of Frédérick and his 'jolies filles'. When Jéricho, who seems to have a
master-key to many of the film's private spaces, comes to find Nathalie
and her son with news that Garance is the mysterious woman who
comes to every performance, the encounter takes place behind the
scenes among stage properties. Nevertheless, Jéricho's freedom of
movement does not extend to the foyer of the theatre where Frédérick
performs his Othello, or the Count's mansion, and derives directly from
his commerce as a receiver of stolen goods and supplier of properties
and costumes. To his indignation the latter function is taken to an
extreme when his persona is 'stolen' for Baptiste's second pantomime,
'Chand d'habits (*The Old Clothes Man*) in which a mime (Baptiste's
father, in fact) imitating the old-clothes seller is murdered by a Pierrot
desperate to obtain the costume that will grant him admission to a ball
in an aristocratic mansion.[18]

If the film's scripted conclusion had been adopted, this would have
been a premonition of the eventual fate of Jéricho, struck down in the
street by Baptiste.[19] Jéricho glories in the multiple punning significances
of his nickname, and from the very beginning of the film repeatedly

announces himself with his chant and his trumpet as a virtual performer. This performance masks a deep sense of his emptiness, glimpsed now backstage when he is accused by Debureau senior of taking too much interest in other people's business: 'Always alone, that's no life. Nobody ever loved me. Nobody. Zero. Nothing!'[20] It is hardly surprising that his ubiquity and inquisitiveness cause suspicion and fear. He is admitted to the theatre and the Rouge-Gorge tavern, and regards himself as a conveyer of news as well as material goods, but he is also suspected as a malicious informant. In both places he is both tolerated and rejected, forcefully by Lacenaire and less threateningly by the actors.

The audiences for both theatres are carefully characterized, in accordance with the evidence provided by such sources as Louis Péricaud's *Le Théâtre des Funambules* (1897) and Georges Cain's *Anciens Théâtres de Paris* (1906). The gallery patrons break bounds, some of them by sitting astride the panels at the front and all of them by partisan applause or shouts of disapproval. The energy of the Funambules, which can only stay within the law by obeying the ban on its artists' speaking, paradoxically derives from its lack of social status. Like the suspicion with which Jéricho's tale-bearing is treated, the theatre's vitality and popular support despite the ban would have resonated powerfully in the context of the Occupation with its stringent restrictions on public assembly. The first sight of a Funambules performance is the pantomime *Les Dangers de la forêt ou le crime et la vertu* ('The dangers of the forest, or crime and virtue'), which degenerates into a brawl between rival families of mimes, and the spectators comment loudly on it throughout, even before the fracas adds to their enjoyment.[21] When the artistic standards of its pantomime performances have been raised through Baptiste's agency the theatre does not lose or change its clientele, but the performances command their silence. The galleryites respect real artistic quality, and reserve their enthusiastic intolerance for sham or incompetence. This is in contrast to the outmoded rules of decorum by which the Count condemns Shakespeare as a 'barbarian', an attitude that would have situated him with the conservatives and against the romantic radicals in the scandal of *Hernani*. The film does little to characterize the intermediate spaces of the auditorium between the gallery and the stage. There are side boxes at the parterre level, one occupied by the Count and his friends during the first pantomime to feature Baptiste, *L'Amoureux de la lune*, the other (evidently on the other side of the theatre) by Garance when she makes her repeated visits to *'Chand d'habits*. The Count uses his stage-side box to isolate himself (and his aristocratic friends) from the rest of the audience, and to provide a privileged point of view for the gaze he directs at Garance in her performance as Diana. She, in turn, uses the privacy of a box to satisfy a real emotional need in watching Baptiste's later performances without his being aware of her.

Both within the theatre and beyond it, *Les Enfants du paradis* identifies in its characters the ability with which they control their presentation of themselves, their free agency being contingent on the social space in which they find themselves but at the same time determined by their quasi-histrionic abilities. In this society, all are actors in one way or another. The correspondences between Lacenaire and the Count – each is a dandy, one criminalized and the other endorsed by society – and the cross-over status of Jéricho contribute to the richness of the film's 'double' effects. As Jill Forbes observes, Part One has to be re-read in the light of Part Two, 'a recurrent dream in which the passage of time is an irrelevance and which certain motifs, desires and repressed tropes and performances recur in similar or in different configurations'.[22]

Woven into this is the film's artfully varied situation of its characters as both actors and spectators. This is also central to the methods by which it addresses and situates its own audience. From the first, as was noted earlier, this has been connected intimately with its central female character, and the film's audience may feel implicated when Garance, in the early scene discussed above, describes the disappointment of the customers who found that she did not live up to showman's promise. Arletty's body, a notable aspect of her attraction as a performer, is seen piecemeal in the film: she shows an elegant leg to Baptiste when she wraps herself in a bedspread at Mme Hermine's, but as the personification of Truth in the well, she reveals little more than the handsome shoulders and upper chest that several of her subsequent gowns also display. As Truth, the mirror she holds conveniently allows her to focus on her reflection, an early intimation of the enigmatic self-absorption she maintains throughout. Garance's smiling refusal to acknowledge emotional connection – strategically broken at times, but reinstated as she sits alone in her coach at the end – is not so much narcissistic as necessarily wary. The first sight of her, navigating her way through the crowd with extraordinary poise and fending off Frédérick's addresses with amused detachment, offers a telling image of a woman making her way through the world, watching her step without needing to look down. For its part the cinematography constantly draws attention to Garance's eyes, and the upper half of her face is repeatedly favoured with a 'special' spotlight that suggests the luminous quality of her gaze. The 'sphinx' maintains her secret, and it is clear that after six years with the Count she still refuses to use the familiar 'tu' to a man who might expect it as of right from a mistress but would challenge anyone foolhardy enough to use it to him without his permission.[23]

Garance's inscrutability is essential to her independence. Neither a streetwalker nor a conventionally chaste woman, her insouciance is proclaimed in lyrics of the song Frédérick hears her humming after Baptiste has left her room. The tune, this time with the words, is heard again in Part Two after the Baron has expelled Lacenaire from his house:

> I am as I am – that is how I was made
> When I feel like laughing – yes I laugh out loud
> I love the man I love – is it my fault
> If it isn't the same one – that I love every time.[24]

Being prepared to adopt whatever circumstances offer does not in itself make an actress of Garance – or anyone. Paradoxically, this theatrical film has at its centre a woman who does not so much play roles as appear in them according to the way she chooses to let herself be viewed. As Truth or as Diana she is qualified more by her looks than any evident histrionic ability, and her 'private' dressing-room scene, the occasion of as much of a showdown as the Count will ever grant a woman, precedes (though not immediately) the scene in which they appear on display in a box at *Othello*. She is not acting in the later scene at the Grand Théâtre when Lacenaire, showman and dramatist and on this occasion Iago to the Count's Othello, draws a curtain in the foyer to reveal the 'ocular proof' of Garance and Baptiste embracing on the balcony outside (Figure 17).

This discovery is a 'double' of the moment during *L'Amoureux de la lune* in which Baptiste, as Pierrot, looked into the wings and saw Frédérick with Garance. There all three were actors behaving in character, as well as *in propria persona*. The short-circuiting of the theatrical illusion is famously emphasized by the remarkable close-up on Barrault/Baptiste/Pierrot as he reacts to what he sees. The sudden jolt is the illegal spoken word, 'Baptiste', from the astonished Nathalie. The solecism is repeated by her during the performance of *'Chand d'habits*, when Baptiste, instead of joining her on stage, rushes from the wings to seek Garance in her box. (The cry is taken up by the gallery, who call the name repeatedly.) Again, a performance is jolted out of its tracks. Baptiste has left the stage, deserting his post and crossing over from a fictional representation of the lovelorn Pierrot to action in his own life. At the Grand Théâtre the moment of transgression, breaching theatrical boundaries, takes place in the privileged territory of the foyer when Frédérick/Othello confronts the Count/Othello. When the

17. *Les Enfants du paradis* (1945): Lacenaire draws the curtain

Count is murdered at the bath-house, he is wearing a robe reminiscent of Othello's costume in the previous night's performance, and dies at the hand of a double of himself, a parody of his own elegance. This melodrama, acted out beyond the theatre's boundaries, is the denouement of the 'play' dictated on his own terms by Lacenaire. It is another variation on the film's extension of playing spaces beyond the theatres, encompassing the Boulevard itself from the very first scenes and shortly returning us to it for the final, desperate (but uncompleted) act between Baptiste and Garance. The end of the murder scene, with Lacenaire sitting down to await arrest, suggests a sequel – allegedly one was planned – which would have brought not only Lacenaire but also Baptiste to trial if the killing of Jéricho had been included in Part Two as scripted. Whether or not a third part would have been possible is irrelevant: the lack of completion in the film as it stands has become part of its pattern.

The central characters move backwards and forwards between public and private performance, and they also bear the additional role of representing Romanticism. The first scenes introduce not only Frédérick and the enigmatic and self-assured Garance, but also Lacenaire, who has impressive credentials as a romantic outsider, being at once dandy, criminal, aspiring dramatist and (possibly) homosexual. Lacenaire's antagonism towards society in general has already been noted: it is akin to the challenging stance taken by others who will impersonate – if not adopt – criminality before the film is over. Both Baptiste and Frédérick fulfil the role of the young aspirant who takes on Paris, like Balzac's defiant hero Eugène de Rastignac who gazes on the city and challenges it to defeat him at the end of *Le Père Goriot* (1835). Both young actors are innovators, but Frédérick makes a career out of setting his face against rules, either the ban on speech (his particular pastime), the right of authors or the canons of taste proclaimed by the Count. Although Garance has no specifically histrionic or artistic talent with which to challenge artistic conservatism, her fashioning of herself as an independent woman constitutes an act of romantic rebellion. She performs for others the role of a muse, inspiring a combination of erotic and artistic aspirations. Her desire to go to India is romantic in its vagueness and yearning for the unattainable. In the film's second part she has achieved this, but has nothing to report from the experience: it seems to be subsumed in the coldness of her life with the Count. His relationship with her appears to be that of connoisseur towards a treasured possession. She embodies both the splendours and miseries of courtesans, but the role is not played to the hilt either by her or the film-makers. Like Lacenaire, Garance perfects a style that gives vivid expression to some aspects of her personality and conceals others.

Among the professional players, Baptiste, for most of the film, is able to express emotion through the persona of Pierrot but is hesitant and relatively inarticulate in his off-stage self. When he does break across this boundary, in the moment of seeing the lovers in the wings or during his final scene with Garance in the bedroom, the effect is shocking. (It also betrays an emotional vulnerability never displayed by Frédérick.) Barrault's performance captures the grace and restraint that Deburau's contemporaries identified as a key to his appeal, the 'lively and profound intelligence' beneath the white mask adopted by the mime.[25] Nathalie, in contrast to both Baptiste and Garance, is a stage actor who does express sincere and undisguised emotions – love for Baptiste and their child, dismay and patient forbearance with the distraught Baptiste. For most of her scenes, Nathalie wears the stylized costume appropriate to her stage roles. In the final sequence at Mme Hermine's lodging house, though, where Baptiste has spent his single night of love with Garance, Nathalie confronts her rival directly. Here Carné frames the wife in the doorway in her fashionable but conventional street clothes, whereas Garance is in the low-cut evening dress and jewels she was wearing when she and Baptiste made their escape from the theatre. Baptiste, clad only in trousers and shirt, rushes out into the street to search for Garance in the crowd of revellers, most of them wearing copies of his white Pierrot costume. The film's constant doubling of characters and situations is reinforced by his encounter with Jéricho, by now a figure on stage as well as in real life. Even without the enactment in the street of the murder only simulated on stage, Baptiste's struggle to free himself from Jéricho's clutches suggests a need to break away from the truth about fictions through which he has lived. Jéricho's final offence is to tell Baptiste what he regards as the truth about Garance: 'You should both be flogged, you and your whore!'[26]

Carné and Prévert create a world that can accommodate the kind of psychological interpretation proposed by Turk in his chapters on androgyny and masochism and 'primal scenes', as well as the varied possibilities of its political significance.[27] These range from detailed analogies between occupied France and its characters and situations to the suggestion that simply by being made in the prevailing conditions it constituted an act of resistance. Within the film any and all of these possible interpretations are supported through the various forms of theatre it represents, and the consistent leakage of theatricality into daily life and *vice versa*. Its title invokes the demonstrative and vocal spectators at the Funambules, of whom Baptiste observes that 'their lives are small but they have big dreams'. In celebrating communal and individual dreaming, *Les Enfants du paradis* also asserts the importance of the intimate relationship between theatre and film, their capacity by complementary means to express but not to explain or resolve life.

Jean Renoir and the theatre as image of society

Jean Renoir's direct involvement in theatre was limited: two plays by him were produced professionally (*Orvet* in 1955 and *Carola* in 1957), and in 1954 he directed *Julius Caesar* in the arena at Arles for a single performance. From an early age, though, the theatre excited him. At the age of five, under the tutelage of his cousin Gabrielle, he was taken to see Guignol, the French equivalent of Punch and Judy, and was so affected by the preliminaries of the show – the trembling of the curtain in front of the stage and the strange sound of the showman's accordion – that he wet himself.[28] Gabrielle also took him to melodramas in the theatres around Montmartre. This chapter will concentrate on two late films whose principal subject matter is the theatre: *The Golden Coach* (1952) and *French Cancan* (1954).[29] His adaptation of Zola's *Nana* (1926) has been discussed in the Introduction; it foreshadows, as Alexander Sesonske notes in his study of the pre-1939 French films, a recurring theme: 'characters who *within their lives* [Sesonske's emphasis] give performances that are deliberately devised, rehearsed and presented to an audience.'[30] The sense of theatre as a metaphor for aspects of human existence recurs in many of Renoir's films from the beginning of his career, either directly through the adaptations of stage works (notably *Boudu sauvé des eaux* [*Boudu Saved from Drowning*, 1932]) or in more general terms as a key element of humanity: the game or play (*le jeu*) whose rules vary, but which enables men and women to deal with passion and desire. In *La Grande illusion* (*The Grand Illusion*, 1937) and *La Règle du jeu* (*The Rules of the Game*, 1939) amateur theatricals provide the medium for impulses otherwise latent but unexpressed. The second of these is particularly significant in tracing the director's engagement with ideas of theatricality. Although it does not deal with theatre as a topic in itself, on account of its stylized 'studio realism' and Feydeau-esque plotting, *Élena et les hommes* (*Elena and the Men*, 1956) is commonly perceived as a 'theatrical' film alongside *The Golden Coach* and *French Cancan*. Renoir's final invocation of theatre was the toy theatre that provided the framing device for his last completed project, the television programme *Le Petit théâtre de Jean Renoir* (1969).

Boudu begins with a patently theatrical performance of *L'Après-midi d'un faune* that turns out to be a dream sequence. Its shallow stage, pasteboard columns and obvious backcloth – and the nymph's clothing – reflect the old-fashioned literary imagination of the bookseller Lestingois. The film's principal storyline is his project of transforming the tramp Boudu (Michel Simon), whom the bookseller saves from an attempt to drown himself in the Seine, into a 'respectable' bourgeois. Boudu is an elemental being, less easily controlled than the faun of the dream. Dressing him up and trimming his hair and beard produce a figure that remains obstinately incongruous. Faced with the need to untangle the overlapping love triangles in and around his household, Lestingois responds in terms of theatrical taste, declaring that 'la moralité du siècle exigera un dénouement qui regularise, comment dire, la situation' ('The morality of the age will demand a denouement that, so to speak, puts the situation in order'). In the end the bookseller's Pygmalion-like plan comes to nothing, and resolution comes with Boudu's return to the water he was saved from, although he is not drowned and, like Chaplin's tramp, walks away to continue in his way of life.

Both *Madame Bovary* (1933) and *La Marseillaise* (1937) offer historical reconstructions of an epoch. In the version of Flaubert's novel the framing of shots repeatedly places Emma Bovary's character on one side or another of a frame – a window or door – or within a carefully constructed composition.[31] *La Marseillaise*, a historical epic of the French Revolution, exploits the potential for performance written into the court's daily life of pageantry and display. The royal actors perceive themselves in dramatic terms. As the threat of revolution increases, Louis XVI and Marie Antoinette discuss strategy: this is the last act of a tragedy, and she will be happy to initiate it with *les trois coups*.

The king, more sensibly, says that he would have preferred a *deus ex machina* role. In the First World War military and social world of *La Grande illusion*, role-playing, in the sense of acting out the behaviour appropriate to one's class, is central to the relationship between the German prison commandant von Rauffenstein and the French prisoner de Boeldieu. It also represents the last defence of the old regime that both aristocrats represent and perceive as being in its death throes. The prisoners' amateur theatricals culminate in an illegal rendition of the Marseillaise when a French victory is announced.

The most explicitly theatrical of Renoir's pre-war films – apart from *Nana* – *La Règle du jeu*, is announced in its screen subtitle as a 'Fantaisie dramatique'. The film is comprehensively indebted to French stage comedies, specifically those of Marivaux, Beaumarchais and Musset.[32] Renoir's continuing interest in those who perform versions of themselves, or the selves they would wish to possess, is enriched by the collision of play and reality throughout the film. In order to sort out the love life of the aviator Jurieu, his friend Octave (played by Renoir) promises to sort things out ('Je m'en occupe') at a weekend house party. During the entertainment got up by the guests to amuse themselves, the camera picks up a real drama developing in the corridor behind the doors of the salon. As one element of the film's intersecting love-plots develops to a climax, the guests assume that the gamekeeper Schumacher's pursuit of his wife's putative lover, the ex-poacher Marceau, is part of the entertainment. Renoir's virtuoso filming of this extended episode owes much to stage farce, turning (as it were) from Musset to Feydau, but is executed in a medium that outstrips it. The camera glides from room to room, as one element of the action tumbles across the path of another. The 'downstairs' backstage world erupts into the 'upstairs' on-stage world when Schumacher, dragging his wife Lisette behind him, hurtles after the terrified Marceau. A gamekeeper – who should not show himself in the state rooms – chases a poacher who is dressed for his new role as a servant. They duck and weave among the guests as the host's newest toy, a massive fairground organ, provides the background music. His declaration that he has had enough of this play-acting ('j'en ai assez de ce théâtre') is repeated later when he commands his major domo to bring an end to the clumsy fisticuffs and pursuits: 'Faites cesser cette comédie.' Corneille, appropriately named after a master of dramatic construction, asks 'which one, sir?' In the final scene, after Jurieu has been shot dead by Schumacher (who mistakes him for Marceau) the host declares that 'la fatalité' – as in classical tragedy – has been responsible for the night's events.

When he returned to Europe in the 1950s, after his years in Hollywood and the adventure of making *The River* in India, Renoir's first completed project was an 'international' Franco-Italian co-production, the second a fully 'French' enterprise marking his return to his cinematic roots. Both *The Golden Coach* (1952) and the engaging but less complex *French Cancan* (1954) continue the exploration of the theatrical elements of human relationships and behaviour by taking them into the theatre itself. Christopher Faulkner, in *The Social Cinema of Jean Renoir* (1986), argues that in these films of the 1950s the political and social dimension of the director's work changes, presenting 'a consolatory rather than an interrogative function for art'.[33] Compared with the pre-war films, in these Renoir is 'no longer interested in representing a social reality subject to the determinations of history'.[34] While it is clear that the performances in both films are effective and successful and, unlike *Nana*, do not use theatre as a symbol of social decadence, in *The Golden Coach* the affirmative effect of the *commedia dell'arte* is nevertheless qualified and it seems that the theatre will always serve its audience best by remaining at a distance from (or at an angle to) reality.

The Golden Coach creates two contending worlds of artifice, with the popular theatre as a mirror to a colonial court. The central character, the actress Camilla (Anna Magnani) is the catalyst for a process that might in other circumstances lead to social and political change. The rules of the court are set against those of the *commedia*, which are just as powerful and, it is implied, less transient. Whereas the comedy of Marivaux, Musset and Beaumarchais lay behind the earlier film, here the director returns to their common roots in the Italian comedy. Vivaldi, Renoir claimed, was his 'collaborator' and inspiration, and the film is carried along on his music (or work in his manner), with its energy and formal grace.[35] The elaborate composite set for the viceregal palace is complemented convincingly by a dusty town square, and appropriate interiors for the inn and a house given to Camilla.[36] Renoir establishes that both groups of characters, the Viceroy and his entourage and the travelling players, are newcomers in Peru, each hoping to make their fortune in their own manner.

The opening titles of this 'fantasy in the Italian style' announce that an Italian troupe has 'crossed to the New World to seek their fortune, driven by hardship and a new vision'. The words are shown against the background of a red theatre curtain, which is raised to reveal a proscenium arch, forestage and footlights. (Renoir's screenplay indicates that the lighting may be electric, gas or even oil: 'The set should not be of any particular period.')[37] On stage is an elaborate structure showing the ground-floor coach entrance

18. *The Golden Coach* (1952): the palace set within the proscenium frame

of the palace, with stairs rising in two flights to a landing from which doors lead to further rooms (Figure 18). The camera moves up and into the set, leaving the 'theatre' behind, and in one deft but elaborately contrived movement the theatricality of the palace has been decisively established. Excitement about the arrival of a golden coach, ordered by the Spanish Viceroy, animates the extravagantly dressed courtiers, but meanwhile the weary Viceroy is bathing his feet in the 'backstage' of his own palace, tended by his barber and wig-maker. As the golden coach is drawn on its cart across the square by a team of oxen, in the background we see the *commedia* troupe's wagon: 'actors – how shocking' exclaims one of the female courtiers. The troupe is astonished by the inn-yard where they will have to perform, and the screenplay indicates that they 'stand around like a group of immigrants'.[38] As their leader goes to negotiate with the innkeeper who has promised them a suitable theatre, Camilla (Anna Magnani) and Felipe – a young man who is evidently her lover but not, it seems, one of the actors – argue about the prospects offered by the New World: she is sceptical, he hopeful. They also differ in their view of the actor's profession. Camilla, discouraged and tired, insists that the other members of the troupe 'still believe ... that those two hours on the stage tonight are worth everything'. He declares: 'I love you, Camilla, not the people you become for those two hours every night.' A montage shows the actors building the platform in the inn yard, painting scenery assuming costumes and masks and – finally – rehearsing music and dance. The opening sequence has shown a stage metamorphosing into a palace, and now we have seen a barn turned into a theatre. In due course the actors will invade the palace – albeit as patronized entertainers – and the court, in the person of the disguised iceroy, will infiltrate the fit-up theatre.

In the palace a comedy of manners is played out to parallel the *lazzi* of the comedians, and at times the two coalesce, as if the situations and character types of the *commedia* were reasserting themselves in the middle of an ostensibly more refined theatrical genre. The actors soon find out that comedy brings in very little in a country where neither the peasants nor the aristocrats are expected to pay, and many middle-class patrons get in free as friends of the landlord. Meanwhile, across the square, there are questions about the cost of the coach and the question of who shall benefit from it. If, as the Viceroy insists, the coach is a government expenditure in the interests of asserting status, whose standing is to be enhanced first? In a telling juxtaposition, after the finale of the actors' rehearsal the film cuts to a shot of courtiers applauding enthusiastically, but when the camera pulls back we see that they are on the other side of the square, and it is the coach they are applauding.

In the court aggression is channelled and moderated through etiquette, but in the theatre disputes are frankly expressed and sometimes violent. The players are citizens of the world: 'we are artists and the world is our own – we move on.' The courtiers' desire for money is rooted in greed rather than the need to survive. Although admission to the Viceroy's premises is to be limited to those who can prove at least eight noble ancestors, there are no children. In contrast to this sterile, anxiety-ridden palace, the players travel with children, and the presence of Isabella, a (presumably) nursing mother, in their number suggests a happy fecundity that does not get in the way of work. Nevertheless, they are not at all indifferent to money. Their first transaction with the innkeeper is an argument about the rent and the takings; they are seen relishing the gold given to them as payment for their court performance, and they embrace any chance for prosperity. Camilla is temporarily seduced by a gold necklace, endowed with symbolic significance very quickly when it causes a violent dispute with Felipe and arouses the jealousy of her third suitor, the toreador Ramon. The Viceroy, at last able to take off his wig and relax in Camilla's company, reflects that 'we're here only for this treacherous gold. No one dreams of anything else', and is disgusted by a society without levity: 'Where gold commands, laughter vanishes.' The significance of money is emphasized by the *commedia* scenario played on the stage: as Columbine she is a go-between urged by Arlecchino to take money for carrying love-letters from all the rivals for her mistress's hand – Pantalone, the Captain and the Lover.

Control of her own body and fortunes is a vexatious matter for Camilla, who has to fend off propositions that would limit her freedom while assuring her of some kind of security. Life as the Viceroy's consort would involve an irksome and patronizing educative process that he takes too lightly. He maintains that the appropriate airs and graces can be acquired, but the terms in which he describes the process betray its real meaning: 'The weaker sex have that extraordinary talent of completely adapting themselves ... One can create the most arrogant of duchesses.' Similarly, the toreador promises that he and Camilla will make an impressive team, 'King of the bullring – and queen of the stage', and that 'every real king and queen will be jealous'. Both propositions will involve pretence and, in the Viceroy's scheme, will require the renunciation of her true self, a performance less honest than that by which she currently lives. The stage gives her a means of measuring sincerity and honesty, and its own etiquette is as powerful as that of the court: the players' *révérence* at the final curtain is no les elegant than those executed by the courtiers every time they leave or enter a room. She is able to taunt an eavesdropping rival by reminding her that 'Isabella, our great lady, never listens behind doors.' Forced to leave the court, she turns to her persecutors on the council of state with an unanswerable rebuke: 'At the end of the second act, when Columbine goes, driven away by her masters, there's a tradition you seem not to know – the comedians bow to her.' Abashed, the courtiers do just that. Magnani endues Camilla with the authority to stand on her dignity, combined with a sense that she will be very hard to please. Repeatedly, her eloquent facial expressions suggest a sceptical disdain for whatever is going on.

The role of spectator is defined and redefined several times. In the fit-up theatre the unresponsive audience turn their back on the stage to greet the popular toreador Ramon when he makes his entrance, and Camilla begins her next scene indignantly facing upstage. Told (in character) by the leader of the troupe that the audience is behind her, she turns and expresses her surprise. Singling out the toreador for banter, she gains his approval and he leads the applause. At court, the troupe seems to have failed to elicit anything more than faint and polite applause, until it is made clear that etiquette requires the courtiers to wait until the Viceroy gives a lead. He invites the women of the company (in fact, he only wants Camilla) to join him for refreshments. The court ladies treat Camilla disdainfully, but to her they become a harmless spectacle whose elegance she admires as she watches the dancing from a gallery. Her relationship with Ramon also entails a shift from actor to spectator. In the theatre it was his lead that the audience followed. She and her companions attend a *corrida*, which is shown to us only through her reactions as she sits among the spectators.

Most of the scene is shot in medium close-up on Camilla, whose face registers distaste at first and then progresses to engagement and finally enthusiasm as the toreador triumphs. The camera has pulled back to show the crowd around her, and he walks into the frame holding up his arms as though offering her the ears of the bull. She throws him the Viceroy's gold chain. In the bull ring and in front of his admirers the toreador's swagger is appropriate to his role, but in private life it is overbearing and absurdly self-confident. Like the Viceroy he is a performer whose style is valid in its own sphere. Unlike the Viceroy, he is unable to unbend. In Camilla's house he remains oblivious to the limitations of his pose. There, like the Viceroy and Camilla's other suitor, he unwittingly becomes an actor in a *commedia*-style farce.

The third lover, Felipe, lacks the kind of charisma that would make him a credible candidate for Camilla's hand, a failing that is especially unfortunate given his opinions and behaviour. Although he lends a hand with the fitting-up of the theatre he is not part of the company and sits watching as they rehearse. In the screenplay's fuller version, Don Antonio lectures him on his inability to cross over into the players' world. Felipe decides to leave and join the army fighting a hard campaign against the 'savages' who threaten one of the chief silver-mining districts:

> Yes, you are doing the right thing – the tortured lovers finish happily only in the theatre – and there, simply because they become ridiculous and amuse the public. Camilla is too much a part of that ...You tried to climb from an aisle seat into the wings. *Ma, caro mio*, Camilla can see you only as part of the audience.[39]

Felipe is absent for a good while in the second half of the film. When he comes back he is a changed man. Captured by the natives who were his enemies, he came to respect them and understand himself, and on his return he asks Camilla to forsake 'this civilization that's making us brutal and dishonest' and join him in a Rousseauesque vision of the ideal, natural life. The golden coach will not be needed. Camilla rejects this proposal, just as she rejects the Viceroy's offer of transformation and the toreador's promise of celebrity.

The climax of this comedy comes when all three suitors turn up at Camilla's house. In an earlier scene at the palace, the Viceroy was unable to keep control of the simultaneous presence in adjoining rooms of Camilla and his 'official' partner the Marquise during a critical meeting of his council. In comparison, Camilla's management of what follows is more adept, as befits a woman of the theatre. She expects the Viceroy, but it is Ramon who arrives first and makes his way in to see her. Camilla seems inclined to accept his proposal that they should unite their forces, and she embraces him, exclaiming 'At last I find a real man', though his authenticity (she explains) comes from his lack of mental complications: 'Ah, such a change.' Felipe arrives, and Ramon is just telling Camilla she must give back the coach, when Isabella comes to whisper the news in her ear. She places Ramon in another room, and steps into the hall to meet Felipe, who describes the plans for 'a new life, close to nature, among rivers, forests', and she seems prepared to accept the idea. Then the Viceroy himself is announced. Felipe is placed in another room, and she goes to see the newcomer, whom she takes into a room where props and costumes are stored. 'This room', she tells him, 'is reserved for persons of quality', adding sarcastically 'eight noble ancestors at least'. Here, against a background of masks, musical instruments and parti-coloured dresses, the Viceroy tells her that he is likely to be ousted by intrigue at court and will soon be an 'ordinary' man. Maybe then there will be a place for him in the troupe? He pulls his wig off and sits down beside a table with a grotesque mask on it: 'Now I can love you like an ordinary man.' She asks wistfully, 'Can I love like a real woman?' Being an ordinary man will involve jealousy, which he admits to, and she immediately decides to organize a confrontation so that he can work out his feelings. This stage-management of her men seems to prompt another rueful reflection on her profession: 'Why do I succeed on the stage, and destroy everything in my life? What is truth? Where does the theatre end and life begin?' Ramon and Felipe meet and begin to fence in the hall, and the noise they make brings the Viceroy to the door of the room where Camilla has joined him again. The three men stand facing her, bewildered, and after a moment's reflection she sends them all away. The Viceroy leaves in his sedan chair and Ramon seems likely to make a fatal lunge at his adversary when the police arrive and arrest them both.

At this point the scene moves out of Camilla's control in the manner of a climactic imbroglio in a comedy. The inadequacy of the men's various propositions is brought home to her only after an initial acknowledgement of her desire for each of them. Although she declares 'I stay, I stay with my work', it is still not clear what her final decision will be, with regard either to them or to the coach. The final sequence returns to the palace, now also a theatre under Camille's as well as Renoir's control. The bishop, an authority hitherto invoked but not seen, is expected. The coach arrives in the carriage entrance and we glimpse Camilla at its window, but it is not yet clear who is with her. The courtiers crowd the galleries, as they had in the scene of the coach's arrival. A line of drummers beats a salute, and after a few moments

Camilla appears, accompanying the Bishop and an attendant monk. The bishop reveals that Camilla has given the coach to the church, so that it may be used to take the Holy Sacrament to the dying, an act of 'pure charity' involving an object that had been the focus of much covetousness. Dressed entirely in black, Camilla stands, inscrutable, as he announces this and tells the company that she has agreed to sing at a solemn Mass to celebrate this gift. 'I would like everyone in the city present – and most especially all of our actors.' The *commedia* troupe, led by their children, take the boards of what is now clearly a stage in the foreground and a drop is lowered to hide the scene as the camera pulls back to reveal the proscenium arch and prompter's box of the theatre.

The introduction here of the bishop, *ex machina*, is another reference to dramatic convention, as is the summoning of every character for the final gathering on stage. The final statement of the film places this in yet another frame. The leader of the troupe is leaning against the proscenium arch. He tells us that he had hoped to offer a melodrama in the Italian manner, but that Camilla is missing. He summons her to the stage, and, still in her black dress, she is warmly welcomed by little group of colleagues in front of what is now a conventional street scene of painted cloth and wings. He admonishes her:

> Don't waste your time in so-called real life. You belong to us, the actors, acrobats, mimes, clowns, mountebanks. Your only way to find happiness is on any stage, any platform, any public place, in those two hours when you become another person – your true self.

Camilla stands in front of the red drop curtain which has by now closed off the street scene from view: 'Felipe – Ramon – the Viceroy – don't they exist any more?' The leader answers her: 'Disappeared. Now they are a part of the audience. Do you miss them?' She closes her eyes and replies 'A little' and looks towards (but not quite into) the camera lens. The film cuts to a long shot of the stage, with her as a small black figure in the centre and the leader in his red costume over to one side, as the title 'The End' appears.

Renoir appears to have shot a more elaborate version of the conclusion, which would have made the transition between the 'real' and 'theatrical' worlds more complex.[40] The bishop's speech would have segued directly into Don Antonio's, which would have begun with an address to the audience from the staircase: 'The destiny of the characters in this comedy in the Italian style is not determined as yet. How do they find their happy endings?' As he came towards the camera, the lighting of the set would have changed to that seen in film's opening moments (the unspecified, possibly modern effect as specified in the screenplay), the curtain would have come down behind him, and he would have introduced a series of tableaux: Felipe with the Indians, Ramon with a bull, the Viceroy with the Marquise. Camilla would then be revealed, alone in front of the stage set, as in the film's final cut, but Don Antonio's speech would have been more explicit in its insistence that playing constituted the only reality worth acknowledgement:

> I saved you for last, Camilla, because you have played the only real part – that of a player ... honestly representing all your brothers and sisters – the acrobats, the dancers, opera singers and street singers, mimes and actors, all ... The others live – rushing about in that so-called real life – lying, killing each other over futile ideas, passing politics, prejudices which die in a few centuries. But us, every evening we suffer and rejoice, die and are born again, without doing harm to anyone – and only for ideas which justify us because they haven't changed since Sophocles and Aristophanes.[41]

The message for Camilla is blunt: 'You see, Camilla, the theater is far superior to life and I hope you now recognize your error in ever doubting it and having a try at this other life.' After the lines in which she is told that her would-be lovers have vanished, and her admission that she misses them, 'a little', the final shot would have shown Camilla slightly less conflicted than she appears to be in the film as released – although the fact that she is only seen there in long shot may have removed the indicated effect:

> Her expression is slightly melancholy. The orchestra begins a triumphant work of Vivaldi. She raises her head and smiles. THE CAMERA BACKS as Camilla bows to the public.

The public, of course, is the cinema audience, 'timeless' in the sense of being outside the historical frame within which the action was displayed.

The Golden Coach was a Franco-Italian co-production but its dialogue was recorded directly in English – not an easy task for all of the actors. The English version was preferred by the director, who disliked the dubbing of the other languages.[42] With *French Cancan*, a 'comédie musicale de Jean Renoir', he made his decisive return to both the French film industry and his childhood world of the Impressionists. Less sophisticated and more light-hearted, in many respects it complements *The Golden Coach*. The characteristics of impressionist art are evoked by the choice of milieu, painterly production design and shot compositions. The film shares his father Pierre-Auguste Renoir's warm appreciation of women and love and his predilection for ordinary details of middle- and working-class life and popular entertainments. Renoir subsequently described it as homage to 'our trade', that of shows: 'En gros, c'est un homage à notre métier, j'entends le métier du spectacle.'[43]

The Golden Coach opposes two irreconcilable social spheres and insists on the special but in some respects difficult nature of the artist's calling. The comedic form evoked is, as Raymond Durgnat points out, appropriate as the 'junction of spontaneity and classicism, bourgeois and even court culture'.[44] The 'fantasy in the Italian manner' was to a considerable extent an exemplary fable about the contradictions inherent in the situation of an independent woman in conventional society: it ends with the isolation of Camilla in the only world where she can find her true self, the stage. *French Cancan* proposes a vision of a society unified in a more optimistic vision of performance as a means of self-expression. It ends with the inauguration of the Moulin Rouge, the exuberance of the new 'French Cancan', and the début of a new star, Nini (Françoise Arnoul). The film frankly admits its status as fiction with a disclaimer in the opening titles. Unlike a Hollywood biopic, it will not have to produce any special pleading about changing names and dates: Danglard (Jean Gabin), its central male character, is not an imitation of Charles Zidler, the real-life creator of the Moulin Rouge, and the story of its creation does not correspond fully to the less romantic reality.[45]

Unlike *The Golden Coach*, the film follows the simpler and more familiar backstager imperatives of bringing out a new talent and putting on the show. After the closure of his sophisticated and upmarket venue Le Paravent Chinois, Danglard needs to get back into business, not by reopening it but by finding a novel attraction. Nini needs to identify in herself the potential that Danglard had noticed in her at the Montmartre dance hall La Reine Blanche. He decides to buy and remodel it, capitalizing on the desire for a brush with the common people that he had observed in his own patrons: 'du canaille pour les millionaires, l'aventure dans le confort' ('lowlife for millionaires, adventure in comfort'). His backer, Baron Walter, suggests that the new establishment will also provide a glimpse of the high life within reach of those with limited means ('la grande vie à la portée des petites bourses'). Danglard corrects him: it will be the *illusion* of high life.[46] He will bring in all the top acts of the dance halls but he has yet to make discovery number two: an old dance – the *Chahut* or *Can Can*, brought up to date. He engages Mme Guibole, a star of twenty years ago, to teach the high-kicking dance to a carefully selected troupe of young women. But what should the new dance be called? She suggests that because English is so fashionable nowadays, the dance's new name should be in that language, and Danglard decides at once that it will be 'le French cancan'.[47]

The professional and love lives of Danglard and Nini converge in a familiar manner, and Renoir weaves the romantic plot ingeniously through a series of vicissitudes involving love and money before the Moulin Rouge can open and Nini can achieve her professional destiny. However, this is not a simple backstage romance. Nini has every chance of overnight stardom, and the new venue is about to open, but Danglard's attachment to a new discovery, the singer Esther Georges, seems to have already become a liaison. On the opening night Nini watches Esther's performance from backstage, and is dismayed by the absorption and delight of Danglard. When Esther comes backstage, she is embraced by Danglard and tells him she will never leave him, and Nini calls out in protest and rushes to lock herself in her dressing room. Danglard and company entreat her to come out, but she refuses until her mother has joined in the argument.

Danglard asks her what she wants. She replies that she wants him for her own, and he tells her that this is not possible – at least, not in the way she implies. She can have a modest domestic life with her first love, the young baker Paolo, or riches and jewels with the Prince who has been wooing her, but she will never capture Danglard. There is only the man of the theatre, and a fireside version ('in slippers') is not available. He cannot be confined. Danglard lives only to create, and he has produced Nini, Esther and many others, because 'all that counts is what the people out there want'. He will be sorry to lose a dancer who promised to become a trouper ('un bon petit soldat'). This is spoken against a background of colourfully dressed and beautiful women, as though Danglard were at the head of his loyal battalion (Figure 19). The other women do not seem to take exception to the simple statement of fact. The backstage location is a reminder of the distinct creative world from which the people out there ('là-bas') are excluded but which cannot exist without them. Irving Singer identifies in this sequence the film's 'most striking declaration about the role of professionalism as a life-sustaining bridge that connects us to our human condition' – a key element of the director's thinking.[48] The speech is the opposite of Julian Marsh's harangue to Peggy Sawyer in *42nd Street* (1933). Danglard does not load Nini with imperatives and reminders of the consequences of failure for her fellow-workers: this is not the insistence that 'you're going out there a youngster, but you've *got* to come back a star'. Instead, Renoir's impresario offers choices, framed not just in terms of loyalty but of what she can expect from him and from life. He

19. *French Cancan* (1954):
Danglard, backed by his
troops

represents a force in both show business and Nini herself that can only
be denied at great personal cost. She hesitates briefly, and then moves
rapidly into an affirmation more spectacular, public and all-embracing
than that allowed to Magnani's conflicted Columbine. Now that both
Nini and the film itself have worked through the complexities of love
and loyalty among the artists, the dance can begin. As Claude-Jean
Phillipe observes, for Nini, unlike Camilla, there is no row of footlights
or curtain, and the performance moves directly into the crowd of
spectators.[49]

To make room for the Can Can, customers at tables on the floor
of the hall are asked to move onto the stage, mingling professionals
and 'civilians' with a promiscuity that is in fact controlled by the
dancers themselves as they rush through the audience and leap down
from the balcony, some flinging themselves literally into the laps of
the spectators. The dynamism of the dance is counterpointed with the
scene backstage, where Danglard sits in a chair, smiling as he imagines
which move is accompanying each piece of the music. He even moves
his left leg in time to the music, kicking out in a seated Can Can of his
own, to the surprise of a passing dresser. Out on the floor, the ranks
of dancers whirl round in a series circular compositions or advance in
waves, sometimes with the shriek, leap and descent into the splits that
places the dance beyond the powers of mere amateurs. Nini is asked
by a fellow dancer whether she still thinks of leaving and affirms her
desire to stay. Renoir leaves the dance in full spate and the final grace
note is a closing shot outside the Moulin Rouge. In the background,
as the music continues, the façade and the red mill glow in the lighted
street. A top-hatted man meanders tipsily across the middle ground of
the picture and raises his hat towards us as the word 'Fin' appears and
the screen fades to black.

Neither *The Golden Coach* nor *French Cancan* harbours illusions about the relation between finance and entertainment. In the former, mutually irreconcilable but related understandings of the value of art (the coach, the performers' work) distinguish the realms of the court and the *commedia*. In *French Cancan*, sex and money are entangled with the motives of Danglard's backers, and this element of the story is treated with realism but without cynicism. The visual effect in both films is that of a world carefully composed by and for the film's purposes, to express truths that mere realism could not encompass. Renoir insisted an artificial setting could often conceal or contain 'inner truth': 'La verité interieure se cache souvent derrière un environnement purement artificiel.'[50] In *The Golden Coach* the world represented was expressly one of fantasy, whether picturesquely tumbledown (the inn yard) or refined (the court.) In *French Cancan*'s studio sets the artificiality of the elaborate illusion is enjoyed. Like Carné's 'poetic realism', this creates a quasi-theatrical cinematic effect that expresses the script's image of a theatricalized society able to express passions, ambitions and desires. Renoir's adoption of a colour palette reminiscent of his father's paintings corresponds to a predominantly pastoral view of the *belle époque*: it contrasts sharply with the darker version of the Moulin Rouge and its urban surroundings created in John Huston's *Moulin Rouge* (1952), a biographical film filled with imitations of scenes and characters as they were depicted by Henri de Toulouse-Lautrec. (Bosley Crowther in the *New York Times* thought that Renoir's 'affectionate picture' didn't quite have 'the class' of Huston's.[51]) Still less does it anticipate the supercharged post-modern version of the venue and its *milieu* in Baz Lurhmann's frenetic *Moulin Rouge* (2001), a fantasy of urban spectacle and decadence with plot elements derived from *La bohème* and *La traviata*. In the book issued to coincide with the release of Lurhmann's film readers are invited to think of the Moulin Rouge 'as a can-can besotted version of Steve Rubell's disco-crazed Studio 54 [in New York] crossed with Bangkok's sex market meets Mardis Gras' carnival.'[52]

French Cancan has been seen as an attempt to identify a definition of 'Frenchness' in the uncomfortable transitional state of post-war France. The charmingly evoked *milieu* of Montmartre, a village not yet fully absorbed by the city, can be compared to the evocation of an 'old' France threatened by modernity in the films of Jacques Tati.[53] Even if one accepts the force of the argument that gratification deferred in *French Cancan* is an expression of the irresolvable conflict in a capitalist society between gratification of the libido (*jouissance*) and its exploitation, Renoir's engagement with the potential for fulfilment seems less qualified than such an account can embrace.[54] John Shaughnessy suggests that 'Danglard does not encourage revolt against the status quo but keeps an alternative, Utopian, set of values alive by preserving the spirit of popular culture within a commodified spectacle.'[55] In this respect it easy to identify Renoir's attitude to the commercial context of his own *métier*, but it must be qualified by acknowledgement of the director's engagement with the craft and aesthetic potential of his art as much as its social significance. In celebrating Renoir, Leo Braudy goes too far in denying that Carné in *Les Enfants du paradis* has anything to offer by way of 'defining what theater means in relation to the world of film'. His claim for the significance of the theatre in Renoir's films, however, seems just: 'In its many mutations of theme and method, from the start of his career, it has furnished an ever-replenishing refuge of order amid the freedoms of nature.'[56] The terms here could be reversed: Renoir locates nature's freedoms in the expressive capacity offered by the theatre and its ordering of the world and the passions.

Jacques Rivette and the incomplete theatre

Jacques Rivette was both a key member of the group that formulated the *politique des auteurs*, and one of its most searching critics. The presence of the theatre in his films is to some extent a response to both critical thinking (in particular that of Bazin) and the practice of his predecessors – notably Renoir, for whom he had great affection and respect and with whom he conducted a series of TV interviews under the title 'Jean Renoir le patron' in 1966.[57] More importantly, it facilitates an artistic exploration of identity and society, and is present in his approach to a variety of genres, including historical themes (*Jeanne La Pucelle*, 1994), and adaptations from novels, ghost stories and thrillers, as well as comedy. For Rivette the theatre often acts as a mirror for the film-making process and – at the same time – as a metaphor for the way his characters perceive and perform their lives. Speaking of *L'Amour fou* (1969), Rivette described the strategy of the performance within the film as 'inevitably an interrogation of truth, using means that are inevitably untruthful' ('c'est forcément une interrogation sur la vérité, avec des moyens qui sont forcément mensongers').[58]

The theatrical performances are seen for the most part in rehearsal, in circumstances fraught with contesting private passions and complicated by often obscure external factors. They might also be hampered by uncertain theories on the part of the director or the group and corresponding misgivings on the part of the actors. These factors coalesce in ways not fully understood by those involved or, indeed, by the cinema audience. Gilles Deleuze observes that 'Rivette elaborates a formula where cinema, theatre and theatricality specific to cinema confront each other'.[59] The director engages in an implicit dialogue with Bazin's essays on the relationship between the media, in particular the contention that there is no 'backstage' (*coulisses*) in film.[60] Rivette rarely shows anything *but* the backstage, and with the exception of *Va savoir* (*Who Knows?*, 2002) the performances are incomplete or deferred. Rehearsal, he decided in the course of working on a film of the stage adaptation of Diderot's *La Réligeuse* (*The Nun*, 1965–1966), was a mysterious process in which the relationships between those involved were closer and more in the nature of conspiracy than he had imagined.[61]

Rivette's work encompasses avant-garde theories and methods of rehearsal and performance developed in the twentieth century, taking the dialogue between cinema and theatre further than most of the directors discussed so far. In his early films he was prepared to have the actors improvize and keep the camera running until a scene seemed to end – or simply stop. Later he would work with the actors on the set to arrive at dialogue which was then 'fixed'. The work was above all actor-centred, and rather than view rushes day-by-day he preferred to wait until editing to judge particular takes as the visual and aural material was shaped. This aleatoric element suggests a degree of like-mindedness with some contemporary theatrical directors, but Rivette's engagement with new ideas in performance does not entail losing touch with the celebration of the theatre's mystery, a tendency evinced in *Phénix*, his unproduced script derived in part from *The Phantom of the Opera*, and his frequent returns to the 'old dark house' *topos*, handled with a strong element of theatricality. The raising of the curtain and the ritual *trois coups* that precede it recur as numinous moments that summon audience and actors across a threshold. The films savour the paradoxical revelation of truth in palpably false representations and performances, and the game of expectation and surprise. *Paris nous appartient* (*Paris Belongs to Us*, 1961), Rivette's first feature-length film, is his initial expression of this multivalent use of theatre within cinema. Although less assured – and less self-evidently experimental – than the four-hour *L'Amour fou* or twelve-hour *Out 1: noli me tangere* (1970), this early work anticipates subsequent variations on theatrical themes.

After a title card quoting the poet Charles Péguy's declaration that Paris belongs to no one ('Paris n'appartient à personne') the opening credits are superimposed on shots from a train speeding through the suburbs towards Paris. The central narrative is the struggle of a young director, Gérard Lenz, to put on *Pericles*. He cannot hold the cast together, and has to rehearse in a number of spaces. Eventually, he finds backing from a major theatre, but is ousted by an artistic director who insists on spectacular effects and indulges the whims of the star actors who have been brought in to replace most of his dwindling band of amateurs and semi-amateurs. Meanwhile a conspiracy plot, never lucidly explained, takes its course, involving an American writer traumatized and exiled by McCarthyism and an obscure (possibly imaginary) international conspiracy. The film ranges across Paris for locations as the hapless theatre company shifts from one rehearsal space to another. When the enthusiast's attempts to direct his own production are hijacked by the 'money', the analogy with radical film-making's struggle with the mainstream is clear. At the centre of the film is a literature student, Anne Goupil. This uncharismatic and naïve outsider is contrasted with an elegant American woman, Terry, who seems very much an insider – although what there is to be inside of is never quite clear. Anne moves into the production with no little or no notion of what is involved. Meanwhile she engages in a quest to locate a tape of guitar music – a Hitchcock-style McGuffin – that allegedly will both hold together the disparate elements of Shakespeare's romance and unravel the conspiracy that seems to be intertwined with the other characters' relationships.

Later films make much of the process of exploration and explication within rehearsal as a mirror both for the characters' off-stage lives and the cinema audience's position as spectators. We find companies working on Racine's *Andromaque* in *L'Amour fou*; Aeschylus' *The Seven Against Thebes* and *Prometheus Bound* in *Out 1: noli me tangere*; Marivaux' *La Double Inconstance* in *La Bande des quatre* (*The Gang of Four*, 1988); and Pirandello's *Come mi vuoi* (*As You Desire Me*) in *Va savoir*. All of these, with the exception of the last, are texts with a claim to canonical status. *Pericles* stands (or, rather, then stood) outside the theatrical and dramatic mainstream. In one of the very few discussions of Shakespeare's late plays in a feature film, the play's director tells his leading actress why he has chosen it.[62] As they sit on a bench on the Pont des Arts, he asks whether she knows the play. She does, and thinks well of it despite its being badly stitched together ('décousue'). He agrees and admits that his friends think he is mad to want to do it, but he believes that it is made to a plan. This *plan terrestre* – a play on words, fusing the play's geographical range with the notion of an earthly as distinct from heavenly level of interpretation – unifies the wanderings of the hero and the other characters, so that they are all brought together in the final act. The actress agrees:

'It's the representation of a world that is chaotic but not absurd' ('C'est la mise en scène d'un monde chaotique, mais pas absurde') and people need to be shown that. The music, of which only a single tape recording exists, had been played by the mysterious Juan, a person whose disappearance is bound up with the political conspiracy vaguely connected with atomic power as well as the McCarthyite witch-hunts. The nearest Lenz comes to a scene of dominance is when he climbs to the roof of the theatre where he has been trying to rehearse and looks out over the city he hopes to possess. This is the point where the film invokes by implication its defiant title, seeming to contradict that quotation from Péguy. By the end of the film the conspiracy has been revealed as probably a chimera (nothing is *quite* certain), Anne's brother has been killed and the director has taken his own life. Paris does not belong to them.

Lenz seems not to have a clear notion of what kind of performance he wishes to elicit from his increasingly disillusioned cast. In complete contrast Sebastien, directing *Andromaque* in *L'Amour fou*, and Lili and Thomas in *Out 1: noli me tangere* seem to know what they want, and situate themselves explicitly within the avant-garde of their time. Sebastien's production will be staged on a white platform with audience seating on four sides in a hall that is not a traditional theatre. (The first shot after the opening titles fades in from a white background to the white of this platform, proposing an equivalence of film and theatre.) The Living Theatre had been seen in Paris several times during the 1960s, and Rivette refers in an interview about *L'Amour fou* to their *Antigone*, shown in Paris in December 1967. Both Lili and Thomas employ rehearsal techniques derived, possibly by way of the Living Theatre and other contemporaries, from Antonin Artaud.[63] However, the approaches of both groups in the film are distinct. Lili and Thomas work in parallel ways on a visceral, ritual-informed exploration. Lili shares the priorities identified by Christopher Innes in Peter Brook's researches into theatre language: 'reversing the traditional priorities of communication, elevating the secondary elements of gesture, pitch, tone and the dynamics of sound or movement that give expressive values, over the primary element of intellectual meaning'.[64] (They practise screaming.) The French *répétition* is more strongly reminiscent of its root sense of repeated action than the English *rehearsal*, a factor underlying the concentration by Rivette on scenes and speeches that are repeated, often without conclusion.

The improvisations employed by Thomas seem near to inflicting actual harm on the participants: in the second episode we see an extended exercise to explore the psyche of Prometheus, in which one actor lies on the floor while the others harass her with noise, physical movement and behaviour that seems only just short of violence. (Although there was a 'camera rehearsal', in the shooting itself Rivette and his camera simply followed the group around as the session developed, and not all the actors had a clear notion of where it might lead.[65]) In *L'Amour fou* Sebastien's production of Racine's play involves respectful attention to the verse together with the rediscovery of rhythms beyond the superficial structure. Both films leave the performances unfinished, but the 'outer' narrative of the theatre company and the director's personal life in *L'Amour fou* are given quasi-classical symmetry as the film concludes where it began, confirming (what the spectator may well have forgotten over four hours) that the audience is waiting for the first performance and the director cannot be reached. The challenge to the film's audience is to watch it again, so that its employment of a flashback can be fully appreciated, and in this sense it shares with Rivette's other films the demand that attention be paid to a degree beyond that assumed in the customary contract between viewer and director. He commented that from the very start the film was nothing but false endings: 'It's a film that never stops ending. That's why it lasts so long.'[66] Not that this will yield resolution: explanation in his work, whether it is afforded in initial viewing or in retrospect, is rarely complete.

In *L'Amour fou* representation is at the heart of the 'private' narrative, that of the relationship between Sebastien (Jean-Pierre Kalfon) and his lover Claire (Bulle Ogier). They have regarded themselves (and are seen by others) as an ideal couple. Sebastien's rehearsals of *Andromaque*, with Claire playing Hermione, are being filmed by André S. Labarthe for a television documentary. During a rehearsal in which she repeatedly fails to stress a line the way Sebastien insists on, Claire claims that the TV crew is making her work impossible and walks out on rehearsal and the production. As Hélène Deschamps points out, this is the first of several moments when the crew's intrusion seems to make the spectator complicit in an intrusion: does Claire object to their presence, or ours?[67] In the café afterwards Sebastien assures André and his crew that filming should continue and telephones his ex-wife Marta offering her the part, which she accepts. Excluded from the community of actors, spending much of her day alone in the apartment she shares with Sebastien and increasingly resentful of her situation, Claire sinks into deep depression. In the apartment she makes a tape recording of herself speaking Hermione's lines from the opening of Act 5, scene 1, a speech that begins 'Où suis-je? Qu'ai je fait? Que dois-je faire encore?/ Quel transport me saisit? Quel chagrin me dévore?' ('Where am I? What have I done? What should I do more?/ What fit took hold of me? What sorrow devours me?') At one point Rivette cuts between Claire sitting on the floor with the microphone and Marta, on stage, delivering the same speech. Marta is now an actress with auditors, whereas Claire has deprived herself of that necessary confirmation of her existence as an artist. As rehearsals continue, Sebastien seems to take on her mental state himself, to the point where he can barely communicate with the actors. After Claire's attempted suicide, Sebastien calls his assistant and announces that he will not be in for two days. The couple seem to find their relationship again by spending two days in the apartment, making love and indulging in a child-like game of make-believe, dressing themselves up as bandits and wrecking the furnishings.[68] Claire leaves the city by train. Sebastien returns to the bedroom and crouches by the tape recorder, listening over and over again to her voice while the telephone rings. In the theatre, as in the film's opening, the actors wait for contact to be made with him and a sparse audience waits for the performance.

Whether or not the show does go on – it seems possible but is hardly likely to be very satisfying – Rivette has got what he needed from it. Effectively *L'Amour fou* is a tale of more than two performances, neither necessarily completed. During rehearsals the TV footage in 16mm is frequently intercut with the 35mm of the film's 'own' camera, which keeps a greater distance from the rehearsal processes: two views are available for much of what goes on. The TV crew at times clamber onto the platform and penetrate what we might assume would be a circle of concentration. Douglas Morrey and Alison Smith point out that in the theatre they 'effectively reconfirm and close the borders of the stage space'.[69] In one sequence the actors move to a completely white Brookian 'empty space' and they and the crew are seen by the more tactful 35mm camera as if framed by its walls and floor on a bare but more conventional box set. In a further complication of the film's meta-narratives, the actors in *Andromaque* were at first under the impression that a full version of the play would be performed and recorded, and Labarthe – a real-life documentary maker of some distinction – was 'acting' as though this genuine process were to be recorded as well as the finished product.[70] This superimposition of levels of mediation and actuality offers more than one level of reflection on the fictional relationship played out (and largely improvized) by Kalfon and Ogier. In witnessing the intimate scenes in the apartment, now turned into an 'empty space' in its own right, the 35mm camera is taken even further beyond the intrusiveness – and embarrassing voyeurism – identified with the 16mm camera and its crew.

Now the 'real' action has moved to the apartment, while the actors and audience in the theatre are left in a state of suspense shared by the film's viewers. We will not know how the story of Sebastien and Claire will conclude and we do not know whether the play will go on. As in most of Rivette's films, whether or not the theatre is their immediate and ostensible subject, the sensation of this boundary-crossing is confused (or enriched) by the frequent shifting of lines of demarcation. As first Claire and then Sebastien move into what might be considered madness, the adjective *fou* takes on a meaning beyond its immediate application to possession by sudden and obsessive desire. *Andromaque*, with its central fable of constancy under trial in a political context and the rivalry of the Greek Hermione and the Trojan exile Andromaque for Pyrrhus' love, does not so much mirror as reflect the situations of the actors around it, much as the mirrors in the café scenes do not merely duplicate but also separate the characters as they talk.

As in *L'Amour fou*, the narrative of *Céline et Julie vont en bateau* (*Céline and Julie Go Boating*, 1974) circles back on itself, this time with the identity of the characters reversed and the conclusion mirroring the film's opening, as first Julie, then Céline, sits on a park bench, sees the other rush past – as Alice sees the White Rabbit – and follows her. The elaborate magic and dream elements of the story are not entirely explicable, involving a mysterious and haunted house in a suburban street. The house itself is entered by one person at a time on the stroke of eleven in the morning. We do not accompany the pair beyond the threshold as they make their journeys to and into it, but subsequently see the enactment of a melodramatic drama, in which whoever has entered takes the role of a nurse. They recall this with the help of a 'magic' lozenge they smuggle out when they leave. Eventually, understanding the likely murderous outcome of the unfolding story, they contrive to enter the house together, taking turns as the nurse and managing to rescue the little girl at danger in this ghostly performance – this element of the plot is from Henry James' novel *The Other House* and would entail her murder by one of the two women aspiring to her father's hand in marriage. In this final repetition the participants are truly ghost-like, unable to perceive the presence of the intruders and locked in versions of their scenes even more halting and rhetorically stylized than those recalled by Céline and Julie after their earlier visits. The house is thus at once a commonplace suburban villa in a garden and the set for a film or a stage play: the costume and speech of the inhabitants are mannered and forced, and the internal geography of the building is obscure.

20. *Céline et Julie vont en bateau* (1974): the melodramatic style

The complexities of *Céline et Julie* have received a good deal of critical attention, not least because the film has many unexplained and probably inexplicable dimensions.[71] The *revenants* (Rivette prefers this term to *fantômes* or ghosts) in the villa are actors in an old-fashioned melodrama, as the young intruders observe. On previous occasions, when they get back to the apartment one of them takes the lozenge in her mouth but both seem able to experience the events recalled. After the penultimate entry into the house Céline has managed to acquire two of the magic sweets, and they have a joint 'viewing', in which the casting of the nurse depends on whose point of view we are adopting. In this rehearsal of the story, which is becoming more intelligible with each repetition of its episodes, they watch the drama from the other side of the screen we are looking at or through, mocking the affected behaviour of the characters in what they perceive as a 'mélo' in terms that are specifically theatrical: 'They talk funny. It's a school [of acting]. The Odéon. A tragedy. They smell of mothballs' ('Ils parlent curieux. Une école. L'Odéon. Une tragédie. Ils sentent la naphtaline'). In their final visit they both manage to get into the house, and prepare for their appearances as the nurse 'Miss Angèle' in a 'backstage' room not previously shown, and the performance is heralded by *les trois coups* and by music on the soundtrack, as if in a theatre. Now the actors within the house are in waxy makeup that suggests their ghostly quality rather than the melodramatic theatricality seen on former occasions, and in one of the repeated scenes the blood flowing from a wound in the hand of the most extravagantly theatrical of the group, Camille (Bulle Ogier), is blue rather than red (Figure 20).

In the following two years Rivette embarked on a further exploration of *la vie parallèle*, to encompass four films, although in the event only two were completed as planned. Among the published texts of the unproduced works, the treatment for *Phénix* revisits both *The Phantom of the Opera* and *Dr Jekyll and Mr Hyde*, with an element of *Jane Eyre*. The period is that of Leroux' novel. In the theatre she has built on the site of an identical building that burned down – and which is therefore in itself a *revenant*, literally a theatre of memory – the actress Deborah, modelled on Sarah Bernhardt, secludes herself in an apartment/dressing room to which she retires after each performance. A mirror, like that in *The Phantom of the Opera*, swivels open onto a secret passage. A succession of young actresses, singled out by Deborah to 'read' to her, have disappeared after failing in performance to meet Deborah's requirements, each incident being heralded by the appearance of an apparition, the 'white lady'. Constance, the sister of the last 'reader' to disappear, infiltrates Deborah's world, intent on uncovering its secrets. A theatre-obsessed oriental potentate, Julian, wishes to add Deborah's voice to his collection of cylinder recordings. She refuses, but discovers that he has been buying up shares to gain control of her in a more sinister way. Late at night she follows him through passages and doorways she did not know existed until she finds herself in a facsimile of her theatre, built by him in his own realm with a room containing effigies of her colleagues and acquaintances, transformed into marionettes.

As if these circumstances were not sufficient as doubling the real world of an actress who lives through the illusions of her art, the figure (ghost?) of Elena, compared by Rivette to Mrs Rochester, exists in a middle-class drawing room on the other side of a door that is permanently locked. (Jeanne Moreau was to play both Elena and Deborah.) Rivette specifies that the impression would be that of a dream opening onto another dream and so on 'to infinity'. Elena's part of the plot is 'less the development of a narrative (like the intrigue of Deborah) than the description and slow worsening of an initial situation, established from the outset as without any exit and based on obsessive repetition [*répétition obsessionale*]'.[72] The plan does not specify the details of Elena's situation but indicates that it would include enough 'reality' to make it unclear whether she was Deborah's dream or vice versa.[73] Like the Opéra in Leroux's story, the theatre would be 'ce palais de mirages', a palace of illusions. In the event, Rivette contrives that the condition of theatrical space is met half way in *L'Amour par terre* (*Love on the Ground*, 1983), where his characters, professional actors, start out in an ordinary apartment being used as a theatre, then find themselves in a *palais de mirages* less grand but almost as 'theatrical' as that envisaged for *Phénix*.

At the beginning of *L'Amour par terre*, after a mysterious – seemingly conspiratorial – rendezvous a group are escorted to an apartment where we discover they are the audience for the performance of a bedroom farce by three young actors. Led from room to room, they are allowed to spy on the scenes as they unfold, but they do not know (as we do) that one of the actors has begun to deviate from the script, causing a panic beyond the performed crises of the farce. Their play has been stolen from the successful boulevard dramatist Roquemaure (Jean Pierre Kalfon, the director in *L'Amour fou*) who is present on this occasion. Rather than recriminating with them, he invites them to come to his house to work on a play he is writing. Soon the sensation of voyeurism that was part of spectators' pleasure in the apartment – itself doubled by the camera's admittance to the backstage comedy – is succeeded by the actors' arrival in a mansion where they are simultaneously performers in a play whose outcome has yet to be found, and witnesses of events that seem to be re-enactments of a possibly criminal and certainly emotionally charged situation.

In this case rehearsal is running alongside the creation of a text (the play) that it is hoped will contain the key to the mystery the actors are experiencing: it is not completed until the performance, which mirrors the film's opening sequence by bringing a group of observers into the house to follow it from room to room. The actors are caught within a house whose grandiose and garish decorations suggest a stage set and which is inhabited by eccentric and vaguely threatening manipulators. The performance there concludes with the introduction of a 'missing' character whose part in the real-life emotional drama that once took place is now revealed. In the film's outcome – a term more appropriate to Rivette's depictions of theatre than 'ending' – Roquemaure's play is taken over by his associates: the actress is literally pulled out of the scene, to be replaced by the 'real' personage. The film's title refers to a statue of Cupid that was knocked to the ground and broke (revealing it as a hollow plaster cast), and which is mysteriously restored: a good deal remains unexplained, but something has been put back in place.

The theme of uncovering the mysteries of a house where a performance is being rehearsed (repeated) is developed with further variations in *La Bande des quatre*. There are two mysterious houses, one a suburban villa where four drama students live, the other the theatre in an obscure backstreet, which has its own secrets beyond those of the play they rehearse there, Marivaux' *La Double inconstance*. Within the theatre there is a double mystery to be penetrated by the students: the craft they are learning at the hands of an enigmatic and demanding mentor, Constance Dumas (Bulle Ogier), and whatever is concealed in the apartment – which we never see – where she lives above the theatre. (The situation recalls that of Deborah in *Phénix*.) The second of these appears to be bound up with the plight of a fellow-student, Cécile, whose boyfriend, imprisoned for a petty crime, has found himself in possession of (or has access to) documents related to a political scandal. The keys to a strong-box containing these are hidden in the chimney-piece of one the rooms in the girls' lodging. Disturbed by what seems to be a poltergeist, Anna leaves her room for the night and a new arrival, the Portuguese student Lucia, quietens the ghost by reciting a charm and discovers the keys. From an early stage in the film the secret of the suburban house has been pursued by Thomas, an investigator who is eventually killed by one of the women. Meanwhile the students work through the script, sometimes in scenes that have a direct bearing on the events unfolding outside the rehearsal. In one of these Cécile breaks down during the dialogue in which the country girl Silvia is distraught at her enforced separation from her lover Arlequin. Another scene, in which the scheming courtier Flaminia instructs her sister Lisette on the techniques of coquetry (Act I, scene 3), is in a lighter mode, juxtaposing the dramatist's satire on learnt behaviour with the teacher's efforts to elicit a convincing performance of naïveté.[74]

The film is more like a conventional thriller than most of Rivette's earlier work but enough of the story remains unexplained to avoid the genre's convention of closure. We do not find out how Constance was involved in the conspiracy, or indeed exactly what it was. As a teacher she demands both emotional truth and respect for the text, and claims that the theatre is a series of *épreuves*: tests, trials or ordeals. She insists that an actor must work with 'la démolition et la doute': performances must be achieved through the actor being taken apart and coping with self-doubt. The choice of play seems significant – the 'double' of the title suggests as much – and there is a sense that the students are acting out something of her emotional experience. They are constantly switched from role to role: in the theatre of their house they at least achieve some sort of stability. In the final scene Constance has been arrested, Joyce (the murderer of the investigator) is in gaol, and the remaining students, at last in costume, are working though the comedy's final scene, in which Silvie declares her decision to stay with the Prince, and her rustic lover Arlequin accepts the situation. Lucia, playing Silvie, breaks down but Anna, as Arlequin, insists that they continue, because Constance would want them to. She takes the Prince's hand to continue the dialogue, but before she can speak the film ends with a cut to another of the shots of the train journey between the two locations with which it began and which have punctuated its episodes.

The shoulder-shrugging title of *Va savoir* (2002) announces it as less earnest and more open to humour: 'who knows?' Again, there is a history to be unravelled, but it has no evident connection with *revenants* of any kind – except in the sense that the central character is an actress coming back to Paris and to aspects of her past love life. Camille (Jeanne Balibar) is appearing in her Italian lover Ugo's production – in Italian – of Pirandello's *Come mi vuoi*. The play's central character, the 'unknown woman' (*L'Ignota*), is taken to be Lucia, the 'lost' daughter of an Italian family, discovered in a night-club in Berlin and brought back to play the role in which others including her ineffectual husband 'desire' to see her. Finding Lucia will resolve a legal and financial situation, the possession of the family estate. Camille's uncertainties combine with those of the character, to the point where she does not know exactly what part she must play in real life or on the stage: in the opening sequence she is picked out in a black void, which at first seems to be expressing her perplexity while a voice from off screen issues orders and the beam from a spot light follows her haltingly around the empty space. After a few moments this is revealed to be a technical rehearsal and the darkness a momentary lapse in the lighting. As she leaves the stage and makes her way to front of house Camille speaks the first of a series of brief 'soliloquies' which consist mainly of exclamations of bewilderment or self-doubt ('ça va, ça va pas...', etc.). Camille's having to perform the play in its original language reinforces the sense when she is on stage of an actress who is not only 'not me' but 'not not me'. Her anxiety is soon revealed as indecision about seeking out her ex-lover, Pierre. At one point she stands by the window in her hotel room pondering this, then turns to the camera and announces 'I'm going' ('J'y vais'). What might ordinarily be an internal monologue is vocalized even as she walks down the street, climbs the stairs to Pierre's apartment – where she encounters his new partner, Silvia – and then goes to the park where she knows he will be sitting on a bench reading a newspaper.

On the play's first night she 'dries' but recovers and then rushes off before the curtain call. L'Ignota has announced that she wants to escape from herself: 'that – yes – to have no more memories of anything – anything at all – to empty myself of all the life that's in me ... I no longer know I'm alive. I'm just a body without a name.'[75] The act ends with her repeating the last phrase, 'un corpo senza nome'. At a later performance we know (she seems not to) that Pierre is watching from the back of the stalls as she speaks lines, including 'as you desire me', in which L'Ignota declares she has come back to her husband. The first of these speeches is an expression of alienation, part of the hesitancy of Camille's off-stage soliloquies. The second reflects the situation with Pierre, although in fact she soon realizes she has no desire to return to him, merely a compulsion to revisit her life of three years ago. At his apartment she insists she is not the woman he knew before, a line echoing the play ('Je ne suis pas celle que tu as connu autrefois').

The emotional correspondences between theatre and reality continue throughout, but for once with Rivette the performance itself is completed. In a converging plot line, Ugo searches for the unique copy of a 'lost' Goldoni comedy, 'une pièce fantôme, inédite' ('a phantom play, unpublished') which is located in the library left by her first husband to the widowed mother of a young student, Dominique. It is as though Ugo is looking for a play without thinking of himself as being in one. There is a conflict of personal agendas between Ugo and Dominique's possessive and semi-criminal step-brother Arthur. He is having an affair with Silvia, who discovers he has stolen a ring from her. Silvia tells Camille about her previous life ('une autre vie très differente'), which included a dangerous but exhilarating period with a burglar and resulted in a term in prison. At this point, it may be simplest to note that complications ensue, and that the final scene is preceded by a 'duel' in which Ugo challenges Pierre to drink a bottle of vodka while balancing on a gantry high above the stage, an episode that incidentally completes the camera's journey through the building as they climb the narrow stair up to the flies. Ugo's opponent falls to his death, or at least would do if there had not been a safety-net that Ugo did not tell him about and which we have not known about until now. Dominique's mother, an enthusiastic amateur confectioner in whose kitchen the lost play has been found, arrives with a huge Black Forest gâteau, to be shared out among them all at the table of the stage set.

Va savoir is Rivette's most comprehensively theatrical film – in the sense of admitting the audience to all parts of the theatre and showing a completed production – and also his least perplexing. It makes no extraordinary demands on the audience's interpretative skills. Given the director's admiration for Renoir, it may not be coincidental that Camille shares her name with his Camilla. At the same time, the Pirandellian dilemma between reality and performance is not as serious a threat as in many of Rivette's other films or the dramatist's own *Six Characters in Search of an Author*. The ghost of the 'phantom play' by Goldoni is laid when it is found – not in the library but among the cookbooks in the kitchen – and the ghosts of Camille's private life have been exorcized, but they were anxieties rather than 'real' spirits from the past. It is as though the film's narrative has been earthed, given a comprehensive and salutary connection with reality only fitfully available to the protagonists of *Céline et Julie* or *L'Amour par terre*.

The denouement is close to a parody of a 'happy ending', a situation hardly associated with Rivette's work: where endings are offered, they are usually at best provisional. Camille's anxieties do not in the end prevent the performance of Pirandello's play. The success of Ugo, identified by Morrey and Smith as 'probably the most collegiate of his directors', seems to betoken some kind of resolution for Rivette himself. But, as they also point out, he is dealing with a play by Pirandello, 'an author obsessed with the paradoxes of authorial authority'.[76] Contrasting Rivette's treatment of theatre with Renoir's, Alain Ménil claimed in 1998 that, for Rivette, art and life do not achieve the fusion the elder director sought to establish, and their point of contact is not an embrace but a collision, a tension and a degree of disengagement shared by the spectator as well as those within the film.[77] In *Va savoir* the 'parallel life' is not located in a realm of haunting or imagination, but in the troubled private life of the protagonist, in effect a return to the dynamic between on stage and off stage in *L'Amour fou*. Claire disintegrated but Camille is only temporarily perplexed. In the scene where she makes her escape from Paul's box room through the skylight and walks on the leads, she maintains her equilibrium, finds a way down and is able to reach the theatre just before the curtain time. Her identity as an actress is confirmed, and the integrity of her performing persona maintained. She achieves a resilience denied to many of her predecessors in Rivette's imagined theatres.

Notes

1 Raymond Durgnat, *Durgnat on Film* (London: Faber and Faber, 1976), p. 59. The chapter, 'Auteurs and Dream Factories', first appeared in the author's book *Films and Feelings* in 1967.
2 An indispensible anthology (and study) remains John Caughie, ed., *Theories of Authorship* (London: Routledge, 1981).
3 Originally published in *Film Culture*, 28 (Spring, 1963), cited from Caughie, *Theories of Authorship*, p. 66.
4 Jacques Rivette, 'Entretien avec Jacques Rivette. Le temps déborde' (*Cahiers du cinéma*, no. 204, September 1968) in Antoine de Baecque and Charles Tesson, eds, *La Nouvelle Vague. Textes et entretiens dans les Cahiers du cinéma* (Paris: Cahiers du cinéma, 1999), p. 303.
5 Irving Singer, *Three Philosophical Filmmakers: Hitchcock, Welles, Renoir* (Cambridge, MA: MIT Press, 2004), p. 1.
6 On the background of the production see Edward Baron Turk, *Child of Paradise: Marcel Carné and the Golden Age of French Cinema* (Cambridge, MA and London: Harvard University Press, 1989) and Jill Forbes, *Les Enfants du paradis* (London: BFI Film Classics, 1997). A

concise account of the film industry during the occupation is given by Jean-Pierre Bertin-Maghit, *Le Cinéma français sous l'occupation* (Paris: Presses Universitaires de France, 1994).

7 Jacques Prévert, *Les Enfants du paradis, le scénario original de Jacques Prévert*, edited by Bernard Chardère (Paris: Editions Jean-Pierre Monza, 2005), p. 53. Subsequent references are to this edition (as 'Prévert') or to the translation by Dinah Brooke (London: Lorrimer, 1968), referred to as 'Brooke'. This translation was based on the earlier publication of the shooting script in *L'Avant-scene du cinéma* (1967).

8 Turk, *Child of Paradise*, p. 250. On Debureau, see Tristan Rémy, *Jean-Gaspard Debureau* (Paris: L'Arche, 1954); on Lemaître, Robert Baldick, *The Life and Times of Frédérick Lemaître* (London: Hamish Hamilton, 1959). In fact Jean-Gaspard Debureau (known as Baptiste) seems not to have performed in the pantomime, whose proper title (with the multiple 'r' imitating the merchant's cry) was *Marrrchand d'habits*, and his début as Pierrot was not simultaneous with Lemaître's appearance at the Funambules. A significant source for Carné and Prévert was Louis Péricaud, *Le Théâtre des Funambules, ses mimes, ses acteurs et ses pantomimes depuis sa foundation jusqu'a sa démolition* (Paris: Léon Sapin, 1897). Péricaud suggests that Debureau appeared in *Marrrchand d'habits*: see Robert F. Storey, *Pierrot. A Critical History of a Mask* (Princeton, NJ: Princeton University Press, 1978), pp. 105–106, citing Rémy. The most influential account of the pantomime is that by Théophile Gautier, 'Shakespeare aux Funambules', *Revue de Paris*, 9/2 (September 1842), pp. 60–66.

9 Mirella Joan Affron, '*Les Enfants du paradis*: Play of Genres', *Cinema Journal*, 10/1 (Autumn 1978), pp. 45–58; 48.

10 On the historical context of the film's events and characters, see, particularly Forbes, *Les Enfants du paradis*, pp. 41–45 and Turk, *Child of Paradise*, Chapter 11. Carné comments on the costuming of Garance in his autobiography, *La Vie à belles dents* (Paris: Jean-Pierre Olivier, 1975), p. 223.

11 Brooke, trans., *Les Enfants du paradis*, pp. 29–30.

12 Ibid., p. 28.

13 Ibid., p. 32.

14 See William L. Hedges, 'Classics Revisited: reaching for the Moon,' *Film Quarterly*, 12/4 (Summer 1959), pp. 27–34; p 29.

15 Brooke, trans., *Les Enfants du paradis*, p. 35.

16 Ibid., pp. 22–23.

17 In Prévert's script this scene in the dressing room follows the rehearsal: the final cut places it after the first performance and the authors' challenge: Prévert, *Les Enfants du paradis*, p. 117.

18 In the original *Marrchand d'habits* the crime has tragic–comic consequences: the ghost of the old-clothes man returns (through a trap) to haunt Pierrot with his repeated cry as he woos and wins the duchess

he has fallen in love with, and in the final scene impales Pierrot on the sabre that is still sticking through his body. Gautier, in 'Shakespeare aux Funambules', celebrates this as a combination of Shakespeare and the Don Giovanni story.

19 In Prévert, *Les Enfants du paradis* (pp. 157–158) the dialogue between Garance and Baptiste takes place in a deserted side-street rather than in the bedroom – Nathalie does not come to find him – and they both encounter Jéricho, who harangues them and pursues them onto the Boulevard du Crime before being felled by a blow from Baptiste's cane. As Baptiste stands gazing at the dead man, Garance flings her arms round his neck, and her cry of 'Mon pauvre Baptiste' is the final line of the film. Brooke, trans., *Les Enfants du paradis* (pp. 216–217) has a different version of the omitted sequence, closer to the completed film.

20 Brooke, trans., *Les Enfants du paradis*, p. 173.

21 The title – but no summary – of the pantomime is given by Péricaud, *Le Théâtre des Funambules*, p. 30.

22 Forbes, *Les Enfants du paradis*, p. 52.

23 When Frédérick visits her in her box he reminds her that as lovers they should surely be able to use 'tu', and she accepts the rebuke.

24 The lyrics are translated in Brooke, *Les Enfants du paradis*, p. 183, together with the second verse: 'Whom I love I embrace,/ And I take no blame/ If each loving face/ Isn't the same' (French text in Prévert, *Les Enfants du paradis*, p. 142).

25 The phrase is from an anonymous pamphlet which synthesizes, without specific attributions, the opinions of a list of critics: *Deburau, par Jules Janin, Gerard de Nerval, Eugene Brifaut ... etc., etc.* (Paris: Imprimerie D'Aubusson et Kugelmann, 1856), p. 9: 'L'intelligence animée et profonde qui vit sous ce masque de plâtre, et qui apparait blanc et immobile.'

26 Brooke, trans., *Les Enfants du paradis*, p. 216. In Prévert's script (p. 159) the attack is more detailed and eloquent. When Baptiste tells him to let go, and that he disgusts them, Jéricho replies, with an 'obscene' wink, 'And her, she doesn't disgust you, eh? Just the opposite. She's cleanliness, purity, heaven in her eyes, the devil in her loins and her legs in the air.'

27 Turk, *Child of Paradise*, Chapters 12 and 13.

28 Jean Renoir, *Écrits (1926–1971)*, edited by Claude Gauter (Paris: Ramsay, 2006), pp. 33–34.

29 *The Golden Coach* was made in French, Italian and English versions – like many 'international' co-productions filmed in Italy in the post-war period – but Renoir recorded the English dialogue directly, and preferred this version to the others.

30 Alexander Sesonske, *Jean Renoir. The French Films, 1924–1939* (Cambridge, MA and London: Harvard University Press, 1985), p. 35.

31 Leo Braudy discusses 'framing' in *Madame Bovary* and other films in *Jean Renoir. The World of his Films* (Garden City, NY: Doubleday, 1972), pp. 80–82.

32 Sesonske, *Jean Renoir*, p. 35.
33 Christopher Faulkner, *The Social Cinema of Jean Renoir* (Princeton, NJ: Princeton University Press, 1986), p. 186.
34 Ibid., p. 167.
35 On Vivaldi see Jean Renoir, *Entretiens et propos*, edited by Jean Narboni (Paris: Cahiers du cinéma, 2005) p. 71; and Jean Renoir, *Ma vie et mes films*, corrected edition (Paris: Flammarion, 2005), p. 248.
36 Renoir hoped to shoot at least some establishing location footage in Latin America, but all filming took place at the CineCittà studios in Rome. On the background of the production see Célia Bertin, *Jean Renoir. Biographie*, new edition (Paris: Éditions du Rocher, 2005), pp. 358–362.
37 Jean Renoir, *The Golden Coach*, shooting script, Hammond French Film Script Archive, Fales Library Collection, NYU: Subseries A-7, p. 101.
38 Ibid., p. 202c.
39 Ibid., p. 616.
40 Ibid., pp. 1525–1528. There are two slightly different version of this sequence, one of which seems to have been shot (as indicated by the crossing out of each shot as it was completed).
41 A French draft of this speech, glued to the back of the script pages, follows Aristophanes' name with 'passing through Shakespeare, Molière and Goldoni'.
42 On the financing, production and reception see Janet Bergstrom, 'The Genealogy of *The Golden Coach*', *Film History*, 21 (2009), pp. 276–294.
43 Renoir, *Ma vie et mes films*, p. 251.
44 Raymond Durgnat, *Jean Renoir* (Berkeley and Los Angeles: University of California Press, 1974), p. 286.
45 The Moulin Rouge was opened in October 1889 by Charles Zidler and Joseph Oller: see John Rearick, *Pleasures of the Belle Époque. Entertainment and Festivity in Turn-of-the-Century France* (New Haven, CT and London: Yale University Press, 1985). Zidler – whom Renoir refers to in notes and interviews as 'Ziegler' – appears under his own name, albeit in a fantastic version of his personality, in Baz Luhrmann's *Moulin Rouge*.
46 Rearick (*Pleasures of the Belle Époque*, p. 62) points out that cabarets and *café-concerts* in Montmartre 'gave visitors the chance to escape their everyday identities', allowing them 'contact with a lower world of colourful Bohemians, high-spirited criminals, and old-fashioned workers'.
47 Renoir simplifies the history of the dance, but is faithful to its trajectory from popular dance-hall craze before the Second Empire to its revival as an exhibition dance at the end of the century. The process is traced by David Price in *Cancan!* (Madison and Teaneck, NJ: Fairleigh Dickinson University Press, 1998).
48 Singer, *Three Philosophical Filmmakers*, p. 172.
49 Claude-Jean Phillipe, *Jean Renoir. Une vie en oeuvres* (Paris: Bernard Grasset, 2005), pp. 400–401.

50 Renoir, *Ma vie et mes films*, p. 247.

51 Bosley Crowther, '*French Can-Can* [sic]; Renoir Movie Offers Colorful Nostalgia', *New York Times*, 17 April 1956.

52 Baz Luhrmann and Catherine Martin, *Moulin Rouge* (London: FilmFour Books, 2001), unnumbered page.

53 See the discussion of 'late Renoir' in Martin O'Shaughnessy, *Jean Renoir* (Manchester: Manchester University Press, 2000), Chapter 6. Tati's *Mon oncle* (1956) situates M. Hulot's 'natural' habitat in the old-fashioned, village-like streets of a quarter that is threatened with demolition to make way for the planned environment represented by the absurdly ultra-modern suburban house of his sister and her husband.

54 The position is argued by Daniel Serceau in *Jean Renoir. La sagesse du plaisir* (Paris: Les Éditions du Cerf, 1985), pp. 312–313. See also Shaughnessy, *Jean Renoir*, p. 200.

55 Shaughnessy, *Jean Renoir*, p. 200.

56 Braudy, *Jean Renoir*, pp. 102, 103.

57 Transcripts from three of these are included in Renoir, *Entretiens et propos*.

58 Rivette, 'Le temps déborde', p. 295.

59 Gilles Deleuze, *Cinema 1. The Time-image*, translated by Hugh Tomlinson and Robert Galeta (London: The Athlone Press, 1989), p. 295.

60 The debate with Bazin in Rivette's criticism and practice is analysed by Alain Ménil, 'Mesure pour mesure. Théâtre et cinéma chez Jacques Rivette', in Suzanne Liandrat-Guigues, ed., *Jacques Rivette, critique et cinéaste* (Paris and Caen: Lettre Modernes Minard, 1998), pp. 67–96.

61 Deleuze, *Cinema 1*, p. 266.

62 In Eric Rohmer's *Conte d'hiver* (1991) the central female character, seeing a performance of *A Winter's Tale*, perceives in its final scene a truth about her own situation.

63 Rivette, 'Le temps déborde', p, 289. European tours are listed in an appendix to Pierre Biner's *The Living Theatre. A History without Myths*, translated by Robert Meister (New York: Avon Books, 1973). Biner's work was first published in Paris in 1972.

64 Christopher Innes, *Holy Theatre. Ritual and the Avant Garde* (Cambridge: Cambridge University Press, 1981), p. 136.

65 Suzanne Schiffmann, 'On a suivi le graphique', in Hélène Frappat, *Jacques Rivette, secret compris* (Paris: Cahiers du cinéma, 2001), p. 143.

66 Rivette, 'Le temps déborde', p. 293.

67 Hélène Deschamps, *Jacques Rivette. Théâtre, amour, cinéma* (Paris: L'Harmattan, 2001), p. 33. Deschamps' book is devoted entirely to the analysis of the film.

68 Bulle Ogier describes the filming as pure improvisation on the final day of shooting in the apartment: Rivette was not even aware that they would be breaking down the bedroom doors with an axe. He did not say 'cut' – 'It was curiosity on his part, almost voyeurism. He wanted to see what the

actors were going to do, what they were going to tell both about this story
and about to themselves' ('On ne pouvait pas aller plus loin', in Frappat,
Jacques Rivette, secret compris, p. 140).

69 Douglas Morrey and Alison Smith, *Jacques Rivette* (Manchester and New
York: Manchester University Press, 2009), p. 152.

70 Rivette, 'Le temps déborde', pp. 272–273.

71 Stéphane Goudet, '*Céline et Julie vont en bateau*. Les spectatrices', in
Suzanne Liandrat-Guigues, ed., *Jacques Rivette, critique et cinéaste*
(Paris and Caen: Lettre Modernes Minard, 1998), pp. 105–116, discusses
wordplay in the film and the significance of the title: 'vont en bateau' ('go
boating') might also signify 'tell a tall tale' or even a drug trip.

72 Hélène Frappat and Jacques Rivette, *Trois films fantômes de Jacques
Rivette* (Paris: Cahiers du cinéma/fiction, 2002), p. 43.

73 Ibid., p. 45.

74 The film also includes texts from Corneille's *Suréna* and Racine's *Esther*.

75 Luigi Pirandello, *As You Desire Me*, trans. Robert Rietti, in *Pirandello:
Collected Plays*, Vol. 4 (London: Calder, 1996), p. 20.

76 Morrey and Smith, *Jacques Rivette*, p. 175.

77 Ménil, 'Mesure pour mesure', p. 90.

Conclusion

THE films that have been discussed invoke the theatre for a variety of purposes. Not only do they confirm their own medium and its institutions with varying degrees of explicitness or forethought as the inheritor and (in a teleological construction of history) successor of the elder medium, but they also draw on the stage's potential to extend or even question assumptions about their own capabilities. It is not uncommon for a film to combine these and related motivations and the effects they achieve or, as with the three *auteurs* discussed in Chapter 6, for a director's work to encompass a developing dialogue with and examination of the theatre.

Other candidates for inclusion crowd round the films selected and the distinct genres of performance that have been identified, inviting separate consideration and development: for example, the specific ontologies and significance of cabaret and circus and European as well as American music halls. However, the central themes that have emerged, enfolding within them varied cinematic uses of theatre, are valid starting points for exploration of the wider field. The defining models of the theatrical career are particularly important, as is the recurring sense of the cinema's tendency to favour the theatre of illusion and approaches to acting that involve the actors' conscious exploration of their own psyche. In this respect, films have used the theatre's status and conditions as an extension of their own project in simultaneously offering to reproduce what is real and exposing what lies beneath or beyond it. (Because of this, it has frequently been necessary to resist the temptation to put inverted commas round the word 'real'.) Another is the fascination with theatricality in itself, construed either in negative terms – outside the theatre, 'theatrical' can denote a perceived excess in behaviour – or as a positive attribute licensed and required by stage performance.[1] In this respect films about filming – such as Truffaut's *La Nuit américaine* (1973) or Almodóvar's *Broken Embraces* (2009) – lack a dimension available to films about theatre, because in the dominant naturalistic regime of cinema since the silent era the film actor's physical techniques have been less demonstrative and self-conscious than those called for by the theatre.

The expression '*the* theatre', with its definite article, is at a level of generalization inappropriate in theoretical analysis of performance, but remains powerful in the imaginative world of film-makers and spectators intrigued by the red curtain and the world beyond it. Imagining the theatre provides a means for cinema to place a frame within its own frame, intensifying the effects of its own techniques, celebrating both independence from and kinship to the live stage and, paradoxically, asserting its own kind of active relationship between spectator and screen. In addition to engaging in processes that have been likened to dreaming and accepting the role of a co-voyeur, when we watch a film we know that by the time we have taken our seat the show has already gone on. Films about the theatre add to this the suspense of a narrative in which the show might just fail to go on, even though almost invariably the curtain does rise. When this does not occur, as in the conclusion of *The Red Shoes*, the effect is all the greater.

Above all, theatres are more easily associated than cinemas with haunting, not only in the sense of the 'mysteries' discussed in Chapter 4, or the quality identified by Marvin Carlson and cited in the Introduction, 'a simultaneous awareness of something previously experienced and of something being offered in the present that is both the same and different, which can only be fully appreciated by a kind of doubleness of perception in the audience'.[2] The buildings themselves are places once filled with illusory activity by actors who have now departed, if only to their next job. The 'ghost light' on the empty stage in American theatres – glimpsed in the opening scenes of *A Double Life* (1948) – and the 'house' full of unexplained 'trous noirs' in *Le Dernier Métro* (1980) share this with the sense of a theatre's backstage area in daytime that Bergman evokes in his script for *Fanny and Alexander* (1989) but does not carry into his film. The image is specific to the theatre's backstage and its status in the 'palace of mirages'. A bird flies in through one of the windows, high in the back wall, which are sometimes opened in the afternoon. It flaps its wings and cheeps incessantly until it flies up 'into the dark toward the catwalk and the blackened rafters'.

> When the bird is silent the stillness becomes magic. Voices then silenced can now be heard; beingless shadows and the imprints of fierce passions can be glimpsed. The dusty air, cut through by the sword blades of sunlight, grows thick with voices long since mute and movements that have ceased.[3]

Notes

1 The uses of the term 'theatricality' are examined with exemplary concision by Tracy C. Davis and Thomas Postelwait, editors of the collection of essays *Theatricality* in the series 'Theatre and Performance Theory (Cambridge: Cambridge University Press, 2003).

2 Marvin Carlson, *The Haunted Stage. The Theatre as Memory Machine* (Ann Arbor: University of Michigan Press, 2001), pp. 11, 51.

3 Ingmar Bergman, *Fanny and Alexander*, translated by Alan Blair (London: Penguin Books, 1989), p. 9.

Filmography

Titles in languages other than English are given in the translation current at the time of writing. An asterisk indicates that the Criterion Collection DVD (region 1) has been used, in addition to other available editions.

Les 400 Coups (François Truffaut, France 1959)
42nd Street (Lloyd Bacon, US 1933)
After The Rehearsal (*Efter repetitionen*: Ingmar Bergman, Sweden 1984)
The Age of Innocence (Martin Scorsese, US 1993)
All About Eve (Joseph L. Mankiewicz, US 1950)
All About My Mother (*Todo sobre mi madre*: Pedro Almodóvar, Spain 1999)
All I Desire (Douglas Sirk, US 1953)
All That Jazz (Bob Fosse, US 1979)
L'Amour fou (Jacques Rivette, France 1969)
Applause (Rouben Mamoulian, US 1929)
Babes in Arms (Busby Berkeley, US 1939)
Babes on Broadway (Busby Berkeley, US 1942)
The Band Wagon (Vincente Minnelli, US 1953)
The Barefoot Contessa (Joseph L. Mankiewicz, US 1954)
Being Julia (István Szabó, Canada/GB/Hungary 2004)
Belle de jour (Luis Buñuel, France/Italy 1967)
Black Narcissus (Michael Powell, Emeric Pressburger, GB 1947)
Black Swan (Darren Aronofsky, US 2010)
Boudu Saved from Drowning (*Boudu sauvé des eaux*: Jean Renoir, France 1932)
The Bride Wore Black (*La Mariée était en noir*: François Truffaut, France 1963)
The Broadway Melody (Harry Beaumont, US 1929)
Broadway Melody of 1936 (Roy del Ruth, US 1935)
Broadway Melody of 1938 (Roy del Ruth, US 1937)
Broadway Melody of 1940 (Norman Taurog, US 1939)
Broadway Rhythm (Roy del Ruth, US 1943)
Broken Embraces (*Los abrazos rotos*: Pedro Almodóvar, Spain 2009)
Bullets over Broadway (Woody Allen, US 1994)

Carefree (Mark Sandrich, US 1938)

Céline and Julie Go Boating (*Céline et Julie vont en bateau*: Jacques Rivette, France 1974)

Champagne Charlie (Alberto Cavalcanti, GB 1944)

The Children of Paradise (*Les Enfants du paradis*: Marcel Carné, France 1945)*

A Chorus Line (Richard Attenborough, US 1985)

Cleopatra (Cecil B. De Mille, US 1934)

The Conversation (Francis Ford Coppola, US 1974)

The Cradle Will Rock (Tim Robbins, US 1999)

Cries and Whispers (*Visningar och rop*: Ingmar Bergman, Sweden 1973)

Dames (Ray Enright, US 1934)

Dancing Lady (Robert Z. Leonard, US 1933)

Daybreak (*Le Jour se lève*: Marcel Carné, France 1939)

Day for Night (*La Nuit américaine*: François Truffaut, France/Italy 1973)

The Devil's Envoys (*Les Visiteurs du soir*: Marcel Carné, France 1942)

The Dolly Sisters (Irving Cummings, US 1945)

A Double Life (George Cukor, US 1948)

The Dresser (Peter Yates, GB 1983)

Easter Parade (Charles Walters, US 1948)

Elena and the Men (*Élena et les hommes*: Jean Renoir, France 1956)

The Entertainer (Tony Richardson, GB 1960)

Evergreen (Victor Savile, GB 1934)

Fanny and Alexander (Ingmar Bergman, Sweden 1982: TV and cinema versions)*

Farinelli il castrato (Gérard Corbiau, Italy/Belgium 1994)

Flying Down to Rio (Thornton Freeland, US 1933)

Follow the Fleet (Mark Sandrich, US 1936)

Footlight Parade (Lloyd Bacon, US 1933)

For Me and My Gal (Busby Berkeley, US 1942)

French Cancan (Jean Renoir, France, 1954)*

The Gang of Four (*La Bande des quatre*: Jacques Rivette, France 1988)

Gaslight (Thorold Dickinson, GB 1940)

Gaslight (George Cukor, US 1944)

The Gay Divorcée (Mark Sandrich, US 1934)

Girl Crazy (Busby Berkeley, US 1943)

Gold Diggers in Paris (Ray Enright, US 1938)

Gold Diggers of Broadway (Roy del Ruth, US 1929)

Gold Diggers of 1933 (Mervyn le Roy, US 1933)

Gold Diggers of 1935 (Busby Berkeley, 1934)

Gold Diggers of 1937 (Lloyd Bacon, US 1936)

The Golden Coach (Jean Renoir, France/US/Italy 1952)*

The Goldwyn Follies (George Marshall, US 1938)

Goodbye, Children (*Au revoir les enfants*: Louis Malle, France 1984)

Good Bye Lenin! (Wolfgang Becker, Germany 2003)

The Good Companions (Victor Savile, GB 1933)
The Grand Illusion (*La Grande illusion*: Jean Renoir, France 1937)
The Great Dictator (Charles Chaplin, US 1941)
The Great Ziegfeld (Robert Z. Leonard, US 1936)
Henry V (Laurence Olivier, GB 1944)
High Heels (*Tacones lejanos*: Pedro Almodóvar, Spain 1991)
The Hollywood Revue of 1929 (Charles Reisner, US 1929)
Hour of the Wolf (*Vargtimmen*: Ingmar Bergman, Sweden 1968)
House of Wax (André de Toth, US 1953)
The Human Beast (*La Bête humaine*: Jean Renoir, France 1938)
Imitation of Life (Douglas Sirk, US 1959)
The Jazz Singer (Alan Crossland, US 1927)
Jeanne la Pucelle, 1. Les Batailles, 2. Les Prisons (Jacques Rivette, France
    1994)
Jezebel (William Wyler, US 1938)
Jolson Sings Again (Harry Levin, US 1948)
The Jolson Story (Alfred E. Green/Joseph H. Lewis, US 1946)
Jules et Jim (François Truffaut, France 1962)
Kika (Pedro Almodóvar, Spain 1993)
Lacombe Lucien (Louis Malle, France 1974)
The Last Metro (*Le Dernier Métro*: François Truffaut, France 1980)*
The Law of Desire (*La ley del deseo*: Pedro Almodóvar, Spain 1987)
A Letter to Three Wives (Joseph L. Mankiewicz, US 1949)
The Libertine (Laurence Dunmore, US/GB 2005)
The Little Foxes (William Wyler, US 1941)
The Little Theatre of Jean Renoir (*Le Petit théâtre de Jean Renoir*: Jean
    Renoir, France 1969)
The Lives of Others (*Das Leben der Anderen*: Florian Henckel von
    Donnersmarck, Germany 2007)
Love on the Ground (*L'Amour par terre*: Jacques Rivette, France 1983)
Madame Bovary (Jean Renoir, France 1933)
The Magic Flute (*Trollflöjten*: Ingmar Bergman, Sweden 1974)*
The Magician (*Ansiktet*: Ingmar Bergman, Sweden 1958)
La Marseillaise (Jean Renoir, France 1937)
Me and Orson Welles (Richard Linklater, US 2009)
Mephisto (István Szabó, Germany/Hungary 1981)
Mississippi Siren (*La Sirène du Mississippi*: François Truffaut, France 1969)
Molière (Ariane Mnouchkine, France 1979)
Molière (Laurent Tirard, France 2006)
Morning Glory (Lowell Sherman, US 1935)
Moulin Rouge (John Huston, US 1952)
Moulin Rouge (Baz Luhrmann, US/Australia 2001)
Mrs Henderson Presents (Stephen Frears, GB 2005)
Mystery of the Wax Museum (Michael Curtiz, US 1933)
Nana (Jean Renoir, France/Germany 1926)

Nosferatu (F.W. Murnau, Germany 1922)

The Nun (*La Réligeuse*: Jacques Rivette, France 1965–1966)

Opening Night (John Cassavetes, US 1977)

Out 1: noli me tangere (Jacques Rivette, France 1970)

Paris Belongs to Us (*Paris nous appartient*: Jacques Rivette, France 1961)

Peeping Tom (Michael Powell, GB 1959)

Persona (Ingmar Bergman, Sweden 1966)

The Phantom Carriage (Victor Sjøstrom, Sweden 1921)

The Phantom of the Opera (Rupert Julian, US 1925)

Port of Shadows (*Le Quai des brumes*: Marcel Carné, France 1938)

Rear Window (Alfred Hitchcock, US 1954)

The Red Shoes (Michael Powell and Emeric Pressburger, GB 1948)*

Rhapsody in Blue (Irving Rapper, US 1945)

Richard III (Laurence Olivier, GB 1955)

The River (Jean Renoir, India 1951)*

Roberta (William A. Seiter, US 1935)

Rope (Alfred Hitchcock, US 1948)

The Rules of the Game (*La Règle du jeu*: Jean Renoir, France 1939)

Safe Conduct (*Laissez-passer*: Bertrand Tavernier, France 2002)

Sawdust and Tinsel (*Gycklarnas afton*: Ingmar Bergman, Sweden 1953)

Scenes from a Marriage (*Scener ur ett äktenskap*: Ingmar Bergman, Sweden 1973)

Senso (Luchino Visconti, Italy 1953)

The Seventh Seal (*Det sjunde insegelet*: Ingmar Bergman, Sweden 1957)

Shakespeare in Love (John Madden, GB/US 1999)

Shall We Dance? (Mark Sandrich, US 1937)

Show Business (Edwin L. Marin, US 1944)

Showgirls (Paul Verhoeven, US 1995)

Sing as We Go! (Basil Dean, GB 1934)

Singin' in the Rain (Gene Kelly/Stanley Donen, US 1952)

Smiles of a Summer Night (*Sommarnattens leende*: Ingmar Bergman, Sweden 1955)

The Sorrow and the Pity (*Le Chagrin et la pitié*, Marcel Ophüls, France 1969)

Stage Beauty (Richard Eyre, GB 2004)

Stage Door (George Cukor, US 1937)

Stage Fright (Alfred Hitchcock, GB 1950)

Star! (Robert Wise, US 1968)

A Star is Born (George Cukor, US 1954)

The Story of Vernon and Irene Castle (H.C. Potter, US 1939)

A Strange Affair (*Drôle de drame*: Marcel Carné, France 1937)

Strike Up the Band (Busby Berkeley, US 1940)

Summer Interlude (*Sommarlek*: Ingmar Bergman, Sweden 1951)

Swing Time (George Stevens, US 1936)

Taking Sides (István Szabó, Germany/Hungary 2001)

Through a Glass Darkly (*Såsom i en spegel*: Ingmar Bergman, Sweden 1961)

To Be or Not to Be (Ernst Lubitsch, US 1942)
Top Hat (Mark Sandrich, US 1935)
Topsy-Turvy (Mike Leigh, GB 1999)*
Twentieth Century (Howard Hawks, US 1934)
Who Knows? (*Va savoir*: Jacques Rivette, France 2002)
Wild Strawberries (*Smultronstället*: Ingmar Bergman, Sweden 1957)
Women on the Verge of a Nervous Breakdown (*Mujeres al borde de un ataque de nervios*: Pedro Almodóvar, Spain 1988)
Yankee Doodle Dandy (Michael Curtiz, US 1942)
Ziegfeld Follies (Vincente Minelli, US 1946)
Ziegfeld Girl (Robert Z. Leonard, US 1941)

Bibliography

Unpublished script material

Hopwood, Avery, *The Gold Diggers. A Comedy in Three Acts*, Lyceum Theatre, New York, 30 September 1919: NYPL typescript, NCOF+ (Hopwood, A. 'Gold diggers')

Maguire, Anthony James, three scripts for *The Great Ziegfeld*, New York Public Library, Bill Rose Theater Collection, Flo Ziegfeld-Billie Burke Papers (*T-Mss 1987-010): (a) Box 12, Folder 1, 'The Great Ziegfeld. He Lived to Glorify Beautiful Womanhood', by William Anthony Maguire, 166 pp., 27 December 1934; (b) Box 125 folder 3, 'Incomplete', 'Script okayed by Mr Stromberg', 21 September 1935, 196 pp., revisions (undated) on pink pages; (c) Box 125 folder 2, 'Incomplete', 'From: Mr Stromberg', 16 July 1935

Powell, Michael and Emeric Pressburger, *The Red Shoes*, continuity script, NYPL, MFLM+ (Red shoes. London)

Renoir, Jean, *The Golden Coach*, shooting script, Hammond French Film Script Archive, Fales Library Collection, NYU: Subseries A-7

Published film scripts

Almodóvar, Pedro, *Todo Sobre mi Madre, edición definitiva del Guión de la Pellicula* (Madrid: El Deseo, 1999)

Bergman, Ingmar, *Fanny and Alexander*, translated by Alan Blair (London: Penguin Books, 1989)

Cohn, Alfred A., *The Jazz Singer*, edited by Robert L. Carringer (Madison: University of Wisconsin Press, 1979)

von Donnersmarck, Florian Henckel, *'Das Leben der Anderen.' Filmbuch von Florian Henckel von Donnersmarck, mit Beiträgen von Sebastian Koch, Ulrich Mühe und Manfred Wilke* (Frankfurt am Main: Suhrkamp Taschenbuch, 2007)

Gelsey, Erwin and James Seymour, *Gold Diggers of 1933*, edited by Arthur Hove (Madison: University of Wisconsin Press, 1980)

James, Rian and James Seymour, *42nd Street*, edited by Rocco Fumento (Madison: University of Wisconsin Press, 1979)

Leigh, Mike, *Topsy-Turvy* (London: Faber, 1999)

Mankiewicz, Joseph L., *All About Eve. A Screenplay by Joseph L. Mankiewicz, Based upon a Short Story by Mary Orr* (New York: Random House, 1951)

Prévert, Jacques, *Les Enfants du paradis, le scénario original de Jacques Prévert*, edited by Bernard Chardère (Paris: Éditions Jean-Pierre Monza, 2005)

—— *Les Enfants du paradis*, translated by Dinah Brooke (London: Lorrimer, 1968)

Renoir, Jean, *Nana, un film de Jean Renoir* [screenplay published with DVD] (Paris: Arte Éditions, 2004)

Truffaut, François and Suzanne Schiffman, *Le Dernier Métro* (Paris: Cahiers du Cinéma, 2001)

—— *The Last Metro*, translated and edited by Mirella Jona Affron and E. Rubinstein (New Brunswick, NJ: Rutgers University Press, 1985)

Books and articles

Acevedo-Muñoz, Ernesto R., *Pedro Almodóvar* (London: BFI, 2007)

Added, Serge, *Le Théâtre dans les années Vichy* (Paris: Éditions Ramsay, 1992)

Affron, Mirella Joan, '*Les Enfants du paradis*: Play of Genres', *Cinema Journal*, 10/1 (Autumn 1978), pp. 45–58

Alatres, Guillermo, 'An Act of Love Towards Oneself' (*Positif*, 1999), in Paula Willoquet-Maricondi, ed., *Pedro Almodóvar Interviews* (Jackson: University of Mississippi Press, 2004)

Allinson, Mark, 'Mimesis and Diegesis. Almodóvar and the Limits of Melodrama', in Brad Epps and Despina Kakoudaki, eds, *All About Almodóvar. A Passion for Cinema* (Minneapolis and London: University of Minnesota Press, 2009)

Altman, Rick, *The American Film Musical* (Bloomington and Indianapolis: Indiana University Press, 1989)

Amiel, Vincent, *Joseph L. Mankiewicz et son double* (Paris: Presses Universitaires de France, 2010)

Anderegg, Michael, 'James Dean Meets the Pirate's Daughter. Passion and Parody in *William Shakespeare's Romeo+Juliet* and *Shakespeare in Love*', in Richard Burt and Lynda E. Boose, eds, *Shakespeare, the Movie, II. Popularizing the Plays on Film, TV, Video and DVD* (London and New York: Routledge, 2003)

Andersen, Hans Christian, *Fairy Tales*, translated by Tiina Nunnaly, edited and introduced by Jackie Wullschalger (New York: Penguin Books, 2004)

[anon.], *Deburau, par Jules Janin, Gerard de Nerval, Eugene Brifaut ... etc., etc.* (Paris: Imprimerie D'Aubusson et Kugelmann, 1856) [anon.] *Petite Encyclopédie illustrée de l'Opéra de Paris*, 2nd edition (Paris: Théâtre National de l'Opéra, 1978)

Artaud, Antonin, *The Theatre and its Double*, translated by Mary Caroline Richards (New York: Grove Press, 1958)

Ash, Timothy Garton, *The File. A Personal History* (London: Harper Collins, 1997)

Atkinson, Brooks, *Broadway*, revised edition (New York: Macmillan, 1974)

Auslander, Philip, *Liveness. Performance in a Mediatized Culture* (London and New York: Routledge, 1999)

de Baecque, Antoine and Serge Toubiana, *François Truffaut*, revised edition (Paris: Gallimard, 2001)

Baldick, Robert, *The Life and Times of Frédérick Lemaître* (London: Hamish Hamilton, 1959)

Bandehausen, Rolf and Peter Gründgens-Gorski, eds, *Gustaf Gründgens. Briefe, Aufsätze, Reden* (Munich: Deutsche Taschenbuch Verlag, 1970)

Barish, Jonas A., *The Antitheatrical Prejudice* (Berkeley and Los Angeles: University of California Press, 1981)

Barnes, Peter, *To Be or Not to Be* (London: BFI Film Classics, 2002)

Barrios, Richard, *A Song In the Dark. The Birth of the Musical Film* (New York: Oxford University Press, 1995)

Basinger, Jeanine, *Silent Stars* (Hanover, NH and London: Wesleyan University Press, 1999)

Bazin, André, *What is Cinema?*, essays selected and translated by Hugh Gray, 2 vols (Berkeley, Los Angeles and London: University of California Press, 1967)

Behlmer, Rudy, *Behind the Scenes. The Making of...* (New York: Ungar, 1982; repr. New York: Samuel French, 1990)

Bennett, Susan, *Theatre Audiences. A Theory of Production and Reception*, 2nd edition (London and New York: Routledge, 1997)

Bergman, Andrew, *We're in the Money. Depression America and its Films* (New York: NYU Press, 1971; Harper paperback, 1972)

Bergman, Ingmar, *Images. My Life in Film*, translated by Marianne Ruuth, introduction by Woody Allen (New York: Arcade Publishing, 2007)

—— *The Magic Lantern. An Autobiography*, translated by Joan Tate (Chicago: University of Chicago Press, 1988)

—— *Sunday's Children*, translated by Joan Tate (New York: Arcade Publishing, 1994)

Bergstrom, Janet, 'The Genealogy of *The Golden Coach*', *Film History*, 21 (2009), pp. 276–294

Bersani, Leo and Ulysse Dutout, 'Almodóvar's Girls', in Brad Epps and Despina Kakoudaki, eds, *All About Almodóvar. A Passion* for Cinema (Minneapolis and London: University of Minnesota Press, 2009)

Bertin, Célia, *Jean Renoir. Biographie*, new edition (Paris: Éditions du Rocher, 2005)

Bertin-Maghit, Jean-Pierre, *Le Cinéma français sous l'occupation* (Paris: Presses Universitaires de France, 1994)

Bianco, Anthony, *Ghosts of 42nd Street. A History of America's Most Infamous Block* (New York: Harper Collins, 2004)

Biner, Pierre, *The Living Theatre. A History without Myths*, translated by Robert Meister (New York: Avon Books, 1973)

Braudy, Leo, *The World in a Frame: What We See in Films* (Chicago: Chicago University Press, 1984)

—— *Jean Renoir. The World of his Films* (Garden City, NY: Doubleday, 1972)

Brecht, Bertolt, 'Erinnerung an Marie A.', in *Ausgewählte Gedichte*, selected by Siegried Unseld, with an afterword by Walter Jens (Frakfurt am Main: Suhrkamp, 1964)

Brontë, Charlotte, *Villette*, edited by Herbert Rosengarten and Margaret Smith (Oxford: Clarendon Press, 1984)

Brownstein, Rachel M., *Tragic Muse. Rachel of the Comédie Française* (Durham, NC and London: Duke University Press, 1995)

Brüggemann, Jörn, ed., *Florian Henckel von Donnersmarck, 'Das Leben der Anderen,' Materialien und Arbeitsanregungen* (Braunschweig: Schroedel, 2010)

Buckner, Robert and Edmund Joseph, *Yankee Doodle Dandy*, edited by Patrick McGilligan (Madison: Warner Bros / University of Wisconsin, 1981)

Burch, Noël, *Theory of Film Practice*, translated by Helen R. Lane (New Brunswick, NJ: Princeton University Press, 1981)

Burke, Billie (with Cameron Shipp), *With a Feather on My Nose. With a Foreword by Ivor Novello* (London: Peter Davies, 1950)

Butler, Judith, *Gender Trouble. Feminism and the Subversion of Reality* (London: Routledge, 1990; new edition, 2006)

Cantor, Eddie with David Freedman and Jane Kenser Ardmore, *'My Life is in Your Hands' and 'Take My Life': The Autobiographies of Eddie Cantor* (New York: Cooper Square Press, 2000)

Capote, Truman, *Music for Chameleons. New Writing* (London: Hamish Hamilton, 1981)

Carlson, Marvin, *The Haunted Stage. The Theatre as Memory Machine* (Ann Arbor: University of Michigan Press, 2001)

—— *Performance. A Critical Introduction* (London and New York: Routledge, 1996)

—— *Places of Performance. The Semiotics of Theatre Architecture* (Ithaca, NY and London: Cornell University Press, 1989)

Carné, Marcel, *La Vie à belles dents* (Paris: Jean-Pierre Olivier, 1975)

Carter, Huntley, *The New Spirit in the Russian Theatre, 1917–1928* (New York, London and Paris: Brentano's, 1929)

Caughie, John, ed., *Theories of Authorship* (London: Routledge, 1981)

Christie, Ian, *Arrows of Desire. The Films of Michael Powell and Emeric Pressburger* (London: Waterstone, 1985)

Cocteau, Jean, *Journal 1942–1945*, edited by Jean Touzot (Paris: Gallimard, 1989)

Cohan, George M., *Twenty Years on Broadway (And the Years It Took to Get There). The True Story of a Trouper's Life from the Cradle to the Closed Shop* (New York: Harper and Brothers, 1925)

Cohan, Steven, *Incongruous Entertainment. Camp, Cultural Value, and the MGM Musical* (Durham, NC and London: Duke University Press, 2005)

Corcy, Stephanie, *La Vie culturelle sous l'occupation* (Paris: Penin, 2005)

Cowie, Peter, *Ingmar Bergman. A Critical Biography*, 2nd edition (New York: Limelight Editions, 1992)

Cox-Ife, William, *W.S. Gilbert. Stage Director* (London: Dennis Dobson, 1977)

Croce, Arlene, *The Fred Astaire and Ginger Rogers Book* (New York: Vintage Books, 1972)

Custen, George F., *Bio/Pics. How Hollywood Constructed Public History* (New Brunswick, NJ: Rutgers University Press, 1992)

Dauth, Brian, ed., *Joseph L. Mankiewicz Interviews* (Jackson: University of Mississippi Press, 2008)

Davis, Tracy C. and Thomas Postelwait, eds, *Theatricality* (Cambridge: Cambridge University Press, 2003)

Delamater, Jerome, *Dance in the Hollywood Musical* (Ann Arbor, MI: UMI Press, 1981)

Deleuze, Gilles, *Cinema 1. The Time-image*, translated by Hugh Tomlinson and Robert Galeta (London: The Athlone Press, 1989)

Deschamps, Hélène, *Jacques Rivette. Théâtre, amour, cinéma* (Paris: L'Harmattan, 2001)

Dickstein, Morris, *Dancing in the Dark. A Cultural History of the Great Depression* (New York: Norton, 2009)

Diderot, Denis, *'The Paradox of Acting' by Denis Diderot and 'Masks or Faces?' by William Archer. Introduction by Lee Strasberg* (New York: Hill and Wang, 1957)

D'Lugo, Marvin, *Pedro Almodóvar* (Urbana and Chicago: University of Illinois Press, 2006)

Duncan, Paul and Bengt Wanselius, eds, *The Ingmar Bergman Archives* (Cologne: Taschen, 2008)

Durgnat, Raymond, *Durgnat on Film* (London: Faber and Faber, 1976)

—— *Jean Renoir* (Berkeley and Los Angeles: University of California Press, 1974)

—— *A Mirror for England. British Movies from Austerity to Affluence* (London: Faber and Faber, 1970)

Dusinberre, Juliet, *Shakespeare and the Nature of Women*, 3rd edition (Basingstoke: Palgrave Macmillan, 2003)

Edwards, Gwynne *Almodóvar. Labyrinths of Passion* (London and Chester Springs, PA: Peter Owen, 2001)

Eldridge, David, *Hollywood's History Films* (London: I.B. Tauris, 2006)

Ellis, John, *Visible Fictions. Cinema, Television, Video* (London: Routledge and Kegan Paul, 1982)

Elsaesser, Thomas, 'Tales of Sound and Fury. Observations on the Family Melodrama', in Barry Keith Grant, ed., *Film Genre Reader III* (Austin: University of Texas Press, 2003)

Epstein, Joseph, *Fred Astaire* (Princeton, NJ: Princeton University Press, 2008)

Erenberg, Lewis A., *Steppin' Out. New York Nightlife and the Transformation of American Culture, 1890–1930* (Chicago: University of Chicago Press, 1984)

Faulkner, Christopher, *The Social Cinema of Jean Renoir* (Princeton, NJ: Princeton University Press, 1986)

Farber, Manny, *Farber on Film. The Complete Film Writings of Manny Farber* (New York: Library of America, 2009)

Feuer, Jane, *The Hollywood Musical*, 2nd edition (Bloomington and Indianapolis: Indiana University Press, 1993)

Forbes, Jill, *Les Enfants du paradis* (London: BFI Film Classics, 1997)

Fordin, Hugh, *MGM's Greatest Musicals. The Arthur Freed Unit* (New York: Da Capo, 1995)

Frappat, Hélène *Jacques Rivette, secret compris* (Paris: Cahiers du cinéma, 2001)

—— and Jacques Rivette, *Trois films fantômes de Jacques Rivette* (Paris: Cahiers du cinéma/fiction, 2002)

Freedland, Michael, *Jolie. The Story of Al Jolson*, 2nd edition (London: W.H. Allen, 1985)

Freud, Sigmund, *The Uncanny*, translated by David McLintock with an introduction by Hugh Houghton (London: Penguin Books, 2003)

Fulbrook, Mary, *Anatomy of a Dictatorship. Inside the GDR, 1949–1989* (Oxford: Oxford University Press, 1995)

Funder, Anna, *Stasiland. Stories from behind the Berlin Wall* (London: Granta Books, 2003)

Gabler, Neal, *An Empire of Their Own. How the Jews Invented Hollywood* (New York: Doubleday, 1988)

—— *Walter Winchell. Gossip, Power and the Culture of Celebrity* (London: Picador, 1995)

Gallafent, Edward, *Astaire and Rogers* (New York: Columbia University Press, 2002)

Garfield, David, *A Player's Place. The Story of the Actors Studio* (New York: Macmillan, 1980)

Gautier, Théophile, *Le Capitaine Fracasse*, edited by Antoine Adam (Paris: Gallimard / Folio Classique, 2002)

—— 'Shakespeare aux Funambules', *Revue de Paris*, 9/2 (September 1842), pp. 60–66

Geist, Kenneth L., *Pictures Will Talk. The Life and Films of Jospeh L. Mankiewicz* (New York: Scribner's, 1978)

Gibbon, Monk, *The Red Shoes Ballet* (London: Saturn Press, 1948)

Gilbert, W.S., *The Savoy Operas, being the Complete Text of the Gilbert and Sullivan Operas as Originally produced in the Years 1875–1896* (London: Macmillan, 1926)

Glenn, Susan A., *Female Spectacle. The Theatrical Roots of Modern Feminism* (Cambridge, MA and London: Harvard University Press, 2000)

Golden, Eve, *Anna Held and the Birth of Ziegfeld's Broadway* (Lexington: University Press of Kentucky, 2000)

—— *Vernon and Irene Castle's Ragtime Revolution* (Lexington: University Press of Kentucky, 2007)

Goldman, Herbert C., *Jolson. The Legend Comes to Life* (New York: Oxford University Press, 1988)

Goodall, Jane R., *Performance and Evolution in the Age of Darwin* (London: Taylor and Francis, 2007)

Gorelik, Mordecai, *New Theatres for Old* (New York, 1940; London: Dennis Dobson, 1947)

Gottlieb, Robert and Robert Kimball, eds, *Reading Lyrics* (New York: Pantheon Books, 2000)

Goudet, Stéphane, '*Céline et Julie vont en bateau*. Les spectatrices', in Suzanne Liandrat-Guigues, ed., *Jacques Rivette, critique et cinéaste* (Paris and Caen: Lettre Modernes Minard, 1998)

Greene, Graham, *The Graham Greene Film Reader: Mornings in the Dark*, edited by David Parkinson (Manchester: Carcanet, 1993)

Greene, Naomi, *Landscapes of Loss. The National Past in Postwar French Cinema* (Princeton, NJ: Princeton University Press, 1999)

Grotowski, Jerzy, *Towards a Poor Theatre*, edited by Eugenio Barba with a Preface by Peter Brook (London: Methuen, 1969)

Guéhenno, Jean, *Journal des années noires, 1940–1944* (1947; Paris: Gallimard, 2002)

Gutner, Howard, *Gowns by Adrian. The MGM Years, 1928–1941* (New York: Abrams, 2001)

Haffner, Sebastian, *Germany Jekyll and Hyde. An Eyewitness Analysis of Nazi Germany*, with an introduction by Neal Acherson (1940; London: Abacus, 2008)

Hambly, John and Patrick Downing, *The Art of Hollywood. A Thames Television Exhibition at the Victoria and Albert Museum* (London: Thames Television, 1979)

Haskell, Arnold, 'Ballet Since 1939', in *Since 1939. Ballet, Films, Music, Painting* (London: Readers' Union / British Council, 1949)

Haskell, Molly, *From Reverence to Rape. The Treatment of Women in the Movies*, 2nd edition (Chicago, IL and London: University of Chicago Press, 1987)

Haver, Ronald, *A Star is Born. The Making of the 1954 Movie and its 1983 Restoration* (New York: Applause, 2002)

Hedges, William L., 'Classics Revisited: Reaching for the Moon', *Film Quarterly*, 12/4 (Summer 1959), pp. 27–34

Hess, Earl J. and Prathiba A. Dadhlkar, *'Singin' in the Rain.' The Making of an American Masterpiece* (Lawrence: University Press of Kansas, 2009)

Higgins, Lynn A., *New Novel, New Wave, New Politics. Fiction and Representation of History in Postwar France* (Lincoln and London: University of Nebraska Press, 1996)

Hirsch, Foster, *The Boys from Syracuse. The Shuberts' Theatrical Empire* (New York: Cooper Square Press, 2000)

Holmes, Diana and Robert Ingram, *François Truffaut* (Manchester: Manchester University Press, 1998)

Howe, Elizabeth, *The First English Actresses. Women and Drama, 1660–1700* (Cambridge: Cambridge University Press, 1992)

Hubner, Laura, *The Films of Ingmar Bergman. Illusions of Light and Darkness* (Basingstoke and New York: Palgrave Macmillan, 2007)

Hughes, John W., *'Mephisto*: István Szabó and "the Gestapo of Suspicion"', *Film Quarterly*, 35/4 (Summer 1982), pp. 13–18

Hyam, Hannah, *Fred and Ginger. The Astaire–Rogers Partnership 1934–1938* (Brighton: Pen Press Publishers, 2007)

Innes, Christopher, *Holy Theatre. Ritual and the Avant Garde* (Cambridge: Cambridge University Press, 1981)

Insdorf, Annette, *Francois Truffaut*, revised edition (Cambridge: Cambridge University Press, 1994)

—— *Indelible Shadows. Film and the Holocaust* (New York: Vintage Books, 1983)

Jacobs, Arthur, *Arthur Sullivan. A Victorian Musician* (Oxford: Oxford University Press, 1996)

James, Henry, *The Tragic Muse*, edited by Philip Hoare (London: Penguin, 1995)

Jung, Carl Gustav, *Collected Works*, ed. Herbert Read, Michael Fordham and Gerhard Adler, 20 vols (London: Routledge & Kegan Paul, 1953–1978)

—— *The Essential Jung*, selected and introduced by Anthony Storr (1984; London: Fontana Press, 1998)

—— *Memories, Dreams, Reflections*, recorded and edited by Aniela Jaffé, translated by Richard and Clara Winston (London: Collins and Routledge & Kegan Paul, 1963)

Kahane, Martine, ed., *L'Ouverture du nouvel Opéra, 5 Janvier 1875* (Paris: Musée d'Orsay / Bibliothèque Nationale, 1986)

Kalin, Jesse, *The Films of Ingmar Bergman* (Cambridge: Cambridge University Press, 2003)

Kamaralli, Anna, 'Rehearsal in Films of Early Modern Theatre. The Erotic Art of Making Shakespeare', *Shakespeare Bulletin* 29/1 (Spring 2011), pp. 27–42

Kantor, Michael, *Broadway. The American Musical, based on the documentary film by Michael Kantor* (New York and Boston: Bulfinch Press, 2004)

Kaplan, E. Ann, ed., *Feminism and Film* (Oxford: Oxford University Press, 2000)

Karsavina, Tamara, *Theatre Street* (London: Constable, 1950)

Kibler, M. Alison, *Rank Ladies. Gender and Cultural Hierarchy in American Vaudeville* (Chapel Hill and London: University of North Carolina Press, 1999)

Kiernander, Adrian, *Ariane Mnouchkine and the Théâtre du Soleil* (Cambridge: Cambridge University Press, 1993)

Kinder, Marsha, 'Reinventing the Motherland: Almodóvar's Brain-Dead Trilogy', *Film Quarterly*, 58/2 (Winter 2004–2005), pp. 9–25

Kirle, Bruce, *Unfinished Show Business. Broadway Musicals as Works-in-Progress* (Carbondale: Southern Illinois University Press, 2005)

Kline, Michael B. and Nancy C. Mellerski, 'Structures of Ambiguity in Truffaut's *Le Dernier Métro*', *The French Review*, 62/1 (October 1988), pp. 88–98

Knabe, Hubertus, *Gefangenen in Hohenschönhausen. Stasi-Häftlinge berichten* (Berlin: List Taschenbuch, 2009)

—— *Die Täter sind unter uns. Über das Schönreden der SED-Diktatur* (Berlin: List Taschenbuch, 2009)

Knutson, Rosalyn, *Playing Companies and Commerce in Shakespeare's Time* (Cambridge: Cambridge University Press, 2001)

Kobal, John, *People Will Talk*, 2nd edition (London: Aurum Press, 1991)

Lambert, Gavin, *On Cukor*, edited by Robert Trachtenberg, revised edition (New York: Rizzoli, 2000)

Lanier, Douglas, *Shakespeare and Modern Popular Culture* (Oxford: Oxford University Press, 2002)

Lazar, David, ed., *Michael Powell Interviews* (Jackson: University of Mississippi Press, 2003)

Leigh, Mike, '*Topsy-Turvy*. A Personal Journey', in David Eden and Meinhard Saremba, eds, *The Cambridge Companion to Gilbert and Sullivan* (Cambridge: Cambridge University Press, 2009)

Leroux, Gaston, *Le Fantôme de l'Opéra* (1910; Paris: Le Livre de Poche, 1981)

Levenson, Jill, 'Shakespeare in Drama Since 1990: Vanishing Act,' *Shakespeare Survey 58: Writing about Shakespeare* (Cambridge: Cambridge University Press, 2005)

Lorca, Federico García, *Three Plays*, translated by Michael Dewell and Carmen Zapata (New York: Farrar, Straus and Giroux, 1993)

Lower, Cheryl Bary and R. Burton Palmer, *Joseph L. Mankiewicz. Critical Essays with an Annotated Bibliography and a Filmography* (Jefferson, NC and London: McFarland, 2001)

Luhrmann, Baz and Catherine Martin, *Moulin Rouge* (London: FilmFour Books, 2001)

Macaulay, Alastair, 'Nice Work, Darling, Nice Work', *Times Literary Supplement*, 27 February 2004, pp. 18–19

McCabe, John, *George M. Cohan. The Man who Owned Broadway* (New York: Doubleday, 1973)

McDonald, Kevin, *Emeric Pressburger. The Life and Death of a Screenwriter* (London and Boston: Faber and Faber, 1994)

McGilligan, Patrick, *George Cukor. A Double Life* (New York: St Martin's Press, 1991)

McLean, Adrienne L., *Dying Swans and Madmen. Ballet, the Body and Narrative Cinema* (New Brunswick, NJ and London: Rutgers University Press, 2008)

—— 'The Red Shoes Revisited', *Dance Chronicle*, 11/1 (1988), pp. 31–83

MacLean, Albert F. Jr, *American Vaudeville as Ritual* (Lexington: University Press of Kentucky, 1965)

Maddison, Stephen, 'All about Women: Pedro Almodóvar and the Heterosexual Dynamic', *Textual Practice*, 14/2 (2000), pp. 265–284

Mankiewicz, Joseph L., *More About 'All About Eve', a colloquy by Gary Carey with Joseph L. Mankiewicz, together with his Screenplay 'All About Eve'* (New York: Random House, 1972)

Mann, Klaus, *Briefe und Antworten, Band I: 1922–1937*, edited by Martin Gregor-Dellin (Munich: Edition Spangenberg, 1975)

—— *Mephisto. Roman enier Karriere* (Reinbek bei Hamburg: Rowohlt, 1981)

—— *Der Wendepunkt. Ein Lebensbericht* (Munich: Edition Spangenberg, 1989)

Marais, Jean, *Histoires de ma vie* (Paris: Albin Michel, 1975)

Maslon, Laurence, ed., *Kaufman and Co. Broadway Comedies* (New York: Library of America, 2004)

Massine, Léonide, *My Life in Ballet* (London: Macmillan, 1968)

Mast, Gerald, *Can't Help Singin'. The American Musical on Stage and Screen* (Woodstock, NY: Overlook Press, 1987)

Maugham, W. Somerset, *Theatre* (Garden City, NY: Doubleday, Doran and Co., 1938)

Mellencamp, Patricia, *A Fine Romance. Five Ages of Film Feminism* (Philadelphia, PA: Temple University Press, 1995)

Ménil, Alain, 'Mesure pour mesure. Théâtre et cinéma chez Jacques Rivette', in Suzanne Liandrat-Guigues, ed., *Jacques Rivette, critique et cinéaste* (Paris and Caen: Lettres Modernes Minard, 1998)

Metz, Christian, *Film Language. A Semiotics of the Cinema*, translated by Michael Taylor (New York: Oxford University Press, 1974)

Michalzik, Peter, *Gustaf Gründgens. Der Schauspieler und die Macht* (Munich: Ullstein Econ List Verlag, 2001)

Mizejewski, Linda, *Ziegfeld Girl. Image and Icon in Culture and Cinema* (Durham, NC and London: Duke University Press, 1999)

Mordden, Ethan, *Ziegfeld. The Man who Invented Show Business* (New York: St Martin's Press, 2008)

Morrey, Douglas and Alison Smith, *Jacques Rivette* (Manchester and New York: Manchester University Press, 2009)

Moynet, J.P., *L'Envers du théâtre* (1873); translated and augmented by Allan

S. Jackson and M. Glen Wilson as *French Theatrical Production in the Nineteenth Century* (Binghamton: SUNY Press, 1976)

Mueller, John, *Astaire Dancing* (New York: Knopf, 1985)

Murphy, Robert, *Realism and Tinsel. Cinema and Society in Britain, 1939–49* (London and New York: Routledge, 1989)

Nathan, George Jean, *The Theatre of the Moment. A Journalistic Commentary* (New York: Alfred A. Knopf, 1936)

Navarro-Daniels, Vilma, 'Tejiendo nuevas identidades: la red metaficional e intertextual en *Todo sobre mi madre* de Pedro Almodóvar', *Ciberletras*, 7 (2002), pp. 1–13

Newnhan, John K., 'Dance Film Notes: "Red Shoes" and "The Unfinished Dance"', *Dancing Times* (September 1948), pp. 647–648; 653

Nichols, Bill, ed., *Movies and Methods* (Berkeley and London: University of California Press, 1976)

Nicoll, Allardyce, *Film and Theater* (New Haven, CT: Yale University Press, 1936)

O'Shaughnessy, Martin, *Jean Renoir* (Manchester: Manchester University Press, 2000)

Pavis, Patrice, *Theatre at the Crossroads of Culture*, translated by Loren Kruger (London and New York: Routledge, 1992)

Péricaud, Louis, *Le Théâtre des Funambules, ses mimes, ses acteurs et ses pantomimes depuis sa foundation jusqu'à sa démolition* (Paris: Léon Sapin, 1897)

Philippe, Claude-Jean, *Jean Renoir. Une vie en oeuvres* (Paris: Bernard Grasset, 2005)

Pirandello, Luigi, *As You Desire Me*, translated by Robert Rietti, in *Pirandello: Collected Plays*, Vol. 4 (London: Calder, 1996)

Place, Janey and Lowell Peterson, 'Some Visual Motifs of Film Noir', in Alain Silver and James Ursini, eds, *Film Noir Reader* (New York: Limelight Editions, 1996)

Plachta, Bodo, *Erläuterungen und Dokumente, Klaus Mann: 'Mephisto'* (Stuttgart: Reclam, 2008)

Powell, Michael, *A Life in Movies. An Autobiography* (London: Heinemann, 1986)

—— 'The Shape of Films to Come', in Peter Noble, ed., *British Film Yearbook, 1947–48* (London: Skelton Robinson, n.d.)

—— and Emeric Pressburger, *The Red Shoes* (New York: St Martin's Press, 1996)

Prawer, S.S., *Caligari's Children. The Film as Tale of Terror* (Oxford: Oxford University Press, 1980)

Price, David, *Cancan!* (Madison and Teaneck, NJ: Fairleigh Dickinson University Press, 1998)

Propp, Vladimir, *The Morphology of the Folktale*, translated by Laurence Scott, 2nd revised edition, edited by Louis A. Wager (Austin: University of Texas Press, 1968)

Pullen, Kirsten, *Actresses and Whores. On Stage and in Society* (Cambridge: Cambridge University Press, 2005)

Rancière, Jacques, *The Emancipated Spectator*, translated by Gregory Elliott (London and New York: Verso, 2009)

Rearick, John, *Pleasures of the Belle Époque. Entertainment and Festivity in Turn-of-the-Century France* (New Haven, CT and London: Yale University Press, 1985)

Rémy, Tristan, *Jean-Gaspard Deburau* (Paris: L'Arche, 1954)

Renoir, Jean, *Écrits (1926–1971)*, edited by Claude Gauter (Paris: Ramsay, 2006)

—— *Entretiens et propos*, edited by Jean Narboni (Paris: Cahiers du cinéma, 2005)

—— *Ma vie et mes films*, corrected edition (Paris: Flammarion, 2005)

Rentschler, Eric, *The Ministry of Illusion. Nazi Cinema and its Afterlife* (Cambridge, MA: Harvard University Press, 1996)

Riding, Alan, *And the Show Went On. Cultural Life in Nazi-Occupied Paris* (New York: Knopf, 2010)

Rivette, Jacques, 'Entretien avec Jacques Rivette. Le temps déborde' (*Cahiers du cinéma*, no. 204, September 1968) in Antoine de Baecque and Charles Tesson, eds, *La Nouvelle Vague. Textes et entretiens dans les Cahiers du cinéma* (Paris: Cahiers du cinéma, 1999)

Roach, Joseph, *The Player's Passion. Studies in the Science of Acting* (Newark, NJ: University of Delaware Press / Associated University Presses, 1985)

Roddick, Nick, *A New Deal in Entertainment. Warner Brothers in the 1930s* (London: British Film Institute, 1983)

Rogin, Michael, *Blackface, White Noise. Jewish Immigrants in the Hollywood Melting Pot* (Berkeley, Los Angeles and London: University of California Press, 1996)

Rosenstone, Robert A., *History on Film/Film on History* (Harlow: Pearson Education, 2006)

Roud, Richard, *The Cinema. A Critical Dictionary of the Cinema* (London: Secker and Warburg, 1980)

Rubin, Martin, *Showstoppers. Busby Berkeley and the Tradition of Spectacle* (New York: Columbia University Press, 1993)

Rühle, Günther, *Theater in Deutschland, 1887–1945, seine Ereignisse, seine Menschen* (Frankfurt am Main: S. Fischer, 2007)

Sagalyn, Lynne B., *Times Square Roulette. Remaking the City Icon* (Cambridge, MA: MIT Press, 2001)

Sanders, James, *Celluloid Skyline. New York and the Movies* (New York: Knopf, 2003)

Sartre, Jean-Paul, *Kean*, edited by David Bradby (Oxford: Oxford University Press, 1973)

Schädlich, Hans Joachim, ed., *Aktenkundig* (Reinbek bei Hamburg: Rowohlt Taschenbuch, 1993)

Scott, Virginia, *Molière. A Theatrical Life* (Cambridge: Cambridge University Press, 2000)

Seldes, Gilbert, *The 7 Lively Arts* (New York: Harper and Brothers, 1924)

Serceau, Daniel, *Jean Renoir. La sagesse du plaisir* (Paris: Les Éditions du Cerf, 1985)

Sesonske, Alexander, *Jean Renoir. The French Films, 1924–1939* (Cambridge, MA and London: Harvard University Press, 1985)

Shakespeare, William, *The Complete Works*, edited by Stanley Wells and Gary Taylor, 2nd edition (Oxford: Clarendon Press, 2005)

Shargel, Raphael, ed., *Ingmar Bergman Interviews* (Jackson: University of Mississippi Press, 2007)

Simon, Alfred, *Molière*, 2nd edition (Paris: Seuil, 1996)

Singer, Irving, *Ingmar Bergman, Cinematic Philosopher. Reflections on his Creativity* (Cambridge, MA: MIT Press, 2007)

—— *Three Philosophical Filmmakers: Hitchcock, Welles, Renoir* (Cambridge, MA: MIT Press, 2004)

Skirov, Ed, *Dark Victory. The Life of Bette Davis* (New York: Henry Holt and Company, 2007)

Smith, Paul Julian, *Desire Unlimited. The Cinema of Pedro Almodóvar* (London and New York: Verso, 1994)

Snyder, Robert W., *The Voice of the City. Vaudeville and Popular Culture in New York* (New York and Oxford: Oxford University Press, 1989)

Sofair, Michael, '*All About my Mother*', *Film Quarterly*, 55/2 (Winter 2001–2002), pp. 40–47

Spotts, Frederic, *The Shameful Peace. How French Artists and Intellectuals Survived the Nazi Occupation* (New Haven, CT and London: Yale University Press, 2006)

Staggs, Sam, *All About All About Eve. The Complete Behind-the-scenes Story of the Bitchiest Film Ever Made* (New York: St Martin's Press, 2001)

Stedman, Jane W., *W.S. Gilbert. A Classic Victorian and his Theatre* (Oxford: Oxford University Press, 1996)

Stevens, Anthony, *On Jung* (London and New York: Routledge, 1990)

Storey, Robert F., *Pierrot. A Critical History of a Mask* (Princeton, NJ: Princeton University Press, 1978)

Storr, Anthony, ed., *The Essential Jung* (1983: London: Fontana, 1998)

Stratyner, Barbara, *Ned Wayburn and the Dance Routine. From Vaudeville to the "Ziegfeld Follies"*, *Studies in Dance History*, no. 13 (New York: Society of Dance History Scholars, 1996)

Strauss, Frederic, ed., *Almodóvar on Almodóvar*, revised edition (London: Faber and Faber, 2006

Strobl, Gerwin, *The Swastika and the Stage. German Theatre and Society, 1933–1945* (Cambridge: Cambridge University Press, 2007)

Studlar, Gaylyn, *This Mad Masquerade. Stardom and Masculinity in the Jazz Age* (New York: Columbia University Press, 1996)

Thiéry, Natacha, *Photogénie du désir. Michael Powell et Emeric Pressburger,
    1945–1950* (Rennes: Presses Universitaires de Rennes, 2009)
Thomas, Tony and Jim Terry, with Busby Berkeley, *The Busby Berkeley Book*
    (London: Thames and Hudson, 1973)
Tribble, Evelyn B., *Cognition in the Globe. Attention and Memory in
    Shakespeare's Theatre* (Basingstoke: Palgrave Macmillan, 2011)
Truffaut, François, *Hitchcock*, with the collaboration of Helen G. Scott,
    revised editon (New York: Simon and Schuster, 1984)
—— *Le Plaisir des yeux* (Paris: Flammarion, 1987)
—— *Truffaut sur Truffaut*, edited by Dominique Rabourdin (Paris: Chêne,
    1985)
Tucker, Sophie, *Some of These Days* (London: Hammond, Hammond & Co.,
    1957)
Turk, Edward Baron, *Child of Paradise: Marcel Carné and the Golden Age
    of French Cinema* (Cambridge, MA and London: Harvard University
    Press, 1989)
Turner, Graeme, *Film as Social Practice*, 3rd edition (London and New York:
    Routledge, 1999)
Vinen, Richard, *Unfree French. Life under the Occupation* (New Haven, CT
    and London: Yale University Press, 2008)
Wills, Nadine '"110 per cent woman": the crotch shot in the Hollywood
    musical', *Screen*, 42/2 (Summer 2001), pp. 121–141
Wilson, Edmund, *The American Earthquake. A Documentary of the Twenties
    and Thirties* (New York: Farrar, Strauss and Giroux, 1958)
Wollen, Peter, *Singin' in the Rain* (London: BFI, 1992)
Wood, Robin, *Hitchcock's Films Revisited*, revised edition (New York:
    Columbia University Press, 2002)
Woodruff, Paul, *The Necessity of Theatre. The Art of Watching and Being
    Watched* (Oxford: Oxford University Press, 2009)
Ziegfeld, Richard and Paulette, *The Ziegfeld Touch. The Life and Times of
    Florenz Ziegfeld, Jr* (New York: Abrams, 1993)
Zola, Émile, *Nana*, ed. Henri Mitterand (Paris: Gallimard / Folio Classique,
    2002)
Zuckmayer, Carl, *Geheimreport*, edited by Gunther Nickel and Johanna
    Schrön (Göttingen: Wallstein Verlag, 2002)

Index

Note: films identified in the text with a particular director are listed under his or her name. All films are listed by their current English title. Page numbers in *italics* refer to illustrations.

DATE DUE